Best

'A lovely read'
Bella

'Hardship, courage and hope on the Home Front'
Kate Thompson, *Secrets of the Lavender Girls*

'A sweeping tale of friendship and hope against the odds'
My Weekly

'A heart-warming tale of the brave women
who stepped up to become the
backbone of Sheffield's steel industry
during the Second World War'
Yours

'A heart-warming story perfect for saga lovers'
Nancy Revell, *The Shipyard Girls on the Home Front*

'A great read'
Yorkshire Post

'A tale of friendship, hope and love.
I couldn't put it down'
Alexandra Walsh, *The Music Makers*

'An excellent history of the Sheffield female
factory workers during the Second World War

Michelle Rawlins is an award-winning freelance journalist with over twenty-five years' experience working in print and digital media. After learning her trade, Michelle began her freelance career writing for national newspapers and women's magazines concentrating on real-life stories – living by the mantra: 'it's always the most ordinary people who have the most extraordinary stories.' Michelle currently teaches journalism at the University of Sheffield.

She is the author of *Women of Steel* and *The Steel Girls* was her debut novel. You can follow Michelle on Twitter @Mrawlins1974 and on Facebook/MichelleRawlinsAuthor.

The Steel Girls series
The Steel Girls
Christmas Hope for the Steel Girls
Steel Girls on the Home Front

Steel Girls
on the
Home Front

Michelle Rawlins

ONE PLACE. MANY STORIES

HQ
An imprint of HarperCollins*Publishers* Ltd
1 London Bridge Street
London SE1 9GF

www.harpercollins.co.uk

HarperCollins*Publishers*
1st Floor, Watermarque Building, Ringsend Road
Dublin 4, Ireland

This edition 2022

1
First published in Great Britain by
HQ, an imprint of HarperCollins*Publishers* Ltd 2022

Copyright © Michelle Rawlins 2022

Michelle Rawlins asserts the moral right to be
identified as the author of this work.
A catalogue record for this book is
available from the British Library.

ISBN: 978-0-00-842735-1

MIX
Paper | Supporting
responsible forestry
FSC™ C007454

This book is produced from independently certified FSC™ paper
to ensure responsible forest management.

For more information visit: www.harpercollins.co.uk/green

This book is set in 11.3/16.5 pt. Sabon by Type-it AS, Norway

Printed and Bound in the UK using 100% Renewable Electricity at
CPI Group (UK) Ltd, Croydon, CR0 4YY

To my two wonderful children, Archie & Tilly, who never cease to make me smile.

Chapter 1

Monday, 29 January 1940

'I'm so sorry.' Archie smiled weakly, taking hold of Patty's slender hand, as she sat next to his hospital bed, concern etched across her face. 'I promise, I didn't mean to scare you.'

'Well yer didn't do a very good job!' she blurted out before she could stop herself. 'It's just, I've been so worried, and you kept telling me nothing was wrong, but I just knew in my heart of hearts, summat weren't right,' she tried to explain. 'How are yer feeling now? Have you eaten anything? What have the doctors said?' As usual Patty didn't draw breath, unable to get her words out quick enough.

Sheepishly, Archie looked down at his starched white bedsheets, guilt coursing through his tired and fragile body.

Less than thirty-six hours earlier he had been rushed to hospital after collapsing in the front yard of Vickers, in the middle of the Vicktory Knitters Wear and Share event. Archie had known for weeks he was ill and getting weaker by the day but, ignoring the concerned protests from his family and Patty, he'd refused to rest. He'd insisted he was okay, despite the relentless cold weather that had left his lips blue and him fighting to catch his breath. It was nothing he hadn't experienced before. Ever since Archie could remember, he'd suffered from nasty colds that always seemed so much worse than his friends' due to his weak heart.

'I promise I'm all right. My pride and downright pig-headedness just got in the way,' Archie finally conceded, colour flushing his cheeks – a welcome sight as far as Patty was concerned, hoping this meant he was getting stronger and more like his old self.

'What do yer mean?' Patty asked gently. She was still cross with Archie for not listening when she'd begged him to take it steady but also knew that it wasn't the time to say *I told you so*. The most important thing now that Archie was laid up in hospital was supporting his recovery.

'Oh,' he sighed, knowing he owed Patty an explanation. He'd left her in such a state of panic when he'd been carted off in the back of an ambulance on a stretcher and rushed to the City Hospital. The doctors had told Archie that Patty had tried to see him the previous night, hours after he'd collapsed, but he'd been flat out and wired up to God-knows-how-many machines while the medical staff assessed his condition. Although he'd spent his childhood being prodded and poked, listening to his childhood consultant's grave warning about how weak he was, he was fully aware what a shock his sudden turn must have been for Patty, especially because he'd tried to convince her it was just a heavy cold. 'I reckon I better start at the beginning.'

'Always a good place to start,' Patty mused. Her head was still a whirlwind of conflicting emotions; frustration mixed with angst as she desperately tried to ward off the fears which had sent a shiver down her spine since Archie's collapse.

'It's a bit of a long story but I'll do my best,' Archie said.

'I've got as long as it takes,' Patty insisted, relieved that Archie was finally going to tell her the truth about what had been going on.

'According to my mum, not long after I was born, doctors told her and m' dad I had a weak valve in my heart. It was a reyt old shock for them and left them and my nannan worried sick. Apparently I was nothing more than a scrap of a lad and my mum never stops reminding me I was knocking on death's door more times than sense. She says she lost count how many times she called the priest to the hospital, convinced I was about to take my last breath. When my pals get a cold, they are over it in a few days, but that could leave me at death's door.'

'Oh,' Patty gasped, struggling to imagine how terrified Archie's family must have been.

'It's not so bad.' Archie smiled encouragingly. 'I'm still here, aren't I?'

'Go on,' Patty encouraged.

'Well, somehow I would always miraculously pick up, even when the doctors thought there was nothing else to be done for me. Apparently my nannan refused to leave my bedside for weeks at a time and would only have a doze when nurses assured her I was stable, and they would check on me every ten minutes.'

'That must have taken its toll on everyone,' Patty said.

'I think, well, I know it did.' Archie nodded. 'It was all a bit of a roller coaster for them. Due to how poorly I would get and never sure of what was around the corner, my mum and dad decided not to have any more children.'

'Gosh,' Patty whispered, her voice breaking.

'Yes, my mum told me a few years ago they were frightened they wouldn't be able to give me all the love and care I needed, but my nannan explained they were also really scared that if they did lose me, they would be left childless.'

'Oh, Archie,' Patty sighed, wiping away the stream of tears that she could no longer hold back. 'Yer poor parents and nannan. They must have been out of their minds. Could they not do anything to make you better?'

'Well, as I said, I'm still here.' Archie smiled, trying to lift the mood.

'Do you ever take anything seriously?' Patty protested, making to tap his arm but thinking better of it, frightened that even the smallest jolt could have unthinkable consequences. 'I really thought you were a gonner yesterday. You reyt scared me.'

Patty closed her eyes to try to compose herself but the memory of Archie's ashen face and his blue lips, gasping to catch his breath, still haunted her. Thank goodness everyone had been there to help: Nancy and Betty consoled her, as Dolly calmy coaxed Archie to stay awake, while Frank and her dad propped Archie up on a chair and wrapped him in coats, to try to abate his violent shivering, telling him Patty would have his guts for garters if he didn't keep fighting. Someone had also run to the office and called for an ambulance quickly.

'I'm ever so sorry,' Archie apologized again, cross with himself for all the unnecessary trouble and worry he'd caused. His whole reason for keeping quiet about his illness was to stop his workmates fretting about him and to avoid being labelled as sickly, but his Yorkshire stubbornness, an all too familiar family trait, had achieved exactly that. 'It really was the last thing I wanted to do. I know it's hard to believe, but as well as trying to convince myself I was okay, I was trying to protect you. I didn't want you fretting. I really thought I had it all under control.'

'I could have looked out for yer more,' Patty sniffled.

'That's just the thing,' Archie added. 'I've been wrapped up in cotton wool by my parents and nannan all my life. I know it's because they love me and care, but I just want to be treated like everyone else. I don't want any special attention.'

'But I'm yer girlfriend,' Patty said, a little more sharply. 'You should have told me. We're not meant to have any secrets. Surely you could have been honest about something so serious?'

Regret momentarily silenced Archie. The whole reason he hadn't told Patty was because he didn't want any fuss but look where that had got him.

'It's hard to explain . . .' he replied, taking a deep breath.

'Try me,' Patty interjected. It took all her effort to be patient and understanding but she couldn't help be somewhat miffed Archie hadn't felt he could share his 'big secret' with her.

Archie bowed his head, a wave of shame overtaking him. 'I just want to feel like a real man,' he muttered.

Stumped by Archie's heartfelt confession, Patty bit her lip. In her eyes he was a 'real man'; he worked in a steel factory and hauled great chunks of metal across a shop floor. As much as she was cross with him for not confiding in her, Patty also knew he didn't need her nagging at him right now. This was one battle she might have to leave for another day. Besides which, it wasn't just brawn and muscles that made Archie a man, he was also one of the kindest and caring blokes she knew.

'Please don't be mad at me,' Archie whispered, lifting his head and looking straight at Patty.

Seeing how exhausted he was, Patty let her frustration subside.

'Oh, yer daft thing,' she said, squeezing Archie's hand a little tighter. 'If I didn't love yer so much, I would bloody well throttle yer, but promise me you won't be so bloody stupid ever again.'

'Aw, Patty, I love you too, with all my heart and I promise I won't lie to you again. Scout's honour,' Archie vowed, raising his other hand into his usual three-finger salute. If the truth be known, this latest scare had really frightened him. It was a long time since he'd had such a close call. After the heart specialists, at the very hospital he was once again a patient in, had found medication for him as a young teenager to keep his condition at ease, he'd managed to survive most winters by staying wrapped up and keeping himself protected against the bitter cold air.

Of course, it still meant he couldn't do everything his mates could. Playing football had been virtually impossible, with doctors warning him anything that caused his heartbeat to race was dangerous. He'd happily taken the title of having two left feet, preferable to being labelled sickly and weak, which in reality is how he'd felt. But the years of hospital appointments, and his family insisting on wrapping him in cotton wool, had taken its toll on his confidence. It was why months ago when they had first met, he'd wrongly assumed Patty had chosen factory lothario Tommy chuffin' Hardcastle over him. He'd resigned himself to never being good enough.

'Yer best not,' Patty said, pulling Archie back to the present. 'But what's done is done, so let's not dwell on it. No point crying over spilt milk as me mom always says.'

'Well, I'm grateful all the same,' Archie replied. 'I was worried you would be so cross that you might decide that I wasn't the right—'

'Now stop that right now,' Patty interrupted, feeling uncharacteristically grown up, and despite her frustration, she was grateful her sweetheart was here to tell the tale. 'It wasn't all that long ago you were running to my rescue when

I was acting like a stubborn old mule and went flying down that godforsaken ladder.' It was true: despite Archie being convinced he wasn't the man of Patty's dreams, it hadn't stopped him running to her aid after her near fatal accident, and in actual fact, it was what had finally brought them together, when a couple of weeks later they had confessed their true feelings for one another.

'Well, I'm one lucky fella, is all I can say,' Archie said, stroking Patty's hand tenderly.

'Yes, you are!' she teased. 'But I could get used to all these compliments.'

Right on cue, Archie's cheeks turned their usual crimson, as they always did when anyone paid him attention.

'Anyway, I'm glad we got everything cleared up,' he said, trying to draw a line under their conversation and move on. 'How's work been today?'

'Well,' Patty said, instinctively dabbing down her mucky khaki overalls, 'it was as busy as ever and everyone was asking about you, wanting to know if you are okay.'

Guilt soared through Archie once again. He really had caused quite a fuss, which was the last thing he'd intended. 'Oh dear, and dare I ask how the rest of the event went yesterday? I hope I didn't ruin it all after everyone's hard work.'

'I'd be lying if I didn't say it didn't 'alf cause quite a to-do.'

'Oh.' Arche slumped. The idea of him bringing the Vicktory Knitters big event to a premature and abrupt end only enhanced how daft he already felt. Patty's friend,

Betty, had been planning the occasion for months, determined to make sure the locals of Attercliffe had enough winter woollies to get them through the rest of the season. She had somehow managed to convince virtually every female steelworker to start knitting hats, gloves, jumpers and cardigans to give away at the event. 'I'll apologize to Betty, Dolly and everyone else as soon as I'm back at work, which hopefully won't be too far away.'

'Hang on a minute,' Patty butted in. 'You're racing ahead of tha'sen, in more ways than one.'

'What do you mean?'

'Well, after you got carted off in that there ambulance, there was a bit of a lull. M' dad took me inside and Dolly forced me to have a very sweet cup of tea, but I'm sure it wasn't just sugar she added to it. Whatever it was, it stopped me shaking anyhow,' Patty explained.

'Oh, Patty,' Archie audibly sighed once again, feeling even worse for all the trouble he'd caused, something he hadn't thought was physically possible.

'I'm not saying it for that reason, and I haven't finished yet!' Patty shook her head. 'Anyway, by the time I'd supped Dolly's concoction and come back out in the yard, Betty and her landlady had somehow managed to appease everyone.'

'So, they didn't have to cut short the event?' Archie asked hopefully, adjusting the pillow behind his back. One of the nurses had used it to prop him up after he'd had another long and much needed sleep.

'No!' Patty exclaimed. 'Yer know what Betty's like. She's reyt good at organising everyone. I have no idea what she and Ivy said to everyone but when I got back into the yard, they'd roped in Frank to take over my table and there were women coming and going, and Dolly soon got to handing out mugs of tea and sweets for the kids.'

'Well, that's one good thing,' Archie answered with an enormous sense of relief, a huge grin appearing across his face.

'So yer can turn that frown upside down once and for all.' Patty smiled, repeating Archie's nannan's phrase, which had become somewhat well-known throughout Vickers to help them get through the difficult times they were facing.

Unable to stifle his laughter, Archie quietly counted his blessings. *I really am a lucky bloke*, he thought to himself.

'I'm just pleased after all the effort you women went to, especially Betty, that the day was still a huge success.'

'I'd fair say it was,' Patty agreed. 'I know when we started clearing up, you could count on one hand how many jumpers and pairs of socks we took back upstairs and put in the Swap Box. I reckon we might have kitted out of 'alf of Sheffield with new winter woollies yesterday. Nobody left empty-handed, that's for sure.'

'Will you tell Betty I'm chuffed to bits for her and apologize again that I wasn't there to carry on helping out?'

'Yes, if you insist!' Patty rolled her eyes in mock frustration, knowing everyone would just be relieved Archie was okay and wasn't, well . . . Patty refused to allow her mind to think about the ifs and maybes. Her sweetheart was sat up in bed, with colour in his cheeks and thankfully no longer looking like he was on death's door.

'Now, tell me,' she said, her tone turning more serious. 'What have the doctors said and are you going to be okay?'

Archie glanced around the long ward of beds, which resembled what he imagined a dormitory in a boys' boarding school would look like, and checked that the much older patients weren't listening. 'I think I've had a very lucky escape,' he whispered.

Patty sensed he didn't want to gloat about the life he still had ahead of him. Some of the old men in the beds nearest Archie looked so frail, their skin transparent and their breathing laboured, she couldn't imagine they were meant for this world much longer.

'I should say so,' Patty replied. 'In fact, I would go as far to say that's the understatement of the century.'

'Yes, you're right. To put it simply, the cold air combined with a bit of a chest infection, well quite a nasty one, played havoc with my breathing and circulation, but the good news is there's no lasting damage. The doctor said I just need to be careful and stay wrapped up.'

Once again Patty's eyes filled with tears. The sheer relief combined with the shock of the last thirty-six hours was all too much.

'Hey, come on,' Archie said gently, edging himself towards Patty and pulling her close, so her head lay on his lap. 'I'm here and nothing bad happened,' he added reassuringly. 'Please don't get upset.'

But now the floodgates had opened, Patty couldn't stop, and she allowed Archie to soothe her; the fears which had soared through her caused her whole body to shudder.

'I was just so frightened I would lose you,' she sobbed, her voice broken. 'I was terrified you wouldn't wake up.'

'But you didn't and here I am, sat up in bed,' Archie said, trying to comfort her. 'And more to the point, I've realized what a daft apeth I've been and won't ever be so stupid again.'

Patty raised her head and looked straight into Archie's eyes, which were also brimming with emotion. 'Really?' she asked.

'When I came to in the hospital,' Archie replied, 'you were the first person I thought about and all I could think was thank God I'm still alive, as the idea of not being able to spend years and years with you by my side would feel like such a waste.'

It wasn't an outright proposal, but the heartfelt sentiment wasn't lost on Patty. 'Oh, Archie,' she whispered. 'There's no one I would rather spend the rest of my life with either.'

For the next few minutes, the pair remained perfectly still, safely encased in one another's arms, oblivious to the constant bleeping of machines, or the clicking of the nurses' heels as they dashed up and down the ward and the rattle of the tea lady pushing her trolley.

'I could stay like this forever,' Patty thought aloud.

'Me too,' Archie agreed.

'Can I get you lovebirds a cuppa?' interrupted the cheery,

plump woman, who was already letting the hot brown liquid flow into two blue-and-white striped enamel mugs, anticipating their answer.

'That would be lovely, thank you,' Archie replied, releasing Patty from his strong, protective arms, not wanting to seem improper.

'Yes, me too,' Patty chirped, her voice returning to normal, even if her blotchy red eyes betrayed how overwrought with emotion she felt.

Regaining their composure, the couple sat upright as they nursed their welcome cuppas, both grateful the other was by their side.

'I really don't want to leave you, but I suppose I better be getting home,' Patty said, as she drained her mug. 'Me mom will have me guts for garters if m' tea ends up ruined.' She'd somehow managed to persuade the ward matron to allow her in to see Archie before the visiting time had officially begun. Patty couldn't be sure, but she was convinced the robust and rather officious-looking woman had weakened when she'd explained she had come straight from the factory. There had been a lot of chatter across the city about what a grand job the women of Sheffield were doing, stepping up to 'do their bit' wherever they could to help the war effort.

'Well, we can't be having that,' Archie laughed, 'I don't want to be getting into any trouble with your parents. I'm sure they are already cross with me for putting you through all this worry.'

'I don't think you have anything to worry about there,' Patty replied. 'M' mom adores you and will just be relieved you are okay. I can guarantee she will insist you come round for tea as soon as you are home and back on yer feet.'

'Well,' Archie grinned, 'that is always an offer I can't refuse. And hopefully it will be sooner rather than later too.'

'Really?' Patty quizzed, realizing she hadn't actually asked Archie when he might be allowed to go home.

'Yes,' he answered, beaming. 'The doctor said this afternoon, if I'm still okay tomorrow, I could be discharged, as long as I promise to stay out of the cold air until my chest is clear.'

'Oh, that's brilliant news.' Patty bent over and kissed Archie on the cheek, before pulling on her navy duffle coat that she had hung on the back of the wooden hospital chair. 'Thinking about it, I haven't heard you cough once since I got here.'

'That will be down to how warm it is in here and the concoction of medicine the nurses keep feeding me.'

'Well, you must do what the doctors said. You ain't coming back to work straightaway, are you?' Patty affirmed, more than asked.

As much as she would miss not seeing Archie every day at Vickers, she would much rather he make a full recovery than try to rush back and have another setback.

'No. I'm going to do as I'm told this time. I reckon I've well and truly learnt my lesson.'

'Good,' Patty said firmly. 'As much as I would like to

stay longer, I better get home. It's already pitch-black out there and I should let you get some rest now.'

'Will you be all right?'

'Yes, don't fret. I can catch a tram and be home in less than half an hour.'

'Well, just take care.'

'I will.' Patty leant over Archie to kiss him goodbye.

'Thank you,' he whispered as their lips parted.

'What for?'

'For caring and not getting angry.'

Patty smiled. 'Just get better and promise never to have any more secrets again and all is forgiven.'

'You have my word,' Archie promised, squeezing Patty's hand a little tighter.

As she left the ward and started heading down the long corridor, she vowed she would take extra care of Archie; after all, isn't that exactly what he'd done for her when she had been recovering from her fall?

'Hiya, luv.' Archie's mum, Gracie, interrupted Patty's thoughts.

'Hello,' Patty greeted brightly in return. 'Sorry, I was in a world of my own. How are you?'

'Well, it's been a while since our Archie has given us such a scare, but I'm getting there.'

'You must be out of your mind,' Patty said, moving to the side of the corridor to make room for a porter who was pushing a frail elderly man in a wheelchair towards Archie's ward.

'It never gets any easier and you never stop worrying,' Gracie sighed. 'That lad has caused me more than a few sleepless nights, that's for sure.'

'I can't begin to imagine how difficult it's been.'

'I don't begrudge it,' Gracie explained. 'He's my son, and that's what mums do. I just wish he'd rest when his body tells him to.'

'Is there anything I can do?' Patty asked, feeling for Gracie, who looked utterly exhausted.

'I dunno, luv. I know what a stubborn old mule our Archie can be. He has me at my wits' end at times.'

'You won't get any arguments from me there,' Patty agreed. 'I'd been pestering him for weeks to take it steady. I just hope he does now.'

'I wouldn't hold your breath, luv. Our Archie is a beggar when it comes to trying to prove to the world he can keep up with everyone else. The only problem is his body can't do it. We've been at this point more times than I've had hot dinners.'

'I'll do my best to try to rein him in a bit,' Patty promised, saddened to see Archie's mum in such a state after his latest turn.

'If you could try, luv, I'd be ever so grateful.' Grace smiled weakly. 'Heaven knows, me and his nannan have tried often enough.'

'I'll do what I can.' Patty nodded.

'Thanks, luv. Well, I best get in and see him. Visiting time will be over before I get there if I don't get a move on.'

'I'm sure Archie will be delighted to see you.'

'Aye, luv. You take care now too. You look as though you need a good night's sleep.'

'I'll be fine, I promise.' As Patty lifted her hand to wave goodbye, she was more determined than ever to make sure she looked after Archie, not only to help Gracie, but to make sure he didn't jeopardise his promise to spend many more happy years with her.

Chapter 2

Tuesday, 30 January 1940

'Patty,' came Betty's familiar voice. The youngest of the three musketeers – the nickname their foreman, Frank, had given them – was just walking through gate three of Vickers, her coat pulled high around her neck, with her workmate Nancy, when Betty caught them up.

'Morning,' Patty chirped, an obvious spring in her step, despite the bitterly cold weather.

'I'm taking from how cheery you are compared to this time yesterday, you got to see Archie, and dare I tempt fate, can I assume he's okay?' Betty asked.

'Yes.' Patty grinned, as the group made their way to the main entrance. 'I've just been telling Nancy, he's not out of the woods yet, and will need to take it steady for a while, but a spell in hospital to rest up and get expert care was just what he needed. He actually had some colour in his cheeks again.'

'Oh, that's marvellous, luv,' Betty said, delighted Archie was as well as could be. He had given them all quite a scare. 'What a relief.'

'Honestly, I thought m' heart was going to burst when I saw him sat up in bed,' Patty said as they made their way through the factory doors and towards the clocking-in machine.

'Well, you must tell us everything over dinner,' Betty insisted, her mind already thinking about what little pick-me-up treats she could muster up for Archie's care package.

'You'll not be able to shut me up, but I need to find a way of making him slow down too,' Patty said, as the three women took it in turns to have their timecards stamped.

'Well, you won't get any arguments from us,' Nancy added, undoing the coat buttons of her navy mackintosh as the trio walked through the maze of corridors towards the factory floor. The heat hitting them was a welcome alternative to the thick frost outside, which had covered the pavements for the last month or so. Everyone who knew Archie had been worried sick after he'd been carted off to the City Hospital. 'I know Dolly will be so relieved he's at least on the road to recovery. You know how much she adores Archie.'

'I do.' Patty nodded. The affectionate, motherly canteen manager had been trying to dose Archie up for weeks with hot water and honey, in a bid to soothe his chest, completely unaware it wasn't just an infection he was suffering from but a lifelong debilitating heart condition.

'Right,' Betty said, as they approached Myrtle – the pet name given to the monstrous crane she had now become an expert in handling and manoeuvring. 'I'll see you both at dinnertime. I've got something I want to chat to you about too.'

'Why doesn't that surprise me?' Nancy laughed, guessing Betty was already planning her next project, after the huge success of the Vicktory Knitters community event.

'She'll never flamin' stop, that one,' Patty added, as the pair made their way over to their respective cranes. 'She's not happy unless she is on a mission.'

'Well, if it keeps her mind busy and helps folk out along the way, it can't be a bad thing.' If Nancy had learnt anything over the past four months since starting at Vickers, it was a busy mind was good at keeping the often overwhelming worries at bay. There wasn't a single hour of the day when she didn't find herself fretting about her beloved husband, Bert, who had been sent to France to support the Allied troops against Hitler. Working as a crane driver had given Nancy a much-needed focus and stopped her falling to pieces worrying about what the future held. So, she understood exactly why Betty threw herself into helping others, first creating a Care Club, to help those in need, which had soon developed into a Swap Club, where Vickers's female workers could donate clothes they didn't need and pick up something for themselves or family members.

'This is true,' Patty agreed, fondly recalling how she had been on the receiving end of Betty's thoughtfulness only a few months earlier, after a nasty fall down her crane ladder had rendered her unable to work for a good few weeks. She had not been able to take home a wage, something her mom and dad heavily relied on to help with the household upkeep.

'Right, luv, see you in a few hours,' Nancy said, taking her coat off and placing it next to her gas mask and bag behind the ladder of her crane, Mildred.

The next four hours passed in what even Patty agreed felt like the blink of eye as they received the non-stop instructions for slabs of steel to be lifted and hauled across the shop floor.

'I reyt thought the day would drag without Archie being around,' Patty confessed as the three women sat down for their dinner. 'But I swear I thought someone had got the timings mixed up when the hooter started – well, apart from the fact m' belly was rumbling.'

'You are a case.' Nancy laughed. 'You're as bad as our Billy when it comes to food. The way he carries on, you'd think I never fed him.'

'Our Tom Tom is the same. M' mom says we've both got hollow legs.' Patty nodded, opening her haversack and pulling out the snap her mom had prepared for her at the crack of dawn. 'Spam sandwich,' she announced, unwrapping the brown greaseproof paper parcel, held together with a piece of string. 'Me favourite, although I'm not s' keen on this brown bread. I prefer the white stuff.'

'I think you might be waiting a while for that, duck,' said Dolly, who had taken a quick break from serving hot dinners to the hordes of hungry steelworkers now filling the canteen. 'Looks like we are stuck with this grainy National Flour for a while.'

'I asked m' mom if she could use a sieve to get all the bits out,' Patty exclaimed, taking a disgruntled bite out of her doorstep sandwich, which to her utter disdain also had only the faintest smearing of butter.

'And what was her response to that?' Nancy asked, somewhat bemused, as she endeavoured to stifle her laughter at the thought of poor Angie finding enough time in the day to honour Patty's presumptive request.

'Well, not to put too fine a point on it, she told me she would shove the sieve where the sun don't shine if I asked her again.'

The whole table, except Patty, burst into a fit of giggles. 'I'm not surprised, duck,' Dolly finally said, tears streaming down her cheeks.

'What?' Patty said, her face poker straight. 'I've heard some women do it and give the grains to the hens.'

'Yes, but you haven't got any hens, luv.' Nancy chortled. 'And I reckon your mom has enough on looking after you lot and running a house, especially with your Tom Tom now on the move.'

'Oh, I suppose yer right,' Patty conceded. 'Did I tell yer she found him at the coal bucket again trying to eat the flamin' stuff? Apparently he was covered head to foot in soot and the only white me mom could see was the rings in his eyes.'

'Yer see, duck,' Dolly said, 'yer poor mom has enough to contend with, without spending hours chuffin' refining bread for you.'

'Our Billy and Linda aren't too keen either,' Nancy added. 'They'd much rather have a slice of good old white bread, with a thick layer of jam, but I think those days are over for a while.'

'It's hard for little ones to understand, isn't it?' Dolly sympathized. 'My granddaughters are the same.'

'It is,' Nancy agreed. 'Especially our Billy, who I'm sure has the appetite of a grown man. He's not impressed that I can't make as many buns and the biscuit tin isn't overflowing with treats anymore.'

'They are too young to have to cope with the ins and outs of a blasted war,' Dolly sighed. 'Anyway,' she turned back to Patty, 'I didn't mean to bring the mood down and I assume by your upturn in mood, our Archie is okay?'

'Oh yes! He's definitely much better than he was, thank you,' Patty trilled. 'To look at him, you would think he is nearly back to his normal self, but he is going to have to look after himself if he doesn't want to have another scare.' The group listened eagerly as she explained how Archie had suffered from a weak heart valve all his life. 'He generally has it under control with medication,' she went on, 'but as soon as he gets the whiff of an infection, it knocks him for six. I think he knew he wasn't right a few weeks ago but he was too stubborn to take a break.'

'I hope he's taken heed and is going to now?' Dolly asked, concern etched across her soft face.

'He says he has!' Patty replied. 'I think he has had quite the scare and the doctors have told him, they will only let him come home on the condition he has some time off, but he really has got to listen to his body and slow down when he's not feeling so good. I've promised his mum I will try and keep an eye on him, but you know how stubborn he can be.'

'Archie and my mum are alike then,' Daisy interjected, as she joined her friends for dinner.

'What's that?' Nancy was secretly praying she had heard Daisy right. 'Have they said your mum can come home too?'

'Yes!' Daisy grinned, her face a picture of elation, as she took a seat at the table, which was conveniently positioned next to the Swap Club box. 'Dad went in to see her after work last night and it looks like she could be home at some point next week.'

Nancy fought back the tears threatening to escape. Her chat, one mum to another, had done the trick. Although when Nancy had sat down with Daisy's desperately ill mum, Josie, a few days before Christmas, she couldn't be sure if the exhausted and frightened woman would take her advice and finally go and get the medical help she needed. Josie had been convinced it would be the last Christmas with her husband and three children and had refused to hand over another penny to a doctor, knowing what a dent it was putting in the already stretched family finances. But after Betty had made sure they wouldn't go without – rallying everyone to donate to the Swap Club collection tin, from presents to mince pies, and paper-chain bunting to a hamper of food – Josie had accepted she didn't want it to be her last. On Boxing Day, she had allowed her husband, Alf, to take her to the City Hospital, where doctors had diagnosed her with an ulcer and a nasty infection, but now, over two months after Nancy had sat down with her, pleading with her to get help, she was finally on the mend and coming home.

'Well, if that's not a reason to celebrate, I have no idea what is,' Dolly cheered. 'After all the worry recently, we needed some good news, and it looks like it's landed all at once.'

'You're absolutely right there,' Patty agreed. 'We should mark the occasion.'

'How about a drink in the Wellington on Friday? I reckon with Archie going to be all right and Josie home soon – not to mention the success of Sunday's event – we all deserve a little toast.'

'Oooh,' Patty trilled at the thought of a bit of excitement. 'Could I invite my friend Hattie too? She ain't 'alf missing her John and it might do her good to get out for a bit.' Like Bert, Hattie's sweetheart had been posted to France at the start of the war.

'Of course.' Dolly smiled. 'The more the merrier and heaven knows, we all need a little boost every now and again.'

'Let me check if Doris minds having the kids for an extra half an hour,' Nancy said. 'If she's okay with it, I'd love to pop in.' Nancy couldn't remember the last time she had been to a pub. It would have been before her Billy came along, when she and Bert would sometimes go for a quick drink on the way to the pictures on Saturday night.

'Don't laugh,' Betty said, nursing her freshly made cuppa she had poured from Dolly's stainless-steel urn, 'but I've never been in a pub.'

'What?' Dolly gasped.

The four women all stopped what they were doing and looked at one another in shock.

'Are you serious?' Patty finally broke the silence. 'Even I've been in a boozer and I don't turn eighteen till July!'

'Did yer dad never take you in as a nipper for a glass of lemonade and a bag of pork scratchings while he had a pint?' Dolly asked, stunned by Betty's revelation.

'Not as far as I can remember,' Betty confessed. 'After my mum died, I think he was so determined to make up for her not being around, that once he'd finished work, he just wanted to be at home with us all. He's never been the sort of man to drown his sorrows in the bottom of a pint pot. He likes the odd drink at Christmas or on a special occasion but that's about it.'

'Well, in that case, we definitely need to introduce you to the Wellington,' Dolly exclaimed. 'What about you, Daisy? Do you think you might be able to make it?'

'Erm, I'll check my aunt and dad don't mind. I just feel a bit guilty putting on my aunt. She's already done so much for us while Mum has been in hospital.'

'Okay, duck.' Dolly nodded. 'Listen, if it's too tricky, we can always do it another time.'

'Let me ask and I'll let you know, if that's okay?' Daisy asked.

'Of course,' Dolly said. 'Same for you, Nancy,' she added, turning to the older of the three crane drivers.

'Thanks, luv,' Nancy replied, finishing off her thinly sliced cheese sandwich, which had also been made using the new National Flour. 'Now, Betty,' she added, 'did you say you had a new idea you wanted to chat to us all about?'

Betty glanced down at her watch. 'I do, but I reckon it will take more than the two minutes we've got left of our break.'

'Jeepers, is that the time?' Dolly said, quickly gathering up the empty mugs. 'I better get back behind that counter before the next load arrives, claiming their throats have been slashed and they are starvin'. But I want to hear more about this new plan,' she added, turning to Betty, already guessing she had another project tucked up her sleeve and keen to get them all involved in.

Chapter 3

Friday, 2 February 1940

'Right, girls, here we are,' Dolly said, as the group all arrived outside the Wellington on the corner of Upwell Street, a few minutes' walk from Vickers.

The women had come to a standstill outside the huge brown-brick pub, the door swinging open every couple of seconds as overall-clad men from the many factories that stood shoulder to shoulder throughout Attercliffe made their way in to spend some of their hard-earned weekly wages.

'Are you all ready?' Dolly asked.

'Yes!' Patty cheered enthusiastically, although she realized she was hardly dressed for a big night out in her mucky boiler suit that seemed to exhale dust no matter how much she or her mom scrubbed it.

'I think so,' Betty muttered, still slightly apprehensive.

'Come on.' Nancy laughed, bemused by her friend's uncharacteristic hesitance. 'You will be fine.'

'Right, well, no time like the present,' Dolly said, pushing open the doors and leading the women into the lounge.

'What's through that other door?' Betty enquired, curious to why they were going into the room opposite.

'That's the tap room, luv,' Dolly explained. 'Where the men like to play darts, cards or dominoes.'

'And according to my dad the beer is cheaper,' Hattie quipped. 'And he would know.' Patty glanced at her friend, but for once didn't say anything, knowing how much it upset Hattie that her dad would spend most nights in the boozer and come home roaring drunk.

'Right, girls,' Dolly said, ushering them to a quiet table in the corner. 'You lot get a seat and I'll go to the bar. What are you all having?'

'Could I just have a lemonade?' Patty asked. 'I can give you the money,' she added, not wanting to assume.

'Get away with yer,' Dolly laughed, 'this is my treat, duck, you've all worked like troopers.'

'As have you,' Betty pointed out, still trying to take in the smoky surroundings. The dark mahogany bar was filling up and there was a steady hum of chatter. On the walls hung black-and-white pictures of Sheffield over the years. The wooden tables were enveloped by chairs on one side and built-in bench-like sofas, with deep-red upholstered cushioning, on the other, against the walls.

'But I don't shift great bulking slabs of steel all day long,' Dolly reasoned. 'Anyway, I insist.'

'Well, maybe just a small port and lemon if that's okay?' Betty replied gratefully.

'It is. Now go and sit down. And what can I get everyone else?' Dolly added, spinning round to face the others.

In turn, Nancy, Daisy and Hattie all politely gave their preferences, as they huddled together, conscious they were the only group of women in the bar and were on the receiving end of several curious and amused glances from members of the opposite sex.

'It's like walking into the factory again for the first time,' Patty whispered.

'I know what you mean,' Daisy agreed, avoiding the blatant stares of the men, who were holding their pints and exchanging smirks.

It was just the ammunition Betty needed to quash her nerves. Despite never stepping foot inside a pub in her life, and having to ask Dolly if women were even allowed in without a man by their side, she suddenly felt galvanized.

'Well, we have as much right to be here as any man,' she said, her steely persona, once again forcing its way to the fore. On the first day she had started at Vickers, Betty had given one of Frank's colleagues short shrift for insinuating women didn't belong in the works, and when Nancy was getting a hard time from the arrogant lad she had initially been teamed up with, it was Betty who had forthrightly insisted her friend shouldn't stand for any nonsense.

'That's the spirit, duck,' Dolly said, as she made her way over to the table, carefully balancing a tray full of drinks. 'They'll all stop gawping soon. Women might be a rarity in here, but we aren't the first and at the rate we are losing lads to the war effort and you lasses are taking their places, we definitely won't be the last.'

'Exactly!' Betty added, now finding her feet in the unfamiliar surroundings. 'We have as much right to an end-of-the-day drink as they do!'

'Get you,' Patty harked. With that the group of women burst into a fit of laughter, bringing even more attention to themselves.

'Right,' Dolly said, raising her glass of pale ale, after they had contained themselves. 'I raise a toast to the Vicktory Knitters and good health to our Archie.'

'I'll definitely drink to that,' Patty cheered.

'Hear hear,' Betty added, as they all took a sip of their drinks.

'Eee, it's nice just to relax a bit, isn't it?' Dolly stated more than asked.

'I won't argue with you there,' Nancy replied. 'I'm looking forward to a bit of time with our Billy and Linda this weekend.'

'I bet you are, luv,' Dolly said. 'It's important. Spending time with my granddaughters is the one thing that really spurs me on and gives me hope.'

Nancy nodded as it dawned on her again that she wasn't alone. Not that she would want anyone else to feel the anguish she was suffering, but knowing she wasn't alone gave her the encouragement she needed to bolster her spirits.

'Now,' Nancy asked, turning to Betty, determined to take a leaf out of Dolly's book and not mope about the ifs and maybes. 'Didn't you say earlier in the week, you had something you wanted to chat to us all about?'

'What's this?' Dolly asked, winking at Betty, in mock surprise. 'Don't tell me, you have another plan up your sleeve?'

'As it happens, I have been thinking about something.' Betty grinned.

'Of course, you have,' Patty said.

'It's just a seed of an idea at the moment,' Betty started.

'Well, come on then. Spit it out. What are you all going to have us doing next?'

Five pairs of eyes turned to Betty, keen to hear what her latest idea was.

'I've been thinking—' she began.

'You never have,' Patty quipped.

'Ssssh.' Hattie gave her friend a gently nudge in the ribs.

'Don't worry,' Betty laughed, raising her eyebrows in jest, 'I'm used to it. Anyway, as I was saying, I was thinking that maybe we could carry on knitting.'

'Hey?' Patty said, looking confused. 'Who for now? Surely we have kitted out 'alf of Sheffield.'

'I agree,' Betty said. 'But how about we join the national campaign to knit for the troops?'

'Oh, luv,' Nancy said, once again taken aback by Betty's thoughtfulness.

'Actually,' Betty said. 'It was holding back those socks for your Bert at the Vicktory Knitters event that inspired me. I heard something on the radio about the government encouraging us all to knit for victory and it made me think of all those soldiers who might benefit from a few extra woollies.'

'That's a lovely idea,' Nancy said, trying to stave off the tears which were filling her eyes. She was sure Bert and men like him would take so much comfort knowing folk back at home were doing their bit to keep them warm and dry.

'My two lads would be reyt grateful, duck,' Dolly added. 'It's a grand idea.'

'I didn't know you had sons away in the forces,' Betty said. 'You never said.'

'Aw, you have all had enough on yer plates these last few months. You didn't need to hear me harping on about my troubles.'

'Are they soldiers too?' Nancy asked, in awe of Dolly's strength. Not once had she bared her soul about how worried she must be.

'No, they are both in the navy. Joined up at the same time. I'm lucky though, as their wives are smashin' girls, and as I said, I get to see both my granddaughters every weekend and usually at least once a week for tea.'

'What are they called, Dolly?' Betty asked kindly.

'Johnny's me eldest, he's twenty-five, and then Michael is twenty-two. A reyt pair of rascals they were as little ones, always thick as thieves, so I'm just taking comfort in the fact they are together at the moment.'

'You really should have said sooner,' Betty sighed.

'Don't be fretting, duck,' Dolly replied, waving her hand, indicating no fuss was needed. 'We can't worry about something that hasn't happened yet, we've just got to stay positive, or we'll not have the strength to get up each day.'

'I honestly don't know how you do it,' Nancy said, taking a small sip of her port and lemon. 'I reckon I need to follow your lead though.'

'Don't get me wrong, duck, I have m' moments, like we all do. I've had m' fair share of sleepless nights but I make m'sen get up each morning and paint a smile on m' face, otherwise I'd fall t' bits and then what good would I be. A bit like you lasses, m' job keeps me going. Ensuring you lot are fed and watered is my way of helping the war effort. If you lot have no energy, you can't make the parts and munitions our troops need.'

'Well,' Betty said, 'that has well and truly cemented my thoughts. Between Bert and your two sons, that's more than enough motivation for us to help our soldiers, sailors and pilots.'

'I'll definitely drink to that.' Dolly smiled, lifting her glass, and once again the women all raised theirs, vowing to start working on their knitting immediately.

'Ivy was telling me the government are producing some patterns, so we can send them exactly what they need. As well as socks, apparently they need knitted helmets to wear under their hats and scarves.'

'Oh, thank God they need scarves,' Patty exclaimed. 'I'm not reyt sure I could do anything more complicated than that. It took all m' time and most of Nancy's patience to teach me that much.'

'Yer not wrong there,' Nancy laughed, recalling how many times she had to unpick Patty's first attempts at following a basic pattern, 'but we got there in the end.'

'Right, well, I shall find out if there are some collection points where we can deliver supplies to and if no one objects, I could use some of the collection tin money to buy more wool.'

'Of course,' came the unison of replies.

'I reckon my mum will be able to do a bit more this time too,' Daisy said.

'Oh gosh, sorry, Daisy. With all my nerves about coming to the pub, I completely forgot to ask. Does it look like your mum might be home as soon as you'd hoped?'

'Yes, actually,' Daisy answered. 'It looks like we can definitely bring her home early next week.'

'Oh, luv, that's wonderful,' Nancy said. 'Between Archie being home and your mum about to be, this really is the best news.'

'Another toast?' Patty proposed, clinking her glass with Daisy's. They didn't need to say another word, but both implicitly understood the importance of good health.

'You'll get no arguments there from me,' Nancy agreed, as they all exchanged delighted grins and emptied their glasses.

'Well, thank you all so much.' Daisy smiled, grateful once again to have been welcomed into this special group of friends. 'But I better be getting off. I promised my dad and aunt I wouldn't be late and would help with tea. Maybe once things have settled down, we could do this more often.

It's been nice to do something that doesn't revolve around work or cooking and cleaning.'

'Yes, we must,' Betty insisted, thinking how good this had been for them all. 'That reminds me,' she said, leaning down to pick up her bag. 'Before we go, I've got a few bits here for your mum.' She handed over a couple of books to Daisy. 'Ivy sent these. She thought they might be useful if she starts to get a bit bored.'

'That's so kind,' Daisy replied. 'The doctors have warned she's got to rest for a while yet, so these and a bit of knitting might stop her trying to do too much too soon. My aunt has insisted she stays for a while longer until mum is back to full health too, as she knows what she's like.'

'I think that's a very wise plan,' Nancy said. 'And if she fancies a natter, I'm happy to pop down one weekend when she's got her strength back.'

'I think she would like that,' Daisy said, carefully placing the four books in her own bag.

'And I haven't forgotten about Archie,' Betty said, passing Patty a pair of woolly socks and a dark-grey knitted scarf. 'These were hiding in the bottom of a bag after the event. I thought they might be useful for him.'

'They will indeed,' Patty said. 'It's flamin' freezing out there and the last thing he needs is getting a cold again.'

'I must admit it does feel like this winter is never ending,' Nancy said, standing up and pulling on her coat. 'I reckon it will be hot pans wrapped in blankets in bed again tonight.'

Chapter 4

'William!' Betty exclaimed as she opened the front door to find her fiancé beaming at her. 'My goodness. What on earth are you doing here?'

'Surprise!' he said, his arms open wide.

'You're not joking,' Betty said in shock. 'You didn't say in your letters you had some leave coming up.'

'I wanted to surprise you,' he said, leaning over to give Betty a kiss. 'Now are you going to invite me in? It's perishing out here. They reckon snow is on the way,' he added, quickly rubbing his arms, exaggerating a shiver. 'These uniforms weren't made for Yorkshire winters.'

'Of course, come on in.' Betty stood to one side as she ushered William, who was dressed in his mid-blue pilot's dress jacket and trousers, inside the house. And despite still being in a state of shock at the unexpected visit, Betty managed to register how dashingly handsome her sweetheart looked in his uniform.

'Now,' he said once Betty had closed the door, shutting out the cold air that had left his cheeks pink, but his lips nearly blue, 'come here.' With that William pulled his fiancée close, wrapped his arms around her slender back and gave her a much longer kiss on the lips.

'I have missed you so much,' he said, after they finally parted. 'And I won't lie, I have missed those kisses even more.'

'William!' Betty blushed, but was secretly delighted. 'I have missed you so much too. Please come and sit down and I will make us a pot of tea. I think Ivy might even have a slice of vinegar cake left you can have.'

'Vinegar cake?' William quizzed.

'Oh, it's her latest recipe. Now eggs are scarce, she's getting rather creative. I have to say, it's really quite nice. Not too heavy.'

'Did I hear my name?' came Ivy's familiar voice from down the hall.

'Hello, Mrs Wallis.' William grinned at the sight of yet another person stunned to see him.

'It's Ivy now, dear,' Betty's landlady said, waving off the now rather Victorian-sounding formality. Ever since she had invited Frank for Christmas Day dinner, she had insisted she be known by her Christian name. 'But more importantly, what are you doing here and why aren't you in Doncaster?'

'Exactly what I would like to know!' Betty chuckled.

'I'll tell you over that cuppa and slice of cake you just promised me,' William said, throwing Betty one of his cheeky smiles. 'I'm parched and my stomach is rumbling.

I've not eaten since breakfast. I was so keen to see you, I quickly dropped my bags at home and came straight here.'

'Oh, I bet your mum wasn't best impressed,' Ivy exclaimed.

'Well, I promised I would have tea with her tonight, so she let me off.'

'You two go and sit down. You will have plenty to catch up on. I'll go and make some tea and muster up a sandwich and a slice of cake.'

'Are you sure?' Betty asked. 'I don't want to put you out.'

'Nonsense, dear. Now go,' she added, shuffling the pair of them into the front room. 'It's warm in there too. I've just put some extra coal on the fire.'

Ten minutes later, William was tucking into a cheese sandwich. 'Despite how limited the rations are, Ivy can't bear the thought of anyone going hungry,' Betty said, as she noted how thickly her landlady had sliced the wholemeal bread.

'Well, we are very well fed but I'm definitely not complaining.' William nodded appreciatively, before taking a slurp of the freshly made cuppa, served, as always, in Ivy's best china crockery.

'Now, are you going to tell me everything you have been up to?' Betty asked, pleased to see her lovely William in the flesh for the first time since he proposed three months earlier.

Suddenly William's cheery demeanour vanished, replaced by a rather more sombre expression.

'What is it?' Betty asked, a cold shiver of apprehension shooting down her spine.

'Please don't look so aghast,' William said, putting his empty plate on the coffee table and wiping the breadcrumbs from his lips.

'But there is something, isn't there?'

Taking her hands, William sat up tall. 'I have some good news and some other news that I would like to talk to you about.'

Betty tensed, closing her eyes for a second. William hadn't said bad news, but she wasn't daft and knew instinctively he was trying to soften whatever the blow was he was about to deliver.

'What's your good news?' she asked, not wanting to destroy the moment and hoping to delay whatever it was William had come here to tell her.

'I have passed all my written exams with flying colours, even algebra and trigonometry, which really were quite hard. Apparently I got some of the highest marks,' he announced proudly, flashing his familiar grin, which would normally put Betty at ease immediately.

'That is wonderful, William,' she said, trying to keep a brave face. 'You have worked so hard and deserve this. I'm so very proud of you.'

'Thank you.' William nodded, still smiling. 'I have to say, I was rather relieved. If I hadn't passed, I don't think they let you carry on with pilot training.'

Betty anxiously bit down on her lip. *This is it. The bad*

news is coming. Pressing her fingertips into the palms and forming tight balls with her hands, she opened her mouth to speak, but no matter how hard she tried, the words just wouldn't come out. *Come on, be brave,* she admonished herself. 'What happens now?' Betty whispered, her voice barely audible.

'My lovely, sweet Bet, please don't worry,' William said, edging closer to her on the brown leather Chesterfield.

'Just tell me,' Betty said, steeling herself for whatever it was William was about to say, but instead of feeling galvanized, she felt as fragile as the lacy covering of snow that was now settling outside on the ledge of the living room window.

William gently uncurled Betty's quivering hands and placed them in his own. 'I have to go away,' was all he could manage.

Betty squeezed her lips together, briefly closing her eyes. 'Where to?' she forced herself to ask.

'Just to a place near Leicester, called Desford to begin with. It's one of the Elementary Flying Training Schools. I'll get to go in a Tiger Moth.'

Betty had no idea what a Tiger Moth was and in this precise moment, she neither cared nor wished to know. 'To begin with?' She repeated the words that had acted as a catalyst for the icy goose pimples that had made her whole body stiffen.

Despite how excited William was about the news his senior officers had delivered, he was also acutely conscious it would terrify Betty. 'Once I've been graded, I will then be sent to join the Empire Air Training Scheme.'

'Empire?' Betty muttered the only word that had really registered. That didn't sound like an English RAF base. 'Where will you have to go?'

This time it was William's turn to bite his lip. The last thing he wanted to do was upset his lovely Bet. 'I won't know until I've been assessed,' he said slowly, trying to break the latest development as gently as possible. 'But we have been warned it could be Rhodesia, Canada or the United States of America.'

'Oh, William,' Betty gasped, no longer able to prevent her tears from falling. 'They are all so far away. How long will you be gone for?'

All the fears Betty had initially felt when William had announced he wanted to join the RAF the previous summer came rushing back. She'd tried to brush it off as a pipe dream from reading too many Biggles books as a little boy, but William's childhood hopes had only grown as the threat of Hitler had advanced. Betty knew William was doing the right and honourable thing by their country, but she had naively assumed it would take much longer for him to be sent abroad.

'I don't know,' William replied honestly. 'They haven't told us a lot yet.'

Betty took a deep breath in. She might not be an expert in pilot training, but she couldn't imagine this would only be a short trip, despite how much the RAF needed pilots. In her heart of hearts, Betty always knew this day would come but she hadn't allowed her mind to travel that far, as she knew it would leave her utterly floored. Betty had always prided herself for being so resilient, but this rotten war would test the patience of even the strongest of people, and whenever it came to anything that involved William, it left Betty's heart physically aching.

'Okay,' was all she could whisper, scared if she said anything else it would only cause her brave and determined William to feel guilty, and no matter how frightened she was, Betty could never deliberately allow that.

'Please try not to worry,' William said, taking both of Betty's hands in his.

Unable to trust she could hide her deflated reaction from William, Betty dropped her head and stared down at her lap, trying with all her might to stop her shoulders from shuddering, but the heavy, salty tears came unbidden, dropping onto her thick emerald-green skirt, unforgivingly creating dark round circles in the weave of the wool.

'Come on,' William said softly, lifting his fiancée's chin with one hand and forcing her to look at him. 'It won't be so bad. I will write to you just like I do now and as soon as I get leave, you will be the first person I come and see.'

'I know,' Betty cried, her voice faltering. 'It just seems so far away.' But what she didn't say was, it wasn't just William travelling to the other side of the world that worried her, but the fact it was now only a matter of time before he would be soaring the skies of Europe, his life at the mercy of Hitler's air force.

William battled with his own conscience. He had known the news would upset Betty, how could he not? But he also knew without a shadow of a doubt, he had to do this. He couldn't stand back and do nothing while a war was raging across Europe. Not much had happened in England yet. There had been lots of false alarms but no actual attacks. William had started to hear the term 'Phoney War', but he wasn't so sure. There was a reason the RAF were keen to get their pilots trained up fast, so mustering the only words he could think of, William pulled Betty into his arms, and as she leant into his chest, he said exactly what she needed to hear, and he firmly believed: 'I will come back.'

For the next few minutes, William held Betty tight as her tears soaked his pilot's jacket. He hated seeing the woman he loved so utterly bereft. The fact he was causing her so much pain made his own heart ache, an overwhelming mixture of guilt and sadness. This was never what he intended.

'I'm sorry,' Betty finally whispered, lifting herself up, her face blotchy and eyes red and swollen. 'What a dafty I'm being,' she added, summoning what little resolve she could.

'No, no, you're not,' William replied. 'I don't like the idea of being so far away from you either and the last thing I wanted to do was come here today and cause you so much upset.'

'It's all right.' Betty nodded, retrieving a pink-and-white handkerchief from the sleeve of her winter cream cardigan and dabbing her eyes.

William poured her a fresh cup of tea. 'It's still warm,' he said. 'Have some. My mum always says a good cuppa makes you feel better.'

Betty couldn't help but smile. That was William, looking on the bright side without fail and never overthinking anything, determined not to dwell on things that might cause him to see the world in a more sinister light. It was hard not to be infected by William's positive outlook on life.

'She's a wise woman,' Betty agreed, taking a sip, the warmth acting as a comfort.

'That she is,' William said. 'And what is it, Archie says? "Let's turn that frown upside down."'

'Oh, William,' Betty said, slowly shaking her head. 'You really are something else.'

But his innocent determination to play down the suffocating gravity of the situation was working as the heavy, foreboding atmosphere began to lift.

'I just think we have to have hope and not dwell on the bad things, and where possible try and stay positive.'

Betty thought about William's words. She was used to his rose-tinted view on life, but she also knew, in many ways he was right. Wasn't this just his way of coping with what was going on around him, in the same way she channelled all her energy into helping people, to keep herself busy? Was there really anything wrong with that?

'You're right,' Betty conceded, all too conscious of the fact that, no matter what her fears, she couldn't transfer those to William, especially when she had no idea when they would see one another again. However frightened she was about his dream 'to be the best pilot the RAF had ever had', Betty knew he had to always believe that he would be coming home and that one day when this godforsaken war was over, they would live normal lives again. 'And we do have so much to look forward to.'

'That's the spirit.' William grinned, relieved Betty's tears had stopped, although acutely aware she was now exaggeratingly stoic. 'And don't forget,' he added, determined to keep his sweetheart buoyed, 'as soon as we have forced Hitler to surrender, we have a wedding to plan.'

'Of course.' Betty smiled, trying to bat away the fears that one wrong manoeuvre or a successful attack from the Luftwaffe could extinguish any wedding plans or wipe out their future together.

A few hours later, after William had tenderly kissed her goodbye, promising he would return the following morning, Betty responded to Ivy's calls from the dining room.

'Come and sit down, dear,' she encouraged, the table already laid and two plates modestly filled with a slice of corned beef hash, carrots and peas. 'No matter what, you still need your strength.'

'I guess you overheard?' Betty asked.

Ivy nodded. 'I wasn't eavesdropping but as I was cooking I caught the gist of it.' What Ivy didn't mention was how it had brought up the painful memories of when her late husband, Lewin, had gone off to fight in the Great War.

'I'm scared,' Betty admitted, almost collapsing into her chair in front of her meal.

'I know,' Ivy said. 'And no matter how hard you try not to be, you are going to be anxious. Sadly, we are humans, and our emotions won't allow us not to feel fretful at a time like this.'

'Does it get any easier?'

Ivy gently placed her knife and fork back down, either side of her plate. 'I don't think it does,' she confessed, 'but you do learn to cope.'

Betty nodded. Ivy rarely mentioned the man who stood pride of place in the black-and-white photo on her front-room mantelpiece and Betty was too polite to pry but had always sensed from the few comments her landlady had made, she'd been left heartbroken and widowed.

'How do you remain strong?' Betty asked, desperate to make sure she didn't fall apart. After all, if Nancy could keep herself together, with two young children to take care of and a husband away in France, then surely she could.

'I found the key was to keep busy. That way your mind can't wander for too long,' Ivy explained. What she didn't have the heart to reveal was, no matter how hard she had tried to keep herself occupied, it still hadn't prevented her from lying awake for hours in the black of night, hoping beyond hope she would one day be reunited with her Lewin.

'I'm trying.'

'You are, dear,' Ivy agreed encouragingly. 'In fact, you

are more than trying. You are doing a truly marvellous job. I'm so very proud of you.'

Betty had to swallow hard to stop another onslaught of tears. Although her dad often said she made him proud, to hear it from Ivy, who had become a surrogate mum to Betty, pulled at her heartstrings. She missed not having a mum to confide in, especially since her elder sister, Margaret, who had helped bring her up after their mum died when Betty was just ten years old, had moved to Nottingham with her husband, Derek, and their daughter, June.

'Thank you,' Betty whispered.

'I mean it, dear. Look at everything you have achieved so far. You rally those girls round at Vickers, keeping them buoyed when life feels tough, not to mention all the good you have done to help others. And now, you have set up another project to knit for troops and sailors. My only worry is you may run yourself ragged if you aren't careful.'

'What do you mean?' Betty asked tentatively. Compared to what Nancy had to juggle, she didn't feel her own list of things to do was too taxing.

'I just worry,' Ivy started, carefully cutting up a potato, 'you aren't having much fun. You are only twenty-three but everything you do revolves around work or helping other people. I just think you need to do something for you too and relax a little, every now and again.'

Betty had always been a hard worker, determined to show she was capable of being independent. Before starting at Vickers she had been employed as a secretary in a solicitor's firm and had every intention of studying for her law exams. But, when war broke out, she had put her plans on hold, her conscience propelling her to do her bit. Before William had signed up to the RAF, they would go to the pictures, have walks around the park and occasionally go to the odd Saturday night dance, but after she'd joined the factory, and William had been posted to Doncaster, apart from two nights out with her workmates, she hadn't even considered that having fun was something she needed to do – there was a war going on after all!

'Just give it some thought,' Ivy added, noting the per-turbed look on Betty's face.

'Okay,' came her reply, but if the truth be known, she really wouldn't know where to start.

The following morning, Betty was waiting by the door, her scarf already tightly tied around her neck and her gloves pulled on, when she heard William approach up the path.

'Have you got your flask?' Ivy asked.

'I have.' Betty smiled, patting her cloth bag with the last two slices of vinegar cake Ivy had insisted she take with her.

Before William could even knock, Betty opened the door.

'I'm assuming that means you're keen to see me?' He grinned, as he pulled his woollen hat down to cover his ears.

'Of course,' Betty said, determined not to ruin their last morning together by getting upset. There was plenty of time for tears, and right now wasn't one of them. She just needed to enjoy this moment with William.

'I know it's a bit nippy, but I thought we could go for a walk around the park.'

'Your wish is my command,' William said, offering Betty his arm. 'Even in this weather, it is still one of my favourite places.'

'Mine too,' Betty replied, linking her arm with William's. There was no need for an explanation. The park had been one of their regular haunts since they'd started courting, as well as the spot where William had proposed.

Ten minutes later, the pair were strolling around the paths which circumnavigated the normally neat green grassy areas now covered in a layer of white lace-like frost.

'I meant what I said yesterday,' William said, breaking their comfortable silence.

'What's that?' Betty asked.

'As soon as all this is over, we should get married and then we can look forward to spending the rest of our lives together.'

'Oh, William, I can't think of anything better.'

'That's a pact then,' William said, leading Betty to the very bench where he'd surprised her with his nannan's engagement ring. 'Let's have a toast with that flask of tea you have brought with you.'

'I have cake too.' Betty smiled, knowing William would never turn down a sweet treat.

'Even better!' William exclaimed.

But just as Betty was about to sit down, William stopped her. 'Hold on a moment,' he said, taking off his own navy woollen scarf.

'What are you doing?' Betty quizzed. 'You will freeze.'

'One bonus of being in the RAF, I now always wear a set of thermals. Going up in those planes can be arctic, so I'm actually not too bad,' he explained, chivalrously laying down his scarf to make a cushion for Betty to sit on.

'You are a true gentleman, William Smith,' Betty said gratefully, quite sure even her trusty thick brown tweed coat wouldn't protect her from the cold park bench.

'Well, what sort of man would I be if I let my fiancée freeze?'

Betty couldn't help but chuckle as she opened the flask of steaming tea and poured it into the lid, which doubled as a cup. 'Here you go,' she said, offering William the welcoming brew.

'Ladies first,' William insisted. 'Besides which, I have a little something for you.'

'Oh,' Betty said, taken aback. William turning up unannounced had already been the best of surprises. 'You really didn't have to.'

'I know,' William said. 'But I wanted to,' he added, handing Betty a long, rectangular gold velvet box.

'What is it?' she asked, curious.

'Open it and you will see.'

Betty popped her tea on the bench as she carefully flipped open the soft-to-touch box. Inside was a beautiful navy-blue fountain pen, with a gold clip on the lid.

'Oh, William,' she gasped. 'It's exquisite.'

'Well, you have no excuse not to write to me and tell me about every single thing you get up to.'

'I would do that anyway,' Betty replied, her voice ever so slightly faltering, 'but I shall write even longer letters now.'

'Good!' William gave Betty a peck on the cheek.

Betty rested her head on William's shoulder, cherishing the moment as she smiled at how thoughtful he was. William had known how hard it would be to tell her he was moving farther away, and then eventually onto heaven knows where, so instead of making the idea of letter writing a heart-rending reminder of the distance between them, he'd found a way to not only soften the blow but to actually make it special.

'I really am very lucky,' Betty whispered, somehow managing to stay composed, not wanting their final morning together to end on a sad note, despite knowing how much she was going to miss William and worrying about whether he would make it through this blasted war.

With that, William wrapped his strong arms tightly around Betty's slender frame. 'I think you'll find I'm the lucky one,' he said, affectionately. 'You are the best fiancée a man could ever wish for and knowing you are here waiting for me is all I need to make sure we are together again soon.'

Chapter 5

'How are you all?' Dolly called as she approached the Swap Club corner of the canteen. 'Did you all have a good weekend?'

'It was grand, thank you.' Patty beamed. 'I spent most of it with Archie.'

'Aw, and how is my favourite young steelworker?' the canteen manager asked, as she gave the stainless-steel tea urn a little shake, checking to see if it needed topping up.

'Well, he's okay, but a bit fed up.'

Patty's answer grabbed the attention of everyone sitting round the table.

'Why, luv?' Nancy enquired. 'Is he getting bored being stuck at home all day?'

'I think so, but I think there's something more to it too.'

'What do you mean?' Dolly probed, burying her hands into her blue striped apron.

'I reckon he's fed up with everyone coddling him, asking if he's okay and fussing round him like he's a sickly kid again.'

'That probably would feel quite suffocating,' Dolly agreed. 'But it's hard as a parent to do any different. You can't help but worry and Archie has had a pretty nasty scare.'

'He has,' Patty nodded, 'and I have to say, I'm firmly on his mum and nannan's side on this one. No matter which way you look at it, he's got a weak heart and needs to be careful.'

'Yer right there, luv,' Dolly agreed, 'but maybe there's a way of keeping an eye on him without him feeling annoyed.'

Sighing, Patty stopped working on her latest knitting project, letting the navy sock fall into her lap. 'That's exactly what Hattie said too. I just don't really know how I can bite my tongue if he's doing too much.'

'Just go gently,' Dolly advised. 'Trust Archie to know his own limits. Wouldn't you all agree?'

'Sorry, what's that?' Betty asked, suddenly aware she hadn't been following the conversation.

'Is everything all right, duck?' Dolly checked. It wasn't like Betty to be so distracted.

'Sorry,' Betty apologized again. 'It's just William – well, he came to visit at the weekend.'

'What?' Patty gasped. 'You kept that quiet!'

Nancy glanced across at her workmate. Now she thought about it, Betty had been very quiet as they had clocked in this morning. She hadn't thought much of it at the time and assumed Betty was just letting Patty vent about her concerns over Archie. 'Is everything okay, luv?'

Betty picked up her mug of warm tea. 'I'm probably just overthinking things as usual, but William is being posted abroad soon to finish his pilot training and I can't help but worry. He had to get a train to Leicester this morning to complete the final part of his initial training in this country.'

The rest of the women listened as Betty repeated what William had told her. 'I tried to be brave when he was telling me,' she said, recalling Saturday's conversation. Betty explained they had spent most of yesterday together, knowing it could be a while before they saw one another again, but every time she thought about him getting his full pilot's licence, tears had flooded her eyes. Then, as they'd said their final goodbyes, she had once again surrendered to her anguish and crumpled into William's arms. And now he was gone, preparing for the next chapter of his unpredictable, terrifying journey.

'Oh, duck,' Dolly said sympathetically, taking a hand from the pocket of her blue-and-white gingham apron and resting it on Betty's shoulder. 'I know it's hard. Heaven knows I've had many a sleepless night worrying about my two lads since they signed up to the navy, but you can get through this. Don't forget we are all here for you.'

'You don't have to cope with this on your own,' Nancy echoed. 'Sometimes just talking it through helps. Look at how many times you have pulled me out of the doldrums when I've struggled to think about what the future holds.'

'I would do that regardless.' Betty smiled.

'That's my point,' Nancy said. 'You don't think twice

about helping anyone else out, whether it be lending a shoulder to cry on or starting a whip round. You are an inspiration and this what you need to keep on doing. The world needs more people like you and it will keep yer mind busy too.'

'Oh, I don't know about that. I have my low moments too.'

'We all do,' Nancy interjected. 'I know how hard it is saying goodbye to someone you love 'n all the fretting that comes with it, but we're here to help you through it.'

'Thank you,' Betty whispered, her voice ever so slightly breaking.

'Don't be daft,' Nancy replied encouragingly. 'That's what friends are for, and like I keep saying, you would do exactly the same.'

'Nancy's right, duck,' Dolly added, taking Betty's now nearly empty mug from her and topping it up from the urn. 'This flamin' war is going to test the best of us but we will get through it. Just don't try and do it alone.'

'You are all so kind,' Betty said, grateful for the freshly poured cuppa.

'Like Nancy says, it's only what you have done for all of us in the past,' Daisy, who had been sat listening, reaffirmed. 'Maybe it's our turn to look after you for a bit.'

'Yes!' Patty exclaimed, feeling a surge of guilt. Here she was having a bit of a moan about Archie, but at least he was still just around the corner, where she could keep a close eye on him. 'We are all here for you.'

'You are all very kind,' Betty said, as it once again dawned on her how this tremendous group of women, who were strangers less than six months ago, had now become such a pillar of support.

'How about once my mum is back on her feet, me and you go to the cinema every now and again, or nip into town for shopping on Saturday and grab a cuppa at a café?' Daisy suggested. 'I can even do your hair like I've been promising.'

'But won't your mum need you at home to help with your sisters and the cooking?' Betty replied.

'She does at the moment,' Daisy agreed. 'But she's getting stronger every day. Even yesterday, despite only coming home on Saturday, she insisted on sitting at the kitchen table to peel the veg for dinner. I reckon in a few weeks' time, she will be able to cope without me for a few hours here and there.'

Betty thought about the advice Ivy had given her about relaxing a little more and having some fun. Maybe this was her opportunity to take heed of what her wise landlady had said.

'That would be lovely.' Betty smiled. Although she wasn't in the mood right now to go out gallivanting, she was astute enough to realize she also couldn't mope about forever. It just wasn't in her nature. At some point, just like she always had, she would have to brush herself off, and carry on. Wasn't that the British bulldog spirit that had got so many through the Great War?

'And I'm always up for another after-work drink in the

Wellington,' Patty added, now laboriously unpicking the last few rows of knitting which she'd made a dog's dinner of.

'Aw, well, we can definitely do that, duck.' Dolly smiled. 'I'm always up for a little tipple after a hard week here.'

'Right,' Dolly added, glancing at the huge clock that adorned the canteen wall. 'I best get back behind that counter and give the lasses a hand. The next lot will be arriving soon for their scran, moaning that they're starvin'."

'Chuffin' 'eck, is it that time already?' Patty exclaimed, shoving her somewhat bedraggled knitting into her cloth bag. 'Dinner breaks never last long enough. Nancy, I'll have to get you to show me what I'm doing wrong with these socks tomorrow. I'm making a right mess of them. They are a lot harder than scarves.'

'Don't worry,' Nancy chuckled, collecting the empty mugs to pop on the tray next to the tea urn, 'you'll be a dab hand by the end of this war.'

'Mmmm,' Patty said. 'I'm not convinced but I'll keep going.'

As the huddle of women made their way back through the maze of factory corridors, Nancy slowed down to walk with Betty, who still wasn't looking her normal chipper self.

'I know it's hard and none of us know what's round the corner, but yer going to be all right, yer know,' she said reassuringly, linking her friend's arm in hers, in a bid to lift Betty's spirits. 'I can't promise everything will turn out perfect, but whatever this war throws at us, you will always have us as friends, and we will get through it together.'

'Aw, Nancy, thank you,' Betty sighed. 'I'm sorry for being a bit gloomy today. I will come out of it. It just hit me hard, William announcing he's going overseas. I really hadn't expected him to leave Doncaster so soon and I don't even know if he will get any more leave before he finishes training at this place near Leicester. I reckon that's why he came home this weekend, to soften the blow in case I don't see him before he gets sent off to God knows where.'

'Of course, it did,' Nancy said, empathizing. 'You wouldn't be the caring woman you are if you weren't upset but remember what you always tell me. Have hope and stay positive. William might be going overseas, but he's still only training, which means he's the safest he can be right now.'

'You're right there,' Betty replied, squeezing Nancy's arm as a way of thanks. She knew what Nancy was saying made a lot of sense. She needed to try and keep some perspective if she could, especially when she was well aware that Nancy's Bert was in France, which if rumour was right, was Hitler's next target. 'Thank you,' Betty added. 'I really am lucky to be surrounded by such good friends.'

'We all are,' Nancy replied, seconds before their voices were drowned out by the ear-piercing screech of metal on metal, and another afternoon of hard work lugging and shifting steel slabs began.

Chapter 6

Sunday, 25 February 1940

'I'm sorry there's no Yorkshire pudding starters today,' Ivy apologized as she encouraged Frank to tuck into the Sunday roast she had prepared for them. 'I'm trying to save my eggs, now we are rationed only one each.' There was just the two of them for dinner after Betty explained she had promised to cook for her dad and brother.

'Gosh, please don't worry,' Frank said, waving away Ivy's concern. 'This all looks absolutely splendid and I'm fairly sure my waistline might benefit from cutting out a few extras here and there,' he added, patting his slightly rotund tummy, barely visible under his navy V-neck sweater and polo shirt.

'Oh, Frank.' Ivy laughed. 'You are hardly overweight, besides which, you are in a physically intensive job and need to keep your strength up.'

'That's what I keep telling myself.' Frank chuckled, cutting up a finely sliced piece of beef.

'Anyway, the main reason I didn't make any puddings today is I'm trying to save a couple of eggs in case I need them for a special occasion.'

'Aw well, I can't fault you. But, I must say it really is quite remarkable how everyone is adapting to rationing and making sure what they have got goes that little bit further. It's been a tough old winter but everyone is doing a grand job of coping.'

'You're not wrong there,' Ivy agreed. 'But we are nearly through it. Let's keep our fingers crossed, we start to see the early signs of spring in the next few weeks.'

'Now that would be lovely,' Frank said. 'It's hard to believe that this time last year, we weren't even seriously considering being at war and now we are working out how to make every scrap of food count.'

'On that note, there is something I would like to get your advice on, if you don't mind, that is?'

'Of course not. I can't promise I can help but I'll do my best.'

'Well,' Ivy began, 'I've been reading about the Dig for Victory campaign and looking at my garden. I've only ever had the odd blackberry bush down at the bottom, which is lovely in the autumn for jams and pies, but I wondered if I could maybe create a vegetable patch. I've got plenty of land out there and as much as it's lovely to look at and sit in during the summer, it all feels a little wasteful, so I was wondering if I could put it to better use.'

'That's a grand idea,' Frank enthused, admiring Ivy's thoughtfulness. 'Heaven knows how limited food is going to get, so if you can produce some of your own, that can only be a good thing.'

'Well, I think Betty and I will probably be okay. Neither of us have huge appetites, but it would be good to do my bit and share with other families that do need extra so nobody goes without.'

'I should imagine people at Vickers would snap your hands off,' Frank encouraged. 'With Daisy's mum not working and Nancy helping Doris with rations as much as she can, along with Patty's parents feeding five kids, the odd bag of carrots or potatoes would go down a treat and make a big difference.'

'That's what I was thinking too.' Ivy smiled. 'Now, here is where I may need your assistance once again.'

'Go on.' Frank chuckled, but was secretly delighted at the idea of having a valid excuse to keep popping over to see Ivy. 'I should warn you, though, I'm not exactly what you would call green-fingered.'

'Don't worry,' Ivy said. 'You don't need to be. My parents used to grow their own vegetables when I was a girl, so I think I can manage that side of things. What I will need help with is digging up some grass to create the vegetable patches, if you think you can lend a hand.'

'Now that's something I can help you with,' Frank beamed, 'and you never know, I might actually learn a thing or two about gardening along the way. I grew up with a backyard, and that's all I have now, so I've never really learnt how to grow anything.'

'In that case, we will make the perfect team!'

'To gardening,' Frank toasted, raising his tankard of pale ale, which Ivy had bought especially for his visit.

'And sharing,' Ivy added, excitedly clinking her glass of sherry with Frank's drink.

'Teamwork at its best.' Frank threw Ivy a warm smile, and instead of feeling pangs of guilt at the thought of betraying his late wife, Mary, he accepted it was good to finally be happy again.

Across town, plans of a different nature were also being discussed.

'Are you sure you are ready to go back to work tomorrow?' Patty asked gently, as she washed and dried pots with Archie. She'd had a lovely afternoon joining his family for a roast chicken dinner and didn't want to spoil things but she couldn't help but worry he was rushing back too soon.

'Yep,' Archie replied, trying to remain jolly despite how much the question irked him. He had been forced to try to reassure everyone countless times in the past week. It wasn't just Patty who insisted on probing him every ten minutes, his mum and nannan had incessantly nagged him.

'I just wanted to be sure,' Patty added, pulling off Gracie's Marigolds, the last of the pans scrubbed to within an inch of their life.

'I've had nearly a month off,' Archie snapped, a little too quickly. 'I reckon that's plenty of time taking it easy, don't you?'

'Okay,' Patty whispered, unsure what else to say for the best.

'Oh, I'm sorry,' Archie said, seeing the flash of hurt

appear on Patty's now forlorn face. 'Come here.' He pulled her into his chest. 'I'm just going a bit stir crazy being at home all the time and I need to get back to work now. I hate the fact that I'm not bringing in any money while I'm sat at home. M' mum would never say anything, but I know she and my dad rely on m' wages and I haven't had any for weeks. I don't like the fact I'm not contributing a single penny right now. Besides which, I promise I feel a million times better.'

Patty looked up at the man she loved with all her heart. She knew only too well after her own spell off work, how hard it was when the family budget was spread a little thin because they were down a wage. 'I just worry,' she said. 'I don't want you to get poorly again.'

'I know.' Archie kissed the top of her head, a mass of strawberry blonde curls. 'But I can't stay at home forever. I will go mad looking at the same four walls.'

Patty nodded. She didn't want to argue with Archie, even if she wished he would just take a little more time off. He still hadn't put back on all the weight he'd lost and although his cough had subsided, it hadn't completely vanished.

'Anyway,' he added, 'what sort of man would I be if I couldn't do my bit while there's a war going on?'

How can I argue with that, without making Archie feel worthless? Patty thought to herself. She just hoped beyond hope he would take it steady and not go hell for leather, trying to prove himself and overdo it all for the sake of his silly pride.

'What's that yer saying?' came Archie mum's voice.

'Nothing!' Archie snapped, once again quicker than he really intended.

The two women exchanged knowing glances. 'We just worry, luv, that's all,' Gracie said gently. 'That's my job as your mum.'

'Well, you really don't need to. I'll be reyt, I promise. Please believe me,' Archie pleaded, his tone softening. 'Besides which, the weather isn't as bad now and I can almost guarantee Frank won't let me out of his sight.'

Well, that's one good thing! Patty thought, immediately thankful she had stopped herself from saying the words out loud, sensing it might have just been the straw that broke the camel's back.

'Why don't I make us all a fresh cuppa,' she said instead, hoping it would lighten the mood. Since first being introduced to Archie's family on Christmas Day, they had made it clear she should treat their home as if it was her own.

'Now that sounds like a grand idea, lass,' Archie's dad, Don, replied, as he walked into the kitchen.

'Let's leave these women to it, son,' he said, putting his fatherly hand on Archie's shoulder. 'We'll only get under their feet. Come and have a game of cards with me in the front room.'

'Why not?' Archie said, relieved, following his dad out of the kitchen and down the hallway. Although Don worried about his son, he'd always avoided smothering him, often acting as a mediator or the calming influence. He knew they had to let Archie make his own way in life, even as he prayed any mistakes Archie made weren't irreparable.

Patty looked at Gracie. 'I'm just worried,' she confessed, filling the kettle before placing it on the hob.

'Story of my life, luv,' she said, somewhat deflated. 'I've worried about that boy since the second he entered the world. He was such a sickly child, always weak, and I would dread every winter, knowing his heart might not be up to it.'

'That must have been hard,' Patty sympathized.

'It was,' Gracie added, nipping into the pantry to fetch a fresh jug of milk from the cold stone. 'He's scared the life out of me too many times, that's for sure. I hoped as he got older the worrying would get less, but it's true what they say, no matter how big they get' – she took some mugs from the cupboard next to the sink – 'they are still your babies and it's hard to let them go. And not that it should make any difference, but he's my only one. My life wouldn't be worth living if I lost him.'

Patty couldn't even begin to imagine the fear Gracie had been forced to endure over the years. She loved Archie and had only known him five months, so she dreaded to think how his own mum felt.

'You'll keep an eye on him, won't you, luv?' Gracie asked, pleased Archie had a nice girl who cared for him.

'Of course,' Patty said, scooping fresh tea leaves into the pink flowery teapot. 'I just hope I don't push him away with my constant worrying. I don't mean to sound like I'm nagging him, but I don't seem to be able to get the words out right. I only get worked up because I care.'

'It's all a tricky balance, luv,' Gracie agreed. 'If it makes you feel any better, in the twenty years I've been his mum, I don't think I've mastered it yet either.'

'Do you think deep down, he knows we mean well?' Patty asked, her vulnerable side revealing itself.

'I reckon so.' Grace nodded, preparing to lift the tea tray and take it into the front room. 'At least I hope so anyway. My biggest worry has always been that Archie will rebel against all my fussing. I just have to pray he keeps himself fit and healthy if he does.'

As Patty followed Gracie into the living room, it dawned on her: loving someone doesn't always go smoothly. Like Gracie had said, she had to let Archie make his own decisions and all she could do was hope she could carefully navigate the path ahead without too many bumps in the road.

Chapter 7

Friday, 1 March 1940

'Hello, you lot.' Dolly beamed as Betty, Nancy, Daisy, Patty, Archie and Frank made their way to the front of the dinner queue. 'How are you all?'

'Starvin'!' came Patty's instantaneous and almost predictable reply.

'Aw, well, it's a good job I've got your Friday treat in store then.' Dolly chuckled, already picking up a warm plate and scooping a generous portion of mince and onion pie onto it. 'I'm afraid there's more gravy than mince but it still tastes good, I promise yer, and there's plenty of mash.'

'I'm sure it will be flamin' gorgeous,' Patty replied, gratefully taking her dinner, her eyes nearly popping out of her head at the thought of tucking in.

'No fear of Hitler making us go hungry with you leading the ship.' Archie, who was next in line, grinned.

'Aw, how are you, luv?' Dolly asked. 'I've seen you over at the Swap Club corner this week, but I've been that busy, I've not had chance to come over and say hello. I reckon they've been recruiting again. There's more women than ever; we're run off our feet.'

'It looks it.' Archie nodded, the cacophony of chatter reverberating around the busy canteen. 'We'll be fighting for yer dinners soon.'

'There will always be a plate of snap here for you, Archie lad, don't you be fretting,' Dolly said, handing over a fuller than normal plate of her much-loved Friday delicacy. 'I've got to keep your energy levels up. We don't want you getting poorly again.'

Archie sighed. Not Dolly too. He knew she only meant well, but was there no reprieve from this constant henpecking? He'd had people fussing over him all week since he'd come back to work.

'Oh, luv, I'm sorry,' the now perturbed canteen manager apologized. 'I didn't mean to cause you any upset, Archie. Just my natural maternal instinct kicking in. Once a mother, always a mother.'

'It's okay,' Archie replied. 'I know people are just being kind, but I promise I'm all right. I just want to crack on now and do m' job as normal.'

'Point taken,' Dolly accepted. 'Now go and enjoy yer dinner while it's still hot and I promise I'll keep my bloody great size-fives firmly on the ground, where they belong.'

'Thanks, Dolly.' Archie smiled, before following Patty over to their designated table next to the Swap Club corner, where women were already milling around the box of donated clothes, carefully pulling out jumpers, scarves and even the odd dress and pair of high heels.

As Archie took a seat at the quieter end of the table, next to Patty, he placed his dinner down and concentrated on keeping a smile on his face, hoping to avoid any more *well-meaning* comments, but as he began to tuck into his extra big portion of pie and mash, his mind wandered. Archie knew without a doubt he was going to have to do something to prove he was not only living a normal life, but also that he was more than capable of doing something worthwhile to contribute to the war effort. His job at Vickers was fine and he loved the hustle and bustle of the factory, especially now they were making parts for planes and tanks. But it just didn't feel enough. He needed to do something on his own, away from people who were always fussing over him. He needed his own purpose in life.

'Penny for them?' Patty interrupted, discreetly touching Archie's knee under the table.

'Oh, sorry,' Archie answered, bringing himself back to the present moment. 'I was just thinking about everything we needed to do to get through this afternoon.' *One white lie wouldn't hurt, would it?* To be fair, Frank had explained there had been yet another increase in orders and it would have to be all hands on deck to get through the ever-increasing workload. But when Archie had offered to help manage the extra work and even put in more hours, Frank had blankly refused, joining the army of concerned friends who were adamant he needed to go steady.

Patty wasn't convinced by Archie's excuse. She had learnt a lot over the last few months, and she instinctively suspected Archie was once again keeping something from her, only this time, she decided, despite her own growing frustrations, to keep schtum, and give him the space he clearly craved – for the time being at least. Patty knew deep down though, she wouldn't be able to stop herself from saying anything indefinitely.

'Yes, I think we are going to be busy, aren't we?' she said, keeping her tone neutral.

'I'll be back in a minute,' Betty said, breaking the moment, as she carefully placed her dinner down and went to chat to the women having a good rummage through the swap box.

'Hello, Carol,' she greeted one of them. Carol had become a regular visitor to the Swap Club, and had also knitted blankets for babies for the Vicktory Knitters event in January along with some of her work pals.

'Oh, hiya, luv,' Carol replied cheerfully. 'I was just seeing what you had. M' sister is struggling. She's got three bairns and a husband away at war and would never dream of spending a penny on her'sen. I've just found this,' she added, holding up a fine emerald-green knitted cardigan. 'You don't mind if I take it for her, do you?'

'Of course not,' Betty said. 'That's what it's there for. Actually, I wondered if I could ask, have you and your friends heard about our latest knitting mission for troops and sailors?'

'Oh, we have indeed, duck.' Carol grinned. 'I think a few of the younger ones might have ulterior motives though.'

'What do you mean?' Betty asked, looking slightly perplexed.

'Haven't you heard?' Carol chuckled. 'Some of those lasses over there' – she tilted her head to the long table she always sat at for dinner, where a group of women were all knitting away – 'are planning on putting little love notes and their addresses in their finished products, in the hope they will find a fella.'

'Really?' Betty was stunned. She knew the number of available men was decreasing as the war carried on, with so many of them being conscripted or signing up, but she had no idea girls were going to such extreme lengths to bagsy themselves a bloke.

'Oh, they are all at it.' Carol laughed, tickled by Betty's innocence. 'Start off as pen pals and end up as brides.'

'Well, you learn something new every day,' Betty said, still a little befuddled by the revelation. 'Anyway, please do take anything that will be useful for your sister and thank you all again for joining in the latest Vicktory Knitters campaign – even if some of those girls have their own intentions.'

'Aw, thanks, luv,' Carol said. 'It really is greatly appreciated. And don't you worry about those lot. The chances are, far more socks will be knitted if they think they will end up with a man at the end of it.'

'I suppose so, yes,' Betty agreed.

Feeling somewhat astonished, Betty joined her friends at her own table.

'Are you all right?' Nancy asked, noting the baffled look on her friend's face.

Betty repeated the story and was met by amused smiles. It would appear Betty really was the only one who hadn't heard of this rather opportunist method of finding a fella.

'Maybe you should try yer luck?' Patty encouraged Daisy. 'Yer never know, you might find a reyt Prince Charming who will come home and sweep you off your feet.'

'Oh, I don't know about that.' Daisy blushed. 'Knowing my luck, I would end up with yet another Jack the Lad. I think I'm happy just the way I am right now. But,' she added, turning to Betty, 'my mum is doing much better now. Do you fancy a night out or a trip into town?'

Betty's natural reaction, even a month ago, would be to quickly find an excuse and politely decline the offer, but as she recalled her landlady's advice and thought about how fed up she had felt lately knowing William was about to start the next part of his training, she had accepted the only way to survive this war was to keep busy and have things to look forward to.

'That would be lovely,' Betty said, picking up her knife and fork. 'How about the pictures?' she suggested. Betty wasn't quite ready to paint the town red but going to see a film, something she and William had always enjoyed, felt like a good compromise.

'Perfect!' Daisy smiled. 'I would really enjoy that. I must

admit the last few months have been hard with mum being so poorly, so it would be lovely to do something nice again and have a bit of fun. How about you come over to mine just after tea and I'll do your hair? It's the least I can do after how much you helped us.'

As well as organising a Christmas package for Daisy and her family, Betty had insisted on buying her friend's lunch every Friday – something she still did, despite Daisy's protests.

Betty had to force herself to fight back the idea she was being disloyal to William by getting dressed up for a night out.

'I'll just set it in curlers for you,' Daisy added, sensing Betty's trepidation. 'Nothing too dramatic.'

'It would do you a world of good,' Nancy encouraged, touching her friend's arm, guessing what was going through her mind. 'You will have a lovely time and I have no doubt William would say the same.'

'Okay, thank you.' Betty smiled graciously, even if she did still feel slightly apprehensive. 'That would be super, and it would be nice to see your mum again too.'

'Oh, yes, she will be delighted you are popping round.' Daisy grinned. 'I'll warn you now though, she will want to thank you all over again.'

'There's really no need,' Betty replied, shaking her head in protest. 'Besides which, it was a team effort.'

'I know but she was and still is immensely grateful. Anyway, I'm glad you are up for a night out,' Daisy said. 'How does tomorrow sound?'

'Tomorrow!' Betty exclaimed, slightly taken aback. She had assumed Daisy meant in a few weeks and it would give her time to get used to the idea.

'No time like the present, duck,' Frank interjected. 'You've been working hard, luv. A night out will be just the tonic.'

Betty looked around the table at her friends who were all smiling back at her. 'All right,' she conceded, accepting no one was going to let her back out. 'Count me in.'

'While we are on the subject of having a little bit of fun,' Nancy piped up. 'I know it's not quite the same, but I was thinking of having a little party for Linda's sixth birthday in a couple of weeks and I wondered if you would all like to come?'

'Ooh, yes,' Patty trilled. 'That sounds lovely. What date is it on and would I be able to bring my little sister and Tom Tom? They don't get out much at the moment so it would be lovely for them to have something to look forward to.'

'Of course.' Nancy smiled, delighted at Patty's enthusiasm. 'It's on seventeenth of March. I would love you all to come and, Daisy, you must bring your sisters too. It won't be the same without Bert being here and I know Linda will be upset her daddy isn't around to help her unwrap her present and blow out the candles on the cake, but if I can make a real day of it, she might not feel as sad.'

'Thank you,' Daisy said. 'I reckon we could all do with something to look forward to. Hopefully my mum will be feeling a little better by then too and can come along.'

'The more the merrier,' Nancy grinned, 'although God knows how I'm going to conjure up a birthday cake with these pesky rations in place. Doris and I barely have enough eggs and butter to go round as it is with six hungry kids between us.'

'Maybe we could all club together?' Betty suggested. 'I'm sure Ivy and I can manage without the odd fresh egg, in fact she's been saving some for a special occasion, and if all else fails I've noticed shops have started selling dried ones.'

'I reckon I might be able to spare the odd bit of butter too,' Dolly added. 'In fact, why don't you leave the cake to me? It could be my birthday present to Linda. Sorry, unless of course you wanted to make it yourself?'

'No, not at all. I barely have a spare minute, so this would be a great help, but are you sure? Don't you have enough to do on your days off helping with your own granddaughters?'

'They can help me.' Dolly winked. 'They are a dab hand at whisking up some cake mix. I've trained them well.'

'Well, in that case, you must bring them along,' Nancy insisted. 'They aren't much younger than Linda, are they?'

'Thanks, duck, as long as you are sure. They will love that. Milly is three and Lucy is four, so they will be delighted to play with some bigger girls.'

'Of course, I don't mind,' Nancy reiterated. 'It really is very kind of you to offer to make the cake.' Then turning to the rest of the group, she added: 'I really am so pleased you can all come along. Our Linda will be made up.'

'What are friends for?' Betty said. 'Besides which, we wouldn't miss it for the world.'

'You'll get no arguments from me there,' Dolly added. 'I reckon a little party is what we all need to keep us smiling.'

Chapter 8

'Come on in,' Daisy greeted as she opened the front door and welcomed Betty into the house, excited to see her friend. 'I was a bit worried you would have second thoughts and back out.'

'Well, I'd be lying if I said it hadn't crossed my mind,' Betty admitted. 'It just feels a bit strange going out on a Saturday night without William.'

'Aw, I bet,' Daisy sympathized, 'but, remember we are only going to the cinema and I'm sure William would rather you have a nice night out than stay at home feeling fed up.'

'Have you been talking to Ivy?' Betty laughed. 'She said exactly the same thing to me this afternoon.'

'I haven't but we can't both be wrong. Now come on in to the kitchen. I've just made a fresh cuppa and my mum wants to say hello.'

As Betty followed Daisy down the hallway, the atmosphere in the house couldn't have been any more different to the last time she and her workmates had visited, just a few days before Christmas. Instead of a heavy dread lingering in the hushed quiet, Betty could hear Daisy's sisters giggling and skipping in the back yard and her parents chatting away in the kitchen, Alf insisting they treat themselves to a chippy tea.

The joyous mood also sparked a series of memories in Betty's own mind of when she and her elder sister had lived at home; they shared all their secrets and barely left each other's side. There wasn't a day that went by when she didn't miss Margaret, but maybe her friendship with Daisy would help fill the void in her life.

'You'll join us, won't you, luv?' Alf insisted, interrupting Betty's thoughts, as she stepped into the kitchen.

'What's that?' she asked politely.

'In a fish and chip tea before you girls go out.'

'I don't want to trouble you,' Betty exclaimed. 'I'm sure I'll end up filling up on plenty of chocolate caramels in the cinema. You really don't need to get me any tea.'

'Nonsense,' Alf asserted. 'Our Daisy has been telling us how you insist on getting her dinner every Friday and, I know it's not much, but it would be my way of saying thank you, especially for everything you did for our family at Christmas.'

'There's really no need . . .'

Before she could finish her sentence, Alf stood up from his chair, kindly waving away her protests. 'It's my treat and I won't have any arguments.'

Betty looked to Daisy, who shrugged and said, 'I did warn you.'

'Right then, I'll go and check what the girls would like, then I'll nip to Flathers chippy,' Alf said, making his way into the back yard.

'Thanks, luv,' Josie replied, 'what would I do without you?'

'I'll leave you ladies to it,' Alf laughed, brushing off the compliment. 'See you in a bit.'

'Betty, please come and have a minute,' Josie, who was sat at the kitchen table, insisted, turning her attention to her. 'Let me pour you a cuppa. It's freshly brewed.'

'That's very kind,' Betty said gratefully. 'You're looking well,' she added, pulling out a chair.

'Here, let me take your coat first,' Daisy said, as Betty undid her brown tweed jacket.

'Thank you.' Then turning to a rosy-cheeked Josie, Betty added: 'You look like a new person. Daisy has been telling us how much better you are feeling.' Although Betty hadn't actually seen Josie in December, when she was at her weakest, Nancy had explained how frightfully frail and underweight she had been.

'Aw, I am, luv. I feel like a new woman and it's all thanks to you and your friend Nancy. I don't think I'll ever be able to thank her enough for talking some sense into me. It doesn't even bare thinking about how things could have turned out if you hadn't all come to see us that day.'

'Well, all's well that ends well,' Betty said modestly, just pleased Josie was much better, and Daisy and her sisters were spared the same heartache she'd endured as a little girl, after her own mum had died far too young in life.

'So, what are you two off to watch tonight?' Josie asked, pouring three cups of tea.

'*21 Days*.' Daisy beamed. 'With Laurence Olivier.'

'Oooh!' Josie smiled. 'Well, you are definitely in for a treat then. I might be getting on a bit, but I have to admit, he is a bit of a dish. It will do you girls good to go and have some fun and relax.'

Then, handing Betty her freshly made brew, she said: 'It sounds like you are all pretty pushed at the factory.'

'We really are,' Betty agreed. 'I've lost count of how many slabs of steel I move in a day. As soon as I've positioned one in place, Frank is shouting from the floor for another to be lifted.'

As the words left her mouth, Betty felt herself stiffen, fighting back the constant simmering worry of what the reality of increased orders meant. But for the next few hours at least, she was determined not to let her fears for the future overtake her first evening out in months.

'You are all doing a grand job,' Josie praised. 'I must admit, I feel a little useless. Now I'm nearly back to full health, I keep thinking I'd like to do my bit too.'

'Mum!' Daisy gasped. 'It's too soon, besides which, Polly and Annie need you.'

Sensing her friend's understandable angst, Betty quickly racked her mind. 'Did Daisy mention our latest knitting mission to send some much-needed necessities to the troops?'

'Oh yes, she did, luv,' Josie replied. 'I'm so sorry I wasn't much use at your big event in January but I'm sure I could help with this.'

'Don't worry about that,' Betty insisted. 'But if you are feeling up to a bit of knitting now, it really would be well received. I should imagine there's a lot of soldiers and sailors who would be grateful for some new socks.'

'I can certainly help with that,' Josie confirmed. 'But I don't know, I can't help feeling it isn't enough.'

'What do you mean?' Betty asked, taking a sip of her tea.

'It's just I see you girls making parts for planes and I feel like I should be doing something constructive too,' Josie sighed.

'Please, mum, one step at a time,' Daisy protested. 'You don't want to get ill again.'

'Don't worry, I promise I'm not going to do anything daft. I'm just saying at some point, I'd like to be able to do my bit too.'

Betty looked to Daisy, the concern evident in her eyes. She completely understood why Daisy felt so anxious after watching her mum come back from death's door. 'Shall we have a go at sorting my hair out?' she asked, hoping it would distract her friend, for the time being at least.

'Yes.' Daisy smiled. 'Let's nip up to my room and I can pop some rollers in, and they can be setting while we have tea?'

'Sounds fun,' Betty grinned, looking forward to going out and hopefully keeping Daisy in good spirits too.

A couple of minutes later, Betty was sat at Daisy's wooden dressing table, staring at herself in the pine-framed mirror.

'Try not to worry,' Betty said sensitively. 'Your mum is most likely just feeling a bit guilty with you at Vickers and your dad down the pit. She probably feels like she needs to help out a bit too.' Betty understood only too well, the need to do something worthwhile.

'I know you're right,' Daisy conceded, carefully brushing Betty's glossy crown of thick dark-brown hair. 'It's just the thought of her doing too much too soon and getting ill again.'

'There must be some slightly less demanding jobs your mum could maybe consider,' Betty suggested. 'She doesn't have to go hell for leather in a factory.'

'Maybe,' Daisy mused. 'I reckon she'll keep going on about it until she finds something. I know what she's like. Now she's feeling a lot better, she won't want to just stay at home while everyone else is "doing their bit".'

'Let me put my thinking cap on and see if I can come up with something, or Ivy and her friends might have a few suggestions,' Betty offered.

'Thank you, that would be grand,' Daisy replied appreciatively. 'But enough about that now. Tonight is about us having a good time. How about I put some rollers in for you and create some big curls to lift the front of your hair?'

'That sounds rather lovely.' Betty beamed, a little bemused but determined to let herself go a little. She was happy to see what Daisy would do with her normally conservative hair. 'I've never been very adventurous, so I'm intrigued to see what wonders you can do with it,' she added.

'I think if this war hadn't broken out, I'd have trained to be a hairdresser. I love creating different styles. I'm always messing with Annie's and Polly's,' Daisy explained, in her element, as she lifted a section of Betty's hair and carefully positioned it around a roller.

'Well, you never know. When it's all over, you could make a go of it.'

'If we all get through this in one piece, I think I might you know.'

'You should,' Betty encouraged. 'We all need hopes and dreams. I was aiming to train as a solicitor before war broke out.'

'Do you think you will go back to it?'

'Maybe,' Betty mused. 'I mean I do hope so, but if the last six months have taught me anything, it's that you never know what's around the corner.'

'I won't argue with you there,' Daisy agreed, as she fixed the final roller into place. 'But as much as I wouldn't want to repeat mum getting ill or that awful episode with Tommy Hardcastle, there's been a lot of good too.'

'I know exactly what you mean.' Betty nodded. 'It really does go to show, that sometimes it's when you are in the midst of the hardest of times, you witness the best of human nature.'

'I couldn't have put it better myself,' Daisy said. 'Folk can be so kind.'

'They can,' Betty replied, watching in the mirror as Daisy set to work on transforming her.

'Now,' her friend added. 'Would you like me to add a bit of rouge and mascara?'

'Oh, why not?' Betty grinned, really getting into the spirit of things. It had been a while since she'd dolled herself up and she had to admit it was fun pampering herself. 'In for a penny, in for a pound, and all that.'

'That's the spirit.' Daisy rubbed pink creamy blusher into Betty's porcelain cheeks. 'Aw, you look lovely,' she said once she'd finished and stood back from the mirror, admiring her handiwork.

'Wow!' Betty gasped, taking in the reflection staring back at her. It was a million miles away from the woman who spent most of her days thirty-foot high in a crane cab and covered in a thick layer of grimy dust. 'You have done a marvellous job. I don't think I've looked this glammed up since the war started.'

'Just wait until your curls have set!' Daisy said excitedly, delighted Betty was pleased with her made-up look. 'As soon as we've had tea, I'll take them out and set them with a bit of sugar and water and you will be all set.'

'Daisy. Betty,' came Alf's call from downstairs, almost on cue. 'Tea's up.'

'Coming,' Daisy replied. 'I don't know about you,' she added, looking at Betty, 'but I'm ravenous. I was so busy after I got home at dinnertime, helping Mum with the cleaning, I forgot to eat.'

Once again, Betty counted her blessings. As soon as she'd walked through the door after her final shift of the week, Ivy had a bowl of home-made vegetable soup ready for her and a slice of freshly baked bread. She'd even coated it in a thin layer of butter, despite how careful they were not to waste their rations.

'Oooh, you look pretty,' Annie said as Betty sat down at the table.

'Thank you.' Betty blushed at the compliment.

'Right, tuck in,' Alf encouraged. 'No need for airs and graces. We don't want it going cold.'

Even though the chippy dinner was obviously a rare treat, Betty acutely aware the family were still recovering from Josie not being able to work, she noted how the family didn't wolf down their fish and chips, but took their time, chewing slowly, as if they were savouring every mouthful.

'So which picture house are you girls off to?' Alf asked.

'The Pavilion, darncliffe,' Daisy replied, as she cut up her final piece of battered fish.

'Aw, me and your dad used to go there when we were courting, didn't we, Alf?'

'Aye, we did that, luv,' Alf smiled, 'many moons ago now.'

'Hey,' Josie laughed, 'we ain't that old!'

'Right, well, we're going to leave you to argue that one out,' Daisy said, standing up from the table, 'and finish getting ready.'

'Oh, let me wash up the dishes first,' Betty offered.

'You will not!' Josie gasped. 'You are a guest. You girls work hard all week. Annie and Polly will help me, won't you, girls?'

Daisy's younger sisters nodded in unison. 'As long as Annie washes,' Polly said. 'I'll dry.'

'Deal!' Annie said, already picking up the empty plates and taking them over to the white ceramic Belfast sink.

'Go on,' Josie encouraged, looking at Daisy and Betty. 'You'll be late if you don't get a move on.'

Fifteen minutes later, the two friends were back in the kitchen, wearing the latest shade of red lipstick and Betty's hair was immaculately coiffed into voluminous victory curls on the top of her head.

'Well, you two really do look a picture,' Josie gushed proudly. 'It reyt takes me back to my younger days. I loved nothing more than getting dolled up for a night out.'

'You will have to come with us next time,' Betty suggested.

'Aw, maybe, luv.' Josie chuckled. 'Although, you wouldn't want me cramping your style. Now go and have a good time.'

'And make sure you wear a scarf each,' Alf added. 'It's still nippy out there.'

'Dad!' Daisy laughed in mock frustration, rolling her eyes.

'You know what he's like, luv,' Josie said. 'You will always be his little girl.'

'I know,' Daisy said, pecking her dad on the cheek. 'But don't worry. We'll be fine.'

'Thank you again,' Betty said, as they made their way to the back door. 'It really has been lovely to see you all.'

'You must come back and visit soon,' Josie insisted. 'Next time. Sleep over too and it will save you traipsing miles home.'

'Oh yes, you must,' Daisy echoed.

'I might just take you up on that, if it's not too much trouble,' Betty replied gratefully.

As the pair headed out the back door, they linked arms and sauntered down Coleridge Road, smiles plastered across their perfectly made-up faces. 'Thank you for this,' Betty said. 'It was just what I needed and has made me realize how much I've missed having time with girlfriends.'

'Don't be daft. Thank *you*!' Daisy exclaimed, delighted she could now return the long-overdue favour and pamper Betty. 'Besides which, it's been so long since I've had a night out. It feels nice to do something normal and fun again.'

'It really does,' Betty agreed. 'And I'm determined to enjoy every minute of it.' Despite how apprehensive she'd felt about a night out while her William was away training, she had to admit dolling herself up and spending some time with Daisy was the perfect balm to lift her from the doldrums she'd been experiencing of late.

Chapter 9

Friday, 8 March 1940

'Hiya, luv,' Doris greeted her neighbour, as Nancy made her way into the kitchen, holding a bulging shopping bag. 'Good day?'

'Not bad. Can't complain really. It's busy but it makes the hours pass quicker.'

'Let me make you a cuppa. I'm sure you could do with it.'

'You know me. I'll never say no.' Nancy grinned. 'Are all the kids upstairs?'

'They are, luv. I think they are making dens again – another *Swallows and Amazons* reenactment. They played in the yard after school for a bit and then settled down to do their homework. Your Linda loves her writing, doesn't she? I did some spellings with them, and she was meticulously writing her letters to make sure they were as neat as could be.'

'Yes, she likes everything to be neat and gets cross with herself if she makes a mistake.'

'Bless her,' Doris replied. 'I reckon it's a girl thing. Our

Alice and Katherine are the same, but I can hardly make out Joe's scrawl.'

'Billy's the same. More interested in playing than writing!'

'And how's your day been?' Doris asked.

'Oh yes, fine. Nothing to worry about at all. I actually feel as though I'm getting into a bit of routine now.'

'That's because you are,' Doris encouraged. 'And a grand job you are doing of it too.'

'Well, I couldn't do it without all your help.'

'Nonsense!' Doris shrugged off the compliment. 'Now, tell me what have yer got in yer bag. Looks like you have been shopping.'

'I have actually.' Nancy beamed. 'I nipped into Woollies before the butcher's on my way home and bought Linda a few bits for her birthday, so I was going to show you. I just didn't want her to see.'

'Aw, I see. Well, I gave them some sliced apple after school, so I reckon we have time for a cuppa while you show me, before they all start complaining they are starving and need their tea.'

'You are good.' Nancy smiled, emptying the gifts onto the wooden kitchen table, keeping one eye on the door and listening for the clatter of feet.

'Oh, these are lovely,' Doris gushed, bringing over a fresh pot of tea, as Nancy showed her the jigsaw, writing set and French knitting doll. 'I'm sure she will love them.'

'I hope so,' Nancy said, carefully placing the gifts back

into her bag before Linda appeared. 'It's going to be hard for her without Bert, so I've been putting a bit of money aside every week to buy her a couple of extra bits.'

'Try not to fret,' Doris said reassuringly, as she poured them both steaming hot mugs of tea. 'We will all help make it as special as possible. I was thinking, why don't I create a few bundles for pass the parcel, with sweeties in the middle, and a little bag of treats for a few rounds of musical chairs?'

'That would be lovely,' Nancy said, 'but haven't you got enough on? You already help us so much and have washing coming out of ycr ears!'

'If I can't help make a little girl's birthday special, then there's something very wrong. Now talking of which, one of my customers has passed on a haul of clothes today. As well as a load of misshapen woollen jumpers she has said I can have to unpick for the wool, after I told her about the latest Vicktory Knitters campaign. She sent a pile of girls' clothes too. She must have twin daughters a little bit older than Linda and Alice. There's a couple of lovely little long-sleeved sailor dresses. Would you like me to wrap onc up for Linda? They're in immaculate condition, she'll never know it's a hand-me-down. I think there's some matching socks too.'

'Oh, Doris. That would be perfect. You know how much Linda loves dresses – a new one for her birthday will make her day, but wouldn't you like to give it to Alice?'

'There's two! So, I can put Alice in one for the party

– well, only if you think it won't take the attention away from Linda?'

'No, not at all. Linda will love that. She loves Alice as if she were her own sister. She will be delighted to be matching.'

'Right, well, you just leave it to me, and I'll make sure they are freshly laundered for the day. Now, did you manage to pick up some sausages? I'll get them in the pan and I've already boiled some potatoes to go with them and made some gravy. No doubt they will all be down in a minute complaining they are starving.'

'I did but you have done enough,' Nancy protested. 'Enjoy your cuppa while I finish tea. It's the very least I can do.'

'But you have been working all day,' Doris said, about to stand up.

'And so have you!' Nancy insisted, gesturing for her neighbour to sit back down. 'Just because you are at home, doesn't make it any less tiring, and you have had the kids before and after school, not to mention trying to juggle all this washing with Georgie to look after. Besides which, you cook for us all most nights. It's my turn.'

'Okay, if you insist,' Doris laughed, 'but I'll do the dishes.'

Nancy knew there was no point in arguing, so instead, picked up the pack of sausages and went over to the hob.

'I also meant to tell you,' she added, lifting a frying pan out of the cupboard, 'Dolly from the canteen at work has said she will make Linda's cake. Isn't that good of her?'

'It really is,' Doris agreed, taking a knitted jumper from

a bag under the table to start unpicking it. 'They are a good bunch. I know it isn't easy working at Vickers, luv, but you landed on yer feet with those lasses.'

'Oh, I know,' Nancy said, adding a dollop of lard to the pan. 'They really are kind. I don't think I would have survived this long without them. They are a tower of strength.'

'And have you heard from Bert lately?' Doris asked tentatively, hoping the mention of his name wouldn't upset her friend.

'Actually, a letter has arrived today,' Nancy said, pulling the airmail envelope from her pocket. 'I nipped in at home to drop my work bag off and it was waiting on the doorstep. I've not had chance to read it yet.'

'Right, that's it,' Dolly said, immediately standing up. 'Sit back down and read that letter while I fry the sausages.'

'I didn't say it for that reason,' Nancy replied, guilt coursing through her.

'I know you didn't, but have a minute, while the kids are still playing,' Doris said, already topping up Nancy's mug with the remainder of the tea.

'Thank you.' Nancy nodded. 'But I'll be the one washing up.'

'Whatever,' Doris shook her head, shrugging off the offer, 'just see what your Bert has to say – that's far more important.'

Sitting back down at the table, Nancy carefully opened the envelope, her heart thumping as it did every time a letter from Bert arrived.

My dearest Nancy,

Nothing new to report here really. Thank you for the socks you sent me. They are perfect and keeping my feet toasty. If you have any more going, I'm sure a few of the lads would be very grateful. It can get quite nippy of a night.

Anyway, I hope our Linda is getting excited for her birthday. Tell her I'll be thinking of her and hope she is looking forward to it. I'm so sorry I can't be there, but I know you will make sure she has the best day ever. Can you believe she is going to be six? Where did that go, aye? I swear it only feels like two minutes ago since she was born. Do you remember when our Billy met her for the first time and prodded her to make sure she was real? It still makes me chuckle when I think about it.

Now listen, you stay strong, Nancy. I'm so proud of you and remember, I'm doing everything I can to get home to you all soon.

As always, Bert had signed off in the same way he always did.

It's the thought of seeing you all again that keeps me going.
All my love, forever and always,
Bert xxxx

Nancy noted he used four kisses, one to represent each member of their little family unit. As always she read his words over and over again, envisaging his voice as though he was sat across the kitchen table talking to her.

'Is everything all right?' Doris asked gently, the emotion on Nancy's face obvious.

'It is,' Nancy whispered. 'He seems fine and as upbeat as ever, more for my sake I'm sure. I think he's probably feeling it a bit that he can't be here for our Linda's birthday.'

'He'll be here in spirit, luv,' Doris said kindly. 'He might not be able to make it in person, but you will be carrying on with all the traditions as though he is. That's what I try to remind myself of when it comes to all our birthdays. George might not be here, but I can feel his presence. I'm sure of it.'

'You're right,' Nancy agreed, as she thought about how as a family they had celebrated Billy's and Linda's special days in the past. Bert might not be with them, but Nancy would ensure the day would go as normally and her little girl would have as much fun as possible – knowing that's exactly what her husband would want.

'Mummy!' Right on cue came Linda's squeal of excitement, as she ran into the kitchen. 'You're home.'

'I am, poppet,' Nancy greeted, as her daughter wrapped her little arms around her waist. 'Now tell me, how was your day at school?'

'It was good. We've been learning how to write on the line, so I'm going to practise by writing a letter to Daddy. Do you think he will be proud of me?'

'Of course, he will,' Nancy replied, bending down so she was at Linda's level. 'Your daddy is always proud of you and loves receiving your letters. He will be so pleased to see you are working on your handwriting and I know he will treasure your letter and keep it in a very safe place.'

A grin that could compete with that of the Cheshire cat

appeared across Linda's rosy-cheeked face. She had always been a daddy's girl, so the idea of him taking such good care of the notes she sent was enough to keep her on cloud nine for hours.

'Right, why don't you go and tell everyone else tea will be ready in ten minutes. I'm just going to help Doris finish cooking dinner and then serve up. No doubt your brother and Joe will be starving.'

'Okay, Mummy,' Linda replied, obedient as ever, before rushing back upstairs.

'You see,' Doris reassured Nancy, 'just letting Linda know her daddy is thinking of her, which he obviously is, will go a long way. And it looks like that writing set is going to go down a treat too.'

'Yes! And you're right – as ever,' Nancy said gratefully. Linda's birthday would be different, this blasted war and all it entailed had made sure of that, but that wasn't to say it wouldn't be full of love and laughter; if nothing else, that was the one thing Nancy could make sure of.

Chapter 10

Thursday, 14 March 1940

'How are you all?' Patty sang, as she plonked herself down at the canteen table, grabbing her home-made Spam sandwich from her bag.

'You're full of the joys of spring today,' Nancy commented. 'Has something happened?'

'Well, apart from the fact this one,' Patty said, giving Archie, who was sat next to her, a playful nudge, 'has just offered to take me to see a picture tomorrow night. And I dunno, just the weather picking up has put me in a good mood. For the first time since God knows when, I wasn't actually freezing m' socks off by the time I got to work. I didn't even put my gloves on this morning.'

'Spring is definitely on the way,' Nancy agreed. 'I think I even spotted a few daffodil stems starting to appear, and not before time. It's been a long winter.'

'When the sun shines, the world shines,' Archie piped up, unwrapping the greaseproof paper enveloping his own snap.

'What?' Patty coughed, spluttering on her generously sliced butty, causing everyone else to burst into laughter.

'Have you been listening to your nannan again, son?' Dolly, who had popped over to the table, asked.

'That obvious?' a now pink-faced Archie replied.

'Afraid so.' Dolly chuckled. 'But I know what you mean. Even the factories look less filthy when it's sunny, and I bet she's just relieved if it means yer chest won't cause you any problems now it's a bit warmer.' But as soon as the words left Dolly's mouth, she instantly regretted them. A cloud had appeared and Archie's smile vanished quicker than a rat down a drain.

'Oh, I'm sorry, lad.' She kicked herself for putting her clumsy size-fives in it again. 'Just ignore me. One day, I'll put m' brain into action before opening m' mouth.'

'It's fine,' Archie muttered, keen to avoid yet another discussion about his health. Despite how often he reassured his family and workmates that he was okay, their fussing seemed to rear its ugly head far too often for his liking.

Patty bit her lip, knowing from experience this wasn't the time to add fuel to the fire, even though she had been thinking the same about the upturn in temperature. Instead, she gently placed one of her hands on Archie's knee under the table, but despite her attempt to appease him, she could tell by how rigid he had gone that Dolly's well-meaning comment had annoyed him.

'Nancy, are you all sorted for Linda's party on Sunday?' Betty chirped up tactfully, sensing Dolly's discomfort and eager to lighten the heavy atmosphere. 'I bet she's getting excited, isn't she?'

'Aw, yes, she is.' Nancy grinned. 'It helps that Doris's daughters have been buoying her along. Every night this week when I've got home, they have been colouring in pieces of paper to make their own rainbow bunting. It keeps her mind off the fact Bert won't be here to watch her open her presents and blow out the candles.'

'Bless her,' Dolly started, grateful for the change in conversation. 'I hope she isn't too sad, but talking about her birthday, I'm going to make the sponge on Saturday so it's nice and fresh. Thanks to Betty and her landlady donating some of their rations, I've got more than enough eggs and butter.'

'Oh, thank you both,' Nancy said. 'This really is ever so kind of you.'

'Nonsense,' Dolly said, waving off the compliment with a quick flick of her hand. 'Birthdays are very special when you are little and I'll be damned if I can't do my bit to ensure Linda has a lovely day.'

'Even so,' Nancy insisted. 'It's a godsend and Linda will be made up.'

'We wouldn't have it any other way,' Betty chipped in. 'Now, have you got anything else planned for the birthday girl? Before the party, that is.'

'I have actually,' Nancy said, taking a quick mouthful of her tea. 'I'm taking her and Billy and a couple of Doris's children roller-skating late Saturday afternoon as a little treat.'

'At The Skates?' Patty asked, coming to life again.

'That's the one,' Nancy said. 'You would be welcome to bring your sisters and the same for you, Daisy.'

'Oooh,' Patty enthused. 'I did love going there when I was little, although I did spend most of it on my knees. It took me months to learn how to stay upright.'

'Why am I not surprised?' Archie butted in, feeling guilty for bringing the high spirits down a peg or two earlier, and now trying to join in the excitement.

'Hey!' Patty exclaimed, giving him a mock menacing glare, but equally relieved he was smiling again. 'I got it eventually. It just took me longer than my friends, that's all.' Turning to Nancy, she added: 'Let me ask my sisters, but I can't imagine they would say no.'

'Same here,' Daisy added. 'It's been a while since Annie and Polly have been, so will be a lovely treat for them.'

'Can I come too?' Archie chirped. 'I was never allowed to go as a kid, and it sounds great fun.'

Patty stiffened. 'Do you really think you should?' she quizzed, the thought of him speeding around the rink instantly making her nervous. 'Aren't you supposed to be taking it steady?'

Archie bit his lip, and momentarily closed his eyes. 'Don't make a scene,' he sternly whispered in Patty's ear, unsure how much more of all this fussing he could take.

'I think you should just give it a couple of months,' Patty said, doing nothing to soften the icy atmosphere that had suddenly emerged between them.

'It's fine,' Archie snapped, deliberately shifting his knee

to knock Patty's hand off. All he wanted to do was have a bit of fun. Was it really too much to hope for?

'I'm sure I can find something a little less strenuous,' he added with an uncharacteristically sarcastic undertone.

The cutting reply wasn't lost on Patty. Clutching her hands together, her eyes burnt with sharp tears.

'Well, I reckon this Sunday will be the bit of fun we can all enjoy,' Betty interjected, sharing a glance with Nancy. 'Is there anything we can do to help?' she added, trying to change the subject to diffuse the rising tension.

'I think I'm about sorted,' Nancy said, also hoping to move the conversation on. 'I managed to wrap all her presents last weekend and Doris has offered to help me make the sandwiches on Sunday morning, but please do come along. It would be lovely to see you.'

'Thank you. Ivy and I will definitely be there. She's planning on bringing a few treats too.'

'That's very kind,' Nancy said. 'She really doesn't have to.'

'Well, you know what she's like. There's no way she would turn up empty-handed and she sees it as her way of doing her bit, she likes to feel useful.'

'Oh, tell me about it!' Daisy gasped. 'My mum is still going on about doing her bit.'

'What's that, luv?' Dolly asked, one eye on Patty and Archie who now both looked close to tears. 'Is your mum well enough to even be thinking about anything extra?'

'She is,' Daisy replied, carefully folding up the brown

baking parchment her thinly sliced cheese sandwich had been wrapped in, so it could be used again. 'To be fair, she is a lot better and looking the best she has in months and her energy levels have returned but I just don't want her to get poorly again.'

'Mmmm,' Dolly mused. 'I might have an idea.'

'Really?' Daisy quizzed. 'Please don't put any more thoughts in her head. I'm sure she would sign up for nearly anything right now. I know it sounds mean-spirited, but it's taking every spare ounce of my patience to not snap at her. We are only just getting back to normal. I really don't want a repeat performance of the last six months.'

'Well,' Dolly started, picking up the empty mugs and piling them onto a tray, 'it's getting busier by the day here, with more and more mouths to feed. Do you reckon your mum would be up for a few hours here in the kitchens every lunchtime, or even just two or three days a week?'

Betty looked at her friend as she considered the idea. She knew how much Daisy was worrying but also could empathize with Josie, remembering how determined she was to give up her comfortable legal secretary role to help the war effort. 'It's got to be better than her going down to the Labour Exchange and signing up to work on a factory floor up to ten hours a day.'

'If it makes you feel any better, luv,' Dolly added, 'I could offer her the job on a trial basis. That way, if after a month I think it's making her poorly or she's struggling, I don't have to keep her on. And, if it helps, I'll promise to keep a close eye on her and make sure she has a decent meal on the days she's working.'

Daisy had to admit, it did seem like an ideal opportunity. Not only would it keep her mum from doing something more arduous, but the idea of her having a nutritious meal every day was almost too good to be true. And on top of that, she would once again be earning a much-needed wage, something Daisy knew her mum was desperate to do, ever since her downturn in health had caused her to give up her cleaning job.

'You promise to keep an eye on her?' Daisy asked, mulling it over.

'I do.' Dolly nodded empathetically. 'But not only that, so can you. You're here every dinnertime. If you think your mum is looking a bit pasty, you can give me a nudge and I'll make an excuse to let her go home for the afternoon.'

'She's bound to give us slightly bigger portions too,' Patty chirped up, attempting to distract herself and not dwell too much on her tiff with Archie.

'Flaming 'eck, Patty!' Archie exclaimed. 'Do you ever stop thinking about your belly?'

'I'm just thinking of the advantages,' Patty said in defence, not sure if Archie was joking or having another pop at her in retaliation.

'To be fair, the idea of Dolly making sure my mum eats properly would be a godsend,' Daisy tactfully interjected. 'I know she's still giving herself smaller portions, so we can all eat more.'

'Well, it sounds like you have just answered your own question,' Betty suggested.

'What do you say, love?' Dolly prompted. 'I know it's a worry, but you have my word, I'll look after your mum.'

'You really are so kind,' Daisy said appreciatively. 'I'll speak to my dad tonight, but I have a sneaking feeling he will agree it's a splendid idea.'

'Right, well, if you and your dad are happy with the idea, give me the nod on Sunday at Nancy's and I'll have a word with her. I assume she will be coming to the party?'

'Yes.' Daisy nodded. 'Is that okay, Nancy? As you can imagine, she's keen to get out.'

'Absolutely,' Nancy replied. 'I think we're all ready for a little get-together – even if it is just a sixth birthday party.'

'Without a doubt,' Patty agreed, keen to ensure the moment wasn't ruined for Nancy, after she'd clearly upset Archie. She'd try to have a chat with him on the way home. 'And obviously, there's going to be cake!'

The comment did the trick, and the group of women couldn't help but chuckle; a little celebration was just what was needed to keep their spirits up.

'Oh, and Dolly,' Daisy said hesitantly, 'I don't want to sound ungrateful, but you won't tell my mum we've had this conversation, will you? It's just she might feel like I'm trying to control her life. As much as I'm worrying, I don't want her to think I'm interfering.'

'Don't you worry, duck.' Dolly winked, tapping the side of her nose. 'Mum's the word. She'll never know.'

'Thank you.' Daisy smiled. 'I really don't know what I'd do without you lot.'

'Aw, well,' Betty interjected, standing up, their lunch break coming to an end. 'That's what friends are for.'

Chapter 11

Sunday, 17 March 1940

Quietly opening the door, Nancy and Billy tiptoed across Linda's room and climbed into her bed. It was a family tradition to wake up whoever's birthday it was with early morning snuggles, and one Nancy was determined to keep up despite Bert being away.

Her dreams interrupted, Linda started to stir and slowly her sleepy eyes began to open.

'Happy birthday!' Nancy and Billy cheered in unison, kissing a cheek each – another tradition. A huge grin appeared on Linda's face, as she stifled a yawn and adjusted to the light creeping in from the edges of her bedroom door, which had been left ajar. 'Six today, poppet,' Nancy sang. 'Such a big girl now.'

Even though she was still coming round, the growing excitement in Linda's eyes was unmistakable. 'Is it really the morning and my birthday?' she whispered.

'It is.' Nancy smiled affectionately. 'Overnight you have magically grown from five to six, and I'm quite sure you have got a little bit taller too.'

'Really?' Linda asked, her childhood innocence making Nancy's heart pound with happiness.

'Yes!' Billy added. 'But you still aren't as tall as me.'

'Billy!' Nancy mock chided.

'Sorry,' he grimaced, then quickly changed the subject. 'Anyway,' he said, 'do you want to open your presents?'

While Linda had been sleeping, Nancy had taken on Bert's role and sneaked into their daughter's room to pile the gifts at the foot of the bed, determined to maintain their usual birthday routine and make the day as special as possible.

'Yes, please.' Linda grinned and lifted herself up the bed until she was sat up on her stripy pink-and-white pillow.

'Because Daddy's not here, can I hand them out?' Billy almost pleaded.

'Of course,' Nancy agreed, biting her lip at the bitter-sweet moment, knowing how proud Bert would be that Billy had taken on his role, without having to be asked.

'Yippee,' Billy cheered, diving to the bottom of the bed, and raising the first neatly wrapped present, which Nancy had sealed with a shiny pink ribbon. 'I've always wanted to do this.'

'Here you go, sis,' Billy said. 'This one is off Mummy and Daddy.'

'Is it?' Linda asked, her eyes widening at the thought of her daddy helping to choose her birthday gifts.

'Of course,' Nancy confirmed. 'Daddy was very keen you had this one in particular.'

Linda cheerfully accepted the gift from her brother and carefully undid the bow and the brown wrapping paper. 'A writing set!' she exclaimed, looking at the pastel-coloured flowery paper and pen.

'I told you Daddy would want to see how hard you have been working at your handwriting,' Nancy encouraged, planting a kiss on her daughter's mop of blonde curly hair.

'I'm going to write to him straight after breakfast and tell him how we all went roller-skating yesterday and how much fun it was, and that I only fell over once, but didn't cry!' Linda exclaimed, clearly over the moon with her present.

'He will like that,' Nancy said, pleased that the previous day's activity had gone down so well and that they could make a weekend of the celebrations.

'But you've got more presents yet,' Billy interrupted, thrusting another gift onto his sister's lap, stunned she could be thinking about letter writing when there was a pile of surprises still to be opened.

'Don't worry.' Nancy laughed at her son's enthusiasm, knowing how he always tore his gifts open at a rate of knots, the complete opposite to his far more patient sister, who liked to take her time and marvel at each one in turn.

For the next half an hour, Linda did exactly that, taking delight in all the presents bestowed upon her, continually thanking her mum as she opened each one, grateful for her jigsaw, French knitting doll, new knickers and socks, and the shiny pink hair ribbons Nancy had also bought for her.

'And this is from me,' Billy announced, proudly handing over the last perfectly wrapped gift.

When Linda took off the paper to reveal a new rag doll, with brown woollen hair and a red cotton dress, her eyes once again lit up. 'I love her,' she exclaimed, wrapping her arms around Billy, who grinned at his mum over his sister's shoulders, delighted she had allowed him to give Linda her main present.

'Right, I think it's time for breakfast,' Nancy said, carefully scooping up all the paper and ribbons, which would come in useful again.

Gripping her new dolly with one hand, Linda pulled on her moccasin-style slippers with the other, and followed her mum and a now ravenous Billy downstairs.

'Is that white bread?' Billy asked, as Nancy lifted the loaf onto the chopping board. 'And not that grainy stuff?'

'It is.' Nancy chuckled. She had spent an age after they had all come back from roller-skating sifting the grains from the bag of National Flour. It was becoming common knowledge that women were now resorting to the trick to keep their disgruntled families happy, saving the grains for hens that more and more folk were keeping in a bid to ensure a fresh supply of eggs. Although Nancy didn't think she had the time to raise animals, she'd hijacked the tip as a birthday treat for Linda, knowing how much she and Billy loved hot buttered white toast and jam.

'I guess I should let Linda have the crust,' Billy conceded generously.

'You can have one end each,' Nancy said, carving up the loaf. 'I'm using the rest for sandwiches for later anyway.'

'Thank you,' both kids squealed simultaneously.

Nancy had to bite back the tears, which were threatening to prick her eyes, as she recalled how Bert would always tease Billy and Linda that he was going to steal the heel of the loaf if they didn't get dressed and downstairs fast.

'Come and sit down and I will get you each a glass of milk while your bread is toasting,' Nancy instructed.

And that's when Linda saw it – the pretty embroidered envelope propped up on the kitchen table, with her name written across the front.

'Is this for me?' she asked, surprised.

'It is.' Nancy smiled. The special letter had arrived a couple of days earlier and Nancy had instantly recognised Bert's handwriting. She had heard about the delicate paper and envelopes soldiers were permitted for occasions but had never actually seen one, until now. It was typical of Bert to use one for Linda's birthday.

'Why don't you open it, poppet, and I can help you read it,' Nancy encouraged.

Marvelling at the beautiful stationery, Linda gently ran her hand over the floral envelope, before carefully placing a finger under the sticky seal, and prizing it open to reveal a letter written on matching paper.

'Thank you,' Linda whispered as she held the precious words close to her chest.

Lifting up the delicate piece of paper, her hands trembling, she took a deep breath in a bid to stop her voice from breaking, and along with her mum, to help her with the tricky words, began reading. . .

My dearest little poppet, Linda,

Happy sixth birthday!

I'm so sorry I can't be there with you to open your presents in bed or watch you blow out your birthday candles, but I am thinking about you and know Mummy and Billy will make sure you have the very best day, with all your friends. It's going to be lots of fun.

Enjoy your party and make sure you get the first piece of cake, before Billy tries to steal all the jam, and when you play pass the parcel make sure you remember my secret trick of holding on to the package for an extra couple of seconds just in case the music stops.

I hope you like the writing set and maybe you could tell me all about your day in your next letter. Mummy can slip it into a special envelope, so it gets to me. You could even draw me a picture of all the presents you have got and then I can pin it to my wall above my bed.

Although I can't be with you today, at five o'clock when you blow out your candles I will also be singing happy birthday to you. Don't forget to make a special wish and I will do one too.

Have the very best day and I will get home to you all as soon as I can.

Lots of love and birthday kisses,

Daddy xxxx

'Oh, Mummy,' Linda gasped, her head flopping onto Nancy's lap, tears cascading down her flushed cheeks.

'Come on, Daddy wouldn't want you to cry on your birthday.'

'They are happy sad tears,' Linda sniffled. 'It's the best letter I've ever had and I'm going to keep it forever, I just wish Daddy was here.'

'We all do but remember he's doing everything he can to get home. Now come on, let's have the best day, otherwise we won't have lots of happy things to tell Daddy in your letter.'

'Okay.' Linda nodded bravely, wiping her eyes on the sleeve of her thick white cotton nightdress.

'Pinky promise!' Billy piped up, offering Linda his little finger across the table.

'Pinky promise.' She smiled, parroting the expression, their fingers interlinking in their oath.

'Right,' Nancy said, sensing this was the time to change the mood. 'Let's have breakfast?'

The rest of the morning passed in a flurry of activity. As Linda played with her new toys, Nancy made trays of cheese sandwiches, sliced up the pork pie she had got from Oliver's, and hung the bunting – which Alice and Katherine had created – in the yard. Doris and her excited quartet of children popped in with cards and, of course, the beautiful blue-and-white sailor dress.

'Can I wear it for the party?' Linda asked, thrilled at the thought of having a brand-new outfit for her special day.

'Of course,' Nancy agreed, as she mouthed a quiet 'thank you' to Doris.

'You're very welcome,' Doris nodded, taking as much pleasure in Linda's delight as the little girl herself.

'Right,' Doris added, keeping Georgie firmly on her hip, 'I've got some almond biscuits in the oven, so I better go and rescue them.'

'Gosh, you really didn't have to do that,' Nancy exclaimed.

'Nonsense!' Doris argued with a smile. 'Besides which, I made them with that dried egg powder, after hearing a tip on the radio, so I'm keen to see how they turn out. I'll be back in a bit to help you set out the food.'

By one o'clock, Nancy's kitchen table was an array of sandwiches, pie, biscuits and even an eggless quiche Doris had somehow mustered up. And right on cue, the chatter of familiar voices, and footsteps in the gennel, announced the arrival of the first guests.

'Hello! Come on in,' Nancy greeted as she welcomed Betty, Ivy and Frank into the kitchen. 'Thank you so much for coming.'

'We wouldn't miss it,' Betty said, pecking Nancy on the cheek.

'I hope I haven't overdone it, but I made a few bits,' Ivy added, handing Nancy a tin. 'It's just some jam tarts. I had jam left over from last summer, so thought I would put it to use, and I made a few drop scones.'

'This really is very generous,' Nancy said, gratefully accepting the sumptuous offerings.

'Not at all,' Ivy retorted. 'Now where is the birthday girl?'

'I'm here,' Linda said, appearing from the hallway holding her neighbour and best friend Alice's hand, the pair dressed identically in their new dresses, hair plaited with ribbons.

'Oh, don't you both look a picture?' Ivy beamed at the sight of the two girls.

'Thank you.' Linda smiled graciously.

'This is for you,' Ivy said, handing over a beautifully wrapped gift, finished with an intricate twirl of pink and silver ribbons.

'Thank you,' Linda whispered again, looking up at her mum, slightly abash at suddenly becoming the centre of attention.

'It's okay, poppet,' Nancy said. 'You can open it.'

Obediently, Linda undid the bow and carefully took apart the wrapping to reveal a tiny red velvet box. Again, her eyes darted from the gift to her mum. 'Go on,' Nancy prompted, also slightly taken aback by the unexpected jewellery box.

As Linda lifted the lid, she instinctively let out a little gasp as she took in the delicate ballerina pin badge. 'It's so pretty,' she whispered, hardly able to say the words.

'Oh, Ivy,' Nancy said. 'You really didn't have to.'

'Honestly, every little girl deserves a little something to make them smile on their birthday. I'm just glad Linda likes it. That's all that matters,' Ivy said, waving off the thanks.

'Can I wear it now, Mummy?' Linda asked.

'Of course,' Nancy said, carefully taking the pink-and-silver brooch from the soft cushion and pinning it to her daughter's dress. 'Why don't you go and look in the hall mirror at how pretty it looks on you?'

Her eyes twinkling with excitement, Linda, taking up Alice's hand again, did as she was asked.

'I've brought these too,' Ivy said, handing Nancy a cloth bag full of newspaper-clad packages.

'What are they?' Nancy asked, intrigued.

'Oh, just a few bits for a few games of pass the parcel.'

'You really are very thoughtful. I don't know what to say,' Nancy exclaimed, turning to Ivy.

'Well, don't say anything at all.' The staunch but motherly landlady smiled. 'You do me the greatest of honours, letting me indulge in the things that give me the greatest pleasures.'

'Thank you,' Nancy said again.

'I have a gift too,' Betty jumped in.

'Me too,' Frank added.

'Linda,' Nancy called.

'Yes, Mummy,' came the little girl's happy reply.

'You have a few more presents here,' Nancy explained.

'Thank you,' came her naturally polite reply. 'Am I allowed to open them now, Mummy?'

'Of course!'

Linda carefully unwrapped each parcel to reveal a pretty pink cotton cardigan from Betty and a game of Ludo from Frank.

'Thank you so much,' Linda repeated, delighted by the gifts.

'You are very welcome, sweetheart,' Frank replied.

'I'm just glad you like them,' Betty added.

'Now, shall I pop the kettle on?' Ivy suggested.

'That would be wonderful,' Nancy responded.

Within minutes, the neat three-bedroom terrace was overflowing with guests and the house was a frenzy of excitement. Patty had arrived with her family and Archie, followed by Daisy, her mum and sisters, alongside Doris and her remaining brood. With each new knock on the door came more generous deliveries of food, the result of meticulously saved rations, along with gifts for Linda. The kitchen now housed a buffet fit for King George VI himself.

Then last but by no means least, Dolly let herself in through the back door. She was holding a huge white box and flanked by two angelic-looking little girls, wearing navy pinafores and white Peter Pan–collared blouses, complemented by matching ribbons at the ends of their neat auburn plaits.

'Aw, this must be Milly and Lucy.' Nancy beamed.

'That's right,' Dolly confirmed, looking to each of her granddaughters in turn, who gave Nancy a shy smile.

'Would you like a biscuit each?' she asked, in a bid to help the girls feel at home.

'Yes, please,' came their polite response, and just as quickly they were whisked away by Doris's eldest daughter, Katherine, to join the rest of the children.

'Well, that was easier than I thought,' Dolly said, placing the box she was holding in the only free space on the table.

'Is this the cake?' Nancy asked, although she suspected it couldn't be anything but.

'It certainly is.' Dolly nodded, carefully taking off the lid to reveal a scrumptious double-layer Victoria sponge, oozing with a strawberry jam centre and topped with pink icing.

'My goodness,' Nancy cooed. 'This is truly wonderful. I don't think I can ever thank you enough.'

'Aw, it was a team effort,' Dolly said, throwing Ivy a grateful smile.

'Well, I really am very touched by what you have all done,' Nancy said, looking at all her friends.

'Not at all,' Dolly said, never one to bask in compliments. 'I reckon a happy occasion and a good get-together was what we all needed.'

'I'll toast to that,' Josie interjected, raising her mug in the air.

'Oooh, I can do better than that!' Patty's mom, Angie, chipped in, pulling a bottle of Rémy Martin brandy from her bag. 'I hope you don't mind, but I brought this, thinking we could all do with a little celebratory drink.'

'I'll not say no to that.' Doris grinned, already fetching a selection of glasses from the cupboard.

As glasses were poured and clinked, Nancy couldn't help but smile – cherishing the moment and feeling very lucky to be surrounded by such good friends who had rallied together to make Linda's day so special.

'Right, who's up for a game of pass the parcel?' Archie called from the yard, holding a box of packages wrapped in pages of the previous week's *Sheffield Star* that Doris and Ivy had put together.

'Me,' came a cacophony of excited squeals, as a thunderclap of children raced outside.

'He's like the Pied Piper.' Daisy laughed. 'He'll make a great dad someday,' she said, turning to Patty.

'He would,' Patty murmured, then, her face turning more serious, added: 'As long as he flamin' looks after himself.'

'I'm sure he will,' Dolly replied. 'Try not to fret. He's had a scare. I'm sure he will be more responsible now.'

Patty nodded, not wanting to detract from the celebrations, but if the truth be known, she wasn't so sure. Archie had taken the hint the day before and hadn't insisted on going roller-skating with herself, Daisy, Nancy and all the kids, but he seemed hell bent on proving he was capable of doing what any fit and healthy man of his age could do, despite the reservations she'd tried to express.

'Right, I think I might go and see what fun all the kids are having,' Nancy said, aware she'd barely seen Linda since all her friends had arrived.

The women watched as Archie, Frank and Patty's dad, Bill, acted as referees for one party game after another. When several rounds of pass the parcel had been exhausted – with Linda remembering her dad's trick and consequently rewarded with a handful of strawberry bonbons – countless raucous games of musical statues began.

An hour later, finally working up a hunger, the cheerful rabble of children headed to the kitchen to satisfy their rumbling tummies. Nancy had discreetly popped the lid back on the box holding the birthday cake, to keep it as a surprise, while the young ones tucked into the sandwiches, jam tarts and biscuits, and the adults indulged in the pork pie, quiche and scones.

'This really is quite a feast,' Frank praised, as Ivy passed him a handkerchief to wipe the crumbs from around his lips. 'You lot don't 'alf know how to put on a good spread.'

'Apart from giving me something to do, it was nice to have a reason,' said Josie, who had made a selection of dripping and Spam sandwiches.

Remembering their conversation, Dolly looked towards Daisy, slightly raising one eyebrow, the silent question answered with the hint of a nod.

'Actually, Josie,' Dolly said, 'if you are looking to fill your time, I could do with an extra pair of hands at the work's canteen a few hours a day, if yer interested?'

'Really?' Josie asked, oblivious to the conversation between her daughter and the canteen manager a few days earlier.

'Aye, we are run off our feet with all these new lasses starting, and I could do with another good cook.'

Instinctively, Josie turned to Daisy. 'Would you mind your old mum working at the same place as you?'

'Not at all. It would be nice.'

'I'm not averse to turning a blind eye to an extra scoop

of mash either to our favourite steelworkers.' Dolly winked at Daisy.

'Well, I have been going round the bend being at home all the time,' Josie replied, popping her empty plate next to the sink and pulling on Nancy's Marigolds to start the washing up.

'There's no need to do that,' Nancy said, rushing towards the sink.

'Yes, there is,' Josie insisted. 'You've been at it all day.'

'Anyway,' Josie carried on dismissing Nancy's protests, and turned to Dolly, 'I'd love to take the job.'

'Reyt you are, duck. Shall we say you start at ten o'clock tomorrow, or do you need a few days to get sorted?'

'No, tomorrow is perfect!'

Betty threw Daisy a knowing smile, sensing her friend would be delighted by the outcome. 'Thank you,' Daisy mouthed, without her mum noticing. She was grateful her fears had been resolved, all thanks to her new friends.

Twenty minutes later, with the dishes washed, dried and put away, Nancy picked up the birthday cake. 'Shall we go into the yard where there is more room?' she suggested.

'Good idea,' Doris agreed, picking up the box of matches. 'We'll be like cramped sardines in here.'

'Looks like there's a surprise coming kids,' Archie called, naturally taking on the role of shepherding the little ones.

Within seconds, the horde of kids were all gathered in the back yard, with Nancy in the middle. 'Are you ready?' she asked Linda, quickly glancing at her watch. *Perfect*, she thought to herself, noting they were moments away from five o'clock.

'Yes,' Linda squealed, her grin extending to her eyes.

And with that, as Doris lit the candles while Nancy proudly held the cake, an excited and loud chorus of 'Happy Birthday' began.

'Hip hip, hooray,' Archie cheered as everyone finished singing.

'Time to blow out the candles,' Nancy encouraged.

Her beaming little girl knew exactly what she was going to wish for. 'Please let Daddy be home soon,' she whispered.

Linda took a deep breath and in one mighty and determined puff, extinguished the six glowing miniature candles. Looking up at her mum, she said: 'This has been the best day ever and I can't wait to tell Daddy all about it.'

'Oh, poppet, he will be delighted for you.'

As all the guests tucked into generous slices of birthday cake and the adults enjoyed another tipple of Angie's brandy, Nancy looked around the yard and, for the umpteenth time that day, smiled. She would have given her right arm for Bert to be there by her side, cherishing the moment, but she knew, with the best will in the world, that wasn't to be. Instead, she counted her blessings that the day had been a roaring success, all thanks to her newfound friends. It may not have been how she'd have planned Linda's birthday, but thanks to their kindness, it turned out better than she could have ever hoped.

Chapter 12

Friday, 22 March 1940

'Hiya, luv.' A nervous-looking Josie smiled from behind the canteen counter, as her daughter and her friends reached the front of the queue.

'Are you getting the hang of it?' Daisy asked.

'I think so,' her mum nodded, 'I haven't broken any plates yet or dropped anyone's dinner!'

'She's doing just grand,' Dolly exclaimed proudly. 'She's only been here a week, and already yer mum has taken to it like a duck to water, just like I knew she would.'

The compliment caused Josie, who was kitted out in an identical blue-and-white gingham as her new boss, to blush. She had been working at Vickers a few hours a day since Linda's birthday party and had settled in without any bother at all.

'I must admit it's wonderful to be doing something again,' Josie said contently. 'It's just nice to be around people and have a good old natter. It's like I've got a purpose again, not to mention I'm not trapped at home staring at my own four walls all day. Everyone has been so kind and welcoming.'

Dolly threw Daisy a conspiratorial wink. She loved it when a plan came together, and Josie had been just the extra pair of hands she needed. Daisy was equally delighted to see her mum so happy, hoping this would satisfy her British bulldog spirit to do her bit for the war effort.

'Right then, I assume you all want a hot dinner?' Josie asked.

'Yes!' Patty chirped, rubbing her stomach over her mucky brown overalls. 'I'm starvin'! I've been thinking about Dolly's mince and onion pie all morning.'

'Well, you're in luck then, luv,' Josie said, as she scooped a generous portion of the traditional weekly fodder onto a plate and handed it to her daughter, before beginning on the next helping for an almost salivating Patty.

A few minutes later, the gang of workers were all comfortably positioned in their usual spot, tucking into their Friday treat. Well, all of them except Betty, who was stood chatting to a few women who had been rummaging through the Swap Box but were now in possession of a couple of balls of wool each.

'She never stops, does she?' Frank chuckled, as he tucked into his dinner.

'No,' Nancy laughed, 'I think it's in her blood, but it makes her happy, which is the main thing.'

'I've heard you lasses have started going out a bit too?' Frank asked, turning to Daisy.

'We have,' Daisy said, quickly swallowing a mouthful

of pie. 'And we are going roller-skating again tomorrow afternoon!'

'Are you?' Patty exclaimed.

'Yes,' Daisy replied. 'We had such a giggle at Linda's party, we thought we would go again. You would be very welcome to come with us. We might even nip into the pub for a quick drink afterwards.'

'Aw, I would have loved to.' Patty smiled. 'But me and Archie are going to the matinee, aren't we?' she added, tapping her sweetheart on the knee.

'We are.' He nodded. 'But if you wanted a bit of fun with the girls, I wouldn't be offended.'

Looking slightly conflicted, Patty glanced from Daisy to Archie.

'You don't need to make a decision now,' Daisy said, sensing her friend wasn't sure what to do and didn't want to put her on the spot.

'Thanks,' Patty said. 'I'll let you know then, if that's all right?'

'Absolutely.' Daisy nodded in between bites of her steaming hot pie.

'Right,' Patty said, placing her knife and fork on her empty plate, the first to finish, and reaching into her cloth bag. 'I better get cracking on these socks or Betty will have me guts for garters.'

'Did I hear my name being mentioned?' Betty asked, finally pulling up a chair to sit down and eat her dinner.

'Do you have elephant ears?' Patty laughed. 'I was just saying I better get a shufti on with these socks.'

'Oh, yes,' Betty replied. 'You must as Ivy and her friends have been unravelling old jumpers. I have an abundance of wool for us all now. Dolly said her sons and their shipmates are desperate for as many pairs as we can produce, and I thought we could send some supplies to the platoon Bert is with too.'

'Aw, thanks, luv,' Nancy said, taking a sip of tea. 'He was made up with the last pair of socks I sent and said the other soldiers would snap his hands off for some.'

'Well, that's that then,' Betty said authoritatively. 'We shall knit for Bert and Dolly's sons and all their comrades.'

'Well, if that's not motivation to keep going, I don't know what is,' Nancy said. 'It certainly helps keep me going too.'

'I'm pleased,' Betty said. She could testify first-hand how doing something positive kept your spirits up. 'It just makes you feel better, doesn't it?'

'Yes,' Nancy agreed. 'I know we are doing our bit here, but sending something tangible to Bert, thinking it's helping him, even in a little way, really keeps me going. And when I can't sleep at night, I just get out my knitting bag and it helps me relax. The rate I'm going I'll have knitted enough for the whole battalion!'

'Well, I bet they will go down a storm,' Betty said encouragingly. 'And if we do have too much, I'll do some research and find out where else we can send them, but I reckon between your husband's platoon and the ship Dolly's sons are on, we will have our hands full for a while. I think

I might need to find out how to send big care packages through the post, though – there's a lot of women knitting for our boys right now.'

'You are a good 'un,' Frank applauded. 'Hitler didn't have a clue when he started this flaming war, the strength of you lasses.'

'Oh, it's a team effort,' Betty said modestly. 'Anyway, you're doing your bit too with all your work here. And Ivy mentioned you're going to help her turn the garden into a veggie patch and am I right in thinking you have even persuaded her to keep hens?'

'Have you?' Nancy exclaimed in admiration. 'Think of all those fabulous fresh eggs and a regular supply of vegetables.'

'Aye, I know, duck,' Frank agreed. 'It was just an idea, but Ivy seems keen. And if I know Ivy, she'll be more than willing to share out everything we grow and produce.'

'She's already talking about how much she wants to make life a little easier for everyone else,' Betty added.

'When are you starting the groundwork, boss?' Archie asked, knowing as soon as he mentioned the idea to his nannan, she would be pestering him and his dad to do the same, even if their back yard was only the fraction of the size of Ivy's garden.

'Actually, I'm going shopping for some chicken wire and wood tomorrow after work,' Frank replied. 'And hope to make a start on the coop for the hens this weekend. Then with the weather warming up, I'll start digging out for the veggie patch in the next few weeks too.'

'And you say I never stop.' Betty laughed. 'You're just as bad, Frank.'

'Well, I suppose there's no time like the present and it keeps me out of mischief, duck.'

'I'm sure Ivy will rustle you up a roast dinner as a thank you.' Betty knew how much Frank and her landlady enjoyed each other's company. There wasn't a weekend that passed when her boss wasn't at the house. It was wonderful to see them both so happy and have something to smile about.

'Actually, gaffer,' Archie added, 'could I come with you to have a look at the materials? I just know my nannan will be on at me when she hears about this.' Turning to Patty, he added: 'Would you mind? We can go to the later showing at the pictures if you like instead.'

'No, I don't mind at all,' Patty said, her face lighting up at the prospect of having a bit of fun with her friends. 'But please don't start digging up yer back garden and exhausting yerself.'

'It's hardly going to kill me,' Archie snapped brusquely, tired of the constant mollycoddling.

'I'll take care of him, lass,' Frank interjected, trying to quickly defuse the situation, but inadvertently making Archie feel even worse.

'I don't need looking after,' Archie blurted out before he could stop himself. 'I am a grown man, yer know.'

'All right.' Patty stiffened, she and Frank taken aback by how defensive Archie was being. Catching Frank's eye, she discreetly shrugged. She might have been worried, but Patty certainly didn't want to cause a scene in front of everyone.

'Means I get the best of both worlds,' she added, cheerily. 'I can go skating now too. Is it okay if I invite Hattie?' she asked, turning to Betty and Daisy. 'She's struggling a bit with her John being away.'

'Of course,' the two women said in unison, before looking at one another and smiling at their timing.

'Gosh, we better get a move on,' Betty said, regaining her composure as she glanced up at the clock on the canteen wall.

'It always goes too fast,' Patty sighed and shoved her half-completed knitted sock back into her bag. 'But at least I got a bit more done.'

'It does, duck.' Frank nodded. 'And I hate to say it, but I think our workload is set to get even harder. We've got orders coming out of our ears.'

'I guess that's why more and more women are being taken on?' Betty asked.

'It is,' Frank replied, standing up. 'We'd be in a reyt old pickle without all the new recruits.'

'You see,' Betty cheered. 'We women know how to get a job done.'

It was now Frank's turn to smile to himself. His feisty steelworkers had come so far since they'd started working at Vickers, all of them changing and growing in different ways, but ultimately finding strength from each other as they navigated their way through this godforsaken war. They had all had their own battles to fight, but as a team, they had shown time and time again, they could tackle whatever was thrown at them.

Chapter 13

Saturday, 23 March 1940

'How was your morning, dear?' Ivy asked as Betty took off her coat and hung it on a hook in the cupboard under the stairs.

'Not so bad,' Betty replied as upbeat as ever. 'There's never a dull moment, but at least it's the weekend now.'

'Aw, yes and you are going roller-skating, aren't you?'

'Yes.' Betty grinned. 'In fact, I better get cleaned up and get changed. I said I'd meet the others at about three o'clock.'

'Before you do,' Ivy interrupted. 'I think you have a letter from William. It came this morning. I recognized his handwriting. I've left it on the table for you with a sandwich and I've just made a fresh pot of tea. I'll bring it in.'

'Thank you,' Betty said gratefully, delighted by the prospect of hearing from William. Despite how regularly his letters now arrived, she still always felt a tingle of excitement when another appeared.

Making herself comfy in the dining room, Betty picked up the envelope and carefully opened the seal and began reading William's letter, which as always started with

My lovely, sweet Bet.

But as Betty pored over the words that eventually followed, her body stiffened; the thrill of receiving the correspondence swiftly turned into devastation at William's news.

> *I'm writing this letter quickly as we have been told this morning that we will depart for Canada in the next couple of days. I'm so sorry, Bet, but by the time you read this, I may already be on a ship to cross the Atlantic or at least in Gourock in Scotland, waiting to board.*

'Oh, William,' Betty gasped, just as her landlady walked into the dining room, holding a fresh tray of tea.

'What is it?' Ivy asked with concern, her heart already racing ten to the dozen for Betty, as she took in how distraught she looked.

'He's . . . he's going,' Betty sobbed, tears now streaming ferociously down her dust-coated cheeks.

'Oh, my poor dear,' Ivy said, placing the tray on the table and wrapping Betty into her chest. 'You poor girl.' She remembered all too vividly her own breathtaking sadness after her Lewin had been sent abroad when she was a similar age to Betty. The unbearable pain had felt insurmountable as the worry she would never see her new husband ever again overwhelmed her. *Please don't let Betty or her dear William suffer the same fate*, she thought. *Life shouldn't be this cruel.*

'Come, come,' Ivy soothed. 'He's not fighting

Chamberlain's war yet. He's still training,' she added, knowing she needed to remain upbeat for Betty's sake. 'There's a long time to go before that happens.'

'I know,' Betty cried into her landlady's cream blouse, soaking the fabric. 'It's just . . .' But the words lodged in her throat, and she couldn't finish her sentence.

'It's okay,' Ivy said gently, stroking Betty's mop of dark-brown hair, wishing she could take away her heartache. 'You don't have to say anything.' Canada was such a long way away and Ivy knew how much Betty had been dreading William leaving. She'd hoped they might get at least one more weekend together, but this war wasn't accommodating of niceties, merciless in its endeavour to empower Hitler and his unthinkable plans.

'But I promise you one thing, though, you don't have to do this alone. We will all be there to help you through this,' Ivy said reassuringly.

'Thank you,' Betty sniffled, taking a deep breath. 'I know you're right. It could be much worse. It's just the not know-ing that's so horrible. I have no idea if I will ever see William again.' Saying it out loud cemented Betty's fear and as the enormous reality of the words hit her, she crumpled into Ivy's chest once more, tears cascading down her flushed face. All Ivy could do was comfort Betty as she wept, until her sobs gradually subsided.

'I don't think I can go out this afternoon. I'll be no company at all,' she muttered. 'I don't want to ruin the day for the others.'

'Take a minute,' Ivy insisted. 'Let me pour you that cup of tea first? I think it will still be warm.'

'Thank you.' Betty reached for the handkerchief she always kept under her sleeve and dabbed her puffy wet eyes.

'Here you go,' Ivy said, popping the cup and saucer in front of Betty. 'There's very little in the world a nice strong cup of Brooke Bond can't solve.'

As Betty took a sip, she drew in a deep breath. 'I'm sorry,' she sighed. 'I just don't know what to do. What if—'

'Come now,' Ivy stopped her firmly. 'You can't think like that. Thinking the worst won't get us through this dastardly war.'

'It just feels like everything is coming all at once.' Betty's voice wobbled, her hands trembling around the china cup.

'You've had a shock and it's perfectly understandable you feel upset.' Ivy empathized. 'But there's a good chance we are all going to have to deal with a few more knocks yet, and take it from me, crumpling at the first huddle won't do you any good.'

'I know you're right,' Betty replied. 'But I just don't know what to do.'

'I'll tell you what you are going to do,' Ivy stated. 'You are going to pick yourself up and carry on. You have a lovely bunch of friends who will be there to help you through.'

'I just don't want to dampen their fun. They deserve to enjoy themselves after how hard they have all worked this week.'

'Betty, dear,' Ivy said firmly. 'From what I've seen of your friends, I think they would be more than a little bit cross if you didn't let them look after you right now, especially after what you have done for all of them since you started at Vickers. Every now and again, I'm afraid you have to allow others to take care of you, no matter how fiercely independent you are. Take it from me. I had to learn the hard way.'

Betty took a minute to let the words sink in. Despite how rotten she felt, she knew Ivy was right.

'Think about what you would be saying to any of those girls if the shoe was on the other foot,' Ivy added. 'It doesn't take a genius to know you would be there, pulling them along and keeping their spirits up.'

'I don't seem to be very good at heeding my own advice,' Betty finally conceded, wiping her tear-stained cheeks.

'I know I sound a little harsh, but it's only because I've been in your shoes and I know from experience no good will come of moping about, but at the same time I don't want you to be too hard on yourself either,' Ivy said kindly. She knew from her own ill-fated past how difficult it was to pick yourself up when you were down, but also how important it was to let others support you.

'So, do you think you can manage to meet up with your friends?' she asked tentatively.

'Oh gosh,' Betty answered. 'I'm still not sure I will be much company. I don't want to bring their mood down. If Daisy or Patty had a phone, I would call them and rearrange but they don't, so I really don't know what to do.'

Ivy considered her answer for a few seconds, remembering

how she too had withdrawn into herself after Lewin had gone off to war. As much as she knew Betty was made of stronger stuff, Ivy was all too aware of how easy it was to shut yourself away. 'Maybe the roller-skating will take your mind off things for a few hours?' Ivy suggested. 'And you girls do seem to have a way of lifting one another's spirits.'

Betty knew in her heart of hearts her landlady was right. What good would moping about the house do her? She would only dwell on the fact her beloved William was hundreds of miles away and she had no idea when she would see him again. The last thing she needed was more time on her hands to fret. She was already trying to work out what else she could do to help the war effort as she couldn't bear to think her free time could be better used.

'You're right,' Betty said, gradually regaining her fighting spirit. 'I need to buck up my ideas. There is no point sat here watching the milk turn sour.' There was a strong chance William was going to be away for months on end, so she needed to keep herself busy and a few hours with her friends would be far more enjoyable than getting herself into a flummox again. There was certainly no point in maudlin if she was going to survive this blasted war in one piece. 'I'll have this sandwich and go and get myself cleaned up.'

'Good for you,' Ivy cheered proudly.

'And thank you.' Betty smiled.

'What for?'

'For just being here,' Betty said, grateful to have a mother figure in her life again. It was times like this she desperately missed her own mum, so to have Ivy, not only as a shoulder to cry on but there to pick her up when she was at her lowest, meant so much. 'I'd probably still be in a heap, drowning in tears if it wasn't for you,' Betty added.

'Well, I'm not sure about that,' Ivy replied, 'but I'm glad I could help a little.'

'You really have,' Betty insisted, the colour now returning to her cheeks.

Just over an hour later, Betty was pacing down Attercliffe Road towards Zion Lane and the Palais De Danse, the posh-sounding name for the roller-skating rink.

'Here she is,' Patty said, as she, Hattie and Daisy caught sight of their friend.

'I'm sorry.' Betty glanced down at the watch her dad had bought her for her twenty-first birthday, and noticed she was ten minutes late.

'It's okay, we've got loads of time,' Daisy said. 'But are you all right?' She knew it wasn't like Betty to be late for anything and she did look a little out of sorts.

'Oh,' Betty replied, taking a deep breath, realizing there was no point trying to hide the truth from her friends. 'I did have a bit of a shock when I got home from work.'

'What's happened?' Daisy asked instinctively.

'I got a letter from William,' Betty started. 'He's on his way to Canada.'

'Oh, luv,' Hattie gasped, imagining how ghastly Betty must be feeling. Her own sweetheart, John, had been sent off to France at the start of the war. 'I'm so sorry. It's a horrible shock, isn't it?' She reached out and touched Betty's arm comfortingly.

'You can say that again,' Betty agreed. 'I'm afraid I was a bit of a mess, but I'm feeling better than I did a couple of hours ago.'

'That's perfectly understandable,' Hattie added. 'I cried myself to sleep for a week after John left. I think you're doing incredibly well to actually have made it here.'

'Hattie's right,' Daisy echoed. 'Are you sure you want to go roller-skating? We can just go to a café instead if you like and have a chat.'

'No, no. I'm okay, I promise, and a bit of fun is probably just what I need.'

As Patty listened to her friends, she took a moment to take stock of what each of them had been through. They'd had to cope with so much, yet here they were, determined to carry on, painting a smile on their faces despite the anguish they'd suffered. It put her own concerns about Archie into perspective. At least he was close by, where she could keep an eye on him. *I really am very lucky in comparison*, Patty thought to herself.

'Right, well, if you are sure, shall we go in then?' Hattie asked the group.

'Yes, let's,' Betty agreed, adamant to make the most of her limited free time.

A couple of minutes later, the four women were swapping their shoes for roller boots. 'We don't need to go downstairs to Mugs Alley today, do we?' Daisy asked, referring to the beginner's rink, as she popped her gas mask next to her practical brown leather Oxford lace-ups.

'No!' Patty concurred. 'I reckon if I can lift great slabs of steel, I can stay upright on these things,' she said, glancing at the clunky boots on wheels.

For the next hour, the women sped around the busy hall, practising their turns and racing against each other, squealing with laughter as they narrowly avoided colliding with other skaters. At one point, Patty nearly went head over heels, as she attempted a fancy crossover, only for Hattie to grab her arm and stabilise her in the nick of time. Betty spun from one side of the room to another, reminiscing how she and Margaret had loved skating when they were younger. Exhilarated, with adrenalin soaring through her veins as she went faster and faster, Betty's fears were forgotten, for the time being at least, and she allowed herself to have some much-needed fun.

'That was marvellous,' she said, beaming, when they all eventually collapsed onto a bench, panting for breath. 'I can't remember the last time I skated as fast!'

'It was probably just what you needed,' Daisy said, once she could speak again.

'I reckon it was,' Betty added. 'I haven't had that much fun in months.'

'Me neither,' Daisy agreed. 'I've been so worried about my mum, and if I'm honest, I'm still a bit worried the new job might end up being a bit too much, but I know I've got to let her get on with it. She is a grown woman after all.'

As Patty untied her roller skates, Daisy's words struck a chord. *Am I being too hard on Archie? He's an adult too and maybe needs to find his own way?*

'We should definitely do this more often,' Daisy added, breaking into Patty's thoughts.

'I would really like that,' Betty agreed, as she began to accept life didn't have to be all work and no play. As much as she was still determined to do more for the war effort and would find a way of using some of her free time productively, she was also starting to realize having time to relax with friends was important too. Not only that, Betty knew if she didn't cherish times like this with her friends, she would end up spending hour after hour sick with worry about William and missing him terribly.

'Me too.' Hattie smiled. 'I don't get out much with John being away.'

'Well, we need to put a stop to that,' Betty enthused. 'This war is testing us all. We need to have something to smile about and look forward to. Now, how about we nip to the King's Head round the corner?'

'I knew you would like going to the pub once you'd been for the first time.' Patty laughed.

'Oh yes, I suppose I did rather enjoy it,' Betty conceded.

'You'll get no complaints from me. I've been accompanying m' dad to the boozer since I was knee high to a grasshopper and I'm not meeting Archie for a couple of hours yet, so I've got plenty of time.'

Feeling far more confident than she had on their recent

visit to the Wellington, Betty led the way as they left the skating rink and headed to the King's Head.

'This one is on me, girls,' Betty announced as they headed inside the traditional boozer, with a tap room on one side and a lounge on the other.

'You don't have to do that,' Daisy protested, conscious of how generous her friend had been towards her while her mum was poorly.

'I'd like to,' Betty insisted. 'You have all pulled me out of the doldrums this afternoon and it's my way of saying thank you.'

'That's very kind,' Hattie added, as the group noted how once again they were receiving curious glances from the regulars perched at the bar.

No longer as self-conscious, five minutes later, the quartet of women were all enjoying their glasses of refreshing lemonade. 'Cheers,' Betty said.

'Here's to friendship and always being there for one another,' Patty cheered, raising her glass. 'To the best friends a girl could ask for.'

'Hear hear,' came the synchronised reply, the friends all smiling, as their glasses clinked together.

Chapter 14

A few miles away, in the city centre, Frank and Archie had just left a hardware store, laden down with rolls of chicken wire.

'This will keep me busy tomorrow,' Archie said, tucking the big roll of wire under his arm. 'My nannan is determined I start building the hen run.'

'You and me both, lad.' Frank chuckled. 'Although, honestly, I don't mind. Ivy has been good to me. It's the least I can do.'

'She certainly seems to be looking after you,' Archie agreed. 'And seems like a nice woman from what I can gather from Betty and the women at work.'

'Aye, she is that son,' Frank replied. 'A real diamond.' There was no denying the fact: he'd grown rather fond of Ivy and was sure the feelings were reciprocated.

'I'm chuffed for yer, gaffer,' Archie said. Frank had always been a good sort and deserved a bit of happiness in his life, especially right now, when no one really knew what the future held. Hitler's lack of assault on Britain was resulting in what some were calling the Phoney War but no one really knew what the power-hungry dictator had up his sleeve. The air of uncertainty had most people in a constant state of flux and bewilderment.

'Thanks, son,' Frank replied. 'And you and Patty are still going strong, I assume?'

'Yeah, we are,' Archie answered. 'Well, at least I think we are. She's a real sweetheart and I'm a lucky bloke. I just worry I'm a bit grumpy at times.'

'What's worrying yer, son?' Frank asked, pleased Archie was beginning to open up about his feelings.

'I dunno, boss,' Archie started. 'I'm just fed up with everyone wrapping me in cotton wool. It's been the same for as long as I can remember. I just want to live my life without people constantly asking me if I'm okay or if I'm sure I should be doing something. I don't mean to snap at people when they ask me, it's just I want to be treated like my own man.'

Frank took a few seconds to consider what Archie had said. Like everyone else at Vickers who knew Archie, he had a soft spot for the young steelworker and couldn't help but feel protective towards the lad. As he thought about the way they'd fussed over Archie recently, he could see why the young lad might feel a little suffocated.

'It's a tricky one,' Frank said diplomatically. 'I guess we all got quite a scare after you collapsed at the Vicktory Knitters event. I don't think anyone means any harm. They just worry but I get how it must feel overwhelming at times.'

'It really does,' Archie insisted. 'I just want to be treated like anybody else, without any special attention. Is that too much to ask?'

'No, son.' Frank saw how much this had got to Archie. 'Would you like me to have a word, maybe ask everyone to stop coddling as much?'

'No,' Archie sighed. 'They will just feel even sorrier for me then and make the problem a million times worse. What I'd really like is for everyone to treat me like any other bloke.'

'All right, lad.' Frank nodded, seeing how frustrated Archie was. 'But please, let me know if I can do anything.'

'Actually, there was something else I was going to talk to you about.'

'Go on.'

Archie had always been close to Frank and felt he could confide in him, especially after his boss had also asked him several times if he was all right.

'I'm thinking of signing up for some voluntary war work,' Archie confessed, relieved to say the words out loud after thinking on the idea for quite a while now.

'I get it, son, I really do,' Frank eventually said, clearly not trying to overstep the mark. 'Have you given this some serious thought? I don't want to put a downer on yer plans, but have you considered how yer family and Patty will feel?'

'Yep.' Archie nodded. 'I should imagine they are going to go barmy, but I can't carry on feeling like a spare part, and a worn-out one at that.'

'I'm fairly sure that's not how anyone sees you.'

'I dunno. Maybe not,' Archie conceded, his mind a whirl of emotions. 'But they certainly don't think I should be doing what most blokes my age are doing and it's really wearing me down.'

Frank was wise enough to know what Archie needed was support, not a lecture on knowing his limitations. 'Have you mentioned this to anyone else?'

Archie bit his lip and looked down.

Frank swallowed back a sigh. 'You don't need me to tell yer son, secrets only end up causing ill feeling. Nothing good ever comes of them.'

'I know,' Archie muttered. 'But there's no guarantee I'll be accepted yet, so I'm thinking there's no point causing a whole lot of fuss for nothing.'

'Okay, son,' Frank accepted. He didn't want to push Archie away, and despite the fact he felt slightly uncomfortable being privy to this information before Archie's parents, he was glad the lad felt he could open up to him.

'Just do me a favour,' Frank added.

'What's that?'

'Don't keep it from those who love you for too long. I know you're fed up, but I assure you, people are only getting on at you because they care.'

The words struck a chord. Archie knew deep down Frank was right, but he also had to carry out his plans without any interference from his parents or Patty, who he knew would do everything in their willpower to talk him out of it.

'I won't, gaffer,' Archie promised, but actually, he was exhausted just thinking about what everyone would say if he was accepted as a volunteer.

'And remember, I'm always around if you fancy a chat over a pint.'

'Thanks, boss,' Archie replied gratefully.

'Right then, I'm going to head to the tram stop,' Frank said. 'Are you coming?'

Archie took a deep breath. 'Actually, I'm going to go and see if I can sign up for a role today.'

Frank tried to hide his concern. 'And there's nothing I can do to try and persuade you to sit on the idea for a while longer?'

'No,' Archie said firmly. He knew if he didn't act now, it might be weeks before he got the chance to set the wheels in motion.

'All right, lad, but remember, yer know where I am if yer need a chat.'

Twenty minutes later, standing outside the Air Raid Precautions offices on Church Street, Archie took a deep breath. 'You can do this,' he murmured, bolstering his own determination in a bid to shrug off the fact he had never made a major decision without consulting his family first. They had been at his side at every pinnacle moment in his life, from his endless stays in hospital, finishing school and deciding what job he would do, but he knew there was no point in worrying about that now. If he allowed his parents' or Patty's concerns to seep into his mind, he would walk straight back out and end up sat on the tram home feeling as miserable as sin, knowing once again he hadn't been able to carry out the one thing he'd been yearning for. The one thing that would prove to himself, and show everyone else, that he was a *real* man and could play a vital and significant role in this blasted war.

Putting his best foot forward, Archie pushed open the door and made his way into the busy hall. Blinkered to the hub of activity, he headed straight to one of the desks.

'All right, son?' asked a burly man, with a deep receding hairline and a greying moustache, as Archie presented himself. 'How can I help yer?'

This was it. 'I want to help,' Archie started, the resolve in his voice giving him the confidence he needed. 'I want to sign up to be an air raid warden.'

Although the last few months had felt like a phoney war, with only the odd air raid siren, which were either false alarms or tests, Archie had heard from one of his mates at Vickers that the government were still pushing forward with the Civil Defence in all key towns and cities. His pal's brother had begun working with the air raid patrol a few months earlier and had been involved in ongoing practice drills. Despite the fact Hitler hadn't attacked Britain yet, all the preparations could only mean it was just a matter of time and Archie wanted to be there, in the thick of the action, doing his bit to protect his home city.

'Reyt, lad,' the man replied, flicking through a pile of

paperwork. 'A worthy cause too. We need as many volunteers as possible.'

'I just want to be useful,' Archie explained.

'That you will be, son. Now, where do yer live and let's see where I can allocate you to.'

'Darn Cliffe, near the works.'

'Are you working at one of them too?' the officer asked, pushing a form and a pen towards Archie.

'I am,' he replied proudly, putting the roll of chicken wire and his gas mark on the floor and taking a seat.

'Then take it from me, yer already doing yer bit. This war is dependent on what you lot are producing in those mills. Yer all doing a grand job.'

But it wasn't enough. 'I just want to do everything I can. If I'm not off fighting, then I want to put all my efforts into helping on the home front,' Archie reiterated, praying they didn't ask him if he had any underlying health conditions.

He needn't have worried. 'Yer a credit to the country, lad,' the man behind the desk praised. 'Now fill me those forms in and there is an air raid warden on Coleridge Road in Darnall we can assign yer to. Not too far away from home then.'

'Thank you.' Archie nodded, feeling somewhat buoyed after finally taking control and doing what he wanted to do for a change.

A couple of hours later, excited at the thought of spending the evening with Patty, Archie tapped on the back door of 56 Thompson Street. But as he waited for someone to answer, Archie began to worry this wasn't the right time to tell her about his latest plans, unsure how she would react. The last thing he wanted was for them to fall out, especially as he didn't want to spoil their evening together and felt so happy with his decision.

'Hiya, luv, come on in,' Angie said, breaking Archie from his thoughts. As he stepped inside and poked his head into the kitchen, the aroma of corned beef and chips instantly hit him. 'Patty's still getting ready. I don't think she was expecting you for a little while yet,' Angie added.

'I'm early,' Archie explained. 'I thought we might go for a drink first if Patty fancied it.'

'I'm sure she'd love to. I'll let her know you're here. Would you like a cuppa while yer waiting?'

'I'll never say no.' Archie grinned. 'Shall I put the kettle on?'

'You will not!' Angie protested. 'You work hard enough and besides which, it's not long boiled, so it will only take me a minute to make us a brew. Just give me a sec while I tell one of the girls to let Patty know yer here.'

As Angie nipped into the hall and commandeered Emily, who had been sat in the front room, Archie nervously played with his fingers; he thought about what, if anything, he should tell Patty.

'She'll not be long,' Angie said, as she bundled back into the kitchen, now with Tom Tom on her hip. He was in pyjamas and looked ready for bed.

'Archie,' he squealed, reaching his arms out.

'Hello, you!' Archie laughed, taking the delighted-looking toddler from Angie, happy for the distraction. 'And what you have got there?'

'Biscuit,' Tom Tom grinned, stuffing the almond and oat treat into his mouth.

'Would you like one, luv?' Angie asked Archie, handing him a mug of hot steaming tea.

'Oh no, I'm fine. Thank you,' he said, accepting the welcome brew.

'That's not like you. You're not sickening for something, are you?'

Archie winced, Angie's innocent comment hanging in the air. But he quickly realized she didn't mean anything by it and was just making conversation.

'No, no, I'm fine,' Archie said, keeping his tone neutral.

'Your nannan keeping you well fed?' Angie asked, oblivious to the impact her words had had.

'Something like that.' Archie smiled politely, happy for Angie to believe he just wasn't hungry, but if the truth be known, he'd hardly touched the meat pie his nannan had served up for his tea, his stomach turning somersaults. It had been quite the afternoon and after breaking the news to his parents and nannan, he just wanted to see Patty and have a couple of hours where they could relax together. His mum and nannan had been furious and upset by his decision, protesting he was deliberately putting his health at risk, and they wouldn't be able to rest for a second while

148

he was out guarding the street. Maybe it was best if he left it a while before telling Patty, keen to avoid ruining their evening in case she shared their concerns. It wasn't like he would never tell her, but a few days wouldn't hurt, would it? *Maybe I can just test the water instead.*

Right on cue, Patty skipped into the kitchen. 'Hello, you.' She grinned, pecking Archie on the cheek. 'Did you have a good afternoon?'

'Hey?' Archie asked, feeling slightly discombobulated by the question.

'With Frank.' Patty laughed, taking in the confused look on Archie's face. 'Did you get what you were looking for?'

'Oh, yes, sorry,' he said in a sigh of relief. 'We got the chicken wire and my nannan has already made plans for me and my dad tomorrow.'

'It will be worth it for all those fresh eggs every day,' Angie said.

'You'll save us the odd one, won't you?' Patty said, playfully nudging Archie in the ribs.

'Of course,' he replied. 'Right, shall we get going?' He stood up, carefully placing Tom Tom on the chair, keen to go and enjoy the evening and avoid any questions about what he'd been doing all afternoon. 'I thought we could nip into the King's Head first for a drink.'

'Sure,' Patty said. 'Although that will be the second time I've been in today. I'll be getting a name for m'sen.'

'Hey?' Archie asked for the second time.

'What is up with you tonight?' Patty laughed, pulling on

the red cape Angie and Bill had bought her for Christmas. 'Have you forgotten, I went to The Skates this afternoon with the girls?'

'Of course,' Archie apologized, his mind a whirl. 'Did you have fun?'

'We did.' Patty nodded. 'But Betty had a bit of a shock. Her William is on his way to Canada, so we nipped for a drink afterwards. Yer know what she's like though, she's refusing to let the news get her down.'

'She really is a force of nature, that one,' Angie said. 'Anyway, you two get yerselves off or you'll not get time for a drink before the pictures.'

'Thanks, Mom,' Patty said, giving her a quick kiss.

'And me!' Tom Tom called from the chair.

'How could I forget?' Patty said, ruffling her brother's mop of strawberry blonde curls.

'Thanks again for the cuppa,' Archie added, as Patty led him out the back door.

'No bother at all,' Angie replied, watching the pair head out. She couldn't put her finger on it, but she was sure something wasn't quite right with Archie. 'I hope to God he's not poorly again,' she muttered to herself, but Angie dismissed the thought as soon as it came into her head on the grounds Archie looked the best he had in months. 'Whatever it is, it will come out in the wash,' she mused.

Angie wasn't the only one to pick up on the fact Archie wasn't his normal chipper self. As Patty sipped a glass of cold lemonade in a quiet corner of the King's Head, she reached her hand across the table to Archie's. 'Is everything all right?' she tentatively asked, praying he wasn't going to announce his heart was playing up again.

'Yes, why?' Archie answered slightly too sharply, instinctively defensive.

'You just seem a bit funny, that's all.'

'Sorry,' Archie apologized. 'It's just a bit wearing everyone asking me if I'm all right all the time.'

Patty knew she was treading on thin ice. The last thing she wanted was another tiff, but at the same time, she couldn't be with Archie if he was going to be moody.

'Are you sure that's everything?' she gently tried again, hoping it wouldn't be the catalyst for another argument.

Archie was also keen not to spoil their night out. He knew he needed to divert the attention away from him. Thinking on his feet, he said: 'All this news of the Germans expanding, it makes yer think, doesn't it?'

'Hey?' Patty quizzed. It was the last thing she expected Archie to say. 'But Hitler hasn't even attacked Britain,' she said. It was true. After all the concerns about mass land and air attacks from the Germans, when war had been announced six months earlier, none had come to fruition, and up to now Blighty had survived completely unscathed.

'I know but I was reading in m' dad's *Daily Mirror* how the Soviets have taken over Finland. Hitler ain't going to like that. He wants Europe. The Germans attacked a naval base on the Orkney Islands last week and six sailors were killed.'

'Really?' Patty asked, oblivious to the fact. 'And where's the Orkney Islands?'

'Just off the north coast of Scotland,' Archie explained. 'And they bombed a village, killing a man – the first British civilian.'

Patty went very quiet as she took in the enormity of what she'd just been told. Is that what had been playing on Archie's mind? 'Do you think Hitler will really attack us?' Despite carrying her mask everywhere and rushing to the communal air raid shelter a handful of times when the sirens sounded, she had never really considered Britain could actually get bombed. The idea of war didn't seem real. She didn't pay any attention when the news came on the family wireless, never read the papers, which in her eyes were as dull as dishwater, and never watched the Pathé newsreels when they burst onto the screen at the start of a film at the picture house. Even as she worked all the hours God sent at Vickers, making parts for planes, an actual war seemed inconceivable.

'Nobody knows for certain, I don't suppose,' Archie conceded. 'But they must think it's likely, otherwise they wouldn't be advertising for people to volunteer for jobs to help with the war effort.'

'What sort of jobs?'

'Oh, yer know. The Home Guard, fire wardens and air patrol wardens.'

Patty took a sharp intake of breath. She really didn't want Archie getting any ideas, not with his dicky ticker. 'Those jobs sound awfully dangerous.'

'Someone's got to do them though,' Archie retorted.

'Well, not you!' Patty said, kissing Archie on the cheek, trying to keep her tone light.

Archie swallowed the last mouthful of his pint. 'Why not me?' He felt somewhat affronted.

'Yer know why,' Patty said, trying to soothe the situation. 'After everything you have been through, it's just too much for yer.'

The smothering comment irked Archie. 'How do you know it's too much for me?'

'It's just what you said about easily getting ill when you were little. I don't want to see you getting poorly again. That's all.'

Archie knew by not confessing how he'd spent the afternoon he was only making the matter worse in the long run, but right now he couldn't face ruining their night out. Seeing how upset Patty was just at the thought of it was all the confirmation he needed to know: for sure she would be furious when he finally plucked up the courage to tell her the truth.

'All right,' he said, quickly changing the subject. 'We better get moving or we'll miss the start of the picture.'

'It's still a bit early, isn't it?' Patty asked, looking at her watch. They still had a good thirty minutes.

'We want to get the best seats,' Archie pointed out, already on his feet and reaching for his jacket.

Patty shook her head in mock frustration at how oddly Archie was acting. Maybe all this talk of war *was* getting to him, especially because she understood how frustrated he felt about not being able to go off and fight. 'All right then, if you insist.' She laughed, linking her arm with Archie's, still oblivious to what was really bothering him. Instead she was determined to leave their past squabbles behind them and enjoy the rest of their evening without any more cross words.

Chapter 15

Pushing his fork into the ground, Frank looked round and smiled as he watched Ivy meticulously remove stones from the nearby patch of soil she was working on. Next to her, Betty was marking out rows where the veggies would go with a ball of string. The carrots, cabbages, potatoes and peas were all ready to sow.

Despite Frank's protests that he could manage preparing the garden by himself, Ivy and Betty had insisted on getting their hands dirty too and had been outside with him since just after nine o'clock. While they decided where the seeds and saplings would be placed, Frank made space in the corner of the garden for the hen coop.

'By the summer we will have a reyt crop on the go,' he enthused, standing up and stretching his back for a moment, pleased with how the plan was coming together.

'Oh, I do hope so.' Ivy grinned. Ever since she'd heard about the Dig for Victory campaign, she had been keen to turn her once immaculately kept lawn into a mini allotment. She wasn't alone as families up and down the country were turning green-fingered in a bid to ensure they could harvest a healthy supply of vegetables now Hitler was hell bent on putting obstacles in the way of trade routes.

'It would be nice to be able to share some of what we grow. With the best will in the world, there's no way Betty and I can eat all the veggies we're planning on growing – even if you come for a roast every Sunday between now and the end of the year.'

'Well, I won't turn that down, but I think, looking at the size of these veggie patches, you're probably right,' Frank replied, chuckling.

'And with rationing now being extended to include all meat, cheese and eggs, every little will help,' Betty added.

'It will be well received, I'm sure of that much,' Frank said, straightening his back after spending the last couple of hours hunched over.

'I agree,' Betty said. 'When you think about Angie and Josie and all those little ones they need to feed.'

'They will be first on my list,' Ivy said, also standing up and stretching. 'And I have to say, I'm sure all the gardening is exercising muscles that I've not used in years.'

'I'll not argue with you there.' Frank laughed, massaging his lower back to release the knot that was forming.

'Why don't we stop for a few moments and get a drink?' Ivy suggested, conscious Frank and Betty were already engaged in backbreaking work six days a week. The last thing she wanted was for either of them to end up with a bad back or pull a muscle.

'I wouldn't say no,' Frank accepted. 'And we have achieved a great deal already this morning.'

Five minutes later, Ivy reappeared holding a tray of refreshments. 'Here you go,' she said, handing Frank a tall glass of cold lemonade.

'You are a good 'un,' Frank thanked her.

'I think it's the very least I can do.' Ivy smiled fondly as they all stood back appreciating their morning's work.

'I think another couple of weekends and we'll have it cracked,' Frank said.

'I know I keep saying it, but this really is very good of you both,' Ivy praised. 'Especially after working a full week at Vickers.'

'Not at all,' Frank said. 'It keeps me out of mischief and it's all for a good cause.'

'Hear hear!' Betty enthused, wiping her muddy hands down her old trousers. Despite her newfound determination to have fun and make more time for herself, she could never pass up the opportunity to help out and do her bit, especially when Ivy had been so good to her.

'How many hens do you think I should get?' Ivy asked.

Frank eyed up the space he'd left for the hen enclosure. 'I'm no expert,' he pondered. 'But I reckon you could maybe start with four and see how you get on.'

'I'm rather looking forward to having a few animals to look after,' Ivy said. 'It will be nice to feel like I'm doing something useful.'

'I don't think you need to worry about that,' Frank

countered, finishing his glass of lemonade. 'You and Betty never stop.'

'Actually,' Ivy said, 'there was something that caught my eye this week while I was out and about that I meant to mention to you, Betty.'

'Really?' Betty asked, her interest instantly piqued.

'Yes, but why don't we go inside, and I'll get us a few biscuits to keep us going,' Ivy suggested.

'Oh, I think I can manage a bite to eat,' Frank said, also intrigued by Ivy's cryptic announcement.

Ten minutes later, the trio were sat around the kitchen table, far too mucky to even think about making themselves comfortable in the front room.

'So,' Betty started, turning to Ivy as she finished pouring everyone a fresh cup of tea, 'are you going to tell us about this idea you've had?'

'Oh yes.' Ivy smiled, placing a plate of Anzac biscuits on the table. 'I went to see my friend Winnie this week in Fulwood and noticed the Women's Voluntary Service have opened a hospital supply depot and they are looking for volunteers. Anyway, Winnie and I have signed up to help out a couple of days a week making hospital clothing, bandages and swabs.'

'I had no idea they had set something like this up,' Betty replied.

'From what I could gather, there's quite a need for it,' Ivy said, lifting her cup and saucer from the table. 'And they are crying out for extra volunteers so I thought you'd want to know.'

'It does sound like a useful thing to be involved in, but I must admit I hadn't realized hospitals were in need of extra supplies,' Betty said thoughtfully.

'I wasn't either, dear,' Ivy agreed. 'I think they are maybe sending some of what they produce abroad.'

'Oh, I see,' Betty said, the cogs in her mind turning. 'Do you think I could help out too of a weekend or the odd evening?'

'As much as I think you are doing enough and don't want you overdoing it and ending up exhausted,' Ivy said, taking a small sip of her still steaming hot tea, 'I assumed you would want to help out if you had the time.'

'Yes, I would,' Betty stated firmly. 'If you think I can be of some use?'

'I'm sure you could,' Ivy affirmed, knowing there was absolutely no point trying to convince Betty otherwise. 'It really did sound like they needed as many hands as possible.'

Betty nodded. She knew why they were in need of extra help but she couldn't allow herself to dwell on that now because if she did let her mind wander, Betty knew she would end up getting upset about the danger these brave men were facing and fretting about what the future held for her own William.

'Maybe I could pop in one night after work this week,' Betty suggested, already starting to work out how many hours she could commit to.

'Aw, Betty duck, I know how you like to keep yerself

busy but don't be taking on too much,' Frank said, his concern evident.

'I won't,' Betty promised, instinctively picking up on the hint of worry in her foreman's voice.

'I just don't want you exhausting yerself. The orders for parts are coming in thick and fast and I don't want you to run yerself ragged. You need time to relax too.'

'I promise I won't do too much and if work is going to be busy, I could go down next Saturday instead.' Now with the WVS setting up a depot to produce essential supplies for the wounded and Vickers being overwhelmed with orders too, it certainly didn't feel like a phoney war anymore and the gravity of the situation struck Betty.

Frank and Ivy exchanged a concerned glance. 'Try not to overthink it all, dear,' Ivy reiterated, as if she was reading Betty's mind. She knew only too well how the 'not knowing' could be more torturous, with your mind going into overdrive, leaving you unable to sleep and always assuming the worst. She remembered all too well the agony of having no idea if and when she would see her husband again after he'd been conscripted into the Great War, and how it had left her sick with fear.

Betty nodded, as she quietly told herself to stay positive. *There's no point falling to bits now*, she silently chastised. *That will be no good at all. I need to be strong if I'm going to survive this blasted war.*

'Ivy's right, duck,' Frank added. 'None of us know what's around the corner. It could all be a precaution. I'm sure

Chamberlain wants this over as quick as the rest of us. No one wants a repeat of the last war.'

'I'm sure you're right,' Betty said optimistically. 'We've just all got to do what we can to help and keep up morale. No point moping about. We won't win this war if we all give up hope now. Hitler doesn't need any extra ammunition.'

'Oh, you really are incredible,' Ivy said, gently patting Betty's arm. 'I don't know where you get your determination and spirit from, but it will take you far, my dear. You're a force of nature, that's for sure.'

'Well, I don't know about that,' Betty said. 'But if it helps us get through, then I'm happy with that.'

'I have no doubt,' Frank added. 'What do they call it? The British bulldog spirit. It will take us all far.'

'You are so right, Frank,' Ivy agreed. 'I spent a lot of the last war worrying and then burying my head in the sand. It did me no good at all. I'm adamant that Hitler won't pull me down this time. Just helping Betty with all her campaigns and now preparing our mini allotment, thanks to you, as well as volunteering with the WVS have helped keep me focused and given me a reason to carry on.'

'You're doing a grand job,' Frank affectionately reassured Ivy. He'd never asked her about her husband or how she'd lost him, not wanting to rake up painful memories. After all, he knew only too well how hard it was to lose someone you loved, but he'd picked up enough to realize the Great War had left Ivy a widow and the heartache she'd suffered had understandably lived with her for a long time, casting a devastating shadow over her life.

'Well, it's not much compared to what you and Betty here are doing, working long hours at Vickers, risking life and limb, but if I can do something, even if it's just something little, I don't feel quite as useless,' Ivy said.

'As I said earlier, you will never be useless!' Frank said, the words leaving his mouth before he had chance to think about the impact.

'Oh erm, erm,' Ivy stuttered, her cheeks flushing at the compliment.

Betty had to bite her lip to stop herself giggling out loud, as she watched the affection flow between her landlady and foreman.

'I just meant,' Frank said, also blushing, and now feeling somewhat self-conscious, 'that you shouldn't doubt how much good you are doing. Look at how much you have helped Betty, and her friends when they needed some support, and now you are planning on growing vegetables and keeping hens, just so you can donate food to others more in need.'

'Anyone would do the same,' Ivy said, not used to being showered with compliments and praise.

'I'm not sure *everyone* would,' Frank replied. 'There's a lot of selfish people in the world, who wouldn't be as keen to share what they have.'

'Frank's right,' Betty agreed, looking at Ivy. 'You really shouldn't underestimate what you are doing to help us all.

I for one am very grateful for how much you have helped and supported me, especially in the last few weeks since I got the news William was being sent to Canada.'

Ivy carefully placed her rose-patterned china cup back on its matching saucer. 'I don't know what to say,' she said. Ivy's voice was barely a whisper and Betty was sure her landlady's eyes were glistening. 'You are both very kind.'

'Not at all,' Frank encouraged. 'Credit where credit is due.'

'Now,' he added, keen to lighten the mood, not wanting to upset Ivy. 'I think I'll have another one of these rather tasty biscuits, if you don't mind?'

'Not at all. It's a new recipe I've been trying out. Apparently you can store them for weeks. In the Great War, wives in New Zealand used to send them to their husbands on the front, as they didn't spoil in the time it took for them to arrive,' Ivy replied, also happy to move the conversation on, to avoid making a spectacle of herself by bursting into tears at the kindness of her friends. 'I heard them talked about on the radio so thought I'd give it a go.'

'Well, I'm rather glad you did,' Frank said, after taking a bite of the crunchy biscuit. 'They're delicious. Are you not having one, Betty?'

'I might have one after dinner,' she replied, stifling a yawn as she stood up, determined to give Ivy and Frank some time together, just the two of them. 'Unless you need a hand with dinner, I thought I'd go and get cleaned up and write William a letter. I'd normally do it later but I just have a sudden urge to tell him what we've been up to. I'm sure he will be amazed when I explain how we have completely turned the garden upside down and wait until I tell him about the hens we are planning – he will be tickled pink!'

'Of course, dear,' Ivy said. 'Off you go. I have it all in hand. There's a joint of beef in the oven and the vegetables are ready to boil, so I'll let you know when it's ready.' Then turning to Frank, she added: 'I hope you will be staying for dinner too?'

'Well, if you are sure,' he replied, dabbing his lips and patting away the biscuit crumbs. 'Only if you have enough and I'm not putting you out?'

'Not at all,' Ivy insisted. 'I think it's the very least I can do. You've definitely earned it after all your hard work today.'

Betty quietly left the kitchen, smiling to herself. This war was certainly testing her spirit at times but seeing her landlady and foreman's friendship blossom and their affection for one another grow, showed there was some things Hitler couldn't destroy. In fact, Betty thought to herself, as she made her way upstairs to her bedroom, if it wasn't for Neville Chamberlain announcing the country was now at war against Germany, Ivy and Frank would never have met. As her foreman said, you just never know what's around the corner. Who would have thought something so wonderful could come from such a difficult and treacherous time.

Chapter 16

As Archie and Patty gloomily trundled across the shop floor, Frank instantly picked up on the tension. Although he hadn't spoken to Archie, Frank worried he'd signed up to volunteer for the war effort after they'd gone their separate ways on Saturday afternoon. Archie certainly seemed in quite a pickle.

'God help us,' he muttered to himself, nodding to the pair.

'All right, boss?' Archie greeted.

'Not s' bad, lad,' he answered, but stopped himself from returning the question.

'Morning, Frank,' Patty added, all signs of the usually cheerful lilt in her voice completely vanished. Despite a fairly pleasant night at the pictures, Patty couldn't help feeling Archie was still being rather sullen. She'd tried to ask him about it several times, but he just shrugged off her question without answering, only adding to her fear there really was something wrong.

Betty and Nancy, who weren't far behind, simultaneously

shrugged at Frank, equally bewildered as to the reasons behind the low mood between the normally happy-as-Larry sweethearts.

On the way to work, Nancy had been grateful Patty's dad, Bill, had been there to chat to her to give them some space. Now, as their first shift of the week was about to start, Nancy sensed it was likely to be a long one and just hoped whatever was troubling the couple would soon be resolved.

'Before you all start,' Frank said, breaking the icy silence, 'can I have a quick word?'

'Is everything all right, boss?' Archie asked, suddenly more alert.

'Aye, there's nothing to worry about, son, but I've been asked from upstairs if everyone would be willing to put in a few extra hours here and there. We are stacked up with orders and need to get on top of them.'

'No bother.' Archie nodded. 'Always happy to help.'

'Thanks, lad.' Frank nodded. 'And it goes without saying, you'll be paid for it. No one is expecting you to do it for free so we'll be offering afters for those that can do more.'

'Well, it all helps,' Archie replied gratefully.

'Do you really think it's a good idea to be taking on more work after everything you have been through?' Patty blurted out, incandescent with frustration.

'Patty!' Archie gasped, his cheeks flushing, in a mixture of anger and frustration that Patty was talking to him as though he were a little boy. This was another reason he'd refrained from telling her about volunteering. She was constantly mothering him when he was perfectly capable of making his own decisions. 'I'll be fine.'

'All right. I'm sorry.' She reddened and her voice faltered from the very public reprimand. 'I just don't want you to get ill again.' Didn't Archie realize she only had his best interests at heart? 'Anyway, I need to start work,' she added defensively, already making her way over to Marlene – her hulk of a crane, where she would spend the next four hours hauling huge slabs of steel before the break for lunch. 'Just let me know when the overtime kicks in, Frank. M' mom will be glad of the extra cash.' And with that, Patty stomped off, leaving Archie, Betty and Nancy temporarily speechless.

'Don't worry, lad,' Frank said, patting Archie's shoulder. 'She'll come round. She's probably just worrying and getting herself in a muddle.'

'I hope so,' Archie sighed, now convinced Patty would blow her top when she found out what he'd really got up to on Saturday afternoon.

'Try not to fret,' Frank added reassuringly. 'I bet Nancy and Betty here will be able to make Patty see you are just trying to do the right thing.' If he was brutally honest with himself, Frank had his own reservations, but he was also well aware after their chat two days earlier Archie didn't need him badgering him as well. 'It's a difficult time for everyone and we have all just been a bit worried about you, but I know you need to do things yer own way son. I'm sure things will settle down eventually.'

'Well, I'm sure we could try,' Betty said, 'if we had the faintest idea what had got into her.'

'She's on at me all the time, always fussing that I'm overdoing it. It's driving me mad. I'm not sure how much more of it I can take,' Archie complained.

'We'll have a chat with her at dinnertime,' Betty smiled sympathetically.

'Thanks,' Archie replied. 'I think I might have my snap with a few of the lads and give Patty some space. I don't want us to have another tiff.'

'C'mon, son,' Frank interjected. 'We better get cracking and get some of these orders sorted. If nothing else, it will keep you busy this morning and take your mind off it for a while.'

'No worries, boss,' Archie said, giving Betty and Nancy a weak smile, before he followed Frank across the busy factory floor.

'What on earth do you think has happened?' Betty asked her friend, puzzled.

'Heaven knows,' Nancy sighed. 'I just hope they can sort it out, as they both look utterly miserable. It was ever such an odd atmosphere between them this morning walking in to work. Patty asked if he was okay and Archie shrugged it off, then they didn't speak another word.'

'Yes,' Betty agreed. 'Let's see if we can get to the bottom of it over a nice cup of tea later at dinner.'

'That sounds like a very wise plan.'

As Nancy made her way over to her crane, another

worry niggled at her. She didn't want to let Frank and her colleagues down, but she wasn't sure what to make of his request for extra hours. Nancy wanted to help but she had no idea how she'd be able to fit in more hours at Vickers. She barely saw Billy and Linda as it was and the idea of not being around to eat tea with them and relying on Doris even more left her feeling all of a muddle. Some days it seemed no matter what you did, it never felt like enough and you end up letting someone down.

'We don't want to intrude, but would you like to talk about this morning and what's troubling you?' Betty asked, handing Patty a mug of Dolly's steaming hot tea as she sat picking at her Spam sandwich.

The young steelworker looked up at the supportive smiles from Betty, Nancy and Daisy. 'I just don't know,' she sighed.

'As Betty said,' Nancy added, 'we don't want to pry, luv, and if you'd rather keep it to yerself, that's okay, we're just worried about you. We don't like to see you so upset and yer know what they say; a problem shared is a problem halved.'

Patty considered this, and then let it all out. 'I'm sorry, I didn't mean to cause such a scene this morning. I just couldn't help it, especially when he offered to do overtime here. I just don't understand him at all! We're not allowed to fuss over him and he won't listen to anyone but I'm just worried he's going to overdo it and get ill again.'

Hearing the word 'overtime', Nancy's stomach did a somersault as she was still unsure what she should do, but she temporarily put her own worries aside, determined to be a sympathetic ear to Patty.

'Do you think he's just trying to show Frank he can help out when needed?' Betty asked gently.

'Maybe,' Patty conceded. 'But it's only been two months since he collapsed. I'm just worried it's too much and too soon. And he's been in a really odd mood.'

'What do you mean?' Betty asked.

'It's hard to say,' Patty started. 'He was all of a dither on Saturday when we went out and this morning I could hardly get a word out of him after I asked if he was okay. I know you'll think I'm being paranoid, but it's as though there's summat he's not telling me. I feel like I'm constantly stepping on eggshells. I'm always scared of asking Archie if he's okay as even that seems to rub him up the wrong way. I swear, I'm only trying to help but whatever I say seems the wrong thing at the moment.'

Patty lifted her hands and encased her flushed cheeks within them, as though she had the weight of the world on her shoulders.

'Come on, luv,' Nancy said, instinctively standing up and moving round the table to sit next to Patty. 'I'm sure you two can sort it out,' she added, putting her arm around her friend's back to comfort her.

'It's just so ridiculous and pig-headed of him,' Patty blubbered, heavy tears now dropping onto her thighs, causing dark circles to form on her overalls. 'He's not thinking of all the worry he's causing me and his family by insisting on carrying on as normal and as if nothing happened.'

Nancy allowed Patty, now in floods of tears, to flop onto her chest. 'Now, now,' Nancy consoled her, 'try not to get yerself into a fluster. Archie is just wanting to prove he can do what other blokes his age are already doing.'

'Can I say something?' Daisy, who had been sat quietly, asked.

'Yes,' Patty said, wiping her tears on her mucky sleeve, leaving a smudge of dust across her cheeks. 'I hope it's an idea of how to make Archie see sense and slow down.'

'Well, not exactly,' Daisy conceded, hoping her good intentions wouldn't be misinterpreted. 'Please don't be mad at me. I only want to help.'

'Hey?' Patty quizzed.

'It's just, after seeing what my mum went through, I do sort of understand why he wants to prove himself.'

'What?' Patty huffed, feeling somewhat befuddled after fully expecting *all* her friends to see this whole sorry mess from her point of view.

The last thing Daisy wanted was to fall out with Patty, especially after the shenanigans and misunderstanding over Tommy Hardcastle. It had taken Patty long enough to accept her into the factory fold.

'Well, after my mum recovered, she really needed to do something to help,' Daisy tentatively explained. 'She wanted to feel useful and as though she was doing something worthwhile. I know you're worried, I was too, but I had to try to see it from my mum's point of view, that she couldn't sit around doing nothing forever.'

'But serving hot dinners is a damn sight safer than risking yer heart failing,' Patty retorted sharply, clearly miffed.

'Did I hear my name being mentioned?' Josie interjected, before Daisy had chance to respond.

'Hello, Mum,' Daisy said, keeping her tone neutral. 'I was just telling Patty how you were desperate to do something to help after you got better.'

Digging her hands into her blue-and-white gingham work apron, Josie glanced from her daughter to a distraught-looking Patty. 'Whatever's the matter, luv?' she asked kindly.

'It's Archie,' she repeated. 'He's only told Frank he'll put in a load of extra hours. Wants to prove he's a man or summat like that!'

'I see,' Josie nodded empathetically, 'and I assume you're worried he's not well enough?'

'Yes!' Patty exclaimed, grateful someone finally understood why she was so worried.

'I do understand it,' Josie said thoughtfully, sitting down on the empty chair next to Patty. 'But can I play devil's advocate for a minute?'

'Not you as well,' Patty sighed, deflated.

'Hear me out,' Josie replied patiently. 'As I'm sure you all heard from our Daisy, she really didn't want me to rush into anything after I finally got better and was forever reminding me to take it steady.'

Daisy instantly blushed. 'Only because I care, Mum.'

'I know, luv,' Josie said, reaching over and affectionately patting her daughter's hand. 'But that's my point,' she added, turning back to Patty. 'Daisy and my old man felt exactly like you do now. They were frightened I'd have a setback and land m'sen back in the hospital.'

'That's exactly what I'm scared of,' Patty agreed. 'I thought I'd lost him after he collapsed. I can't bear to think of Archie putting himself in such a daft position again.'

'I get that,' Josie said, 'but, if you can, try to put yourself in Archie's shoes. If he's anything like me, he'll be feeling pretty inadequate and just wanting to prove to himself he is capable of something useful.'

'Oh, I'm sorry, Mum,' Daisy chipped in, guilt coursing through her. 'I didn't mean to nag you.'

'You didn't, luv,' Josie reassured her. 'But what I'm saying is, Archie just needs to do something that makes him feel normal.'

'But isn't a typical week here enough, without the overtime?' Patty quizzed. 'We're already making chuffin' munitions for troops, surely that's plenty!'

'Probably not,' Josie sighed. 'He'll have seen lads he went to school with sign up and go off to war. He'll be feeling pretty inferior that he couldn't do that, so will be trying to find another way to show he's more than doing his bit. He'll be overcompensating, luv.'

'I just can't get m' head around the fact he could make himself ill again or summat even worse,' Patty lamented stubbornly.

'His pride has taken a bit of a battering lately. Yer know what blokes are like, luv, they need to feel strong and in control. From what our Daisy has told me, his mum and nannan have understandably been wrapping him in cotton wool all his life, like we all would, but by the sounds of it, he just wants to be his own man and this is his chance to show he is capable of doing something.'

Patty listened, trying to digest Josie's words, but her mind was a whirl.

'All I'll add,' Josie said, standing up and collecting the empty mugs, 'is don't smother him too much, or you could end up pushing him away. I know it's the last thing you'd mean to do but it would be a crying shame, as from what I've seen of the two of you, you are a match made in heaven.'

'It is the last thing I want,' Patty said. 'M' head's just a mess with it all and I have this horrible feeling there's summat else he ain't telling me. It's just not like Archie to be so quiet and avoid answering m' questions. Maybe I'm being paranoid, either that or he's just biting his tongue to avoid us falling out. I really don't know, but I know my fussing is driving him mad.'

'I'm sure, luv,' Josie said. 'Give yourself a bit of time. It'll all work out in the wash, I promise yer. Anyway, I better get back behind that counter; the next lot will be here in a minute, demanding their snap.'

'Thanks, Josie,' Patty answered, but despite her polite reply, she wasn't convinced. As far as she was concerned,

Archie was being a damn fool for even thinking about putting his health, or even worse, his life, at risk.

'No bother,' Josie replied. 'Now get yerselves back to work. I've heard things are really picking up and it's all hands on deck.'

'Well, at least that will help take my mind off it all. I'll be so busy this afternoon I won't have time to be in the doldrums about it.' Patty tried to look on the bright side and gather herself for a hard afternoon's work. 'And if I'm in a crane cab by m'sen I can't say owt to put my flamin' foot in it, can I?'

Across the table, Nancy grimaced again at the thought of the increased workload. And if the idea of overtime hadn't already sent her into a quandary about how she would manage at home looking after the children, the reason behind the need for more hands on deck to complete orders made her even more apprehensive. In his last letter, Bert had sounded cheery but she couldn't help but worry if he would be safe or soon be in even more danger.

She deliberately hovered behind her friends as they made their way out of the canteen into the noisy bustle of the factory, taking a moment to compose herself. She would be able to work something out with Doris or Frank on the overtime, but she didn't want her worries to add to what her friends were already dealing with, especially when Patty was in such a state of turmoil of her own.

Chapter 17

'Can I walk you home?' Archie asked tentatively, as he caught up with Patty, and they joined the throng of workers leaving Vickers. For the past week, since he'd signed up to be an air raid warden, they'd both been treading on eggshells. Knowing he hadn't told Patty the full truth was tearing at him. If he wanted to sort things out, he'd have to be honest with her.

'S'ppose,' Patty muttered sulkily. 'We're going the same way.' She was still furious with Archie for agreeing to the overtime, but had also spent the last few days feeling thoroughly miserable. They'd barely spent a minute together since they'd quarrelled.

Betty and Nancy, who were walking alongside their friend, swapped a knowing glance, and quickly excused themselves, hoping that the pair could finally sort it out.

'We'll see you tomorrow,' Betty said tactfully, holding back slightly, to give Patty and Archie the space they obviously needed.

'Yes, see you then,' Patty said, with a wave of her hand,

her shoulders slumped as she trundled towards gate three with an equally glum Archie by her side.

As soon as Betty and Nancy were out of earshot, Archie turned to Patty. 'I need to tell you something,' he said, taking a deep breath.

Patty bit down on her lip. *Flamin' Nora*, she silently cursed. *What's he chuffin' done this time?* Instead, she said, 'Go on then, you may as well spit it out.'

This wasn't how Archie had hoped the conversation would go, but he knew the longer he kept his news a secret, the worse it would become.

'Please don't be mad at me,' he started.

Patty eyed him suspiciously. 'You hardly make it difficult,' she scoffed, but immediately regretted her cutting remark.

'All right,' Archie muttered, trying to find his voice. 'Do you fancy going for a drink at the Wellington?'

'I can't,' Patty retorted. 'I promised m' mom I'd get back and help her out.'

'All right,' Archie sighed, wishing there was a better place than stood on the street to break the news to her.

'Just tell me,' Patty entreated, unable to bear the wait. She'd been worried sick about Archie and what he hadn't been telling her so she just wanted to know the truth.

'Okay . . .' He'd really hoped they could have had this chat when Patty was feeling more relaxed and there was chance she wouldn't be so angry but judging by the icy atmosphere that had once again surfaced between them, he realized now it was highly unlikely.

'Are you going to tell me then?' Patty trilled impatiently.

'Yes, yes, sorry.' Archie could feel his cheeks colouring and his heart racing, stopping him from getting the words out.

'Just say it!' Patty gasped, her tolerance wearing thin.

'Please try to understand,' Archie finally started. 'I never meant to lie to you.'

Goose pimples prickled Patty's skin and her blood ran cold as she froze to the spot. She looked at Archie in horror, speechless.

'It's not as bad as you think,' he quickly added, seeing the dread on his sweetheart's face. 'It's just, well, how can I say it? I've, erm, I've signed up to be an air raid warden.'

'What?' Patty quizzed. 'When?'

Archie knew he couldn't lie, despite how much he knew his next revelation would hurt Patty.

'Last Saturday.'

'The same day we went to see a picture?' Patty asked, trying to process what Archie was telling her.

'Yes,' he whispered sheepishly.

As the penny dropped, the fury inside Patty grew. No wonder he had been acting so odd.

'You mean you deliberately lied to me?'

'I'm sorry. I didn't mean to. I was hoping if we could just chat about it, you would be able to understand my reasons behind it.'

Anger, fear and utter bewilderment consumed Patty. *Is Archie really the man I think he is?*

Incandescent with rage, Patty glared at Archie. 'How could you?' she cried.

'Patty, please . . .' Archie pleaded, but before he could finish his sentence, Patty abruptly turned on her heel and raced down Brightside Lane, quickly vanishing into the crowds of workers who were making their way home, heavy tears cascading down her now sodden cheeks.

'I'm such a fool,' Archie sighed, his naive hopes of Patty hearing him out well and truly dashed. 'I'll be lucky if she ever speaks to me again.'

Across the road, Betty and Nancy were still chatting away, oblivious to the explosive fallout.

'I hope they can sort things out, I hate seeing them both so miserable,' Nancy said as she buttoned up her coat. Although spring was making an appearance, the late afternoon air was still nippy.

'Oh, I'm sure they will,' Betty replied matter-of-factly. 'I can see why Patty's upset, but Archie is only trying to prove he is capable of doing his bit. You can hardly blame him for that and beyond all of that, they are clearly madly in love, even if they are doing a pretty good job of disguising it right now.'

'I guess you're right,' Nancy agreed, recalling the very conversation she'd had with Bert before he had gone off to war. His moral conscience and determination to do the right thing had been the driving force behind his decision to go off to war without complaint, never considering his own safety, although aware of how much his family would miss him and he them.

'I do sympathize with Patty though,' Nancy added, as they made their way onto the cobblestones of Brightside Lane. 'The worry never goes away.'

'I know,' Betty agreed. 'But what can we do? We have to carry on, otherwise none of us would get up of a morning and that won't do anyone any good.'

Once again, Nancy was left in awe of Betty's strength. 'I really don't know how you do it,' she praised. 'I'd love to have your determination.'

'But you do,' Betty protested. 'As I keep telling you, you are stronger than you think.'

'But I'm not like you,' Nancy insisted, suddenly welling up. 'I just about get through each day in one piece, but you are always thinking of how to do more.'

'I don't have two children and I also have a landlady who cooks and cleans for me!' Betty reminded her gently, placing her hand on Nancy's arm. 'Now come on, don't be getting upset or feeling guilty.'

'Well, you still always manage to keep your spirits up,' Nancy said in admiration. 'Look at me. I thought I was doing so well, but I feel like I could fall to bits at any moment.'

'You mustn't be so hard on yourself,' Betty insisted. 'Like I have told you and will keep on telling you, you are doing a grand job juggling those little ones and working here.'

'I just feel so guilty about the overtime Frank mentioned. I don't think I can manage it, which makes me feel like I'm letting you all down.'

'You are doing no such thing,' Betty said sternly. 'And don't forget, I have more time on my hands, so I have to find ways to keep myself busy, otherwise I would be in a terrible pickle. Don't get me wrong, I want to help and do as much as I can but if I'm being honest, it helps me too.'

'Really?' Nancy asked.

'Of course! Admittedly, I've never been good at sitting and doing nothing but, at the moment, I'm very eager not to have any free time, as I know I'd be in a terrible kerfuffle worrying about William.'

'Well, I'm still in awe and maybe I need to take a page out of your book.'

'I think you do enough,' Betty reiterated. 'And I also think you should stop worrying about if you could do more and give yourself a pat on the back for what you already do.'

'Thanks, Betty, you're a good friend,' Nancy said, dabbing her watery eyes, once again feeling grateful for the support.

'Why don't you have a chat with Frank and let him know how you are feeling? He's a good man. I'm sure he will understand.'

'Maybe I will.' Nancy nodded, accepting she would have to do something. All this worrying was leaving her a nervous wreck. 'Thank you again.'

'Not at all, but I must dash. I've got a few errands to run, but please think about what I've said and maybe talk to Doris too. I'm sure she would hate to think of you suffering like this.'

'I know you're right. I really wish I was more like you. I'm always in such a dither.'

'Nonsense,' Betty said firmly. 'You just have a lot on your mind, that's all. Now go and see those children of yours and make sure you have a good tea and a natter with Doris.'

'I will and thank you again.'

'You have nothing to thank me for,' Betty said, waving off the gesture. 'Just take care of yourself, that's all I ask.'

As the two women went their separate ways, Betty couldn't help worrying about her friend. She hadn't the heart to mention where she was really going: the new depot the Women's Voluntary Service had set up where volunteers were making bandages, swabs and hospital clothing. She was trying not to think about William and just concentrate on doing her bit.

Fifteen minutes later, Nancy opened Doris's back door. 'Hello,' she called, making her way into the warm kitchen, heat radiating from the range.

'Hiya, luv,' Doris trilled as she turned to face her neighbour, little George perched on her hip, munching on a jammy slice of bread. 'I've just put the kettle on. Take the weight off your feet and have a sit-down. I'll make you a cuppa.'

'I can do it,' Nancy offered, keeping her voice from breaking. 'I'm sure you have been run ragged all day too.'

'Don't be daft, luv,' Doris protested. 'At least I'm at home and not in that great mucky factory.'

'It's not so bad. Well, not at the moment anyway,' Nancy said.

Doris threw her friend a quizzical look. She knew Nancy well enough to know when something was wrong. 'Here, you take Georgie and I'll make us a nice hot brew.'

Nancy didn't argue but instead opened her arms and took the sticky-fingered, smiling toddler from Doris. 'Have you been a good boy for yer mummy?' Nancy asked, as Georgie stuffed the remaining piece of bread in his mouth, making his cheeks bulge.

'Mmm,' came the muffled reply, as the happy youngster nodded his head up and down eagerly.

'Well, that's debatable.' Doris laughed. 'I'm not sure I'd call jumping on a pile of freshly laundered bedding behaving, but I guess he hasn't been so bad, and it can get a little bit boring for him while I'm constantly washing and ironing.'

'Oh gosh,' Nancy sighed. 'And then you have my two to look after as well. If it's getting too much, please tell me and I'll try and sort something else out.' But the reality was Nancy didn't know how on earth she would cope without Doris. There was no way she could work at Vickers without her help, and she certainly couldn't juggle this overtime Frank had mentioned. She couldn't possibly ask Doris to do anything else to help her out. She clearly had enough on her own plate as it was.

'Don't be getting yerself in a frenzy,' Doris said, now fully convinced something was worrying her friend. 'It's actually a godsend when I collect the bigger ones from school as they normally take Georgie off m' hands for an hour or so and he's always so excited to see them. He's only come downstairs and left them all playing in their bedrooms because he was hungry – again! I swear these boys are born with hollow legs.'

'You won't get any arguments from me there.' Nancy chuckled, momentarily forgetting her fears, and feeling better for sitting down with a friend over a cup of tea. 'I'm sure our Billy could eat from morning till night and still claim he was starvin'.'

'Well, he's in good company with Georgie here and his big brother, Joe,' Doris replied, fetching the teapot and a fresh jug of milk over to the table. 'Now let me just grab us a mug each. You look in need of a good strong brew.'

'That obvious?' Nancy asked.

'Yep.' Doris nodded, pouring the tea through the strainer. 'Now come on, tell me what's bothering you while the kids are still playing upstairs. I don't want you going home later and getting yer'sen in a pickle and not able to sleep. That's no good for yer when you are in control of that heavy crane all day.'

'I'm probably overthinking everything,' Nancy started, accepting the steaming brew.

'Go on,' Doris prompted.

'It's just everything is starting to feel so real all of a sudden,' Nancy said, tears once again stinging her eyes, as she gently popped Georgie on the floor next to his toy cars.

'What do you mean, luv?' Doris asked. 'Has something happened?'

Nancy took a deep breath, trying to keep herself calm, despite how impossible it felt. 'Nothing major, well, except for that awful bombing on the Orkney Islands last week. It just feels so close to home and more real, doesn't it?'

'It does,' Doris agreed. 'I can't begin to imagine what those poor people went through. It doesn't bare thinking about.'

'I know it probably sounds daft and I'm probably being a bit naive,' Nancy said, raising her mug of tea to her lips, 'but because Britain hasn't really had any bombing or attacks, I thought this Phoney War, as it keeps being called, might just carry on. I suppose, if I'm honest, that's what I was hoping for, and that way Bert would be home soon, and we could all go back to normal.'

'Oh, luv,' Doris said, as she sat down opposite her friend. 'I reckon that's what we all want, but none of us really know what's around the corner, despite how much we hope and pray. We've just got to stick together and deal with whatever happens.'

'You're right – as always.' Nancy nodded, wishing she had just an ounce of Doris's or Betty's resilience.

'Anyway,' Doris added, 'has something else happened? You don't seem right at all.'

'I really am predictable, aren't I?'

'Well, we all have our moments, luv. So, what's happened at work today to leave you feeling so distressed?'

Nancy took another sip of her tea, before biting her lip. 'I keep trying to tell myself it's nothing, but it feels much bigger than that.'

Doris raised an eyebrow, encouraging Nancy to carry on.

'Frank mentioned last week the gaffers have asked us all to do some overtime as the orders are coming in thick and fast. I've been avoiding it but then it came up again today when Frank said they couldn't keep up with all the orders. If we are making more munitions and parts for planes, do they think more attacks are imminent? They wouldn't be doing all this if the war wasn't stepping up a level, would they? On top of what happened in the Orkneys, it just feels like something awful is brewing.'

After blurting out what had been worrying her all day, Nancy put her mug down, and unable to keep herself together any longer, put her head in her hands and the tears she had been trying so hard to repress finally beat her.

'Come on, luv,' Doris said, immediately on her feet and at her friend's side, putting her arm around her. 'Whatever happens we will get through this together, just like we always have. None of us know what the future holds.'

'I know,' Nancy sobbed. 'It just feels so daunting now and I'm so scared.'

'Of course, you are, luv,' Doris soothed, rubbing Nancy's back. 'That's completely normal. You wouldn't be human if you weren't.'

'But what if Bert, if he doesn't . . .' Nancy had never

been able to say out loud the words that kept her awake night after night.

'I know it's hard, but you mustn't think like that,' Doris said gently. 'Like I said, we have no idea what's going to happen, but one thing I do know is that we have to have hope if we are going to survive this blasted war.'

'You're right and so is Betty. She tells me exactly the same thing all the time, and as much as I know I need to listen to you both, I still find myself in a muddle,' Nancy snivelled, wiping her sodden cheeks with a hankie, the river of tears now reduced to a gentle trickle.

'As I keep saying, that's completely understandable,' Doris said, sitting back down. 'Don't forget we can't always keep a stiff upper lip all the time. We are human and we have these pesky little things called emotions that play flamin' havoc with us.'

'Don't they just,' Nancy sighed, once again appreciating Doris's words of wisdom.

'Life is certainly sent to try us, luv,' Doris added, quickly retrieving Georgie and lifting him into her arms, as he made a beeline for the range.

'Isn't it just,' Nancy replied. 'But listen to me harping on after everything you have had to go through. I should be counting my blessings.'

'It's all relative,' Doris replied empathetically. 'Losing George was the worst thing I've ever been through, and I wouldn't wish it on anyone, but I have a lot to be thankful for. I have a roof over my head, the kids are fed and clothed, and I have you as a friend.'

'Aw, Doris,' Nancy said, dabbing her watery eyes. 'Don't. You'll set me off again.'

'A good cry has never hurt anyone.' Doris smiled. 'You have to get it out of yer system, or you will feel a million times worse.'

'Well, I'm grateful that you are happy to listen. You must think I'm a right moaning Minnie.'

'I don't at all. You have done the same for me more times than I can remember. That's what friends are for. Now come on, let's get this tea out before those lot upstairs start complaining they have never been fed.'

'That sounds like a plan,' Nancy said, making her way to the cupboard to get out a pile of plates. 'I must admit, I feel quite peckish myself. I hardly touched m' dinner after getting myself all of a dither.'

'Well, you will be pleased to know I've made a reyt hearty stew, so that should fill you up, and I baked a fresh loaf this morning to mop up the gravy.'

'I really don't know how you do it.'

'You can blame this one,' Doris said, raising her eyebrows as she glanced at Georgie. 'He thought five-thirty was a good time to start the day. The little bugger!'

'Oh, Georgie.' Nancy chuckled. 'You are a monkey. It's a good job yer cute.'

Lapping up the attention, the toddler threw Nancy and Doris his most endearing toothy smile.

'Now,' Doris said authoritatively, 'before those big 'uns pile downstairs, I just want you to know if you need to do some overtime, and you want to take it, then I'm happy for Billy and Linda to be here with me.'

'But I really can't put on you anymore than I already do,' Nancy protested, as she lay the table for tea.

'You're doing nothing of the sort,' Doris insisted, popping Georgie back down on the floor, away from the range. 'They are as good as gold and keep my lot entertained. I hardly notice they are here. Besides which, the extra cash will help you out.'

'It's always handy,' Nancy agreed. 'But we get by as we are. My wages more than make up for the drop in Bert's wages. I think I was more worried about letting everyone down at work as well abusing your good nature.'

'Well, you don't need to worry about it,' Doris replied, lifting the steaming casserole dish from the oven. 'I can cope feeding the kids by m'sen, so if you decide to do it, you won't need to fret about letting yer pals down either. But if it's really worrying you, why don't you have a word with Frank? He seems like a decent enough bloke and from what you've said, he wouldn't want you fretting like this. Maybe you could just do one lot of overtime a week, that way you are still helping yer pals and you still get to see Billy and Linda too?'

'Thank you.' Nancy smiled appreciatively. 'But it goes without saying, if I do have to work extra, I'll help out with more groceries.'

'If it makes you feel better, that's fine, and you'll get no complaints when it comes to extra food from this one.' Doris laughed, glancing towards Georgie, who was now safely encased under the table with his bright yellow Tonka miniature truck. 'But it's really not necessary.'

Nancy knew her friend well enough not to argue but was also quietly adamant she would be making a couple of extra visits to Oliver's for an extra joint of meat as a thank you for all Doris did for them.

Chapter 18

'Well, that was another long week.' Patty yawned as she joined Nancy and Betty at the foot of Myrtle.

'Wasn't it just?' Betty agreed. 'Only one more half shift though, and we are done for the week.'

'Thank God!' Patty exclaimed. 'I'm flamin' shattered. This overtime is nearly killing me.'

It had certainly been a long couple of weeks. After agreeing to the overtime, Betty and Patty had worked until six o'clock through the week, adding an extra two hours to their already physically draining days. Nancy had taken Doris's advice, and Frank had agreed she should do overtime only twice a week, insisting she must spend time with her children.

'I guess it's all hands on deck now,' Betty said resolutely.

'It does feel like that, doesn't it?' Nancy sighed.

'Try not to panic, girls,' Frank said as he came up alongside them, keeping his tone calm, and quickly folding up his copy of the *Daily Mirror*. 'Hitler has still got a long way to go yet before he wins this war.'

'It didn't sound like that on the radio this morning,'

Patty countered. Even she'd stopped eating her porridge and jam to listen to the latest headlines on the BBC with her mom and dad.

Four days earlier Hitler had instructed his warships to enter Norway's ports and called for the country to surrender. After they'd refused, the Germans had begun storming the country from the skies with a parachute invasion.

'Do you think the Allied troops can fight them off?' Nancy asked nervously, wondering if Bert would be transferred from wherever he was in France.

'I can't imagine they will give up without at least trying,' Frank said, but he couldn't be sure if he was trying to convince himself or Nancy.

'It just all feels a little bit close to home.' All the positivity Nancy had managed to muster after Doris's pep talk a couple of weeks earlier was now fading.

'What do yer mean?' Patty asked. 'A bit close to home? I thought Norway was miles away.'

'Not as far we'd like,' Frank said, opening his paper, but taking care not to reveal the headlines, acutely aware they weren't what Nancy, Betty or Patty needed to see right now. 'Look 'ere.'

He showed Patty a map of Europe – 'This is us' – and he pointed to Britain, which seemed so tiny compared to the rest of the continent. 'And this area here below us is France.'

Instinctively Nancy looked over Frank's shoulder. *Where are you, Bert?* she thought. On the map it only seemed like a hop, skip and a jump to the French mainland but she knew in reality he might as well be on the other side of the world. She'd never travelled farther than Manchester, so anything outside of Britain seemed so strange and unfamiliar.

'And this,' Frank added, pulling Nancy back to the moment, 'is Norway.'

Betty was aware of how Europe looked on a map, after excelling at geography at school, but even she looked slightly aghast. She also spotted how close the Orkney Islands were, revealing where that poor man had lost his life at the hands of Hitler.

'Chuffin' 'eck!' Patty finally gasped, vocalising what they were all thinking. 'That ain't far away at all.'

'Aye, but we have the North Sea between them and us, duck,' Frank said, trying to reassure his Three Musketeers.

But they have U-boats and fighter planes, Betty quietly mused, not vocalising her fears, knowing it would send poor Nancy into a frenzy of worry.

Patty was right: the attack on Norway did feel a little bit too close for comfort. Hitler clearly wasn't holding back on his barbaric mission to take over Europe.

'We've also got one of the best armies, navy and RAF in the world,' Frank added, again as much to bolster his own spirits.

'And we are helping them be the best they can be by working overtime to help produce the parts they need,' Betty added. This latest development in Norway fuelled her determination to do her bit, to ensure William and his fellow pilots had everything they needed to defend their country against the Luftwaffe.

'I s'ppose,' Patty said, an unfamiliar sense of impending doom leaving her all of a muddle.

'Think of all those new lipsticks you could buy,' Betty said, playing to Patty's love of shopping and hoping it would lighten the atmosphere.

'Yes,' Patty suddenly beamed, 'I'm overdue a shopping trip with Hattie, but I'm meeting her for a quick drink at the Wellington in a minute. She's really missing John, so it will do her good.'

'Aw, that will be nice.' Nancy nodded. 'And have you and Archie got any plans for the weekend?' Nancy was keen to move away from the subject of war.

'Definitely not. I can barely look at him right now and we haven't been speaking.'

'Has something else happened?'

'You could say that.' Patty sniffled, her eyes glistening with tears.

'Take your time,' Nancy said kindly.

'It's just too awful,' Patty finally gasped, her shoulders shuddering.

'Surely, it's not that bad,' Nancy said tentatively.

'That's just it,' Patty cried, tears now flowing down her dusty cheeks. 'It is. He still doesn't get how selfish he's being by signing up to be an air raid warden.'

'I'm sure Archie just wants to feel useful,' Betty suggested.

'But at what cost?' Patty moaned. 'Surely, his health has to come first. I can't believe he's been so chuffin' stupid.'

Betty took a deep breath, momentarily stumped for

words. Patty had a valid point. It had only been just over two months since Archie had collapsed at the Vicktory Knitters event. *Was his heart up to that amount of stress, if and when the time came?*

'I'm not sure anything I can say will make you feel better, duck,' Frank interjected. 'But take it from me, luv, you're going to feel a whole lot worse if you don't try and make up. I have no doubt Archie will be feeling as upset as you are. Why don't you have a chat later?'

'I can't even think about speaking to him. It will end in another row. Anyway, the thing is, he is doing some air raid warden thing tonight, so I'm clearly at the bottom of his list of priorities. I'm not even sure what exactly it is he's doing. I couldn't bring myself to ask.'

'Is there no way you could try to talk it through?' Nancy encouraged, dismayed to see her friend and Archie still at loggerheads after his recent revelation. 'Maybe plan a nice night out together and somehow get back on track,' she added, hoping a romantic night might help ease the tension.

'I don't think I can bear to be in the same room as him at the moment. I just need some space,' Patty insisted. 'Not only is he putting his life at risk but he kept the whole flamin' thing from me.'

'I understand,' Nancy conceded. 'But talking it through might help. It really might do you both some good?' she added, a question more than a statement.

'Oh, I don't know, maybe. I'm just not sure,' Patty muttered unconvincingly.

'Maybe you both just need time to get used to the idea?' Nancy suggested.

'Possibly.' Patty nodded half-heartedly. But she'd been livid all week and couldn't even look Archie in the eye after he'd so blatantly lied to her. 'Anyway, you don't need to listen to me harping on. Today's been depressing enough. What are you two up to?'

'Oh, I'm just looking forward to spending some time with Billy and Linda,' Nancy answered, throwing her gas mask over her shoulder as they made their way off the shop floor. 'I'm ready for it now.'

'Are you coping all right?' Betty asked, knowing how hard her friend had been finding everything lately. Nancy already had so much on her plate with looking after the kids and not wanting to put upon Doris, so the extra hours at Vickers had meant even less time with Billy and Linda.

'I've had my moments and a couple of tears,' Nancy confessed. 'I don't think you ever get used to parting with your children. It's been tough only seeing them at bedtime on the nights I work overtime but Doris has been a godsend as ever. I couldn't do it without her. I'm going to make a big roast on Sunday to give her a break as a thank you.'

'Well, I'm sure she will appreciate that,' Betty encouraged. 'But make sure you get a rest too. It's been a long week.'

'Well, if nothing else, I should sleep well.' Nancy yawned, but on second thought she wasn't sure the latest news about Norway would be conducive to a good night's sleep. 'I must make time to write to Bert too. I've not had chance all week.'

'I owe William a letter too,' Betty said, as the women left the ear-splitting cacophony of factory noise behind them and entered the yard.

'Has he got to Canada yet?' Nancy asked.

'I'm not sure. He hadn't in his last letter, but I don't think it will be long now.'

'How are you feeling?' Nancy probed, aware of how good Betty was at putting on a brave face.

'I won't lie, it has been difficult,' Betty confessed. 'But I've started volunteering at the Women's Voluntary Service now as well as helping Ivy and Frank get the garden ready for planting and the hens, so I've barely had a minute to think.'

'I reckon that's the best way,' Patty chirped. 'Sometimes I think half my problem is I have too much time to think about stuff and get myself into more of a tizz.'

'I know what you mean. I'm very guilty of that too, luv,' Nancy empathized. 'If it wasn't for Betty here and Doris, I'd have gone mad going round in circles and constantly whittling.'

'We all cope differently,' Betty explained. 'And there's nothing wrong with that.'

'Mmm, I reckon Archie might disagree,' Patty sighed. 'I think he'd be a lot happier if he thought I wasn't worrying about him all the time. That way he could just carry on working himself into an early grave.'

'Oh, don't say that, luv,' Nancy said, touching Patty's arm. 'You'd be devastated if anything happened to him. We all would.'

'You're probably right but quite frankly, he's only got himself to blame,' Patty replied adamantly. But as she considered her words, a surge of guilt coursed through her. She'd been so busy harping on about what Archie was putting her through, she hadn't stopped to consider how wretched her friends must feel, not being able to see the men they loved.

'I'm sorry,' Patty said. 'I know you both worry so much about William and Bert. It's harder with them being so far away. At least I can still see Archie.'

'It doesn't matter where they are, luv,' Betty empathized. 'You worry. It's only natural, but maybe with a little more time, you and Archie can work things out.'

'Maybe.' Patty nodded. 'We'll see, but as Archie's nannan always says, I better turn this frown upside down, as here's Hattie. She's definitely got enough on without listening to me ranting.'

The three women turned to greet Hattie as she made her way up Brightside Lane.

'Hattie, over here.' Patty waved, quickly painting on her best smile, catching her friend's attention amongst the sea of workers flowing through the factory gates.

'Evening, everyone,' Hattie said as she navigated her way through the crowd and reached the trio of women.

'Good to see you again,' Betty greeted. 'We must all have another get-together again soon, maybe at The Skates?'

'You are very welcome to come with us for a drink,' Hattie offered, 'if you don't have to rush off anywhere?'

'That would be lovely, but are you sure you two don't want a catch-up by yourselves?'

'Not at all,' Hattie insisted. 'The more the merrier. How about you, Nancy? Would you like to join us too?'

'I'd have loved to, but I really need to get home. Doris has had my two since half seven this morning and I really want to spend some time with them before bedtime, but maybe next time when things have settled down at work a little?'

'Yes, you must,' Hattie replied. 'I can't imagine you get much time to relax.'

'I don't,' Nancy confirmed. 'I'm not complaining, mind. Anyway, I better make tracks, but you all go and have a good time.'

'Well, I'll see you in the morning,' Betty said. 'And try and get some sleep if you can.'

'I will. I'm dead-beat, so that should help.' Nancy yawned, as she turned to walk in the opposite direction to her friends.

Fifteen minutes later, Betty, Patty and Hattie were nursing their drinks in a quiet corner of the Wellington.

'I guess you've all heard about Norway?' Hattie said, taking a sip of port and lemon.

'Yes,' Patty replied, sighing. 'We were just talking about it before you arrived. It feels a bit frightening, doesn't it?'

'Yes, I'm more worried about John. He went out to

France as part of the British Expeditionary Force, but I'm scared he could be sent over to Norway now. I know that's what he's there to do but the idea of him being in the middle of all that fighting is too much.'

'I know it's easier said than done,' Betty said, wondering if that was also the same battalion of men Bert was with, 'but try not to think the worst. Surely, it would take a lot of organising to move all those men to Norway, and they will have their own army.' Betty really had no idea, but she hated seeing anyone worrying. Heaven knows, she'd done her fair share thinking about where William would end up.

'I hope so,' Hattie sighed. 'Anyway, you haven't come here to listen to me moan. Patty has been telling me you're all still knitting away. I've been doing some socks for John too. He says in his letters his feet are always cold.'

'We are.' Betty nodded enthusiastically, keen to keep the conversation upbeat and cheer them both up. 'We are hoping to send some woollies to the men working with Nancy's husband and Dolly's sons, but I've also discovered the WVS arrange care packages to be sent out to the Allied troops, so if we get too many, I can send them there.'

'I reckon we'll be sending them by the shipload.' Patty laughed. 'That pile you and Dolly are collecting seems to be getting bigger by the day.'

'You could be right there,' Betty replied. 'I think everyone is just keen to do something to help.'

'It does make you feel better,' Hattie agreed. 'Working

in Woollies doesn't really feel like I'm doing anything very worthwhile and more than ever I want to do something useful.'

'If you have some free time, I'm sure the WVS would always welcome an extra pair of hands,' Betty suggested. 'They have an Air Raid Precautions office on Church Street in town. I'm sure if you nipped down, they would find you something to do, even if it's just some extra knitting.'

'Do you know, I might go and have a chat with them,' Hattie mused. 'It would be good to keep myself busy rather than sitting and fretting. There must be something I can turn my hand to?'

'I don't doubt it for a second,' Betty encouraged, hoping it might also act as a distraction and stop Hattie worrying about John quite as much. It had certainly helped her as it kept her mind busy, and she liked feeling as though she was doing something useful, but on the other hand, the fact she was making bandages for hospitals was a sign this war wasn't going to end any time soon and made her worry about what the next few months might bring.

'Church Street – that must be where Archie signed up at,' Patty piped up, her mind wandering. 'I never actually asked him.'

'I didn't know he'd signed up for that. How's that going?' Hattie asked, concerned.

'Neither did I. We had another t' do the other week. He flamin' kept it from me for over a week and I got so upset at him after he finally confessed that he'd signed up to it.'

'Gosh,' Hattie replied. 'Why didn't he just tell you straightaway?'

'He probably knew I'd go barmy!'

'And did you?' Hattie was fairly sure she knew what the answer was.

'I did,' Patty confirmed. 'Wouldn't you? Apart from being pretty miffed he lied to me after promising he never would hide anything from me again after his scare in January, I'm just scared his heart isn't up to it physically.'

'Maybe you just need a little bit more time to take it all in. I guess Archie is just trying to make up for the fact he can't join up and go and fight and was then worried it might cause a rift between you.'

'That's the top and tail of it,' Patty conceded, taking a mouthful of her lemonade. 'I just can't get over the fact he's putting his health at risk. It's like he's dug his heels in and won't listen to any common sense at all.'

'I can understand why you are so upset, but it sounds like no matter what you say, he's not going to change his mind.'

'I think yer right there,' Patty sighed despondently.

'Well, let's not put a downer on tonight,' Hattie said, in a bid to stop Patty getting herself in a fluster. 'Why don't we arrange a date for that trip into town for a look round the shops and a cake at Lyons? Maybe we could go next weekend? It will be something for us both to look forward to.'

But just as they were about to discuss when would work, a deafening screech drowned out their chatter.

'Typical!' Patty frowned. 'A flamin' air raid.'

'Ay, up, everyone,' boomed the landlord, competing with the high-pitched siren. 'If anyone wants to take their drinks down to the cellar, there's plenty of room, and we definitely aren't short of beer.'

His instructions were met by a chorus of support.

'Sounds like a plan.'

'I'm up for that.'

'What do you think we should do?' Hattie asked, looking slightly anxious, as the siren continued to sound.

Betty took a few seconds to consider their options. 'Well,' she said, trying to be logical. 'We can either make a dash for the communal one you use, Patty, or join this lot in the cellar.'

'Er, I don't know,' Patty replied, unable to think straight in the panic of everyone dashing about.

'I'm sure it's just another false alarm,' Hattie jumped in. 'But maybe it's safer to stay here and go down to the cellar than head out into the streets.'

'Yes, you're right,' Betty said, grabbing her coat and gas mask.

'Come on then, let's go,' Hattie said, as the three women followed the throng of men, clad in overalls, down the steep stairs into the cavernous cellar.

Hit by the distinct aroma of hops mixed with stale cigarettes, they found themselves ushered towards some old wooden chairs.

'You'll be safe here, girls,' an older man said, perching

himself on a wooden bar stool, a pint in one hand and his gas mask in the other. 'Hitler will be hard-pressed to get us down here.'

'Thank you,' Betty said politely, trying to stave off her nerves and ignore the cold shiver which had just raced down her spine. You didn't have to be a genius to work out why the dogged German leader would target the steelworks. Parts for planes and tanks, let alone munitions, were being churned out by the truckload every single day to ensure the Allied troops had what they needed to defeat Jerry. If Hitler could put a stop to production, it would surely bolster his campaign. Vickers was the only factory in the country to home the ginormous fifteen-tonne steam-powered drop hammer which forged the crankshafts for the Rolls-Royce Merlin engine used in Spitfires and Hurricanes – key aircraft for the RAF.

As the pub customers piled into the crowded cellar, which thankfully hadn't been thrown into complete darkness due to a couple of gas-powered lights the landlord had installed, Betty quietly wondered if the Phoney War as they knew it was coming to an end.

Looking across at the terrified look on Patty's face, she was glad she hadn't vocalised her thoughts.

'It's going to be all right,' Betty said, hiding her own fears, giving Patty's knee a gentle tap.

'Do yer think so?'

'Of course,' Betty replied confidently, in a bid to reassure herself as well as her friend.

'But what about Archie?' Patty gasped. 'I have no idea where he is. We've barely spoke. I don't even know if he's on patrol or back at home. I just hope he and his family got to the communal shelter on time. Do you think he's in danger?'

'He'll be okay, I just know it,' Hattie said. 'No doubt my dad will be down the boozer half cut and my poor mum will be in the cupboard under the stairs or in the coal bunker by herself. I know she'll not leave the house, frightened I'll come back and she isn't there.'

'Try not to fret,' Betty said, desperate to keep her voice level, but not entirely convinced she was succeeding. 'I'm sure this will be over as quick as it's started.'

In fact, Betty's thoughts were with her own family and Ivy. 'Please let them all be safe,' she quietly prayed. Worried her landlady would also be at home by herself, Betty hoped she would have the good sense to take herself into either the cellar or the Anderson shelter in the garden. She had no idea what shift her dad and brother were on. As much as she never liked the idea of them being deep underground at the pit, it was probably the best place for them right now.

'Don't you girls be getting yerselves worked up,' the old man next to them chirped up. 'We survived the last war, we'll survive this one too.'

'At what cost though!' Patty blurted out, unable to hold back her emotions a second longer.

'Come on,' Hattie said, instinctively wrapping her arms

around her best friend. 'Like Betty said, it's probably another false alarm.'

'But what if it isn't?' Patty cried, her whole body now shaking. 'I have no idea where Archie is. He could be right in the thick of it as we speak, and I didn't even give him a second glance when he rushed off after work. In fact, I've been pretty off with him for the last fortnight.'

'Don't beat yourself up,' Hattie said, attempting to soothe Patty. 'Archie's a sensible lad. He won't put himself in any danger.'

'But he can't predict where a great flamin' bomb will land, can he? I'm such a fool. Why didn't I just go and give him a hug? If anything happens to him, I'll never forgive m'self, especially as the last thing he'll remember of me is being mardy.'

Betty momentarily closed her eyes. Although she knew Patty had worked herself up into a state, she also knew she had a point – no one had any idea what flight path the Luftwaffe would take, except the pilots and their superior officers. Even if the steelworks were their prime target, Betty was aware this wasn't the time to overthink things. She needed to do what she did best: stay calm and remain positive.

'Why did he have to go and chuffin' become an air raid warden?' Patty sobbed. 'He may as well have gone and signed his own death warrant!'

'Listen,' Betty said, her logical side surfacing. 'Can you hear anything?'

'What do yer mean?' Patty quizzed.

'Tell me what you can hear,' Betty repeated, trying to keep her friend focused.

Patty fell silent and looked around the cellar, which was now full of the pub regulars calmly chatting, exchanging banter, and supping their drinks. A couple of men had started a game of cards to pass the time, and a few others were perched around a crate playing dominoes.

'Just people talking,' Patty finally said.

'Exactly,' Betty replied.

'What do yer mean?' Patty asked, confused.

'Well, if Jerry was bombing the steelworks or anywhere nearby, we would be able to hear it, wouldn't we? From what William has told me, those planes are deafening, and I can't hear anything that would make me think the Germans are overhead, let alone anything that resembles an explosion.'

As Betty's words sunk in, the fear and worry in Patty's face gradually started to fade. Her breathing steadied and her shoulders stopped shaking.

'Betty's right,' Hattie added. 'We would definitely know if an air strike had begun. We might be protected down here from a blast, but we would still know about it.'

'Thank you,' she whispered, looking from Hattie to Betty, as she wiped her tears away with the sleeve of her dusty overalls, leaving a black streak across her cheeks. 'I didn't mean to get m'self in such a mess.'

'It's all right,' Hattie smiled kindly, 'we all get worried. It's normal.'

'Is it?' Patty asked. 'You two look as cool as cucumbers!'

'Looks can be deceiving,' Betty said reassuringly. 'I don't think any of us feel particularly calm when those sirens start, even though they have all been false alarms so far.'

'That's just it, isn't it?' Patty started.

'What do you mean?' Betty asked.

'They have been false alarms so far. But what if the next one is real?'

The three women fell silent for a few seconds. The news about Norway being attacked prevalent in their minds.

'There's nowt you can do but find shelter if those bombs do come,' the old man, who had now finished his pint, chirped up. 'We can't predict what's coming, we've just got to do what we can to stay alive.'

'I guess you're right,' Betty replied politely, slightly taken aback about how blunt he was.

'But while most of us are being sensible, Archie is deliberately throwing himself into the line of fire!' Patty said, her voice increasing an octave. 'I don't know whether to bloody throttle him or give him a medal.'

Betty and Hattie exchanged a worried glance.

'I know what you're thinking,' Patty interrupted. 'I don't want it to drive a wedge between us but it's driving me mad. As far as I know he could be killed tonight and there isn't a damn thing I can do about it. And what's even more frustrating is I haven't even spoken to him. I haven't told him I love him. I've been in such a bad mood with him and now I might never get the chance to talk to Archie again.'

'But Patty,' Betty said tentatively. 'As much as I hate to

say it, and don't even like to think about it, in some ways, isn't that the same for most of us? I can't speak to William, Hattie can't talk to her boyfriend, John, and Nancy is in a tizz about Bert. None of us can speak to each other either and have no idea what every day will bring.'

'Yes. Yes, it is the same in some ways,' Patty partially conceded. 'But Archie had a choice. William, John and Bert had to go off to war. Archie didn't but still he wants to leave me worried sick.'

Betty was wise enough to know she wasn't going to win this battle. Patty needed to find a way of coming to terms with Archie signing up to be an air raid warden, just like she'd had to accept that William was determined to be a pilot.

Before the conversation could carry on any further, the all-clear siren started, reverberating around the cellar.

'I told you we would survive,' the old chap piped up over the screech, sliding off his bar stool. 'Now don't be getting yerselves in a tickle.'

'If only it was that chuffin' easy,' Patty whispered despondently.

A couple of minutes later, the three women emerged onto Brightside Lane, the road looking exactly as it had an hour earlier, with no sign of an invasion or bombing spree, as Betty had reasoned earlier.

'Right,' she said. 'If neither of you mind, I'm going to catch my tram into town and then home. I'll not get to the depot now and want to check Ivy is all right.'

'Not at all,' Hattie replied. 'I need to go and see my mum too. I'm sorry it wasn't the relaxing drink we'd hoped for.'

'It can't be helped,' Betty said, quickly shaking her head. 'It was hardly your fault but let's try and have another get-together again soon.'

'I'd like that.' Hattie nodded. 'And Patty,' she added, turning to her friend, who looked as though she hadn't slept for a week. 'Try to go easy on Archie. I can't imagine he meant to upset you or anyone else for that matter.'

'You're probably right,' Patty replied with resignation, too tired to argue. 'I'll go and see m' mom and dad and then maybe check if he's home.'

But even as the words left her lips, and she waved her friends goodbye, Patty still wasn't sure if once she'd found out Archie was safe, whether she would throw her arms around him in relief or burst into tears of frustration at all the worry he'd caused her. In her heart of hearts Patty knew she desperately wanted to sort things out with Archie, even if she couldn't understand his actions.

'Why can't anything be easy?' she said to herself as she trundled home.

Chapter 19

Saturday, 13 April 1940

Just after midday, Betty, Nancy, Patty and Daisy were grouped together outside Vickers.

'Well, let's hope tonight is quieter than last night,' Nancy said. 'I could do with a decent night's sleep. It took me ages to settle our Linda.'

'Our Polly was the same.' Daisy nodded. 'She hates the shelters and screeching of the sirens.'

'Whereas our Tom Tom can sleep through anything, as long as someone is cuddling him and he has a biscuit,' Patty added.

'Anyway, what are you all up to this weekend?' Nancy asked, trying not to think about the increased frequency of air raids and what that meant.

'I'm meeting Hattie in a bit for a catch-up,' Patty said. 'She's fretting about her John, so I thought it might take her mind off things for a couple of hours. Then I'm supposed to be seeing Archie and going to watch a picture, but I'm not sure I can face it.'

'It might do you both some good if you have a nice night

211

out?' Nancy suggested, trying to repress her own worries about Bert.

'Maybe,' Patty responded, rather unconvincingly.

'And what about you two?' Nancy asked, turning to Betty and Daisy.

'Actually,' Betty beamed, 'I'm off to the WVS, but I wondered if anyone fancied a cuppa and a cake first?'

'Oooh, I wouldn't say no.' Daisy grinned.

'I best not,' Nancy declined graciously. 'I need to get home to Linda and Billy.'

'How about you, Patty?' Betty asked.

'Normally I'd snap yer hand off,' Patty said. 'But I promised m' mom I'd help her out with some jobs and look after Tom Tom before I meet Hattie.'

'Well, a good natter will be lovely,' Betty said, trying to raise her friend's spirits. 'It might be just what you need too?'

'S'ppose,' Patty sighed.

'Come on,' Nancy said, gently tapping her friend on the shoulder. 'Don't spoil your afternoon. You will enjoy seeing Hattie and she will appreciate your support. Then you can see how you feel about tonight.'

'I hope so,' Patty said. 'It's just me and Archie can't agree on this air raid warden thing, and I just feel so fed up.'

'I know yer do, luv,' Nancy sympathized. 'But give it time. I'm sure you will both find a way through.'

'I meant to say, I saw him last night,' Daisy said, turning to Patty tentatively.

'Did you?' Patty quizzed, suddenly alert. 'Archie didn't

say owt this morning.' But if Patty was honest with herself, she hadn't really given him a chance. Every time they talked about his new mission to help the war effort, it ended badly, with neither of them being able to accept the other's point of view.

'Yes,' Daisy replied, now wondering if she should have said anything at all. 'He was on duty with the other air raid wardens on our street.'

'Oh right,' Patty replied, her pride taking a dent at the thought of other people knowing what her boyfriend was doing before she did.

'He looked to be doing a reyt grand job,' Daisy offered, hoping she wasn't on the verge of sparking another rift.

'That's good,' Patty said, aware she was at risk of sounding like a petulant toddler. It's not that she doubted how conscientious Archie would be, far from it. She knew he was a hard worker and would put his heart and soul into the job. That was the problem; would the role be what finally robbed him of his health? 'I'm just glad he didn't come to any harm, and nobody else for that matter.'

'Yes,' Betty said, trying to keep the atmosphere light and prevent it from descending into one of doom and gloom for Patty's as well as Nancy's sake.

'Oh, hello, Archie,' Nancy interjected, as she spotted him walking towards the group.

'Ay up,' he greeted the women.

'I bet you're ready for the weekend, aren't you?' Nancy said, trying to sound as upbeat as possible.

'I am that.' He nodded, stifling a yawn, as he turned to Patty in the hope she was a little less hostile, only for her to abruptly face the other way.

'Right then,' Nancy said. 'I better make a move and get to the butcher's before everything is sold out.'

'Yes, sorry,' Betty said. 'We'll walk with you.' Then turning to Patty and Archie, she added: 'Hope you two both have a good weekend.'

'You too,' Patty replied.

'Ay, take it steady now,' Archie added. 'And make sure you have a rest.'

'I'm off for cake.' Betty laughed, enjoying the fact she was once again allowing herself a little bit of time to have some fun.

'Have one for me.' Archie grinned. 'With lots of cream!'

'I might just do that.' Betty waved as she, Daisy and Nancy headed towards the centre of Attercliffe, giving Patty and Archie some space to sort things out.

Archie turned back to Patty. 'Do you still fancy going to the pictures tonight?' he asked hesitantly.

'I don't know,' Patty sighed, unable to decide what she wanted. She'd deliberately avoided making any plans with Archie and getting into a conversation on the way to work.

'I don't want to fall out with you,' Archie said, as they made their way down Brightside Lane. 'It feels like a long time since we've had a bit of fun together.'

'Well, you know the answer to that,' Patty shot out, the fury inside reigniting. Exhausted after another fretful night, which he had been the cause of, she was not in the mood to try to reason with Archie again.

'Can we—' But before Archie could finish his sentence, Patty had flounced off, leaving him open-mouthed as he watched the woman he loved disappear amongst the crowd of workers.

'I really hope a night out together might help Patty and Archie sort everything out,' Daisy said, as she, Nancy and Betty made their way down Attercliffe Road.

'Yes, me too,' Nancy agreed. 'They've been through the mill together lately but he dotes on her. It would be a shame if they can't find a way to make up.'

'Maybe a night at the pictures and a bit of time together, just the two of them, will do the trick,' Betty added.

A few minutes later, the three women came to a stop outside Oliver's Butchers. 'This is me,' Nancy said, double-checking her ration books were in her handbag as she joined the queue of women.

'I'm sorry you can't join us,' Daisy said.

'Don't be,' Nancy insisted. 'I'm happy to go home and spend time with Billy and Linda. Now you two go and enjoy a good old natter over something nice and I'll see you both on Monday.'

'I hope you can get a bit of time to relax too,' Betty said.

'Well, I won't be thirty feet up a mucky crane,' Nancy replied. 'So, that's a start.'

Betty and Daisy both knew, though, in reality, Nancy

wouldn't stop for a minute all weekend, determined to return Doris's goodwill and help her out, as well as take care of her own children.

'I don't know how she does it,' Daisy said as she and Betty waited for a tram to pass so they could cross the road to Browns teashop.

'Are you kidding?' Betty gasped.

'What do you mean?'

'Well, it wasn't too long ago that you were working all day at Vickers, going home to look after your mum, and care for your sisters, *and* make sure there was a meal on the table.'

'I did have my aunt to help me, so I can't take all the credit.'

'And Nancy has Doris. You are both rather wonderful,' Betty praised, as they walked to the other side of the road.

'Don't laugh,' Daisy said, 'but now Mum is back on her feet, and she doesn't need me to do so many jobs around the house, I would actually like to do a little bit more myself.'

'Let's grab a table and I might have just the solution for you.' Betty grinned, as she opened the door of Browns and spotted a free table by the window.

Ten minutes later, after a waitress had brought over a large pot of tea and two rather delicious-looking plump scones, the two women couldn't help but giggle.

'This does feel like quite the luxury, doesn't it?' Daisy exclaimed, as she carefully sliced her scone in half and, through habit, only used a sliver of butter.

'It does,' Betty agreed, but simultaneously feeling a surge of guilt that while she was out gallivanting and having fun, William was doing God knows what. It had been a good week or so since she'd had a letter from her fiancé. Unlike the last time she'd not received any mail for a while, this time Betty wasn't getting herself in a tizz, confident that he was simply busy with all his training or that his notes were taking a while to cross the Atlantic. Instead of moping about, waiting for an envelope to drop through her door, Betty had made a promise to herself to enjoy the little things in life and be kind to herself.

Pulling herself back to the moment, Betty added: 'I think we deserve it though, what with yet another false air raid alarm, all the hours we've been working and what you have to cope with over the last few months.'

'Well, all's well that ends well,' Daisy said cheerfully, lifting up her dainty blue-and-white teacup to her lips. 'But I'll definitely enjoy our mini celebration.'

'Absolutely!' Betty encouraged. 'Now, are you serious about wanting to fill your time?'

'Yes, I really am,' Daisy said, popping her teacup back down on the saucer. 'I think this war is having the same effect on most of us, isn't it? I feel like I should be doing more, especially now Mum doesn't need me quite as much.'

'Well, I can highly recommend the WVS,' Betty prompted. 'They are crying out for more helpers. The reasons why don't bear thinking about but I'm sure they would be grateful for an extra pair of hands.'

'Do you think they would have me?'

'Have you?' Betty snorted, ready to take a dainty bite from her scone. 'They would snap your hands off. I'm going up to the depot at Fulwood from here, if you fancy coming along?'

'That would be marvellous,' Daisy said gratefully. 'My sisters are going down to The Skates this afternoon and Mum has insisted she doesn't need any help with the housework, so that would be perfect.'

'Right, let's enjoy this rather tasty scone and cup of tea, and we can get the tram over there.'

'Thank you. And this treat is on me, I insist.'

'No,' Betty protested. 'Your money is better spent on your family.'

'Ssh,' Daisy said, putting her index finger to her lips. 'It's the very least I can do.'

'All right,' Betty nodded, 'but it's on me next time.'

'It's a deal,' Daisy said. 'And thank you.'

'What on earth for?'

'For being such a good friend. I really am so pleased we became pals.'

'Oh, Daisy, me too,' Betty replied, popping her scone back down on her side plate. 'I'd become so obsessed with working hard and staying busy, but you have showed me how to have fun again, which I'm so very grateful for.'

'I think we were both in need of that.' Daisy smiled warmly.

'I'll drink to that,' Betty said, raising her teacup, her little finger pointing upwards. 'To friendship and fun.'

An hour later, the two friends were stood outside the entrance of the WVS depot.

'Are you ready?' Betty asked.

'I am! I know it sounds a little bit odd, but I'm actually quite looking forward to it.'

'You don't have to explain to me,' Betty enthused. 'When Ivy first mentioned this place to me, I couldn't wait to come along and start helping out. It feels good, knowing you are doing your bit, and I've met so many wonderful women. I promise you, they are all so kind and will welcome you with open arms.'

'Well, fingers crossed I can be useful.'

'I have no doubt,' Betty exclaimed, pushing open one of the big wooden double doors, ushering Daisy to make her way inside.

'Gosh, it's big, isn't it?' Daisy vociferated above the nosy chatter of dozens of women sat at wooden tables, surrounded by lengths of thin white material.

'It is.' Betty nodded, as always trying not to overthink why so many additional hospital supplies were needed. 'Every week more and more women are signing up to help. The manager, Mrs Rafferty, is glad of it though. Let's go and find her and I will introduce you.'

Daisy followed, wide-eyed, as they passed the uniform rows of workstations, until they reached the end of the hall where a plump, friendly faced woman, not much older than her own mum, was sat behind a desk, a huge pile of papers in front of her.

'Hello, Mrs Rafferty,' Betty said, gently interrupting the auburn-haired woman, who was wearing a greyish-green, long-sleeved flannel dress, from the documents she was reading.

'Hello, Betty. How are you? Come to help out for an hour or so?'

'I have, and I've brought along my friend Daisy, who would like to volunteer too.'

'That's marvellous,' Mrs Rafferty enthused, turning to Daisy with a welcoming smile. 'We need all the help we can get. Thank you so much. Has Betty explained what we do here?'

'She has,' Daisy replied politely. 'I'm sorry I've not been able to come along sooner. It's been a little bit hectic at home.'

'No need for apologies,' Mrs Rafferty said, shaking Daisy's hand. 'It's just lovely to have you here now. If you don't mind, I'll just get you to fill in a form with your details and then I'm sure Betty will be happy to show you the ropes. She's quite the expert and can explain exactly what you need to do. Would that be all right, Betty?'

'Of course,' Betty replied, blushing at Mrs Rafferty's words.

Ten minutes later, the pair were sat at a free table, and Betty was meticulously showing Daisy how to roll and fold the layers of material to make and package the bandages. The next couple of hours passed in a flurry of activity as Daisy quickly learnt the technique, in between introductions to several of the other women whom Betty had got to know since starting at the depot.

At four o'clock the pair picked up the boxes they had filled and placed them next to the pile at the end of the hall. 'Will we see you again?' Mrs Rafferty asked, as she made a note of the work Betty and Daisy had achieved.

'Definitely,' Daisy nodded, 'it feels good to be so productive.'

'Well, we are glad you have joined the service,' Mrs Rafferty acknowledged. 'We are a friendly group and if what I've seen you do this afternoon is anything to go by, I'm sure you will be a splendid asset.'

It was Daisy's turn to feel slightly self-conscious. 'I hope so,' she replied, her cheeks turning pink.

'Right, well, lovely to meet you, Daisy, and hopefully I'll see you both next week sometime if you're able to pop in.'

'You will,' Daisy and Betty answered in unison, before turning to grin at one another.

Chapter 20

'Hello, luv,' Frank said as Ivy opened her front door.

'Lovely to see you.' Ivy smiled, her delight obvious, as she gestured for Frank, who was holding a beautiful bunch of spring daffodils, to step inside. 'I've made some sandwiches. I thought you might be hungry.'

'You're not wrong. Breakfast felt like a long time ago now,' Frank agreed, handing Ivy the bunch of yellow flowers that were just coming into bud. 'These are for you.'

'Oh, thank you,' Ivy replied graciously. 'That's very kind of you, but you really didn't have to.'

'I wanted to,' Frank insisted. Betty had told him Ivy had been a nervous wreck during the air raid and had hidden under the stairs too scared to go outside into the Anderson shelter by herself. The thought of Ivy all alone had made Frank fretful all morning but he hoped his small gesture would be just the tonic to cheer her up.

'I shall get them in some water. It's lovely to see daffodils, isn't it? It always reminds me the better weather is on its way.'

'It does that.' Frank nodded, stepping inside the hall and taking off his overcoat.

'Is Betty not with you?' Ivy asked, half expecting her lodger to come rushing up the path.

'The last I heard she was going for a cake and cuppa with Daisy, and then I think she mentioned nipping to the WVS depot at Fulwood,' Frank explained. 'I told her it would do her good after last night and that you wouldn't mind if she grabbed something to eat a bit later.'

'Not at all,' Ivy agreed, directing Frank into the living room. 'That girl works too hard. It's nice to see her having a bit of downtime too.'

'It is.' Frank gave the back of his overalls a brush before sitting down on the brown leather Chesterfield couch. 'I hope they aren't too mucky,' he added, conscious of how immaculate Ivy kept her house.

'Please don't worry about that,' she said, with a wave of her hand. 'After everything you do for me, I'd be offended if you gave it a second thought. But if it makes you feel more comfortable, you would be welcome to leave a spare set of clothes here, so you don't have to sit in your work clobber all the time.'

Taken aback by the suggestion, Frank was momentarily stumped for words. Nothing would make him happier. He didn't want to jump ahead of himself, but was this confirmation that Ivy was as fond of his company as he was of hers?

'That would be useful,' Frank finally replied. 'I do feel guilty dropping dust everywhere. Maybe I could leave some extra gardening clothes here and some slacks and a pullover to get changed into afterwards?'

'That seems like a very sensible idea,' Ivy said, hoping her offer hadn't come across as a little too forward. 'It saves you carting them over every time. It's no trouble for me to give them a rinse.'

'You really don't have to go to that much trouble,' Frank said, secretly quite pleased.

'Nonsense,' Ivy admonished. 'It gives me something to do. Besides which, I like caring for you and Betty.'

Caring! Frank replayed the word in his head. It had certainly been a long time since anyone except his family had cared for him. 'Thank you,' he answered, his cheeks reddening. 'That really is very kind of you.'

'Now speaking of which,' Frank added, sensing this was a good time to broach the subject. 'How were you last night when the sirens started?'

'Let me bring the pot of tea and sandwiches in first,' Ivy said, making her way into the hallway. 'And then we can have a good old natter and maybe do a bit of gardening?'

Frank wasn't daft. Ivy was as proud as she was caring. Frank knew her well enough by now to understand she hated people worrying about her, so would always put on a brave face. He couldn't criticize her for that, knowing he was guilty of the exact same thing. It had taken him a long time to open up to people after he'd lost Mary and only now, over a decade later, was he allowing himself to have feelings for another woman.

'These are delicious,' Frank said ten minutes later, after taking a bite of the thickly sliced cheese sandwich.

'I managed to get a pork pie from the butcher's too if you fancy a slice,' Ivy said.

'Well, I wouldn't say no, that will be a proper treat,' Frank started, 'but I don't want to be eating you of house and home. I know how tricky it is with rations.'

'Frank,' Ivy warned, with an amused glint in her eye. 'I should hope you know by now, I wouldn't offer if I couldn't afford to.'

'I do,' Frank smiled gratefully, 'I just don't like to take advantage of your good nature.'

'You're not,' Ivy insisted. 'As I said, it's a pleasure to have someone to look after again.'

'And what about you, Ivy?' Frank started, taking a mouthful of tea, hoping it would give him some Dutch courage. 'I know I'm helping with the garden and all of Betty's projects but . . .' Frank paused and took a deep breath, unsure how to articulate what he wanted to say.

After his Mary had passed away, he'd vowed he would never so much as look at another woman, let alone allow any emotions to surface for someone of the opposite sex. Mary had been his soul mate, his best friend, the woman he was sure he would spend the rest of his life with. Frank had resigned himself to living the rest of his years alone, but over the last six months or so, he knew his feelings for Ivy had grown and he was happy to let them flourish, feeling sure his late wife wouldn't want him to get old, lonely and miserable.

'What is it?' Ivy prompted, pulling Frank back to the moment, her voice no more than a whisper.

'Well, it's just when Betty mentioned you were here alone when the sirens started, I couldn't help but worry about you. The idea of you being frightened or scared upset me.' That's it. He'd said it now.

For a moment, Ivy didn't say a word. You could have heard a pin drop; the silence was almost deafening.

I've said too much. Let my feelings get the better of me instead of just letting events take their natural course, Frank thought to himself. But then he thought about how on Christmas Day, he'd woken up from his late afternoon doze with a blanket over him. It could have only been Ivy who'd been so thoughtful. And now she was suggesting he leave spare clothes at the house. But maybe she was just being practical? Caring for him as she would Betty – is that what she meant? Why did these things have to be so difficult? he silently mused, his emotions whirling.

'Thank you,' Ivy finally said.

'What for?' Frank asked tentatively.

'For caring,' came her tender reply. It had been over twenty years since she'd opened her heart enough, to allow another man to show any form of affection towards her.

'Oh, Ivy,' Frank gasped, a mixture of relief and elation, reaching across the coffee table to gently place his hand on hers. 'Of course I care. I would like to be here for you if you'll let me.'

'I would like that very much too,' Ivy replied, her eyes glistening, hoping Lewin, whose photograph stood proudly on the mantelpiece, wouldn't begrudge her this second chance at happiness.

'Maybe I could pop over once or twice in the week, as well as a weekend?' Frank suggested.

'That would be lovely, but only if you put up no arguments about me cooking your meals.'

'I think I can accept that,' Frank replied, smiling. He had no idea where Ivy's invitation for them to spend more time together would lead to, but right now, he was just happy in the knowledge his feelings were being reciprocated.

'Now, can I top up your cup of tea?' Ivy offered.

'That would be grand, thank you,' Frank obliged. 'But as soon as I've had this, I'm going to go and do some more work in the garden while it's dry. I want to check no pesky little birds have been poking their beaks into the seeds we planted and finish the ground ready for the hen coop.'

'Oh, yes,' Ivy enthused. 'Do you think we are nearly ready for them?'

'Yes, I'm just going to make sure the coop is escape-proof and a friend mentioned he had some hens we could have.'

'That's marvellous. Thank you. Between the hens and the veggie patch, we should have enough eggs and fresh vegetables to keep us going all year and plenty to give away to anyone who would like them.'

'They won't go to waste that's for sure,' Frank pointed out.

'I'm so looking forward to having a plentiful supply of eggs,' Ivy mused.

'Folk will be snapping your hands off for them. Not that I've had the misfortune to taste them yet, but I've heard the dried ones aren't much cop at all.'

'They do sound rather unpleasant,' Ivy agreed.

'Hopefully there will be no need for them here. And I meant to mention, I overheard a couple of women at work explaining they are sieving the National Flour to collect the grains and then feed them to their hens.'

'That is a good tip,' Ivy said. 'And quite frankly, can only improve the flour! I'm not keen on this new stuff at all.'

'I don't think you're alone,' Frank laughed, 'I'm not overly partial to it but at the same time I'll happily eat whatever I'm given.'

'Right, I'll just go and get changed into some old clothes,' Ivy said, standing up and collecting their empty plates, 'and I shall give you a hand outside.'

'You really don't have to,' Frank said. 'If you fancy putting your feet up, I can do it.'

Turning in the front room doorway, Ivy threw Frank a flabbergasted look. 'I think you know me better than that by now, Frank Brown!'

'That I do.' He chuckled, the comfortable familiarity adding to how content Frank already felt.

Ten minutes later, the pair, now in their designated gardening clothes, were working side by side in perfect unison, as they turned over the soft soil to plant the seedlings, which had begun to overtake Ivy's once clutter-free and meticulously kept kitchen.

Across town, Patty was pulling on her red cape at home. Despite how cross she was, during their catch-up over a pot of tea, Hattie had persuaded Patty she should still go out with Archie this evening, even after she had flounced off after work when he'd tried to talk to her. On the one hand, Patty was pleased he'd arrived a couple of minutes earlier, holding a bag of strawberry bonbons, but on the other, she was still so confused and wasn't sure what she would even say to him. Archie was equally as perplexed, and had turned up not sure whether Patty would even agree to still go to see the George Formby picture. But the fact she hadn't slammed the door in his face had left him hopeful the night would at least get off to a good start.

'Have a good time, you two,' Angie called from the kitchen table, where she was kneading a ball of dough, ready to pop it into the pancheon to prove overnight. 'Make sure you both relax. You've had a long week.' What she really wanted to say was, *Try and put your differences aside and remember how much you adore one another,* but Patty could be as stubborn as a mule when she put her mind to it so Angie knew better that Patty would have to come around in her own time.

'Thanks, Mom,' Patty replied, hoping she and Archie could have at least one night where they didn't end up disagreeing. But truthfully, his selfish determination to be an air raid warden against her wishes was really grating on her. No matter how hard she tried, Patty couldn't get past the fact he wasn't thinking about anyone else but himself and hadn't considered for a single minute how his actions were impacting everyone else.

'Try not to worry, luv,' Bill said to Angie, when he was sure his daughter and Archie were out of earshot. 'They'll sort it out.'

'I hope so,' Angie sighed. 'Patty has been miserable for weeks. Nothing I say seems to help. She just can't get over the fact Archie is deliberately putting himself in harm's way.'

'He's just a young lad trying to find his place in the world,' Bill added.

'I know, but I can see it from our Patty's point of view as well. Her frustration stems from love.'

'She's always wore her heart on her sleeve, that's for sure.'

As Patty made her way up Thompson Street, Archie linked his arm through hers. 'I nipped and got you some strawberry bonbons on my way to yours.'

'Thank you.' Patty nodded graciously, sending herself into turmoil once again. 'That was good of yer.'

'I just want to make you happy,' Archie said, his heart aching, wishing he and Patty could just go back to having fun together like they used to, without this stormy cloud hanging over them.

'Do you?' Patty retorted, her mind a muddle of conflicting thoughts. 'Sorry,' she apologized instantly, regretting her hasty and somewhat pointed remark, not because it wasn't true; Patty was still finding it difficult to accept what he'd done, especially the fact he'd lied to her, but there was just no point getting into another argument. 'It's just . . .'

'I know,' Archie stopped her. 'You don't need to explain.'

'Don't I?'

'No.'

'But I don't think you realize how much this is killing me.' Again, Patty wished she could swallow her choice of words.

'I promise, I'm not doing it to hurt you,' Archie said, softly pulling Patty round to face him.

'But by putting yourself at risk, that's exactly what you are doing.'

'I'm sorry. That has never been my intention. You mean more to me than anyone else in the world.'

Patty looked up into Archie's crystal blue eyes, the very eyes that had captivated her from the moment she first saw them. 'But you won't give up being an air raid warden, will you?'

'No, I can't do that,' Archie answered. The tone in his voice was as steadfast as it was kind.

'I don't know what to say.' Patty was a cyclone of whirling emotions.

'I just want us to be like we used to be,' Archie whispered. 'I hate all this bickering. It's tearing me apart.'

'Me too,' Patty confessed, the frustration she felt being momentarily outbalanced by the love she had for Archie.

'I know we aren't likely to agree on me being an air raid warden but could we at least just focus on the things we enjoy together?' Archie asked.

'I'd like that too,' Patty replied, her head falling onto his strong, firm chest.

'I love you, Patty Andrews,' Archie said, wrapping his arms around her slender frame.

'And I love you, Archie Howard.'

Neither of them moved for several minutes, enjoying the heartfelt embrace, something they'd both missed. But when they finally broke apart, and although Archie looked the happiest he had in weeks, Patty knew she was forcing her smile. The reality was it was going to be easier said than done to forget about what he was doing and the worry it was causing her.

Thirty minutes later, as they sat on the back row of the pictures and Archie placed his arm lovingly around her shoulders, she could feel the upset she'd been battling for weeks starting to surface again. She tried to ignore it, bat away the thoughts which had caused her one sleepless night after another, but no matter how much Patty attempted to get drawn into the slapstick comedy, as George Formby made one comical quip after another, she couldn't fight off the voice in her head. *How can he love me but still risk his life?* she asked herself. *That isn't how you treat someone you care about.* It was just so selfish of him. Did he really not realize all the worry he was putting her and his family through? Patty tried to tell herself everything would be all right, it would all sort itself out in the wash – isn't that what her friends and family kept telling her? – but she just couldn't see how.

Chapter 21

'I'm home,' Betty called as she opened the front door of her lodgings, her brown tweed coat already slung over one arm due to the welcome rise in temperature.

'Hello, dear.' Ivy made her way down the hallway, a huge smile on her face.

'You look happy,' Betty said. 'Is it the thought of all those hens arriving?' One of Frank's brothers knew someone who could supply him with four hens, and a pal who owned a car had arranged to give him a lift to collect them.

'Well, I must say the idea of a regular supply of eggs is quite exciting but no, that's not the reason.'

'What is it then?' Betty laughed, not used to Ivy being quite so cryptic.

'Go and have a look in the front room.' Ivy gestured towards the lounge with her hand.

'Okay,' Betty said, not sure whether to be excited or nervous, but as she did as Ivy instructed, her eyes were immediately drawn to the mantelpiece. On it a piece of string was hanging from one corner to another, and clipped to it with wooden pegs, hanging proudly like a line of washing, were several airmail envelopes.

'Oh, my goodness,' Betty gasped, instantly recognising William's handwriting. 'Are they what I think they are?'

'I assume so.' Ivy grinned. 'I couldn't believe it when the postman arrived with so many this morning.'

William's letters had been few and far between of late, but unlike last time, when there had been a hiatus in letters, Betty hadn't assumed her fiancé had suddenly lost interest and forgotten about her. She knew he was at sea on his way to Canada and that post would be sporadic. On a couple of occasions, she'd had to stop herself worrying his ship had been attacked, logically telling herself she'd have heard about it on the World News or even worse, received a telegram – neither of which had happened.

'Where do I start?' Betty wondered, overwhelmed at how much William had been writing to her. Canada seemed so far away, but her heart was feeling full that William was okay and she could spend an afternoon reading about his adventures.

'At the beginning of course.' Ivy chuckled. 'Why don't I make you a lovely fresh pot of tea and bring in a slice of my new eggless quiche? And you can take your time reading them all.'

Normally, Betty would have insisted on getting changed out of her grubby overalls first and freshening herself up, but Ivy had relaxed somewhat about keeping her house spotless since they had started their mini allotment in the garden, and for Betty, the idea of holding out even an extra minute to read all those letters was just unthinkable.

'That would be lovely,' she replied gratefully, her eyes beginning to glisten.

'You are very welcome, my dear,' Ivy said. 'Frank will bring the hens in around the back, so don't worry about us. We won't disturb you.'

'Thank you,' Betty whispered, gently fingering the washing line of letters, as she examined the post marks which stretched back over several weeks. She could just imagine William's reaction if he could see how all his correspondence had been hung up. His face would be a picture. It was just like Ivy to make an occasion of all the post, knowing how much it would mean to her.

'If only I had the luxury of a camera,' Betty said out loud, but she knew even without photographic evidence, this moment would be etched in her memory forever.

Ten minutes later, Betty was sat on the couch, the pile of letters on one side of the coffee table, her quiche and cup of tea on the other.

Carefully she opened each letter and then placed them in a neat pile in the order they had been written, grateful William had the foresight to date each and every one.

Every note began the same:

My lovely, sweet Bet.

Closing her eyes, in the quiet solitude of the front room, Betty could hear William say those exact words, as he had done many times throughout their courtship. He might not be physically with her, but as she held each letter, she could feel his presence, smell his woody aftershave, and see his happy-go-lucky smile. The comfort it brought her was immeasurable.

Betty read each letter in turn, taking in every word, trying to visualize what William was telling her. He explained how as they got closer to the American coast, there was a great cheer of excitement to finally see land at last after weeks at sea. Betty noted how William made no mention of the terrifying German U-boats that were responsible for attacking Allied ships; whether this was to shelter Betty and prevent her worrying or due to the fact all mail was censored, or a mixture of both, she couldn't be quite sure.

Instead, William showered his letters with light-hearted anecdotes.

As we passed the Statue of Liberty, one of the chaps called out in a broad Yorkshire accent: 'It's just like Blackpool Tower!', which caused us all to burst into laughter. I'm not really sure what I thought New York would be like, but it seemed very busy and that was just the harbour. I suppose that's what London must be like too. Anyway, I didn't see that much of the city as it was nearly midnight when we departed from the ship and we got straight on a train that took us through the outskirts of New York, but guess what, Bet, they don't have a blackout, so are still allowed streetlights on at night. Last night, after being on the Atlantic for so long, was the best night's sleep I've had since leaving Scotland. It might have still been a bunk bed, but I didn't feel like I was swaying in the waves. I'm writing you this letter as we pass through New England. It reminds me a little bit of the countryside around Yorkshire. The trees are all blossoming and look lovely.

In William's next letters he explained how he had arrived in Monkton, and had to march to a huge camp, but after two days embarked upon another five-day train journey to the Elementary Flying Training School at Moose Jaw, Saskatchewan. He'd stopped at Montreal and then at the Canadian capital of Ottawa.

We stopped there for four hours and were allowed to get off the train to watch the breaking up of the ice on the St Lawrence River, which had frozen over the winter. Bet, I wish you could have seen it – there were blocks of ice as big as football fields. I've never seen anything like it in my life. We saw the Great Lakes from the train as we carried on travelling and all I can see now from the window are the prairies. I'm certainly seeing the world, Bet, and I'm still on the ground!

Despite the worry of what the future might hold for William, Betty couldn't help but smile at his enthusiasm. He was living his big adventure, the one that filled her with dread but William with excitement. His next note revealed to Betty he had finally arrived at the camp to begin the next phase of his training.

It all starts tomorrow, Bet. We've been told for the next eight weeks our days will be split between flying Tiger Moths and lectures. Apparently there's a lot of turbulence over the prairies as the weather gets warmer, so we have to start at six in the morning. I won't lie, Bet, I'm a little bit nervous, not because of the flying, I can't wait to do that. I just don't want to make a mistake and make a fool out of myself. Anyway, wish me luck, Bet, I'll write and let you know how it goes.

'Good luck, William,' Betty whispered, grateful there was one more letter, the front adorned with her fiancé's handwriting, evidence that he must have survived his forementioned training flight.

Oh Bet, the flying is everything and more I could have ever dreamed of. I'm still tingling with excitement as I write you this letter. I went up in the air this morning with an instructor and he showed me the circuits I need to complete. At the moment, he has to fly with me, but it won't be long before I'm up there solo! Can you believe it, Bet? Little old me flying a plane, like I've always dreamed of. Anyway, enough about me. Your last letter made me so happy. I'm so glad you and your new friend Daisy are going out a bit and you are enjoying yourself. You work so hard, between the factory and now at the WVS, and deserve a bit of time to relax. The Skates sounds so much fun. You'll have to teach me how to stay upright on roller skates when I'm next home, but no doubt you will just end up catching me instead! I might be learning to fly a plane but I'm not sure I would be any good with wheels on my feet.

    Write again soon my lovely, sweet Bet. I so look forward to the mailman arriving. It makes my day when he hands me a letter from you.

    All my love,

    William xxx

Betty pulled the letter to her chest, and felt her own heartbeat thumping through her overalls, myriad emotions coursing through her. Relief that her William had landed in Canada, was alive and carrying out his biggest dream, but at the same time fear. Fear that her beloved fiancé would be badly hurt, maimed or, dare she think it, something worse, while flying one of those great monstrous planes. But as much as she worried about him, she was so immensely proud and in awe of William's bravery and determination to be the best pilot he could be. He had travelled halfway around the world to do his bit and fulfil his greatest ambition. He'd never once moaned or complained about what was expected of him. Betty realized this was partially due to the fact he still saw joining the RAF as one big adventure, but she was also well aware that he was making ginormous sacrifices to defend the country against Hitler and his troops.

'I love you so much, William,' Betty whispered, suddenly feeling a stream of silent tears rolling down her cheeks. 'Please stay safe and come home in one piece.' The thought of anything happening to him didn't bear contemplating. Her future was with William. She envisaged them getting married, moving into a house together, having children and eventually growing old together. Once this blasted war was over, she intended to spend every minute she could with her future husband and never have another day apart.

Sitting back in her chair, Betty momentarily closed her eyes. 'You can do this,' she told herself. Part of her wanted to quietly nip upstairs, take off her mucky work clothes, slip into her nightdress, climb into bed, pulling her eiderdown up over her shoulders, and fall asleep – holding William's letters.

Could she allow herself that one indulgence?

Could she forget about the rest of the world for one night, drop into a heavy, contented sleep and dream about the happy future she envisaged for her and William?

She knew Ivy wouldn't mind, that she and Frank would actually be in favour of her straying from her normally stoic attitude. 'It will do her good,' she could almost hear them say. 'A good rest is just what she needs.'

Betty stood and scooped up all of William's letters, so she could add them to the box of correspondence she kept under her bed. He'd told her so much, as well as reassuring her it was okay to have some fun in between working. Betty had suffered moments of unbidden guilt for enjoying herself, as she'd remembered her fiancé was risking life and limb, but his words of encouragement had eased her conscience. Maybe she was finally learning to get the balance right between her relentless determination to do her bit to help the Allied troops and taking care of herself too. Maybe a little nap wasn't such a bad idea after all, but just as she was about to go upstairs and rest, she heard a high-pitched screech coming from outside.

'Quick, Frank. Catch it!'

Ivy's voice followed the unfamiliar cry, then came a succession of: 'Come here, you little rascal' and 'I've got you, yer little minx'.

'What the giddy aunt is going on?' Betty gasped, popping William's letters back onto the coffee table and rushing through the kitchen, and to the garden, where all the commotion was coming from. As Betty reached the back door, all her thoughts of an early night were quickly forgotten as she watched in disbelief as Frank hastily picked up a rather unimpressed-looking red-feathered hen just as it made a bee-line for Ivy's blackberry bushes at the bottom of the garden.

'Oh, well done, Frank!' Ivy cheered, clapping her hands. 'We'll have to keep an eye on this one. She's clearly got a rebellious streak.'

'I'll double-check she can't escape and maybe pop some extra chicken wire up if needs be,' he said, trundling back up the garden with the wriggling hen, which was doing its best to try to get out of Frank's grip.

'Right then, Houdini,' he added, dropping the bird, which was flapping its ruffled wings, into the coop. 'Let's see if you can stay put in here!'

'I was wondering whether I should name them,' Ivy laughed, 'I think you have just made my mind up.'

'It looks like I missed out on all the fun,' Betty chirped up, unable to conceal her amusement. 'Dare I ask what happened?'

'Sorry, Betty!' Ivy said. 'I hope we didn't disturb you. We just had a bit of an incident with one of the hens.'

'Not at all.' Betty grinned. 'I gather one of our new guests wasn't quite behaving.'

'You could say that again,' Ivy replied. 'Houdini here, as she has now been aptly named, tried to make a run for it as Frank introduced them to their new home.'

'How very rude of her.' Betty now laughed, unable to keep her face straight. 'After all that time you spent making them a lovely wooden shelter and run.'

'I know!' Frank exclaimed. 'You would think she would be a little more grateful.'

With that, the three of them all burst into a fit of infectious giggles. 'I can see these hens are going to keep me on my toes,' Ivy said, when she was finally able to catch her breath and string a sentence together.

'I'm sure they will settle down,' Frank said reassuringly. 'They will just be getting used to their surroundings. Give them a day or so and I'm sure they will be as good as gold.'

'I hope so. I wouldn't like them to be in any form of distress,' she added, her compassionate side shining through.

'Don't fret,' Frank advised. 'Hens are known for being quite tame, and dare I tempt fate, a little docile.'

'Mmm,' Ivy mused. 'We'll see about that. Now, how about those sandwiches and a nice cup of tea?'

'That, I will never say no too.' Frank nodded.

'Will you join us, Betty?' Ivy asked.

'That would have been lovely,' she started, though she still felt like taking a little time to digest William's letters – despite the fact her mood had been somewhat lifted by the comical display of Frank chasing the errant hen around the garden – 'but would you mind if I just went upstairs and had a lie down?'

'Is everything okay or do you want to talk about what's on your mind?' Ivy asked gently.

'Everything is quite well. William made it safely to Canada and is enjoying his adventures so far. I'm just feeling a bit tired all of a sudden,' Betty replied.

'Of course, well then, you must go and rest.' Ivy had worried the impact of so many letters would leave Betty emotionally overwhelmed, but also knew from experience, Betty needed to work through it herself. She, of all people, knew how draining it could be to cope with a loved one being so far away.

'Thank you.' Betty smiled, grateful her landlady understood a few hours by herself was just what she needed. This must have been exactly what she went through during the Great War, waiting for letters from her beloved Lewin, followed by the feeling of sheer relief and happiness when some good news finally arrived.

Chapter 22

Friday, 26 April 1940

'I'm ready for this,' Nancy thanked Dolly, as she handed her a steaming plate of pie and mash. If it wasn't for her neighbour, Doris, and her daily hot meal at work, she was sure she would forget to eat. In between the extra hours in the factory and trying to ensure Billy and Linda did their homework and that they spent some quality time together, she didn't know whether she was coming or going.

'Long morning?' the canteen manager asked.

'Aye, that, on top of the fact I barely slept a wink last night. You always feel hungrier when you're tired, don't you?'

'That you do, luv,' Dolly agreed. 'Something happen?'

'Just another letter from Bert. It just left me a bit unsettled.'

Dolly knew exactly how Nancy felt. She'd not felt right since Hitler had invaded Norway. There had been more and more reports of German U-Boats attacking Allied ships. She wasn't a religious woman but had got into the habit of saying a little prayer every night, before she fell asleep, asking God to look after her two boys, Michael and Johnny, who had gone off to join the navy as soon as war had been announced. Despite the fact they always kept their letters jovial and seemed in high spirits, Dolly wasn't daft, and knew that would be mainly for her benefit.

But she also knew it wouldn't do Nancy any good to air her own worries. 'Right, go and eat your dinner while it's still hot and grab a cuppa. I'll be over soon, and we can have a natter. A problem shared and all that.'

'Thanks, luv,' Nancy said as she made her way over to the usual table next to the Swap Club corner, once again grateful for the friends she had at Vickers. Daisy, Patty, Archie and Frank were already tucking into their food, while Betty was taking delivery of a yet another pile of knitted garments from a woman Nancy had seen a few times, donating a pile of woollies or looking through what was on offer in the clothing box.

'I hope you don't mind me saying but you look a bit weary today, Nancy,' Daisy said gently, as her friend pulled up a chair and sat down.

'I am, luv.' Nancy yawned. Her tiredness levels were increasing with each day. 'I was just telling Dolly I didn't sleep that well.'

'Worrying about Bert?' Daisy asked, just as Betty came and sat down between the two women, her arms full of knitted scarves, socks and head warmers designed to be worn under hard hats or helmets.

'Am I that predictable?' Nancy asked, conscious she always seemed to be airing her concerns about her husband.

'It's perfectly understandable,' Daisy said. 'Here, let me get you and Betty a cuppa. That always helps.'

'Is everything all right? Has something upset you?' Betty asked as she placed the huge pile of garments on an empty chair, hearing the tail end of the conversation.

'No more than usual,' Nancy sighed, although if she was honest, she was finding the balance of working and being a mum a tricky one to maintain.

'Go on.' Betty knew how prone her friend was to worrying.

'It's nothing really,' Nancy confessed. 'It's just there was a letter waiting for me from Bert when I got home last night, and it just made me feel a little uneasy.'

'In what way?' Betty asked, picking up her knife and fork.

'As you know, they can't say much, but he just mentioned he could be moving on soon,' Nancy explained.

'Well, that could mean anything,' Betty replied. She knew exactly why her friend was feeling uneasy but wanted to try and remain positive for her sake.

'It's just with the Germans sending all those extra troops into Norway, I'm worried that might mean that's where he's heading. The idea of him being right in the thick of it terrifies me.'

'Now come on, duck,' Frank chirped up, overhearing Nancy's concerns. 'You could be putting two and two together and getting five.' Despite his own reservations that war would soon be on their doorstep, he hated seeing any of his squad getting themselves into a flummox. From what he'd read in the *Daily Mirror*, Norway weren't bearing up too well against the invasion.

'I know. I'm trying my best to stay rational but yer know what it's like, everything seems worse in the middle of the night when you can't think straight.'

Patty, who had also been listening, bit the inside of her lip. She knew exactly what Nancy meant and hadn't slept a full night, waking up from some horrible dream, since Archie had signed up to be an air raid warden. Instinctively sensing what was going through Patty's mind, Archie discreetly put his hand under the table and gently placed it on her knee. He still felt torn by the upset he was causing everyone he loved and his determination to prove he could play his part in the war effort. Patty didn't push Archie's hand away. She was still feeling somewhat discombobulated, angry one minute and sick with worry the next, but at least Archie was here by her side, and she could still see him, unlike Nancy and Betty, who had no idea when they would see their Bert and William again.

'It does, duck,' Frank said, interrupting Patty's thoughts. 'But like my wise old mum used to say, there's no point worrying about summit that might never happen.'

'Frank's right,' Betty encouraged, smiling gratefully towards Daisy, who had just placed two hot mugs of tea in front of her and Nancy. 'I know it's easier said than done, and I'm my own worst enemy at times, but try not to think about the ifs and maybes. None of us know what's going to happen, all we can do is stay strong and hope this war doesn't go on for too much longer.' Since she'd received her abundance of letters from William a week ago, she'd had to give herself a handful of pep talks, reminding herself to stay positive.

'I hope to God you're right.' Nancy nodded, moving her fork absentmindedly around her plate without actually lifting up any food, despite the rumbling protests from her stomach. 'This endless not knowing is horrific.'

'It is and I can't deny it,' Betty agreed, 'but we have to have hope, otherwise we'll all end up in a heap and then we'll be no good to anyone.'

'Now that, I can't argue with.' Nancy nodded, her frown lifting. She was determined not to fall to bits, even if it was for no other reason than to protect Billy and Linda. With their dad away, she had taken on the role of both parents, and they needed her more than ever.

'Reyt then, how's yer dinner?' Dolly said, approaching the table, a tray in one hand and a hot brew in the other.

'I reckon it was just what the doctor ordered,' Frank said, lifting a mouthful of steaming mash to his lips. 'You don't 'alf look after us, duck.'

'Well, I can't be letting m' favourite workers go hungry now, can I?'

'There's no fear of that, Mrs P,' Archie said, gratefully.

'I'm glad to hear it,' Dolly replied, satisfied she was doing her bit to keep the Sheffield steel industry going full throttle.

'Now,' she added, pulling up a chair near Nancy and

taking a rare break from serving up meals to hordes of hungry workers. 'How are yer feeling, luv?'

Sensing the two women might want a quiet natter, Archie moved further along the table to give them some privacy, tactful enough to realize they probably wanted to confide in one another about their shared worries.

'Oh, you know what I'm like,' Nancy started. 'Determined to paint a smile on m' face one minute, but close to tears the next.'

'I reckon that's how most of us feel, luv,' Dolly said. 'I know it's not much use, but I promise you, you aren't alone. There isn't an hour that goes by when I'm not thinking of my lads and willing them to get home in one piece.'

'Gosh, I'm sorry, Dolly,' Nancy apologized. 'Listen to me, always harping on about how I feel. I need to remember that a lot of us are in the same boat.'

'Don't be daft, luv,' Dolly said, brushing off Nancy's concerns with a wave of her hand. 'It's only natural that you're fretting about your Bert especially when you've two little 'uns to look after too. Flamin' Hitler has got us all in a state of flux. I hope t' God, one day in the not-too-distant future, he gets his comeuppance, but I'll not hold m' breath just yet.'

'Me too,' Nancy replied. She's always known being a working mum would be difficult; she just hadn't envisaged exactly how hard it would be. 'Have you heard from your sons recently?'

'Aye, they are good lads and know I'll get m'sen in a tizz

if they don't write regularly, not that they can tell me much, but I'm grateful every time a letter from one of them lands on the doorstep. They are still together too, on the same ship, which brings me some comfort. Knowing they have each other is a godsend. I just hope that way, if one of them is feeling a bit fed up, the other one will spur them on.'

'I bet their little girls miss them too, don't they?' Nancy asked.

'They do, luv. Lucy more so, being four, she's a year older than our Milly, who just accepts her daddy is away. My daughters-in-law are lovely lasses, though, and do a grand job of keeping up the girls' spirits, and I have to admit, having m' granddaughters around gives me a reason to smile too and stay positive. The last thing they need is their nannan moping about but to be fair, they are such happy little souls it's hard not to feel cheerful in their company.'

'That's good to hear,' Nancy said. 'We all need a reason to smile.'

'Aye, we do that, luv,' Dolly agreed, taking a mouthful of her tea.

As Patty finished her dinner, her pie and mash weren't the only things she was digesting. Not being able to help but overhear Nancy's and Dolly's worries about their loved ones being hundreds of miles away, she knew she should be happy and grateful that Archie was still here with her.

'Reyt, enough of all this maudlin,' Dolly said. 'Tell me, Betty,' she added, 'how's our knitting pile looking?'

'Ginormous!' Betty exclaimed. 'Honestly, I wasn't sure

how much we'd get after everyone did so much for the Vicktory Knitters event, but there seems to be no stopping people. I've just been given another load,' she added, glancing at the woollies she'd been handed fifteen minutes earlier.

'I am going to start taking them over to the WVS depot after work tonight. They have offered to get them sent to Bert's platoon and to the ship your sons are on.'

'Oh, that's marvellous,' Dolly cheered. 'That's bound to given them all a little boost.'

'You can say that again,' Betty said, delighted some good would come of her latest plan. 'But I reckon there could be a few additional bonuses.'

'Whatever do you mean?' Dolly quizzed, guessing there was something else Betty was keen to tell them.

'Well,' Betty grinned, 'one of the younger girls was telling me how she and her friends have been popping little messages into whatever they've knitted, asking if whoever received their knitwear would like to write to them.'

'Love letters!' Patty trilled, suddenly alert and happy for a welcome distraction to escape her own worries.

'Yes, I suppose that is what you would call it,' Betty giggled, amused.

'How exciting!' Patty exclaimed, momentarily forgetting about the more pressing reasons why the knitting campaign had been launched. 'Just think, they might find the man of their dreams by knitting a pair of socks! Wouldn't that be romantic?'

'You are a case, luv.' Dolly laughed.

'Well, it's true, isn't it?' Patty said, taking the ribbing in good spirits. 'There's bound to be a few soldiers or sailors who would snap their hands off at a young pretty girl writing to them.'

'I suppose you're right,' Dolly conceded. 'And if it gives a few of those lads, who haven't got a sweetheart waiting for them at home, a reason to keep going, there's no harm in that.'

'Exactly!' Patty affirmed. 'And you never know where that might lead to.'

'Well, I think we all need something to smile about right now, so if it does the trick . . .' Dolly trailed off.

'Now, speaking of which,' she added, turning to Betty. 'Would you like an extra pair of hands to haul some of these woollies across town? I've got nothing on after work tomorrow, so happy to lend a hand and it will keep m' mind busy too.'

'Well, that would be lovely, if you don't mind?' Betty replied. 'We have got quite a haul.'

'That's that then.' Dolly nodded, standing up and piling the empty mugs and plates from the table onto her tray. 'I'll meet you up here tomorrow after your shift finishes and we can bag up what we are taking.'

'Brilliant,' Betty said. 'Maybe we could go for a drink afterwards too and have a natter?'

'Oh, I reckon I can manage that,' the canteen manager smiled gratefully. 'It's gotta beat worrying m'sen sick about m' two lads.'

'Absolutely,' Betty replied, saddened by the thought of Dolly, who was normally so strong and full of life, being so wracked by worry. 'And after we've carted this load across town, we'll deserve to put our feet up with a drink.'

Chapter 23

Saturday, 27 April 1940

'Well, my arms feel a lot lighter for that,' Dolly said. After a full morning at Vickers, Betty and Dolly had traipsed across town and dropped a haul of woollies off at the WVS depot in Fulwood.

'Not that we should complain. All those lasses have worked ever so hard to supply soldiers and sailors with socks and hats. I know my two lads will be ever so grateful.'

'How long have they been away?' Betty asked as they made their way out of the building.

'Since September now, duck. It feels like a lifetime.'

'You must really miss them?'

'Aye, I do that, luv. Until this blasted war started, there wasn't a day that passed when I didn't see or speak to them both. The last seven months have felt like a lifetime. No matter how old yer kids get, they are still your babies.'

'I'm sorry,' Betty replied. 'It must be ever so hard trying not to worry constantly.'

'It is, luv, but as I was telling Nancy, my granddaughters

254

and my daughters-in-law are a real blessing. They really do keep me going.'

'I'm glad to hear that.' Betty smiled, once again realizing what a fortunate position she was in. Although William was thousands of miles away in Canada, he was probably as safe as he could be, whereas Dolly's sons, Michael and Johnny, were on a ship, open to the elements and, heaven forbid, very visible to Hitler.

'Anyway, enough of my maudlin, it'll not do anyone any good. How's your William getting on?'

'Just the same I think,' Betty answered. 'From what I can gather he's got to get a certain number of flying hours with an experienced co-pilot and then he can go solo. I'm trying not to think too deeply about it. A bit like you, I'll worry myself sick if I do.'

'You must miss him too?'

'I do, but as you do, I keep myself busy to stop myself getting in a tizz.'

'It feels like the only way, doesn't it?' Dolly affirmed more than asked.

'Yes, I think so,' Betty agreed. 'I've never been one to mope about. My dad always says I'm not happy unless I'm doing one hundred things at once.'

'Aye, well, we women like to have things to keep us occupied. I'm not sure I know how to sit down and relax.'

'I know exactly what you mean,' Betty chuckled. 'Frank and Ivy are always laughing at me and my latest missions, as they call them.'

'You do seem to be very proactive when it comes to thinking up ways to help people,' Dolly added, as they made their way back to the tram station. 'And speaking of Frank and Ivy, how are things there? I have to say Frank is a lovely fella and deserves to be happy. Losing his Mary hit him hard and as much as he's always put on a brave face in front of the lads, I could tell he was struggling. He's a big softy at heart.'

'Isn't he?' Betty smiled. 'I should imagine he has to be quite firm working with dozens of burly steelworkers, but he's always looked after Nancy, Patty and myself, and I can tell he's pretty smitten with Ivy. They never stop smiling in each other's company.'

'Well, something good needs to come out of this godforsaken war. I'm old enough, duck, to remember the flamin' misery the last one caused. It's nice to see a bit of happiness.'

'You're right,' Betty said. 'Now. Do you still fancy going for that drink?'

'That would be lovely, duck. I must admit, I'm parched.'

'I think there's a pub not far from the tram stop,' Betty suggested.

But before Dolly had chance to answer, a piercing screech stopped them in their tracks.

'Typical!' Dolly sighed. 'Well, that's put sharp shrift to our plans. Where's the nearest shelter, duck? We better make our way there and take cover.'

*

At Thompson Street, with Tom Tom perched on one hip, Patty was using her free hand to set the table, while her mom made a pot of tea.

'What's up, luv?' Angie asked, but if she was the betting sort, she would have waged her last shilling on already knowing the answer. 'You've hardly said a word since you got home at dinnertime.'

It was true, Patty had changed the bedding, cleaned the hearth and even swept the back yard, barely saying a word.

'Sorry, Mom,' Patty sighed. 'I don't mean to be a misery guts. It's just Archie . . .' But, knowing she was at risk, once again, of sounding like a stuck record, she stopped in mid-sentence.

'Has something else happened?' Angie asked, hoping if she could persuade Patty to talk about whatever the problem was, it might help.

'The same old thing,' Patty confessed. 'Archie is doing some air raid patrol thing tonight and I just can't get past the idea he is deliberately putting himself at risk when he doesn't have to. It was a selfish idea of his.'

'Lots of lads are off fighting this war,' Angie said gently. 'They are all doing their bit.'

'I know,' Patty exclaimed, raising her voice a few octaves, causing Tom Tom to stiffen, 'but they have been conscripted. They have no choice, but Archie chuffin' well does. I don't understand why he can't be happy with the fact he's doing more than his flamin' bit working at Vickers and making parts for all those planes and tanks. Ain't that enough for anyone?'

'I can see yer side, luv,' Angie sympathized. 'But maybe that's the point. Archie knows because of his heart, he'll never be called up and he probably feels very guilty, so wants to prove he can do something else equally as worthwhile.'

'But couldn't he have done summit less risky? He collapsed just being in the cold. I dread to think what might happen to him if chuffin' Hitler aims a bomb where he's on patrol.'

'Oh, Patty,' Angie gasped, nearly dropping the teapot she'd just filled with freshly boiled water from the kettle. 'Don't say that. The consequences don't bear thinking about for any of us.'

'I'm sorry, Mom,' Patty said, realizing the impact of what she had blurted out. 'I didn't mean to sound so insensitive. I just can't get my head round why Archie would not only put himself in that position but put me and his family through all that worry too. I've been thinking about it for weeks now and it still doesn't make any chuffin' sense to me.'

Putting the last of the cutlery on the table, Patty collapsed onto one of the kitchen chairs, Tom Tom now perched on her lap, instinctively wrapping his arms around his big sister, sensing how upset she was.

'Maybe Archie is looking at it from a slightly different perspective,' Angie suggested, quickly popping the teapot on the table, next to a jug of milk.

'I know what yer mean, Mom, but no matter how hard I try, I just keep going round in circles in m' own head. I didn't even tell Archie to take care tonight when we said goodbye at dinnertime. I just felt if I did, it would be like me saying I was okay with him being an air raid warden, and I'm just not.'

'Oh, Patty luv,' Angie sighed, accepting her daughter was going to have to find her own way through. 'Just promise me you will take on board what I've said, that's all I ask.'

'Okay, Mom.' Patty nodded, but she had no idea how she and Archie would ever see eye to eye again. They seemed to be at constant loggerheads with neither of them prepared to back down.

'Dad's back.' Sally came rushing in through the back, bringing the conversation to a halt. She had been playing in the back yard with her brother and sister, John and Emily, when the mouthwatering aroma of fish and chips coming up the gennel had alerted them to the fact tea had arrived.

'Chippies,' Tom Tom squealed excitedly, his eyes lighting up, never happier than when he was eating.

'Right, let's get you lot fed.' Angie grinned, as her whole family suddenly appeared around the kitchen table, looking as though they'd never eaten.

'I'm starvin',' John exclaimed, as if to reiterate the fact.

'Aren't we all, son?' Bill laughed. 'Give your mom two minutes and she will have this lot divided up and you can get stuck in. The young lass in the chippy even gave us an extra portion of scraps – she obviously knows you lot have got hollow legs!'

But just as Angie was about to serve up the monthly treat, a piercing siren silenced the family banter.

'You couldn't write it,' Bill said, rolling his eyes. 'Well, we shan't let this lot go to waste,' he added, lifting the bag off the table. 'Come on, kids, grab yer coats and gas masks. Sally, fetch the policy documents bag. We'll take this lot with us and eat it down the shelter.'

As the rest of the family went into autopilot, doing exactly as they had been asked, now familiar with the increasing frequency of the air raid siren, Angie quickly poured the fresh tea through a strainer into a flask. But Patty was frozen to the spot.

'Archie,' was all she could whisper.

Chapter 24

'How are my lovely girls?' Alf called, as he opened the back door and made his way into the kitchen, where Josie and Daisy were just doing the pots.

'Hello, luv.' Josie smiled, turning round from the sink as Alf gave her a peck on the cheek. 'Don't you be covering me in soot! Yer as black as the ace of spades.'

'The pit will do that to yer.' Alf laughed, going to wrap his arms around his wife.

'Don't you dare!' she exclaimed, quickly jumping back, raising her dishcloth in a warning gesture. 'You come anywhere near me before you've got cleaned up and I won't be responsible for my actions! The bath is waiting for you in the front room.'

'What do yer reckon, Daisy? Shall I risk your mum's wrath?'

'At your own peril.' She chuckled, delighted to see her parents laughing and joking again, now her mum was back to full health.

'Oh, I think I might take the risk,' Alf teased, moving a step closer to his wife, who was now virtually pinned next to the sink.

'I am warning you, Alf Smith, if you so much as put a mucky finger anywhere near me, I'll be forced to give yer tea that I've just plated up to the neighbours.'

'That's no way to treat yer hardworking husband, who's just put in an extra couple of hours down a filthy mine!'

But before Alf could carry out his affectionate threats, the increasingly familiar siren, indicating a potential air raid, brought their joking to an abrupt halt.

'Urgh, here we go again,' Josie sighed. 'Daisy, call the girls would yer, while I make a quick flask of tea and butter yer dad some bread to keep him going.'

Like most households, the family had their set and now well-practised routine polished to a fine art and within a couple of minutes, they were all at the back door with their coats on, gas masks in one hand, and a bag of supplies and games in the other, ready to make their way to the communal air raid shelter.

'Right, let's get going,' Alf said, directing his wife and daughters down the narrow gennel, which divided their house from their neighbour's.

'I'm scared,' Polly whispered, tightly gripping her mummy's hand.

'You're going to be all right,' Josie calmy reassured her youngest daughter. 'I'm sure it will just be another false alarm.' But the truth of the matter was, Josie had no idea. Although Britain had not fallen victim to any of the Luftwaffe's aerial attacks, she too had felt unnerved by the German assault on Norway. It had been much talked about in the Vickers canteen at dinner breaks and it sounded like Norway wasn't putting up much of a defence. She worried that this could give Hitler the confidence to continue his rampage and widen his attacks across more of Europe.

'Yer mum's right,' Alf said. 'I bet we'll be home again before bedtime and I'll be reading you one of those books you have in your bag, back in yer own bed.'

Putting on a brave face, Polly allowed herself to be ushered down Coleridge Road, falling into step with the sea of neighbours, who also felt safer in the public shelter, surrounded by friendly faces, than being left scared out of their wits under the stairs or in the coal bunker.

But just as they reached the end of the road and were about to queue for the shelter, Polly began sobbing hysterically. 'Bunny,' she cried. 'I've left Bunny behind.'

Josie and Alf look at each other in alarm. Polly had been given the rabbit teddy when she was born and it only left her side when she was at school.

'Bunny will be fine, sweetheart,' Josie said, trying to reassure her daughter, but even as she said the words, she knew it was going to take more than that to appease her little girl.

'No, Mummy, I can't leave her. I just can't,' she protested, heavy tears dripping down her cheeks.

But it wasn't the teddy Josie and Alf were worried about. They both knew Polly would cry uncontrollably until she had Bunny in her arms. The shelters were daunting enough without their daughter being separated from the one teddy that always guaranteed to settle her.

'I'll run back,' Daisy volunteered, acutely aware of what a state Polly would get herself in without her beloved pink bunny.

'Oh, no you don't,' Alf said firmly. 'If one of us goes, we all go. I'm not risking us getting split up.'

Conscious they didn't have much time, Alf made the quick decision. 'Come on,' he instructed. 'Let's rush back.'

'Thank you, Daddy,' Polly whispered, her sobs easing against the drone of the air raid siren.

Josie glanced at her husband as they navigated their way through the crowd of people now going in the opposite direction.

'Are you all okay?' came a familiar voice.

'Archie!' Daisy said in surprise, relieved to see a familiar face among the throng of panic, then remembering he had been assigned to their street as part of his patrol. 'We will be back in a few minutes. Polly's left her teddy.'

'Don't worry,' Archie said calmly. 'I'll keep the door open for you.'

'Thank you.' Daisy waved, as she gripped her other sister's hand, picking up her pace as she and Annie stepped off the pavement and onto the less crowded road.

As they reached their house, Daisy went to run down the gennel so she could dash in and get Bunny.

'Oh, no you don't, luv,' Alf said firmly, gently taking hold of his eldest daughter's arm. 'You stay with your mum and sisters. I'll be back in a jiffy.'

Josie didn't say a word, but once again reminded herself

why she loved her husband so much. Alf never failed to put her and the girls first, his instinctively protective spirit never faltering.

A couple of minutes later, Alf was rushing back towards his family, holding a very tired, faded pink teddy bear rabbit in his hands. 'Thank you, Daddy. I love you.' Polly grinned, wrapping her arms around Bunny.

'That's okay, sweetheart, Bunny's here now.' Alf smiled. 'We best get going, hold Daisy's hand now so we can stick together. That siren isn't stopping, and I'll feel better when we are all in the shelter.'

With urgency, Josie and Alf led their daughters, who were all holding hands, back along Coleridge Road, trying not to reveal their shared sense of worry. The last place they wanted to be if bombs started dropping from the sky was outside on the street, within spitting distance of the steelworks, which they assumed was what Jerry would be aiming for.

But as the throng of neighbours moved towards the communal shelter, Daisy felt a sudden surge from behind, forcing her grip on Polly's little hand to come loose. Before she could reach out for her, she was violently pushed forward.

'Polly!' Daisy screamed, as she turned to her right and realized she couldn't see her little sister. Desperately scanning the sea of faces, Daisy searched for Polly's mass of long brown hair and bright red anorak but couldn't see her for the rush of people now scrambling to get through the metal door and relative safety.

'Mum, Dad!' Daisy yelled. 'I've lost Polly.'

'What?' Josie gasped. 'How?'

The family tried to stand still but were pushed and shoved, as a hustle of people scurried past them, nearly knocking Annie sideways.

'Polly!' Alf yelled, not even trying to disguise the sheer panic in his voice.

'Mum,' Annie cried. 'Where is she?'

'We'll find her,' Daisy vowed, her eyes darting in every direction, berating herself for not keeping a tighter grip on Polly's hand.

'Is everything all right?' came Archie's familiar voice.

'It's Polly,' Daisy gasped. 'We've lost her.'

'Right, stay by the door in case she appears but I'll go and look for her,' he asserted with the calmness and authority of someone with twice his experience.

Not wasting a single second and leaving the family no option to do exactly what he'd instructed, Archie immersed himself into the bustling crowd, shouting for them to make way. 'Make some room,' he called out authoritatively, before giving a sharp shrill on his whistle. 'There's a little girl missing.'

'I should follow him,' Alf insisted, unable to stand by and do nothing.

'But what if you get lost too?' Annie sobbed, fearful tears now falling heavily down her cheeks.

'Just stay with your mum and sister here. I'll be fine but I need to help find Polly.'

Josie pulled her two eldest daughters into her arms, as

Alf scrambled forward against the tide of bodies heading into the shelter.

The family soon lost sight of him as he became engulfed in the sea of people.

Josie stiffened as she quietly prayed Polly was all right, trying desperately to hide her fear. Every second felt like an hour, and the piercing siren only heightened how frightened she was feeling.

'She'll be okay,' Daisy whispered, in a bid to convince herself, as well as her mum and Annie.

Then, just as the two women thought their resolve was about to falter, Archie re-emerged holding a sobbing and visibly shaking Polly in his arms.

'Oh, luv,' Josie called out, stepping towards Archie and her daughter, who was holding her left wrist with her right hand, and her beloved pink rabbit tucked in between. 'What happened?'

'I think she got knocked over and crushed in the crowd,' Archie explained, with Alf now hurrying back towards them. 'I found her huddled on the ground in a little ball,' he added, carefully placing Polly on the pavement, her family circling her. 'I need to close the shelter so let's get you all inside and we can check if she's badly hurt.'

As Daisy looked at the bewildered look on her sister's face, she knew Polly was in state of shock.

'You're going to be okay,' she whispered affectionately, gently rubbing Polly's clammy cheek, as Alf put his arm around his daughter.

'Come in here and Mummy will give you a cuddle,' Josie said, trying to prevent her voice from breaking.

As they moved to enter the shelter, a dozen people were still clambering to get inside.

'Easy does it,' Archie said, encouraging everyone to take care as they rushed to make their way inside, a sense of panic in the air. 'Please don't worry. There's enough room for everyone.' But since Hitler had invaded Norway, it no longer felt quite like the Phoney War of the last seven months.

'Come on, kids, let's get inside,' Alf said, keener than ever to make sure his family were safe.

But as they shuffled towards the opening, a loud bang sent shockwaves through the crowd. There was another sudden surge from behind, jolting Daisy and her family forward.

'It was just a car backfiring,' Archie said, raising his voice, but remaining calm. 'Please don't panic.'

But it was too late; fear that it had been a bomb dropping caused a mini stampede. Archie firmly blew on his silver whistle again, determined to take charge, get everyone inside and avert another accident. But as everyone jostled through, the family were all knocked off-balance as they stepped into the cavernous shelter.

'Polly, are you all right?' Daisy called out, trying to catch sight of her already shaken sister amongst the rush of people grabbing seats on the benches or bagging places on the floor.

'No,' came a whimper in reply.

'Oh, Polly,' Daisy gasped, spotting her little sister, who was once again in a heap on the floor a few steps in front of her.

'Luv, are you okay?' Josie quickly bent down to be next to her daughter.

'Mummy, it really hurts.' Polly wept, looking down at her left wrist, which was twisted at an awkward angle.

'Oh, sweetheart,' Alf said, now by her side, as fresh tears trickled down her cheeks.

But when he tried to lift Polly up, the surge of people bustling to find somewhere to sit pushed him down again.

'Daddy!' Polly screamed, frightened.

'It's okay,' Josie said, but her voice broke, as she tried, to no avail, to create some space around her family.

'Archie,' Daisy called in desperation, hoping if he could hear her, he could clear some space.

'Daisy,' came the muffled reply. 'Where are you?'

'Down here.'

Within seconds, Archie was standing behind Alf, and beckoning for Josie, Daisy and Annie to get inside the shelter. As soon as they were all inside, he quickly and firmly closed the heavy metal door, which acted as their barrier against the outside world.

'Come on, everyone. Out the way,' the family heard Archie order. 'There's someone hurt. Make some room.' It wasn't a request. It was a demand.

The firm instructions did the trick. As Archie forced his way through the busy communal shelter, the locals responded by creating space. The jostling and pushing stopped and Archie found Daisy and her family surrounding Polly, who was in an awkward heap on the floor.

'Can we all shift up a bit,' Archie commanded, as opposed to asked, turning to the folk who were sitting on the left bench. 'We've got a little girl who needs a bit of room.'

'Thank you,' Josie whispered, her nerves shot to pieces. 'I really thought for a minute there we were going to get trampled on.'

'People are just frightened,' Archie said.

'Well, they listened to you, son. You didn't 'alf manage to get them under control,' Alf praised, now able to lift a terrified and bewildered Polly into his arms.

'Is she okay?' Archie asked as the few people who were still standing managed to find a spot on one of the benches.

'I think she's really banged her arm,' Josie said, no longer able to disguise the concern in her voice.

'Let's have a look at her,' Archie said, keen not to waste another minute after all the commotion.

'Right, Polly,' Archie said, in a gentler tone. 'Would you mind if I take a look at what's causing you all this pain?'

'Okay.' She nodded tentatively, gripping her bunny, her little face crumpled in agony.

'I promise Archie won't hurt you,' Josie reassured her daughter.

'And I've got a bag of boiled sweeties in my bag.' Archie smiled. 'Would you like one? You've had quite the adventure this evening.'

'Yes, please,' Polly replied, a glimmer of a smile appearing.

'Here you go,' Archie said, offering her a strawberry bonbon. 'Why don't you suck on that, while I take a look at your arm and let's see if we can turn that frown upside down?'

'Thank you.' Polly took the sweet and popped it in her mouth.

'Right,' Archie said, positioning himself on the floor. 'I'm just going to take off your jacket and roll up your sleeve. It might hurt a little, but I promise, I will be as gentle as possible.'

'Shall we have a sing-song?' an elderly woman, just further down the bench from Polly, suggested. 'Might help this little one,' she added affectionately.

'That's a grand idea,' someone else replied.

And with that, the older lady burst into a chorus of 'You Are My Sunshine', quickly accompanied by at least a dozen others, all keen to help Polly forget about her injury, and keep their own nerves at bay. The impromptu singalong did the trick. Before she'd even realized it, Archie had Polly's bare arm resting limply in the palm of his hand.

'She'll need to see a doctor,' he said, looking towards Josie and Alf, 'but looking at the size of this lump and how quickly it's swelling up, I reckon it's at least a bad sprain or more likely a broken wrist.'

'I hate to say it, but I think you might be right, son,' Alf agreed.

'What does that mean?' Polly whispered, her eyes smarting.

'Well, we won't know for sure, luv, until we get you to a hospital, but I think it's fair to say there will be no French knitting or playing cat's cradle for a while.'

'Try and be brave for me,' Archie said gently, as he poured some cold water from a bottle onto a towel and carefully wrapped it around Polly's injured wrist. 'Hopefully this will help keep the swelling down a bit,' he said to Alf and Josie.

Turning his attention back to Polly, he added: 'I just need you to keep this nice and high. Maybe rest your arm on your mum's and try not to move it. Then when the all-clear sounds, we can get you to the hospital.'

'Oh,' Polly sighed, looking crestfallen. 'Will it hurt for a long time?'

'It might sting for a bit,' Josie said. 'But hopefully we can get you something to help with that.'

'And what I reckon it does mean,' Archie said, determined to keep Polly's spirits up, 'is you will end up spoiled rotten.'

The befuddled little girl looked up at her parents. 'Really?' she asked.

'Aye, I think Archie here might be right, sweetheart. We will all be waiting on you hand and foot.'

Polly wasn't the type of little girl to demand attention, but even she couldn't help but smile at the idea of so much fuss.

'I'll pass you all your toys if your hand is too sore to pick them up,' Annie promised. 'And we can read together on the couch.'

Polly momentarily forgot about the agonizing pain coursing through her. 'Thank you,' she said, gratefully.

'In fact, why don't I start now?' Annie suggested, pulling her little sister's copy of *Wind in the Willows*, which she had received at Christmas, from her bag. The two girls settled down and began reading about the latest adventures of Mr Toad, Mole, Rat and Mr Badger.

'Thanks so much, luv,' Josie said, turning to Archie now Polly was happily reading with Annie and feeling a bit more comfortable. 'You really have been a godsend. I'm not sure what we'd have done if you weren't around to help.'

'Not all,' Archie said, waving the compliment away. 'I wasn't sure if I would be any good at this job when I first volunteered, so it's nice to know I can do some good.'

'Don't you be undermining yerself,' Josie exclaimed. 'You should be proud of yerself and I'm sure when you report back to your superiors, they will be impressed too.'

'Hear hear,' came a call of support from a nearby bloke, who had witnessed Archie's swift response to Polly's fall and how he had prevented any further injuries by bringing order to the jostling crowd earlier. The accolade acted as a spontaneous catalyst for more cheers of praise, followed by an impromptu and rather raucous round of applause.

'There's really no need,' Archie muttered, his cheeks blazing. For once, the young steelworker was grateful for the dim light emitting from the dozen or so torches people had brought with them, as he hoped his embarrassed blushes went unseen.

A few moments later, as the clapping came to a gradual

stop, the high-pitched screech of the all-clear siren reverberated around the shelter.

'Thank the lord for that,' someone called out.

'Aye, someone must be looking down on us,' another grateful voice replied.

Archie immediately stood up. 'All's well that ends well,' he announced. 'Give me a few seconds and I'll have this door open. Just sit tight for a minute for me, then you can all be on your way and enjoy the rest of your evening.' Then turning to Daisy and her family, he added: 'If you all hang on until everyone else is out, one of my superiors will be along and I'm sure he will give you a lift to the hospital to have Polly checked out.'

'We don't want to put you to any more trouble,' Josie said. 'You've already done so much.'

'Josie's right,' Alf said. 'I'm sure we'll manage and be able to get a tram up there.'

'Not at all,' Archie insisted. 'Part of my job is to look after anyone who gets hurts in a shelter, so it's the very least I can do. If you don't mind hanging on a little while, I'm sure I can get it all arranged. It will take a lot longer on the tram so I'd rather we got her there sooner so she can get the medical help she needs.'

'Thank you,' Alf replied. 'We really are very grateful. You've done a cracking job lad.'

As Archie began directing everyone else out of the shelter, Josie turned to her daughter. 'You really do work with some lovely people, luv,' she said. 'This will be the

274

second time your friends have helped us out in a time of need.'

'I know, Mum,' Daisy agreed. 'I never thought for a minute going to work in a great dirty steelworks would result in me making so many good friends. I just hope when Patty hears what a grand job Archie has done tonight, she might go a bit easier on him.'

'Has she still not been able to forgive him and put their differences to one side? I'd hoped my word with her might have helped smooth things over,' Josie said.

'I don't think so,' Daisy replied.

'Well, he's proved his salt tonight, luv,' Alf added. 'He's a credit to the air raid patrol. I dread to think what we'd have done if he hadn't been here. Polly could have been more seriously injured if he hadn't got to her when he did, and if he didn't get all those people in order, there could have been a dangerous crush.'

Daisy knew her dad was right. Archie had been a real hero, selflessly making sure other people were safe. She'd understood why Patty had been so cut up about Archie signing up and keeping it from her at first, but she hoped hearing about this might help her see what good he was doing.

Chapter 25

'Are you all okay after Saturday night?' Daisy asked as she caught up with her friends trundling through gate three, ready to start their first shift of the week.

'I was just asking Nancy the same,' Betty said. 'It certainly wasn't what Dolly and I had in mind and put wreck and ruin to our plans for a relaxing drink after dropping off all the woollies at the WVS.'

'Did you get to a shelter okay?' Daisy asked.

'We did and thankfully it didn't go on too long. I must admit, I was a bit worried about Ivy, though, especially after the last one.'

'Oh goodness, of course. How was she?'

'Actually, Frank was there, so she felt a lot better. They went into the shelter in the garden with a flask of tea and by the time I got home, there was a platter of sandwiches on the table.'

'That's a relief.' Daisy smiled. 'How about you, Nancy?'

'Oh, it wasn't too bad. We'd just finished tea when the sirens started, so we rushed down to the shelter. Linda gets a bit worried but because Doris's kids were there, and we bumped into Patty and her family, it didn't feel quite as scary, although you always worry that it won't be a false alarm and something awful will happen.'

'You do,' Betty sympathized, touching her friend's arm. 'But all's well that ends well.'

'This is true.' Nancy nodded as the group made their way into the building.

'Unfortunately, ours didn't end quite that well,' Daisy sighed.

'Oh gosh, sorry, Daisy. What happened?' Betty asked. 'Here's me harping on about everything being okay. Are you all right?'

'I am, yes, but our Polly had a reyt old scare and then came a cropper.'

'What do you mean?' Nancy asked, her maternal instinct alerted.

'I'm sure Archie must have told you about it on the way in,' Daisy said, turning to Patty.

'Er, no, he didn't say anything. To be honest we barely spoke. I couldn't bring myself to ask about how he'd got on.'

'Oh, Patty, you must ask him,' Daisy gasped. 'He was a real hero. I don't know what we'd have done without him.'

'What do you mean?' Patty exclaimed, looking utterly bewildered. She wasn't the only one who was intrigued. Betty and Nancy had also stopped in their tracks to find out what Archie had done to deserve such an accolade.

'Maybe Archie should explain,' Daisy said. 'I don't want to steal his thunder. He deserves all the glory.'

'No, please tell me,' Patty pushed. 'Besides which, you know what he's like, he's too modest to talk about any good deeds he might have done.'

'Are you sure?' Daisy asked, conscious there was a reason Archie hadn't mentioned the traumatic series of events to Patty.

'Yes,' Patty sighed, 'I'd actually really appreciate it if you did.'

'Okay then,' Daisy said. And as the women moved further up the line towards the clocking-in machine, she recalled how Archie had jumped into action after Polly had become separated from them but also come to her rescue after she'd tripped going into the shelter.

'He really was very good,' Daisy explained. 'He was so calm. Not only did he find Polly when the rest of us were panicking but he knew exactly what to do after she got hurt. He put our Polly at ease and my dad said when they got back from the hospital, the doctors told him Archie's actions had prevented Polly's injury getting any worse.'

'Oh!' Patty gasped. 'I had no idea.' Her mind was a whirl, but suddenly the penny dropped. *Archie really is doing some – no, not some – a LOT of good. Was this what he meant by proving himself and not always being wrapped in cotton wool because of his heart condition?* Guilt soared through Patty as she began to understand Archie's need to be more than a steelworker, to contribute further to the war effort. She'd been so harsh on him and all he wanted was to feel as though he too could do some good.

'Are you all right, luv?' Nancy asked, breaking into Patty's thoughts and bringing her back to the moment. 'You've gone ever so pale.'

'Sorry, yes, I'm fine. I just feel like I've been so hard on Archie and all he wanted was to show he was capable of doing something worthwhile for the war effort.'

The other three women all glanced at one another, before smiling at Patty. 'Don't be hard on yerself, luv,' Nancy said kindly. 'No one can blame you for worrying. We are all very fond of Archie and none of us want to see him get poorly again, but I guess we have to accept his decisions too.'

'And that's exactly what I'm going to do from now on,' Patty said. 'I feel so stupid and just want to go and wrap my arms around him, but he had to go and see Frank early about today's jobs, so I guess I'll have to wait until we finish now.'

'It will make it all the more special when you see him,' Daisy said. 'I'm just so glad me telling you this hasn't caused a problem.'

'No! Not at all,' Patty exclaimed. 'Thank God you did, otherwise I'd probably never have found out. I can be a right mardy old mule when I want to be!'

'You never can!' Nancy teased.

With that, all four women started chuckling, but behind their laughter, they were delighted, in their own way, that

Patty had found a way to come to terms with Archie's decision to become an air raid warden.

'Oh gosh, I'm sorry,' Patty spurted out. 'Here's me thinking about myself again. How's Polly now?' she asked, looking at Daisy. 'What happened at the hospital?'

'Don't worry,' Daisy said. 'Well, we didn't all go. My dad insisted me, my mum and Annie go home after the all-clear. Archie arranged for one of his superiors to take Dad and Polly to the hospital. Apparently the doctors took one look at her wrist and knew it was broken, but like I said, if Archie hadn't reacted how he did, the damage could have been much worse.'

'The poor little lamb. Is she in pain?' Nancy asked.

'She was last night, but the doctors gave her something to help, and she's in a plaster cast now, so I think it's easing.'

'Can we do anything to help?' Nancy offered.

'I think we are all right at the moment.' Daisy smiled gratefully. 'Although, Dad did tell her we would all be waiting on her! Annie was keen to be her little servant last night, but I should imagine the novelty will soon wear off.'

'Will she be able to go to school?' Nancy asked, as they approached the time machines.

Daisy nodded. 'Mum's hoping so. She is going to nip in and see her teacher today. She could be in plaster for a couple of months, so I hope so, otherwise it will mean someone needs to stay at home with her, and we have only just got back to normal after Mum being so ill.'

'I'm sure they will do their best to accommodate her,'

Nancy said reassuringly. 'I think the teachers know how hard to it is for families right now and it will do Polly no good to be away from all her friends and out of a routine for so long.'

'That's what we're hoping too,' Daisy agreed, taking her timecard from the metal rack and inserting it into the clocking-in machine. 'The one saving grace is that it was her left wrist, and she is right-handed, so can still write.'

'I'll keep everything crossed for you,' Nancy said, picking out her own timecard. 'But, the offer stands, please let us know if we can be of any help.'

'I will. Thank you.' Once again Daisy felt blessed to be surrounded by such a caring group of women.

'And as for you,' Nancy added, turning to Patty, 'make sure you and Archie do something nice this weekend. I think you both deserve something to smile about. It's been a difficult time for you.'

'I just can't wait to talk to him. I'm going to give him the biggest kiss!'

'Oh, Patty,' Betty laughed, 'you are case, but I reckon from what Daisy has just told us, Archie definitely deserves it.'

As soon as the clock struck six o'clock, Patty dashed down her crane ladder at the speed of light, eager to speak to Archie. The additional two hours overtime seemed to last forever, and she'd spent the whole afternoon going over and over in her head what she wanted to say to him. Although she was still worried he would get hurt or his new role might be too much pressure on his heart, she finally understood his reasons. And from what Daisy had told her, he was doing a truly amazing job.

As Patty jumped off the last rung onto the factory floor, which was bustling with workers all keen to finish for the day, she scanned the workshop, but Archie was nowhere in sight.

'You all right, duck,' Frank said, as he came up alongside Patty, his coat on, ready to make a sharp exit and head over to Ivy's house.

'I was just looking for Archie,' Patty said. 'But I can't see him.'

'I think he's just left,' Frank said gently, astute enough to realize this wasn't what Patty would be expecting to hear. The two of them always walked to and from work together.

'Oh, chuffin' 'eck!' Patty gasped.

'What is it, duck?'

'It's completely my fault,' Patty sighed, 'I deliberately didn't ask him this morning how he got on last night in the raid and then Daisy told me what a grand job he did looking after her little sister after she hurt herself. I've been mardy with him for ages about his new role and after this morning, he probably thought there was no point even hanging around to walk home together.'

'If I was you, duck, I'd make haste and go after him. I've known that lad long enough to know, he's probably just hurting. He's always been the same; wears his heart on his sleeve. Go and tell him how proud you are, I'm sure that will do the trick.'

'Thanks, Frank,' Patty said, already spinning on her heels, bag and gas mask in one hand, and her jacket in the other. 'Wish me luck,' she added, before zig-zagging her way through the dozens of steelworkers, all heading for the exit.

'What's the rush?' Betty called, as Patty sped past her and Nancy.

'I'll tell you tomorrow,' she shouted back, as the distance between them quickly increased.

Outside in the yard, Patty dodged through the sea of men and women, in mucky overalls, flat caps and hair nets, and looked for Archie's distinctive mop of blonde hair, but she couldn't see him for love or money.

'Drat!' she muttered, jostling through the crowd until she managed to find herself free of gate three, on Brightside Lane. Staring straight down the cobbled road, knowing exactly the route Archie would take, Patty scanned the throng of workers.

'There he is,' Patty said out loud to herself, spotting him. But her elation of finding him was instantly damped as she saw his slouching shoulders.

'Oh, Patty, you've been such a clot,' she muttered, flustered by her own stubbornness. Determined to make things right, she picked up her pace, her walk turning to a jog, as she rushed towards Archie, oblivious to the fact her gas mask was repeatedly banging against her calves and the heavens had suddenly opened, heavy raindrops quickly drenching her.

'Archie,' she called, as she got within reaching distance. But between the rain, that was now ruining what had started off as a bright spring day, and the clatter of steel-capped boots on the now soaked cobbles, her voice was drowned out.

'Wait up,' she shouted again, now gripping the back of Archie's arm.

'Hey,' Archie said, spinning round, taken off-guard. 'Oh, it's you,' he added, realizing it was Patty who was virtually accosting him.

'You didn't wait after work,' Patty replied by way of an explanation.

'I didn't think you were bothered about talking to me,' Archie said.

Once again, guilt coursed through Patty. 'I'm sorry,' she apologized. Then, without taking a breath, she added: 'I've been such a fool. I didn't mean to make you feel worse. I was just so worried and scared and frightened you would get hurt. Daisy told me what happened and how you helped Polly. I think I get it now. I can see you just want to help. I am sorry. I promise. Will you ever forgive me? I swear I will do my best to be more understanding in future.'

'Hold on,' Archie said. 'I'm just as much at fault. I went about it all the wrong way and shouldn't have lied to you. I should have talked to you first.'

'Well, I didn't help, did I? Storming off in a huff every two minutes. I should have tried to listen to you instead of being so mardy and pig-headed.'

'We've both been a pair of clots.'

'Do you hate me?' Patty gasped, terrified Archie had heard enough of her moaning, and her apology had come too late.

'No!' Archie laughed, the corners of his lips turning upwards, bemused by Patty's outburst that had come out at a rate of knots. As he shook his head, the rain dripped off his nose. 'I could never hate you. You are the only girl I've ever . . . I love you with all my heart.'

'Oh, Archie,' Patty sighed, dropping her gas mask, bag and coat to the ground so she could wrap her sodden wet arms around Archie's neck. Her head felt the familiar comfort of his chest. 'I love you so much too.'

'It's a good job.' Archie laughed.

'What do you mean?' Patty said.

'Well, I'm not sure I would let any old girl soak me to the skin.'

'Oops.' Patty smiled, detaching herself from Archie, who now resembled a drowned rat.

'Shall we treat ourselves to a fish and chip supper and get dried off?' Archie suggested.

'That would be lovely.' Patty nodded, a mixture of relief and happiness soaring through her.

Ten minutes later, the pair were positioned at a table in the corner of Flathers chippy, sharing a large portion of fish and chips, with a side of scraps, which the motherly-looking woman behind the counter had thrown in after taking sympathy on Patty, seeing how soaked she was.

'Tell me everything that happened. Daisy explained you did a grand job of looking after Polly after she got lost in the crowds and then got hurt. She said you were like a true hero,' Patty gushed, filling with pride as she acknowledged for the first time what a splendid job Archie was doing as an air raid warden.

'It was nothing really,' Archie replied modestly, cutting the battered fish in half.

'That's not what I heard this morning,' Patty insisted. 'From what I could gather, you really put Polly at ease.'

'I suppose when you put it like that, I did.' Archie blushed, sill unable to accept a compliment without a surge of blood rushing to his cheeks.

'Daisy and her parents were ever so grateful,' Patty said.

'Do you know how she got on at the hospital?' Archie asked, as ever diverting the attention away from himself. 'I meant to try and find Daisy this morning to ask her.'

'Broken wrist, I'm afraid, but the doctors said it would have been a lot worse if you hadn't looked after her so well.'

'I'm just glad I could be of some use,' Archie replied.

Patty took a second to consider his answer. 'Is this what you meant by wanting to be useful and do some good?'

'Yes.' Archie nodded. 'It is. It's hard knowing I can't go and join blokes like Bert and William, or your friend Hattie's boyfriend, and protect the country against Hitler's troops. It makes me feel useless and not a proper man. All my life, I've had to watch other lads my age do stuff that my heart condition stops me doing and I guess my pride and self-worth have taken a bit of a hammering.'

'And now you've found something?' Patty asked, reaching across the table, and entwining her own fingers with Archie's.

'Yes,' he answered. 'I might not be on the front line or training to be a pilot, but if I can help keep folk safe and help anyone who might get hurt, then I just feel like I'm doing my bit.'

Patty squeezed Archie's hand tighter, tears of love filling her eyes. Although Archie had said the same words to her countless times, it was as though she was only now truly understanding what he was telling her. Of course, she was still going to worry about him, how could she not after seeing him collapse and end up in hospital only a few months earlier? But Patty also knew Archie needed her support, and she was determined to show him how proud she really was.

'I'm sorry it's taken me so long to understand,' she said earnestly. 'I suppose I couldn't see past the fact you might get hurt and I didn't know why you would want to do that, but I get it now. Just promise me you will take care, that's all I ask.'

'I promise.' Archie nodded, leaning over and planting a kiss on Patty's lips, before adding: 'If it makes you feel any better, I would really like to be around to spend as much time with you as possible.'

'Oh, Archie,' Patty said. 'That's all I want too.' And

the weight she had been carrying around on her shoulders for weeks vanished. It had taken a while and a lot of soul searching but Patty was determined to leave their squabbles in the past and enjoy every moment she and Archie had together.

'Why don't you come for dinner on Sunday? Yer know what m' mom is like. She will cook loads and will be really happy if you can make it. And so will I.'

'I'd really like that.' Archie grinned, delighted he and Patty were finally back on track.

Chapter 26

'You look like you've got the weight of the world on your shoulders, is everything okay?' Betty asked, placing her hand on Nancy's as they made their way out of the factory a few minutes after the midday hooter had signalled the end of their shift.

'Oh, I'm sure it will be,' Nancy sighed. 'I just can't shake this feeling in the pit of m' stomach. It's churning all the time. I'm just so worried. I heard on the wireless that blasted Hitler has now attacked France and I haven't had a letter from Bert for over a week. I have no idea where he even is.'

'It's perfectly normal to be feeling anxious at a time like this,' Betty said empathetically. 'Bert's your husband, you are bound to worry.'

'I just need to know he's safe.'

'Of course you do,' Betty said kindly. 'But please try and keep strong if you can. I know it's easier said than done but I'm sure Bert will be doing everything he can to stay safe, so he can get home to you, Billy and Linda.'

'Thanks, luv.' Nancy nodded, silently praying Betty was right. The last twenty-four hours had left her in complete turmoil.

Not only was the additional overtime leaving her run ragged, as she tried to juggle work and give Billy and Linda the attention they deserved, but the latest news from Europe had rattled her. Norway was struggling to hold up against Hitler since his invasion last month, but in his latest move he had invaded Belgium, Luxembourg, the Netherlands and, even more horrifying, France, where Bert was stationed. Owing to the fact, British forces had failed to prevent the occupation across Europe, Neville Chamberlain, who had eight months earlier announced Britain was at war with Germany, had stood down as Prime Minister and Winston Churchill was set to take his place. Nancy was sure all the upheaval would only lead to more uncertainty.

She hadn't been able to think of anything else since the news had started to filter through. She had no idea whether Bert was fighting against German troops in France or Norway or was safely positioned in a camp. Her mind was all over the place, flitting from trying to remain positive to thinking the worst. She hoped her job at Vickers meant she was doing her bit to help the Allied forces but God knows how she was even managing to operate a great hulk of a crane. With the guilt about not getting home some nights until it was Billy's and Linda's bedtime, mixed with the sleepless nights fretting about Bert, it was a miracle she hadn't done someone a serious injury swinging the hook almost on autopilot.

'What are you up to for the rest of the day?' Betty asked, as they approached the factory exit, hoping to distract Nancy from the thoughts that were troubling her.

'I'm going to nip to Oliver's to pick up some meat on my way home. It's definitely my turn to cook tonight. Doris has made dinner virtually every night this week, so I'll go and relieve her of my two and make a casserole. If I don't spend some time with them, they are going to forget who I am at this rate. It's bad enough their dad is away, without them hardly seeing me as well.'

'Now come on' Betty said gently. 'They know you're a great mum. Don't be so hard on yourself and please make sure you stop and put your feet up this afternoon with a cup of tea.' She'd noticed how wrung-out her friend looked. Nancy was growing paler by the day and had started losing weight too. 'You'll make yourself poorly if you don't have a little rest.'

'Thanks, Betty,' Nancy replied. 'I'll do my best.' Though, the last thing Nancy wanted to do was stop; keeping herself busy was the only thing preventing from her falling into a heap on the floor. All the extra hours at work could only mean one thing: the Allied troops needed more munitions, and you didn't need to be a genius to know why. If Nancy thought about it too much, she wouldn't be able to get through the day.

'Enough about me,' she said, conscious she didn't want to be the one her friends always needed to cheer up. Everyone was worrying and missing loved ones, especially Betty, whose William was now in Canada. 'What are you doing this weekend? Have you and Daisy got any nice plans?'

'I'm on gardening duty with Frank and Ivy as soon as I get back. I've promised to do a spot of weeding and check no slugs are attacking the veggies, then I think Daisy and I are going to the pictures later,' Betty said, feeling rather guilty for talking about having fun, given the news coming out of Europe.

Nancy sensed her friend's apprehension. 'That will be lovely,' she said. 'I know how much you miss William. It will be good for you to go and have a relaxing evening. You work so hard, what with everything you do here and all your volunteering at the WVS, not to mention the gardening with Ivy. You deserve it.'

'Thank you,' Betty replied, grateful for Nancy's unfailing support. 'At least the sun is out too, I always think you can't help but feel brighter about everything when there are blue skies.'

Nancy nodded with a smile in agreement.

'Aw, there you two are,' Frank said, approaching Betty and Nancy. 'I must have missed you coming down out of your cabs.'

'Oh, sorry, Frank,' Betty apologized. 'I should have looked out for you. I was just telling Nancy we are planning on getting some more veggies planted today.'

'Aye, it will certainly keep us busy.' Frank nodded. 'And I reckon some of those spring cabbages we planted might be ripe for pulling out now.'

'That's exciting,' Betty exclaimed. 'Our first harvest. Ivy will be thrilled.'

'That she will be, duck,' Frank agreed. 'And no doubt that's what we'll be eating for the next week too!'

'Yes, I'm sure.' Betty chuckled.

'Are you both walking into Attercliffe then?' Nancy asked. 'I'll tag along as I'm nipping to get some meat for dinner.'

'We are,' Betty replied, linking her free arm through Nancy's, hoping to keep her friend bolstered.

Like everyone else, Frank had also heard the news that had been worrying the nation. 'Keep yer chin up, duck,' he said, looking at Nancy. 'I know you must be out of yer mind, but your Bert sounds like a wise man. He won't deliberately put himself in danger.'

'Thanks, Frank.' Nancy nodded, as they made their way out of gate three and onto Brightside Lane. 'That's what I keep trying to tell myself, but you know what it's like, you can't help but worry in times like these.'

'And nobody can blame yer for that, duck, but remember we are all here for yer and if we can do anything to help, then you only have to say.'

'I appreciate that, Frank,' Nancy replied. 'Just having people to talk to really is a godsend. I think I'd go mad if I was at home by myself worrying.'

'Well, you won't have that problem while we're still all here,' Betty said, as they followed the hordes of workers making their way home.

'Thank you,' Nancy said, gratefully. 'I know I've said it a one hundred times before, but I really don't know what I'd do without you all.'

'I think it's fair to say we all help each other along and Frank keeps us so busy these days we don't have time to do much dwelling,' Betty replied.

'Yer not wrong there, duck,' Frank said. 'You lasses have been like a breath of fresh air and I for one am very grateful to have you around.'

'Oh, Frank.' Nancy smiled. Her foreman might outwardly appear to be a burly and hardened steelworker, but the reality was he was a big softy at heart. 'I'm so glad we have been of some use.'

'Yer worth your weight in gold, every one of you,' Frank reiterated. 'But don't be telling the blokes. I don't want them thinking I favour you lasses over them. I will never hear the end of it.'

'Your secret's safe with us,' Betty promised.

A couple of minutes later, the trio had reached Attercliffe Road and had come to a stop outside Oliver's, where a queue of women, chatting about what they were hoping to muster up for tea, had formed.

'Try and take it steady this weekend,' Frank said, patting Nancy on the shoulder as they prepared to go their separate ways.

'I'll do my best.' Nancy nodded, but she knew herself; even with the best efforts, she would struggle to find peace until she heard from Bert and had some news reassuring her that he was safe and well for the time being. She also wanted to make up having to work such long hours by spending the rest of the weekend with Billy and Linda. Maybe they could play some board games, have a tiddly winks challenge or she could help them put on a play using an old sheet for a curtain. They loved re-enacting *Swallows and Amazons*. 'You two have a grand weekend too,' Nancy added. 'I hope you can relax. It's been a busy old week for all of us.'

'It has that, duck. I think all this overtime has left us all in need of a bit of shuteye, but I reckon Ivy has a list of jobs waiting for me.' Frank chuckled. 'Not that I mind. It keeps me out of mischief, and I have to admit, she feeds me well.'

Nancy and Betty exchanged a knowing glance and a warm smile. Despite all the uncertainty going on around them, it was lovely to see Frank so happy. Heaven knows he deserved it.

Forty-five minutes later, on her way to Doris's, Nancy quickly nipped into her own house. Hanging her gas mask on a coat hook just inside the back door, she went down the hall towards the front door.

'Oh dear,' she whispered, sighing heavily, the lack of any letters on the floor making her heart race. 'Where are you, Bert?' Painful tears smarted the back of her eyes. 'Please just let me know you're safe. I need to know you are still with us. We love you so much.'

But Nancy knew deep down, no matter how much she willed Bert to come home in one piece, it wouldn't make a scrap of difference. Despite not being a practising

Christian, only going to church for weddings and christenings, like Dolly, she'd even began saying a little prayer every night before she got into bed. Nancy had no idea what good it would do, but quite frankly she was prepared to try anything. 'Please, God, look after my Bert,' she repeated. 'Me, Billy and Linda need him. I'm begging you, please don't take him from us yet.'

As much as she wanted to collapse onto the floor, or crawl upstairs and hide under her eiderdown, hoping she would wake up and this would all just be a terrible nightmare, Nancy knew she had to remain strong and paint a smile on her face for the sake of her children. They needed her more than ever now, and she already felt like she was only doing half a job, and a pretty poor one at that with the hours she'd been working.

'Right,' she said to herself, turning round and heading back out the way she'd come in. 'Paint yer smile on. All this moping and fretting ain't going to do you much good.'

'Mummy!' Linda called excitedly, bringing Nancy out of the doldrums, after she'd shut the back door and trundled into Doris's yard. 'You're home,' the little girl added, running towards her weary mum and wrapping her arms around her waist. 'I've missed you.'

'I've missed you too, poppet,' Nancy replied, embracing her daughter, wishing she could hold on to Linda like this forever. 'Have you had fun this morning?'

'Yes, Alice and I played post offices.'

'Did you?'

'Yes,' Linda responded.

'And what did you do?' This wasn't a game she'd heard Linda mention before.

'I wrote a letter to Daddy, asking why he hadn't replied to my last one yet, and Alice stamped it before putting it in the mail sack.'

The innocent answer left Nancy momentarily speechless. Although she was very aware a letter from Bert hadn't arrived for a while, it hadn't even crossed her mind it had been in Linda's thoughts too. Yet another pang of guilt paralyzed her. Why hadn't she realized this? If she'd been around more, maybe she would have noticed how Linda was coping. Of course, she knew Linda loved her daddy with all her heart and frequently got upset when the subject of when he would be home came up, but for some reason Nancy hadn't clocked the absence of mail from him had registered in Linda's mind. Probably because she was spending all the hours God sent at the Vickers and not enough with her children. As Linda's mum, she should have realized her own daughter was fretting about the lack of a letter. She should have picked up on this, should have reassured her daughter at the first indication Linda was worrying, but she had failed to spot the signs. *Why didn't I see this coming?* But, deep down she knew why. Between all the overtime, then trying to be a good mum when she was at home despite how exhausted she was amid her own increasing worries about Bert, she was being pulled in all directions and, in her own eyes, was failing to do a good job at anything.

Please let another letter arrive soon, Nancy thought to herself for the umpteenth time. It might not solve the muddle she was in, but it would at least put her mind at rest, and reassure Linda her daddy was all right. Nancy had no idea how on earth she would ever be able to tell her children there would be no more letters from their daddy, and she refused to allow her mind to go any further or think the unthinkable.

'I'm sure one will arrive soon, poppet,' Nancy said, trying to stay strong for Linda's sake. As Betty kept telling her, she had to think positive and to have hope, otherwise she wouldn't be able to get out of bed each day.

'Well, I've told Daddy off for not writing sooner, so hopefully he will send one soon, otherwise he will be in trouble.'

Nancy didn't know whether to laugh or cry. It was good to see Linda wasn't as emotionally drained as she was by the lack of mail from Bert, but there was no disguising the fact, it was clearly bothering her. *Maybe this is her way of coping*, Nancy pondered, thankful her little girl wasn't in floods of tears, which is what she would have expected, yet immeasurably saddened by what must be going on in Linda's mind.

'Nancy,' Doris called, poking her head around the back door, bringing Nancy back to the moment. 'You're back from work.' Little Georgie was in his usual position, perched on her hip.

'Yes. Sorry,' Nancy stuttered. 'I just popped in at home for a minute.'

'Are you all right?' Doris asked, stopping her friend. 'You look as white as a sheet.'

'Do I?'

'Yes,' Doris said. 'Come on inside. I'll pop the kettle on.'

'Thank you. That would be nice, luv.' Nancy nodded, her heart pounding.

Five minutes later, the two women were each nursing a hot cuppa, while Georgie played with his toy cars at their feet.

'Come on, luv, tell me what's happened,' Doris said, dunking a home-made almond biscuit into her brew.

'It's nothing really,' Nancy started.

'You're not getting away with it that easily,' Doris said, raising an eyebrow. 'I've known you long enough, Nancy Edwards, to know when something is wrong. And quite frankly, it wouldn't take a genius to know now is one of those times.'

'Oh dear,' Nancy replied. 'I'm really not very good at this whole stiff-upper-lip and bulldog-spirit thing, am I?'

'I'm not sure many of us are,' Doris revealed. 'We are just all coping in our own ways and some of us are better at disguising our worries than others, not that it's a competition. But are you going to tell me what's caused you to look as though you have just seen a ghost or am I going to have to prize it out of you?'

'It's just something our Linda said as I got here,' Nancy conceded, and then went on to tell the story of Linda playing post offices with Alice and the contents of her own letter she had written to Bert.

'Aw, that makes sense now,' Doris said, nodding before taking a mouthful of her tea.

'What do you mean?'

'I overheard the girls playing a little earlier and Linda said she was telling her daddy off in a letter.'

'Really?'

'Yes, but she said it in such a matter-of-fact way that I didn't really react. It was almost like how they talk to their dollies when they are playing schools.'

'I don't know whether that makes me feel better or worse,' Nancy confessed.

'In what way?'

'Well, it's just if she hadn't even noticed a letter from Bert hadn't arrived for a while, I wouldn't have had to deal with the impact it was having on her, but it now feels like she is almost accepting of the fact, and that doesn't feel very normal either. And not only that, I hadn't even picked up on the fact it was bothering her. What sort of mother am I?'

'Now come on,' Doris said firmly. 'As I've told you a million times, you are doing a grand job, but you are also exhausted and need to take a break. You aren't doing yer'sen any good working all the hours God sends and then trying to do everything at home too. You need to have a bit of downtime too.'

'It's easier said than done though, isn't it?' Nancy stated, more than asked.

'It is, luv, but yer know Billy and Linda can always play

here for a few hours of a weekend while you just have a bit of time to catch up with yerself.'

'You do so much already. I don't like putting on you so much as it is,' Nancy protested.

'And that's what friends are for.'

As much as Nancy was grateful for Doris's offer, she also knew she would feel even more guilty if she put on her anymore. She saw precious little of Billy and Linda as it was without handing them over on her time off.

'Oh, I'm just getting m'sen in a pickle,' Nancy said. 'It's just hard to know what's going on in their little heads, isn't it?'

'I'll not argue with you there, luv,' Doris replied. 'I got m'sen in a right mess after George died, trying to fathom out what the kids were thinking. I went from being pleased if they were laughing and playing, then fretting that they had forgotten about their dad.'

'It's all so confusing, isn't it?' Nancy sighed. 'I really don't know whether I'm coming or going.'

'Don't be so hard on yerself,' Doris encouraged. 'It's only natural you are feeling anxious. All this news of German troops marching through France is bound to leave you feeling uneasy. Bert's your husband, of course you are going to worry, but maybe Linda has just found her own way to deal with not hearing from him. Children can be far more resilient than we give them credit for. Look at Billy and how well he's coped since Bert signed up. And look at my lot now. Yes, we still have tears every now and again, and one of them will wake up having a nightmare, but on the whole, they are just getting on with things.'

Nancy thought about Doris's words. 'Does that mean they are just forgetting Bert?' she said, her voice breaking.

'No!' Doris said authoritatively. 'It's just they think differently to us. They can be quite black and white about stuff. Whereas we analyze everything and overthink every little thing, they just take it as they see it.'

'It's not like our Linda, though. You have seen how upset she can get over her daddy.'

'I know, luv,' Doris agreed. 'And there's nothing to say that tomorrow, or next week, or even later today, something might set her off and she's in floods of tears again, but right now she has found her own little way of dealing with what's going on, and that's got to be a good thing, hasn't it?'

'It is.' Nancy nodded in agreement. She would much rather Linda respond to the situation by playing a game, than coming home from school upset or climbing into her bed in the middle of the night after a bad dream. 'I wish I had her strength sometimes,' Nancy mused. 'I reckon I'd get a bit more sleep.'

'You're still struggling to nod off,' Doris stated, more than asked.

'I seem to be getting worse,' Nancy confessed. 'My mind plays awful tricks on me. I envisage Bert in some dark hole somewhere, badly injured and unable to call for help, or even worse. By the time I realize it's just a nightmare, I'm so shaken, I can't get back to sleep. I can't remember the last time I slept through.'

'Oh, luv,' Doris said, reaching over and placing her hand on Nancy's arm. 'That's the flamin' irony of being an adult. We are supposed to be more logical than our kids, but the reality is, a lot of the time we overthink stuff and get ourselves in a right old state.'

'Yer not wrong there, luv.' Nancy nodded, lifting her mug to her lips. 'I feel like I'm going mad half the time.'

'I'm not surprised,' Doris said. 'I often think the not knowing is worse than hearing news, no matter how hard it is to swallow.'

'I just don't want to fall to bits,' Nancy confessed. 'Billy and Linda need me more than ever. I've got to stay strong for their sakes. No good will come of them watching me crumble. I need to be a mum and dad to them while Bert is away.'

'Now stop this,' Doris said, kindly but firmly. 'Despite what you might be thinking, I can tell you now, Billy and Linda are very lucky to have you. I know you think those kiddies are suffering without their daddy being around, but you are more than making up for it.'

'Do you really think so?' Nancy asked, hoping Doris wasn't just being kind. All she'd ever wanted was to create a happy home and give her children the best life possible, where they grew up feeling loved and secure.

'Yes!' Doris replied adamantly. 'Remember how you and Bert always used to tell me what a grand job I was doing after losing George. I couldn't see the wood for the trees, but you two were always reassuring me the kids were lucky to have me. I was terrified their lives would be ruined and I wouldn't be able to make up for George not being here.'

'And look what an amazing job you have done,' Nancy praised. 'Those kiddies have all come through losing their dad admirably and that's all down to you.'

'But don't you see,' Doris said, taking a mouthful of tea. 'You are doing exactly the same. It's amazing how strong we become when we have to be. I guess it's our maternal instinct to always protect our kids.'

'You don't think Bert's not coming back, do you?' Nancy replied, her heart racing once again.

'No!' Doris insisted, quietly chastising herself, knowing what a worrier Nancy was. 'I know not hearing from Bert is a worry, but remember, no news is good news.'

'I hope so, luv,' Nancy sighed. 'I really do.'

'What I'm saying,' Doris added, 'is as a mum, you will always find the strength to make sure your kids are all right. It's just built into us to always protect them. No matter how hard life seems and what a battle it sometimes feels, we somehow manage it.'

'That might be true,' Nancy conceded, silently admitting that never in a million years had she envisaged working long hours in a steel factory and juggling being a mum with a husband away at war. 'But I couldn't do it without you. I really am very lucky to have you as a friend.'

'We are lucky to have each other,' Doris reminded Nancy.

'As I have said many times before, you got me through the hardest time of my life.'

'We make a good team, aye,' Nancy confirmed.

'That we do, luv,' Doris echoed. 'And no matter what the future has in store for us, we will face it together and there's one thing I can definitely guarantee.'

'What's that?' Nancy asked.

'Neither of us will fall apart.'

Full of admiration, Nancy looked at her friend. More than anything in the world, she wanted to believe she was right, that she, little old Nancy Edwards, could face whatever was thrown at her and not only stay standing, but also ensure her children survived too. But no matter how hard she tried, why did she still have a niggling feel of doubt, a constant worry that something awful was going to happen to shatter the very foundations of her life?

Before Nancy could voice her concerns or Doris could argue her point any further, the thunderclap of footsteps racing downstairs and into the kitchen brought their conversation to a halt.

'Mum!' Billy exclaimed. 'Yer back. You can save me from Joe, he's about to capture my army and make me beg for mercy.'

'I am.' Nancy laughed, despite the bittersweet irony of his innocent comments, her frown was well and truly turned upside down by the sight of her perpetually happy son.

'Does that mean it's time for dinner? I'm starvin'.'

'Me too,' Joe added, holding his stomach for added

emphasis. 'I reckon I might collapse with hunger if I don't eat soon.'

'Listen to the pair of yer.' Doris laughed, supping the last mouthful of her now lukewarm tea. 'You would think you'd never been fed.'

'We haven't!' the two boys replied in perfect unison.

Doris rolled her eyes in amusement, more than used to Joe and Billy complaining their tummies were rumbling.

'Well, it just so happens,' Nancy grinned, reaching down for her bag, 'I managed to pick up some bacon and sausages from Oliver's to see us through the weekend.'

'Yes!' Billy cheered. 'Can you cook them now?'

'There's certainly no rest for the wicked with you around.' Nancy laughed, but at the same time was grateful to Billy, for jolting her out of her melancholy mood.

Half an hour later, as the two families were gathered around Doris's kitchen table tucking into a pile of bacon sandwiches, accompanied by a chorus of 'oohs' and 'aahs', Nancy couldn't help but smile. She might spend virtually every waking moment of her day fretting about Bert and what the future held but moments like this made her realize she still had so much to be thankful for.

Chapter 27

Sunday, 19 May 1940

'I think we earned this,' Betty told Daisy as she took the last bite of the scone they had shared.

'Absolutely!'

The two friends had spent the morning at the WVS and had nipped to a nearby café to treat themselves. Betty was gradually learning to reward herself with a little bit of fun for all her hard work.

'I'm so glad you told me about the depot,' Daisy enthused, as she lifted her mug of tea to her lips. 'I really do feel like I am doing something useful.'

'No need to thank me,' Betty replied. 'I'm just glad you are enjoying the work.'

'I really am. It makes you feel good knowing you are really doing something to help, doesn't it?'

'Yes,' Betty agreed. 'As you know, I'm not very good at sitting still, although, I am getting better at allowing myself time to relax. My problem is if I stop for too long, my mind goes into overtime. I start fretting about William, so keeping busy and knowing I'm making a difference, no matter how little it is, stops me getting into a pickle with myself.'

'I'm sure,' Daisy empathized. She understood no matter how much a brave face Betty put on, it was only natural she would worry about her fiancé and what this godforsaken war might mean for him.

'Anyway, no point in maudlin,' Betty said, her stoic reasoning returning. 'It's good to have some fun every now and again.'

'I think we both deserve it,' Daisy reiterated. 'Remember, we do work hard, so the odd cake and a night at the picture house or in the Welly is just the tonic.'

'It is, and even though I could sit here all afternoon, I better head back. I want to hear this announcement that's supposed to be on the wireless.'

'Of course. I dread to think what's coming next. I'm trying to stay positive.' Daisy reached for her pale-blue cardigan from the back of the chair. 'I promised I'd help Mum with the Sunday roast this afternoon too.'

Across town, Nancy and her neighbour braced themselves as they sat at Doris's kitchen table, their heads turned in the direction of the wireless, as Winston Churchill's sombre voice broke their anxious silence.

'I speak to you for the first time as Prime Minister in a solemn hour for the life of our country, of our empire, of our allies and, above all, of the cause of freedom. A tremendous battle is raging in France and Flanders. The Germans by a remarkable combination of air bombing and heavily armoured tanks have broken through the French defences north of the Maginot Line, and strong columns of their armoured vehicles are ravaging the open country, which for the first day or two was without defenders.'

'Good Lord,' Nancy muttered in horror, vocalising Doris's silent fears.

Doris leant across to her friend and gently squeezed Nancy's arm as she took a deep breath, the enormity of the Prime Minister's ominous words hanging heavy in the air. As they listened with bated breath, the two women struggled to take in every word, but the sentiment and danger ahead weren't lost on them.

'We must not allow ourselves to be intimidated by the presence of these armoured vehicles in unexpected places behind our lines . . .' Churchill continued. 'If the French retain that genius for recovery and counter-attack for which they have so long been famous; and if the British Army shows the dogged endurance and solid fighting power of which there have been so many examples in the past – then a sudden transformation of the scene might spring into being.'

'Please, God, look after my dear Bert,' Nancy whispered, as she tried to digest what the Prime Minister was saying, the panic she had been fighting for weeks now threatening to erupt.

'Try to stay strong,' Doris said. 'You don't know whereabouts in France he is. He may even have been sent to Norway. I know it's easier said than done but try not to think the worst.'

But rumour had it the Allied troops had been retreating from Norway, and were now defending France. Nancy could feel her whole body trembling. This had always been her greatest fear. Hitler's troops were doing their utmost to take over the very country her husband, alongside thousands of others, was defending. She'd only ever known Bert as a gentle and kind man; yes, he was strong and protective, but she wasn't sure if that made him capable of defending himself against a platoon of men whose aim was to destroy the Allied forces. Could he really hold his own in a war? Was he the brave heroic soldier who could take down enemy attackers that Billy boasted about?

On the radio, Churchill continued, 'It would be foolish, however, to disguise the gravity of the hour.'

'Oh!' Nancy gasped, the impact of the words hitting her like a thunderbolt, unable to concentrate on what their new Prime Minister said next.

'Come on,' Doris said, standing up and moving to sit next to Nancy, putting her arms around her now shuddering shoulders.

'How can I possibly cope if Bert . . .' But as always Nancy couldn't finish that particular sentence. If she said it, then she felt sure she was somehow sealing her husband's fate. 'Billy and Linda,' was all she could mutter, her voice breaking.

'You mustn't think like this,' Doris reiterated. 'I can see why you'd think the worst but from what I can gather, there is a long way to go before that happens. As I keep telling you, Bert will not do anything to deliberately put himself in danger.'

'But hasn't he done that already by going off to war?' Nancy said, tears filling her eyes. This moment is what she had been dreading all along.

'Listen,' Doris gently reassured. 'From what we are hearing from Churchill, the German troops have only occupied a small part of France at the moment and the Allied troops are a force to be reckoned with. For all we know they could start retreating after they realize what they are up against.' But even as Doris spoke the words, she knew they expressed wishful thinking more than anything. Hitler seemed hell bent on gaining as much power as possible and any idea of a surrender seemed somewhat unlikely. She knew she had to keep her friend hopeful at this time.

'I just don't know what to think,' Nancy cried. 'I'm so scared. What if Bert doesn't make it—'

'I know you are,' Doris said, tactfully interrupting her friend, pouring two fresh mugs of tea from the pot. 'Let's see what happens over the next few days and weeks. We can't worry about something that hasn't happened, otherwise we would never get up each day.'

Nancy knew Doris was right, but in that moment she was terrified.

Aware the Prime Minister was still talking, the two women once again concentrated on what he was saying.

'My confidence in our ability to fight it out to the finish with the German Air Force has been strengthened . . .'

'You see,' Doris said, hoping the words would give Nancy hope. 'The Germans aren't just stampeding across France.'

Nancy nodded, praying her neighbour was right, trying to focus on the wireless, hoping the new leader would offer a light at the end of the tunnel.

'If the battle is to be won, we must provide our men with ever-increasing quantities of the weapons and ammunitions they need. We must have, and have more quickly, more aeroplanes, more tanks, more shells, more guns,' Churchill rallied. 'They increase our strength against the powerfully armed enemy.'

'Did you hear that?' Doris asked, hoping it would bolster Nancy and give her something to focus on.

'I did,' Nancy replied, unable to listen to anything more the Prime Minister was saying, her head already swimming in confusion and worry.

'I know this is going to sound tough,' Doris started.

Nancy raised an eyebrow in her friend's direction.

'It's meant with the best intentions,' Doris continued. 'But it sounds like your Bert and all those other troops really need woman like you to carry on doing what yer doing in the factories.'

'It's the fact they need so many munitions that's worrying me,' Nancy said, reaching for her mug of tea. 'Hitler's army are clearly a force to be feared.'

Doris knew there was no point in arguing. 'No doubt, luv, but that's not to say the Allied troops aren't giving them a run for their money. From what I can gather, they are still holding their own in France.'

Nancy knew her friend was only trying to keep her spirits

up. 'Let's hope so,' she said. Despite the overwhelming worry which had consumed her over the last couple of weeks, Nancy inwardly berated herself for always thinking about the worst-case scenario.

'I know I need to at least try and think positively,' she admitted. 'I just constantly find myself thinking something terrible is going to happen and we won't see Bert again.'

'And as I keep telling you,' Doris smiled, 'that's completely normal. But it's my job to keep you upright and stop you falling into a heap on the floor.'

'You really are a good friend.'

'Now enough of that,' Doris said. 'All I care about is making sure you and those kiddies are all right.'

'Thanks, luv,' Nancy replied gratefully, finishing off her cuppa, accepting how modest Doris was. 'Now, speaking of which, they have been out in the yard for a long time.'

'Enjoying the sunshine at long last,' Doris grinned, 'not that I'm complaining. This upturn in weather has been a godsend for getting all the laundry dry and it stops them all being under our feet.'

'This is true,' Nancy agreed, equally as pleased Billy and Linda hadn't been privy to the Prime Minister's speech. Despite the rallying tone of his first broadcast as the country's leader, the sentiment was clear – Hitler's attack on mainland Europe revealed this war was far from over and in actual fact, was only just beginning.

Chapter 28

'What does it mean, Frank?' Patty asked, tucking into her Spam sandwich as she peered across the canteen table at her foreman's *Daily Mirror*.

'Do you mean what's going on in Dunkirk?' Frank asked, taking a gulp from his mug of tea.

'Yes,' Patty nodded, 'I keep hearing bits on the radio, but I don't really understand it.'

Frank took a deep breath. The whole country had shuddered at the news that the Battle of France had been lost and Hitler had managed to occupy the country.

'Well, to put it simply, duck, the Allied soldiers were forced to retreat to the beaches of Dunkirk in the north of France after Hitler's army managed to surround them,' Frank explained. 'It looks like there is nothing else they can do right now to defend the country.'

'That doesn't sound good.' Patty had always struggled to understand what was going on in Europe and for the most part was happy not to know and to live in blissful ignorance, but even she couldn't hide from the German dictator's latest victory. 'And these boats everyone is going on about,' Patty added. 'Can they rescue everyone?'

'I hope so, duck,' Frank said, feeling troubled by the terrifying headlines. 'But I have to admit, it's quite a worry. All we can do is keep our fingers crossed and just hope the small ships can get all our troops out of France and quick.'

'Do you think they will?' Patty asked. The emergency call from the Ministry of Shipping for domestic vessels, including pleasure crafts, fishing boats and yachts, to take to the water from Ramsgate and make their way to France to rescue stranded troops had been answered with a vengeance, small crafts risking life and limb to bring soldiers back to Britain.

'Well, they seem to be doing a grand job so far,' Frank said, but conscious of how anxious Nancy, who was stood by the tea urn, looked and how frightened she must be feeling, he restrained from saying it would be nothing short of a miracle to bring every one of those men home in one piece.

'There's nothing like the British bulldog spirit to get a job done,' Dolly said, who had come over to the table to see her friends, taking a quick break from serving up dinners.

'You're not wrong there, duck,' Frank agreed. 'It's extraordinary how many of those owners are willing to offer up their boats. Rumour has it some of the fishermen are even sailing their own, instead of handing them over to the Royal Navy. I bet there's a fair few of them that have never even crossed the channel before, but they are willing to risk their own lives to help.'

'Is it a long way?' Patty asked. 'Across the water to France, that is, and to the place all the soldiers are?'

'I don't know the exact distance, duck, but it will take a good few hours, I bet five or six, and that's if the water is calm.'

'I hope some of them are wearing our knitted vests and hats,' Patty said. 'Sounds like they are going to need them.'

'That they are, duck,' Frank agreed, lifting up his knife and fork to start his dinner.

'Anyway,' Dolly interjected, also conscious that Nancy would be finding the conversation difficult. 'We have to stay positive. Our Allied troops are a force to be reckoned with.'

'Shall I play mum?' Nancy asked, who was still stood by the stainless tea vessel, trying to keep herself busy. The thought of chatting about the latest developments filled her with dread. She'd barely slept a wink, tossing and turning all night, worrying about Bert, and knew it wouldn't take much for her to burst into floods of tears. No matter how hard she tried, Nancy couldn't shake the feeling that something awful was about to happen. More than ever, she wished she had just an ounce of Betty or Doris's strength, knowing it wouldn't take much for her to crumble into a million tiny pieces right now.

'That would be lovely,' Betty replied, bringing Nancy back to the present. 'Would you like a hand?'

'No, no. I'll be fine,' Nancy insisted. 'Would everyone else like one too?'

'That would be grand, duck,' Frank replied.

'I wouldn't say no,' Archie added.

'Me too,' came Patty's response.

'Coming up.' Nancy nodded. 'What about you, Daisy? Would you like a nice hot cuppa?'

'That would be lovely,' she answered. 'But I do feel guilty while I'm just sat here.'

'Don't,' Nancy asserted. 'It's nothing and it will only take me a minute.'

'Thank you all the same,' Frank reiterated. 'I'm feeling very spoilt at the moment. I could get used to all these women spoiling me. I don't know I'm born.'

'I wouldn't complain, boss.' Archie laughed, gently nudging him in the ribs.

'Oh, I'm definitely not.' Frank grinned. 'In fact, I'd go as far to say, I'm quite enjoying it.'

Betty couldn't help but smile to herself. There weren't many positives coming out of this blasted war but seeing Frank and Ivy's friendship blossom was definitely one of them.

'I might have to get Patty here trained up,' Archie added, winking at his sweetheart, who was sat next to him and about to take a bite out of her Spam sandwich.

'I don't think so,' she scoffed. 'I reckon it's you who should be waiting on me. Isn't that what a real gentleman does to woo the woman of his dreams?'

'I'm only pulling yer leg,' he teased. 'You know your every wish is my command.'

'Actually,' Patty said, turning to Archie and lifting

a red-and-white package from her bag, 'I've bought you these.'

'What are they?'

'It's nothing much. I just nipped to the sweet shop last night and got you some bonbons to get you through your next air warden shift.'

'Aw, thank you.' Archie's whole face lit up, before he quickly gave Patty a discreet peck on the cheek. It wasn't just the sweets that made him smile, but the fact Patty was finally supporting him in his mission to do his bit. It was the latest in a thoughtful line of supplies Patty had got him over the past few weeks: a pair of socks she knitted for him 'to stop him getting cold' and a wrapped-up slice of pork pie she'd bought from the butcher's.

'Well, I can't be letting yer go hungry, can I? What sort of girlfriend would I be?'

Betty, Daisy and Frank all shared a bemused glance, pleased to see Archie and Patty back on good terms after weeks of bickering. It was certainly a welcome change to the icy atmosphere that had enveloped them after he volunteered as an air raid warden. Hearing about Archie's heroics had finally helped Patty see things straight and realize what a good job he was doing to help the people of Sheffield when the sirens sounded. She had finally accepted it was Archie's way of proving himself and they were back to resembling love's young dream.

'How's Polly?' Betty asked, turning to Daisy, the happy banter reminding her it had been the girl's accident that had acted as a catalyst to repair the rift between Patty and Archie.

'Just the same, really,' Daisy said, unwrapping her cheese sandwich. 'She's managing to go to school, which is a great help, and I think, if the truth beknown, she's rather enjoying all the attention.'

'Thank goodness you were there to help her,' Patty said to Archie, now full of enthusiasm for his voluntary wartime role.

'It was nothing,' Archie said, his cheeks flushing.

'Well, I would beg to differ,' Daisy added.

'I'm just glad she's doing all right,' Archie said, keen to move the attention away from himself. 'Anyway,' he added, now looking towards Betty. 'Frank here tells me Ivy's garden is coming along a treat.'

'Oh, it is.' Betty beamed. 'In fact, you have just reminded me, I have a little something here for you all,' she added, reaching down for her cloth bag and pulling out a Jacob's biscuit tin.

'Ooh, has Ivy been baking?' Patty asked, her eyes lighting up at the thought of the landlady's sweet treats.

'I'm afraid not,' Betty chuckled, 'but I think your mom might be pleased with what I have got.'

'What?' Patty quizzed, looking intrigued.

Betty opened the tin to reveal half a dozen brown speckled eggs neatly encased in a cotton tea towel to prevent any breakage.

'Well, it's not the jam tart I was hoping for,' Patty

exclaimed, her excitement dwindling. 'But yer right, m' mom will be reyt pleased.'

'There's two each for you, Daisy and Nancy.'

'That's lovely of you, thank you,' Daisy said. 'My mum will also be over the moon. She hates using those dried eggs.'

'If I'm honest, I think this is why Ivy decided on getting hens. She wanted to do something more to help.'

'Well, please thank her from me,' Daisy reiterated. 'And I'm sure my mum will say the same.'

'Archie, I didn't bring you any as I assume your hens are laying eggs too.'

'They are,' Archie said. 'We only have two hens, so they aren't quite as prolific as your lot, but we've had a couple of eggs. My nannan is sending my dad for a couple more hens, though, now she knows they will actually do what she intended. She's promised she will make us all a big cake if they produce enough eggs.'

'Well, that will be worth waiting for,' Patty said, grinning again at the thought of a rare treat after months of enduring rationing.

'Sorry, did I hear my name being mentioned?' Nancy asked, handing everyone a mug of steaming hot tea.

'You did and thank you for this,' Betty said gratefully, taking the freshly poured cuppa from Nancy. 'Ivy has sent you two eggs.'

'That's ever so good of her,' Nancy said, beaming. 'Are you sure she can spare them?'

'Absolutely,' Betty enthused. 'Houdini and her pals seem to be on a roll. I should imagine there will be plenty more where these came from.'

'Houdini?' Nancy quizzed.

'Did we not tell you,' Betty stated more than asked, glancing at Frank, who was already chuckling away to himself.

'I don't think so,' Nancy said curiously.

'One of the hens desperately tried to escape on the first day we got them, and poor Frank had a bit of an adventure trying to catch it.'

'I'd have paid good money to have seen that.' Archie laughed.

'I bet you would, son, that blighter was running rings around me.' Frank laughed, shaking his head. 'But I'm hoping that it's an experience not to be repeated any time soon.'

'Well, quite selfishly, I hope no more of the hens try to do a runner either, as these eggs are like gold dust.' Daisy grinned.

Normally, the light-hearted banter, and such a tale of Frank chasing a hen around the garden, would have Nancy in stitches too, but she was struggling to think about anything but Bert and where he might be. Instead, she pulled her knitting out of her bag and carried on with the latest pair of socks she'd started in the middle of the night when sleep had once again evaded her.

'That reminds me,' Patty said, looking over at Nancy's

handiwork. 'I'm meeting Hattie after work tonight and I think she has a few bits to donate to the knitting pile.'

'That's marvellous,' Betty said, lifting her sandwich to take a bite. 'Daisy or I can take another pile to the WVS depot one night this week or at the weekend. I tend to pop in two or three times a week, depending on how much overtime we have on here.'

'Is it still busy?' Patty asked.

'Yes, but they are still crying out for more volunteers,' Betty explained.

'And it really is a marvellous place,' Daisy enthused. 'Everyone is so friendly, and you really feel as though you are doing something worthwhile.'

'I think Hattie might be interested in coming along,' Patty mused. 'I think she feels as though she isn't doing anything constructive just working at Woollies.'

'They definitely won't turn her away,' Betty encouraged.

'How is Hattie?' Nancy asked Patty, assuming she too would be getting herself in a state about what was happening in France.

'Not good if I'm honest,' Patty confirmed, finishing her snap and taking her half-finished knitting from her own bag.

'Has something else happened?' Daisy interjected.

'No. She hasn't had any bad news or anything,' Patty explained. 'But her John is in France and all this recent news about Dunkirk has made her on edge. I've never seen her so anxious.'

I know the feeling, Nancy thought to herself, but didn't dare vocalise for fear she wouldn't be able to control her emotions and might burst into tears.

'I'm sorry,' Daisy replied, feeling foolish for not realizing the obvious.

'Please, don't be,' Patty said. 'Hattie is just desperate to hear from John. Once she does, I think she will feel a bit better.'

'Oh,' Nancy audibly gasped, unable to stop herself.

The group of workers turned to face her. 'Come on,' Betty said, touching her friend's arm. 'A letter will arrive any day now. I'm sure of it. Just keep strong if you can.'

'I'm sorry,' Patty apologized, guilt coursing through her. 'I didn't mean to upset you.'

'Don't apologize,' Nancy said, gripping her mug of tea, hoping it would somehow magically stop her from bursting into tears. 'I'm just overly sensitive at the moment.'

'As I keep telling you, it's perfectly understandable,' Betty reassured her. 'And we are all here for you.'

'I know,' Nancy nodded, 'and for that alone, I'm so very grateful.'

'That's what friends are for.' Betty smiled.

'Thank you,' Nancy replied. 'Anyway,' she turned to Patty, keen to take the focus off herself, 'will you wish Hattie all the best from me and tell her I'm thinking about her.'

'Of course,' Patty said, still silently admonishing herself for being so tactless.

'Hey, be careful.' Archie gently nudged her.

'What?' Patty quizzed, paranoid she had put her foot in it again.

'Yer knitting,' Archie said, looking down at the slowly unravelling navy-blue woollen hat.

'Oh drat,' Patty moaned. She'd been so worried about upsetting Nancy, she hadn't noticed the wool freely slipping off her needles. 'This took me chuffin' ages. I'm not sure I can even salvage it.'

'Give it here,' Nancy said, managing the smallest hint of a grin and more than happy to have something to distract her. Since teaching Patty how to knit, she'd lost count how many times she'd had to rescue a lost stich, or in this case a row.

'Sorry!' Patty exclaimed, handing over the pile of messy yarn. 'I'm such a clot at times. I swear I have no idea how I even manage to control that huge monstrous crane when I can't even manage to knit a hat without making a dog's ear of it. You should have seen the socks I knitted for Archie, they have got more holes in them than sense.'

Archie reached under the table and patted her knee, letting her know, despite how bedraggled the socks looked, he appreciated the effort regardless.

'Don't be saying that, duck,' Frank chuckled, 'you'll give me heart failure at the thought of what damage could be caused. Besides which, as I keep saying, you are all doing an absolutely grand job. Talking of which, are you all still okay to carry on for a bit longer with the extra hours? We still have quite a mountain of work to get through.'

Nancy bit her lip and tried to concentrate on salvaging Patty's mishap, fully aware Frank was trying to be subtle and not spell out the obvious. The continuation of overtime must mean more orders, and there was only one reason for that. *You can do this*, she told herself, remembering her chat with Doris from the previous afternoon, and the rallying words Winston Churchill had broadcast to the nation. '*If the battle is to be won, we must provide our men with ever-increasing quantities of the weapons and ammunitions they need.*'

'I'll see if Doris is happy to keep having our Billy and Linda a couple of evenings a week,' Nancy announced, looking at Frank. She wasn't sure how else she could help Bert right now, but if doing her bit, when she could, to help manufacture the munitions he and the Allied troops needed, then that's what she would set her mind to. Doris had been right when she'd said that the country needed people like her more than ever.

'Thanks, duck, but don't worry if it's too much. You are already putting enough hours in as well as looking after those little ones,' Frank said.

'Thank you for being so understanding,' Nancy said appreciatively, as she began rethreading Patty's wool onto one of her needles.

'You can count me in,' Betty said.

'And me, if you can trust me?' Patty grinned. 'M' mom will always be grateful for anything extra in m' wages.'

'I reckon you have more than proved how capable you are,' Frank replied, half laughing.

'Our supervisor over on the turner's floor has asked us the same thing this morning,' Daisy chirped up. 'It looks like we will all be here a bit later this week.'

'We should maybe arrange a drink in the Wellington on Saturday night then to reward ourselves,' Betty suggested. Ever since her workmates had introduced her to the local public house, she had accepted life was too short for all work and no play. The odd night out to the picture house, an afternoon at The Skates, alongside a port and lemon with her friends had allowed Betty to have a bit of fun, instead of constantly working. For years she had trained herself to always keep busy, but she'd slowly come to realize that enjoying time with her friends was just as important and was equally as effective at stopping her from worrying about her William every single hour of the day.

'I'd definitely be up for that,' Patty piped up. 'It will be the very least we deserve.'

'Me too, if my mum can spare me,' Daisy added.

'What's that, luv?' came Josie's voice as she approached the table, holding an empty tray.

'Hiya, Mum.' Daisy smiled. 'The girls here are just planning a drink on Saturday night, but I was going to check if you needed me at home before I agreed to go.'

'Of course, you can, luv,' Josie enthused. 'You deserve a few things to look forward to, after all the hours you put in,' she added, placing the tray on the table and collecting up the empty mugs. 'I might even join you all, if yer dad doesn't mind watching yer sisters for an hour or so.'

'You should,' Betty encouraged.

'Did I hear the Wellington being mentioned?' Dolly, who had nipped over to see friends, asked.

'You did that.' Frank nodded. 'These lasses are planning a bit of a night out on Saturday after agreeing to some more overtime.'

'Well, you can count me in,' Dolly said. 'It'll beat staying at home by m'sen.'

'You are always very welcome,' Betty encouraged, conscious Dolly must also be worrying about her two sons, following the latest developments across Europe.

'Sounds like a date then,' Dolly grinned, 'as long as you don't mind us oldies joining you young 'uns.' She chuckled, winking at Josie.

'Not at all,' Betty enthused. 'It would be lovely for us all to have a little get-together outside of work.'

Then turning to Nancy, she added: 'I know you might not want to leave Billy and Linda, especially if you'll be seeing less of them with more overtime over the next few weeks, but if you can make it, that would be lovely.'

'Thanks, luv,' Nancy said, holding up Patty's knitting that she'd miraculously managed to salvage. 'Can I let you know?'

'Of course,' Betty replied, realizing how difficult it must be for her friend to be away from her children so much.

'Right, you lot,' Frank said. 'Now you've got your social lives sorted, I'm afraid we need to get back to work.'

'You are a spoilsport,' Patty teased, throwing him a mock

scowl. 'I thought we were going to get away with an extra ten minutes.'

'Believe me, duck, if I could wrangle it, I'd happily let you, but I wouldn't 'alf get it in the neck, especially with the increasing workload we are having to cope with.'

The innocent comment made Nancy flinch once again. *Stop it*, she silently chastised herself, fully aware this war wasn't coming to an end anytime soon, and she needed to somehow try to find a way of getting through each day, without constantly being on edge.

'How have you been?' Patty asked Hattie as they walked around the make-up counter at Banners, a few minutes' walk from Vickers. They had originally thought about nipping to see a picture after work, but Patty had the good sense to realize what her friend really needed was a good old natter.

'I won't lie,' Hattie sighed, 'I haven't been great.'

'Still no news from John?'

'Sadly not,' her friend replied, shaking her head. 'I know there's a good chance he's just too busy to write, what with everything going on in France, but it leaves me on edge. I need to know he's all right.'

'I'm sure he will be,' Patty said. Though she still didn't fully understand enough about what was happening across Europe to be certain of her words, she was also savvy enough to realize, after seeing the state poor Nancy was in, that what Hattie needed now was hope. No good would come of dwelling on the ifs and maybes or the worst-case scenarios. She knew it was easier said than done, but there really was no point in worrying about something that hadn't happened yet. It was more important Hattie focused on the here and now.

'We are planning a drink at the Wellington on Saturday night. Why don't you come with us?' Patty suggested, hoping the company might be good for Hattie. 'It might help keep your mind off things a little, or we could have a trip to The Skates at the weekend?'

'As much as my heart isn't in it, I think I'll take you up on the offer,' Hattie said. 'It definitely beats moping about at home and worrying about what Hitler is going to do next or listening to my dad rant after he's had one too many.'

'Is he still drinking a lot?' Patty enquired.

'Yes, and all the news seems to have made it worse. I try to understand why he gets so angry. God knows what he saw in the last war and I'm sure Hitler invading France is bringing back awful memories. On top of that I think he feels frustrated that he's too old now to sign up.'

'It must be very hard for him,' Patty empathized.

'You're probably right,' Hattie agreed. 'I just feel a bit helpless.'

'I'm sure,' Patty said, as she absent-mindedly picked up a pale-pink lipstick.

'It's just all so draining.'

'Do make sure you come on Saturday then,' Patty said, convinced Hattie was better off with friends than enduring another one of her dad's drunken episodes. 'Hopefully Nancy will come along too. She definitely needs a break.'

'I'm sure. It must be so hard for her too,' Hattie said, as the pair moved towards the women's clothing section.

'It is but she hasn't made her mind up yet. She doesn't like to leave her two little ones for long, especially after working all day,' Patty explained.

'I can understand that. Being a mum as well as a dad, while her husband is away, must put a lot of pressure on her.'

'I think it does,' Patty agreed. 'I can understand it, though. I know how torn m' mom would feel if she had to go out to work and leave my brother and sisters. She would be in a reyt state.'

'I'm sure.' Hattie nodded, picking up a lemon blouse with a delicate Peter Pan collar. 'This would suit you,' she added.

'Thank you,' Patty said. 'I haven't treated myself in a while and I could do with something new for Saturday night.'

'You should get it,' Hattie encouraged. 'I'm sure Archie would like you in it too.'

'I think I might,' Patty replied gratefully, imagining how she could also wear it for her next date with Archie, now things were much better between them.

'Is everything back on good terms with you two now?'

'It is.' Patty beamed. 'I obviously still worry about him, but I realize now why being an air raid warden is so important to him. And honestly, I feel like a bit of a fool for not being as understanding as I should have been from the beginning.'

'Don't be fretting about that now,' Hattie said, not only pleased Patty had found a way to come to terms with Archie's decision, but very proud of her too. It was no secret Patty could be headstrong and as stubborn as a mule at times. *Maybe with what the war was throwing at them, Patty was growing up*, Hattie thought.

'All that matters is you both found a way to work it out,' she continued out loud.

'Thanks, Hattie,' Patty replied, thinking about her friend's words. She'd never really considered *how* you reacted to a situation was probably more important than the actual fallout, but made a mental note to always try and bear it in mind for the future, fully aware she had a lot to be grateful for.

While Hattie, Nancy and Betty were all worrying about their loved ones, for the most part Patty had hers by her side and was determined to do her best on making sure it stayed that way.

'Dare I ask how Nancy is coping with her husband away?' Hattie asked tentatively.

Patty thought very carefully before she answered, not wanting to add to her friend's worries. 'I think she's trying to keep her mind busy. As well as working and looking after her Billy and Linda, I'm convinced she has done enough knitting to keep the whole British Army, Navy and RAF in hats and socks.'

'Oh, speaking of which,' Hattie said, glancing down at the bag that was hanging from her arm, containing several pairs of woollen socks, hats and scarves. 'I've got a few more to add to the pile. I've probably been a bit like Nancy. When I'm struggling to sleep, I just start knitting and it helps me relax.'

'As much as I don't like to think of you fretting like that, Betty will be delighted.' Patty smiled. 'I'll take it in tomorrow.'

'The rate I'm going, I'll probably have a few more to add to it by the end of the week,' Hattie added.

'I'm sure they will go to good use,' Patty said, peeking into the bag of woollen garments, 'and looking at how lovely they are, I should imagine any soldier would pick one of your pieces over mine. Anything beyond a basic scarf and I end up in a reyt mess. Nancy had to salvage the hat I was making today after it all fell off the knitting needle.'

'You really are a case, Patty.' Hattie chuckled, a smile appearing on her face for the first time since they'd met up.

'That's probably one way of putting it.' Patty laughed. 'It's a good job Nancy is so patient is all I can say.'

Chapter 29

'You made it.' Betty grinned, as Nancy walked towards her. Betty, Daisy and Josie had arrived at the Wellington a few minutes early and had decided to wait outside until the rest of their workmates and friends arrived.

'Doris insisted,' Nancy said, raising her eyebrows. 'I still feel guilty but as soon as I mentioned it, she was adamant I came along, although I'll probably only stay for one drink if you don't mind?'

'Not at all. I'm just glad Doris persuaded you,' Betty said. 'It will do you good to have an hour or so to relax.' As the week had worn on, the anxious frown marks on Nancy's forehead and the dark circles under her eyes had increased, not to mention the fact her clothes were virtually hanging off her.

'I'll make a Sunday roast tomorrow to make up for it. Heaven knows, Doris deserves a break too.'

'Well, there you go then,' Betty encouraged. 'You can let Doris put her feet up tomorrow in return for you relaxing this evening.'

'I suppose so,' Nancy replied. She knew her friend only

meant well, but Nancy really couldn't remember the last time she'd relaxed. It had now been nearly a month since she'd had a letter from Bert and she still worried no matter how much she tried to tell herself that if there was something to worry about, she would know by now. *There's bound to be a logical explanation*, she thought to herself, remembering how Betty didn't hear from William for weeks on end after his letters went astray in this country, let alone having to wait for post to cross the channel. But the sense of dread she felt was mounting by the day, especially after Hitler had successfully invaded France and troops were being rescued from the shores of Dunkirk. Once again, Nancy had tried to remind herself if something had happened to her husband, surely she would have received a telegram or some form of notification from the army, but even that didn't seem to be putting her mind at rest. She'd lost track of the last time she'd had a full night's sleep, waking nightly, haunting images breaking her sleep, and when Linda had hugged her earlier this week, she'd announced: 'Your bones are sticking out, Mummy.' Nancy hadn't even noticed she had lost weight until then but as she'd pulled on her peach cotton skirt and cream blouse, to come out this evening, they hung off her far looser than they used to.

'You're here already,' came Dolly's cheerful greeting, bringing Nancy back to the moment.

'We are,' she replied, wondering whether she should just make her excuses and go home. That way she could at least write Bert another letter and let him know she was thinking of him.

But her friends were all so keen to have a night out and she had to agree it was probably the best thing for her to be with friends, taking her mind off everything if only for a few hours.

'Are Patty, Angie and Hattie inside?' Dolly asked, as she realized three of their gang were missing.

'No, we're here,' Angie panted, pacing towards the group, her daughter and her best friend struggling to keep up alongside her.

'Sorry,' Patty trilled. 'It's my fault we're late.'

'Let me guess,' Betty chuckled, 'you couldn't decide what to wear?'

'Am I that predictable?' Patty answered, turning her free hand upwards, the other holding her gas mask and handbag, in mock surprise.

'Well, you look lovely,' Daisy said, complimenting her friend, who was wearing a baby pink satin skirt and a lemon blouse she'd never seen her wear before.

'Thank you, and so do you,' Patty replied, admiring Daisy's very modern flared navy trousers, which were fast becoming all the rage.

'Do your really like them?' Daisy asked. 'I wasn't sure at first, but I picked up one of those women's magazines that was hanging around in the canteen the other day and they were described as the latest fashion must-have for women. Anyway, Mum insisted I treated myself, so I nipped into Banners after work today.'

'You deserve it, luv. You work so hard,' Josie insisted. 'And it's not very often you spend any money on yourself.'

'They really suit you,' Patty praised, delighted that Daisy was enjoying life again after the months of worry she'd endured. 'You've definitely got the height and legs to pull them off.'

'Well, you young 'uns look as though you are getting ready for a night on the town. You do know we are only at the Welly, don't you?' Dolly laughed affectionately at the local boozer.

'It doesn't matter!' Patty exclaimed. 'It's a Saturday night, and we have come out. We have to look our best.'

Dolly, Angie, Nancy and Josie all exchanged amused glances, knowing they would have done exactly the same at Patty's age.

'Now, is everyone here?' Dolly asked.

'Yes, I think we are,' Betty answered.

'Reyt then! What are we waiting for? Let's get inside and find ourselves a table,' Dolly encouraged.

Ten minutes later the gaggle of workers were all positioned round two mahogany wooden tables which had been pushed together to accommodate them all in the snug.

'I reckon we all deserve this,' Dolly said, raising her half a pale ale into the air, initiating a toast. 'It's been another busy old week.'

'I'll drink to that,' Josie agreed, clinking her glass with Dolly's. 'I've never seen so many hungry workers. We must have served literally thousands of dinners this week.'

'Aye, we will have,' Dolly nodded.

'And you girls should all be very proud of yourselves too,' Dolly encouraged, looking towards the rest of the group. 'The workload doesn't seem to be easing up.'

'You can say that again,' Patty replied, lifting up her glass of lemonade. 'Cheers!' she added, clinking her half-pint glass with her friends.

'Cheers,' came the united reply.

'I'm not sure I can take any credit, but I have no doubt you are all doing a grand job,' Hattie said, taking a sip of her port and lemon.

'You are doing more than your bit,' Betty protested. 'Patty brought in that big pile of knitting you did. You are helping so many by just doing that.'

'That's very kind of you to say.' Hattie smiled. 'I've actually got a couple more bits in my bag. Please don't let me go home without giving you them.'

'Gosh, you really have been busy,' Betty praised. 'I think you and Nancy are my most productive knitters!'

'My mum taught me to knit when I was knee high to a grasshopper, so I can almost do it in my sleep,' Hattie explained. 'And to be honest, it's helping me out too. I'm struggling to settle of a night and besides which, I want to help. Working at Woollies isn't exactly helping the war effort. As much as I thought Patty was bonkers for leaving the shop to start at Vickers, I'm almost envious of her now. You are all doing so much good. I feel a little bit like a spare part selling lipsticks and mascara.'

'You can always come and join us,' Patty enthused. 'From what Frank says, they are still crying out for women to come join the works and you'll probably earn a bit more cash than at Woollies.'

'Well, I'll never say no to that!' Hattie replied. 'The extra cash would definitely help my mum, it's probably something I need to give some proper thought to.'

'Is she struggling, luv?' Dolly asked, her naturally caring side shining through.

'A little bit, but I should imagine we're only in the same boat as everyone else,' Hattie said, her cheeks blushing. Patty didn't say a word, but momentarily placed her hand on her friend's knee under the table, knowing the real reason Hattie's mum was scraping Peter to pay Paul was due to her dad's drinking habit.

'You would be very welcome at Vickers, luv,' Dolly reiterated, not wanting to press the issue, conscious Hattie was looking a little embarrassed, but also keen to let her know she would be welcomed with open arms. 'We really are a friendly lot.'

'Or come and join Daisy and myself at the WVS?' Betty suggested.' We are off there again tomorrow for a few hours if you fancy lending a hand for a few hours.'

'Thank you,' Hattie answered. 'Maybe I'll have a chat with my mum and see what she says.'

'And just think, you get to see more of me if you come and work at the factory,' Patty trilled, also keen to make sure her friend was okay.

'And who could resist that!' Betty chuckled.

'You could also help her out with her knitting,' Nancy, who was sat on the other side of Hattie, added.

'Hey,' Patty protested. 'I thought I was doing all right now.'

'Apart from dropping the whole lot off a needle,' Nancy gently reminded her.

'Oh yeah, I forgot about that,' Patty said coyly. 'But at least you rescued it.'

'Exactly my point,' Nancy reiterated. 'I could do with someone else, just to make sure your knitting doesn't end up in a heap on the floor.'

With that, the group of workers all burst into laughter, Patty's escapades never failing to entertain them.

As the women's laughter subsided and they all began different conversations, Nancy turned to Hattie. 'If you are serious about joining, there is also another advantage.'

'What's that?' Hattie asked, curious.

'It does help keep your mind busy and stops you spending the whole day fretting.'

'Do you mean about your husband?' Hattie quizzed.

'I do.' Nancy nodded. 'Not only that, but this lot also keep me upright too. Whenever I'm having a bad day, which seems to be most of the time right now, they are there to spur me along. I'd be in a reyt old pickle without them.'

'I must admit, apart from Patty, I only really chat to my mum about how worried I am about John. There's no one at work I can talk to.'

'Oh, luv,' Nancy sympathized. 'Try and keep strong if

you can and like Betty said, you are always welcome to come and see us.'

'Thank you,' Hattie said. 'I do appreciate it.'

'I mean it,' Nancy insisted. 'Don't try and do this alone. Take it from me, it's just too hard.'

'Can I ask one question?' Hattie enquired.

'Of course, luv. What is it?'

'Apart from talking to your friends, have you got any other tips on how to keep positive? I have to admit, I feel like it's getting harder by the day.'

'I know exactly what you mean,' Nancy confided. 'But there is one thing I do, which does help.'

'Do you mind if I ask what it is?' Hattie asked tentatively.

'Not at all,' Nancy replied, a warm melancholy smile appearing across her face at the thought of what she was about to say.

Hattie didn't say a word for the few seconds it took for Nancy to speak again, instinctively sensing whatever it was she needed a moment to compose herself.

Taking a deep breath, Nancy said: 'I think about how we first met and with it I recall how happy and carefree we were, without a worry in the world. I can lose myself in that daydream for what feels like an eternity but is probably only ten minutes, maybe a bit more, but it helps me smile as well as spur me on.'

'That's lovely,' Hattie said, also remembering how she had been on cloud nine when John had asked her out and they first started courting.

'Oh, please tell us about it. It sounds so romantic.'

'It really was,' Nancy grinned, the memory lighting up her eyes. 'I was only twenty-two but convinced I was going to end up an old spinster as apart from the odd date and trip to the picture house with the occasional boy, I hadn't been one for much courting and certainly hadn't found a man I thought I could spend the rest of my life with.'

'Bert must have been very special then?' Hattie asked.

'He was, luv, sorry, *is*,' Nancy agreed, correcting herself. 'Do you know, I think I knew from the very first moment I set eyes on him, Bert was the man for me.'

Hattie smiled, but didn't interrupt, allowing Nancy to tell the story that obviously brought her so much comfort.

'I was on the tram. He was a conductor and when he came to take the money for my ticket, I realized I didn't have quite enough money. I'd left my purse at home and only had a couple of coins in my bag. I was convinced I'd be thrown off the tram and would have to walk the rest of the way home from town. I remember I was really tired after being on my feet all day working in the co-op. The idea of having to walk a few miles back to my parent's house virtually had me in tears. Anyway, when Bert came to ask for my payment, he must have seen I was in a reyt old pickle and took sympathy on me, as he took some change out of his own pocket and paid it himself. But do you know what I remember most?'

'What?' Hattie asked.

'His smile,' Nancy continued. 'It was so warm and gentle.

There was just something about it that captivated me. Looking back now, I know that's the moment he stole my heart.'

'What happened next?' Hattie prompted, mesmerised by Nancy's story.

'Well, just before I got off the tram, he came back over to me and asked if he could take me out on a date. I honestly thought I was dreaming. Nothing like that had ever happened to me before. If he hadn't sounded so genuine, I really would have thought someone had dared him as a joke to ask me out. Anyway, I somehow managed to say yes, gave him my address and he promised to pick me up a couple of nights later. When I got off the tram, I had to pinch myself, as I was still so shocked this good-looking man, with the kindest smile had asked me, little old Nancy Collins, as I was then, out. I walked home on a cloud, but that night I managed to convince myself he would think better of it and wouldn't turn up. Of course, on the day we'd arranged, I still got myself ready, just in case, but had prepared myself to be let down. I'd never had much self-confidence. I was always the shy one at school and all my friends were married by then, let alone courting. Anyway, to my absolute surprise, as he had promised, Bert knocked on my front door at the time we'd agreed, holding a lovely bunch of pink-and-white chrysanthemums. When I close my eyes, I can still remember how dapper he looked in his sharply pressed polo shirt, slacks and his hair greased back, like one of those famous Hollywood movie star actors. You could have literally knocked me over with a feather. I felt like the happiest girl in the whole of Sheffield.'

'Oh, Nancy,' Betty said. 'I recall you telling me you met Bert on a tram, but that story is the loveliest thing I've heard in a long time.'

'It really is,' Josie added, dabbing her eyes with a handkerchief. 'He sounds like a really lovely man.'

'He is,' Nancy smiled, 'and over the last few weeks, whenever I've been at rock bottom and I'm lying awake in bed, engulfed in darkness or knitting away at the kitchen table, that's the moment I remember and it somehow keeps me going, reminds me about why I need to have hope, because I love that man with all my heart.'

Suddenly remembering where she was, Nancy looked around and realized the rest of her friends had all stopped their own conversations and were sat in silence looking at her.

'Sorry, I didn't mean to get so carried away with myself,' she blushed.

'No need to apologize,' Dolly insisted. 'You deserve an amazing fella. And if recalling those special memories helps you get through right now, then I for one am happy to hear them.'

'Hear hear,' Josie encouraged.

'It's like something out of a romantic picture,' Patty enthused.

'I suppose it is.' Nancy chuckled. 'You don't realize in the moment how perfect everything is, it's only when you look back and remember how happy you were.'

'True enough, duck.' Dolly nodded, taking a sip of her drink. 'My two lads used to run me ragged when they were kids, always playing tricks on me and running into the kitchen with their muddy boots on but actually when I look back they were the best days. The house was always full of laughter and there was never a dull moment.'

'Oh yes,' Nancy laughed, 'it was the same at our house. Whenever our Billy came in caked in dirt, and stealing the end of the loaf, instead of telling him off, Bert would race him for the crust.'

The next hour passed in no time at all as the women all reminisced, sharing their favourite pre-war memories, and instead of grieving for a bygone age, they smiled as they recounted the stories that had been stored away in a safe place at the back of their minds. As well as taking their mind off what was playing out in Europe, it gave them hope at how good the good times would be again when this war was finally over.

The night out had done exactly what Betty had hoped it would when she'd suggested a little get-together – it had given the group the motivation they needed to carry on, knowing no matter how hard life seemed right now, no one could take their memories away.

'So, what is everyone up to tomorrow?' Dolly interjected, taking the last sip of pale ale from her glass. 'I know Daisy and Betty are off doing their bit at the WVS. Have you any plans, Patty?'

'Hattie and I are going to The Skates in the morning and then I'm hoping Archie will make it for Sunday dinner if he isn't on air raid duty,' she replied with a big grin.

'That will be nice,' Betty enthused. 'Ivy and Frank have promised to make a roast for when I get back from the depot, and I believe we may even be having some of their freshly grown veg.'

'Isn't that marvellous?' Dolly exclaimed. 'It's lovely to see Frank so happy.'

'And how about you?' Betty asked.

'Aw, I have my granddaughters and their mums coming over, so that will be a treat.'

'Aw enjoy it luv,' Nancy said, standing up to pull on her blue mackintosh.

'Are you not staying for another?' Dolly asked.

'I best not,' Nancy replied. 'I'm quite tired and don't want to take advantage of Doris's generous nature any more for one night.'

'Well, you take it steady, duck, and please promise us you will try to relax a little tomorrow.'

'I will.' Nancy smiled, as she bid her friend's goodnight.

A few minutes later, as she headed down Prince Street, the thought of what lay ahead over the weekend was enough to spur her on. She'd planned to cook a big meal and promised Doris she would take the girls roller-skating afterwards, followed by a cosy evening snuggled up on the sofa with Billy and Linda, reading their bedtime stories.

It would be a lovely way to end their weekend. Excited to give her children a huge hug, Nancy picked up her pace, vowing she wasn't going to let her constant worries about Bert spoil a single minute of her only day off. As Archie's nannan would say, '*There's no point worrying about what hasn't happened.*'

And isn't that what Bert would want too? He'd told her countless times in his letters to rest when she could and just enjoy time with their two children, so tomorrow, she was going to heed his words. She'd even find time to write him an extra-long letter and maybe Linda could draw him a picture – that was bound to boost his spirits, wherever he was.

I can do this, she optimistically thought to herself, a welcome contrast to the self-doubt and worry she'd felt for the last few weeks.

Feeling unusually positive, Nancy was home before she knew it. In a world of her own, she hadn't spotted the solemn-looking soldier, dressed in a khaki uniform and matching beret, about to knock on her front door.

It was only when she was about to turn into the gennel between her house and Doris's that Nancy noticed him and froze in her tracks.

'Mrs Edwards?' asked the official-looking older man, with a bushy greying moustache. He was holding a brown envelope.

'Yes,' Nancy whispered, praying with all her might she was in the middle of one of her terrible dreams and would wake up at any second. Only she wasn't, and there was only one of two reasons the army would send one of their own to her house.

'I'm afraid I have some bad news.'

Author's Note

I started The Steel Girls series after spending two years researching the true-life stories of the women who worked in the factories that lined the River Don during World War Two. Their tales of hardship, strength and resilience left me humbled and in complete admiration of what this tremendous generation endured.

Many were mums or young girls, with no experience of what it was like to be employed in one of the ginormous windowless factories, which were described on more than one occasion as entering 'hell on earth'. The deafening, ear splitting cacophony of noise mixed with the perilously dangerous, but accepted working conditions, alongside the relentless and exhaustingly long shifts, was a huge culture shock for so many of the women who walked through those factory doors for the first time.

Those who had young children had no choice but to hand their precious sons and daughters over to grandparents or leave them in the care of older siblings, some of them only just out of school themselves, but were expected to grow up fast and also do their bit to help.

What struck me in the course of my research, though, was how little resistance was offered to this new arduous, strangely unfamiliar, and frequently quite terrifying way of life. 'We were just doing what was needed,' was an all-too-common answer when I asked the women I had the privilege of talking to why they so eagerly took on the somewhat risky roles they volunteered for. 'We had no choice. It was what was needed to keep the factories going.' This is true, the foundries desperately needed workers, with so many of the opposite sex signing up to begin a 'new adventure'.

It soon became clear to me that this band of formidable, proud and hardworking Yorkshire women were not going to just stand by and let Hitler and his troops reap havoc across Europe and beyond without them doing what they could to aid their husbands, brothers, sons and uncles, who were off fighting someone else's war.

Over and over again, I was left in complete awe of how much the women of Sheffield sacrificed, day in and day out, for six long years. It's hard for most of us to comprehend now what a difficult and seemingly never-ending length of time this was. As well as working night and day as crane drivers, turners, making camouflage netting or working next to a red hot and at times fatal Bessemer Converter, they were also terrified by the very realistic fear they may never see their loved ones ever again.

One lady, Kathleen Roberts, told me whenever a shooting star was seen going over a factory, it was a sign another soldier had fallen and a telegram bearing the bad news would be delivered soon afterwards. To live with that level of sheer terror, let alone cope with the ominous air raid sirens that indicated the Luftwaffe could be on their way, is truly unimaginable. But this is the harsh and constant reality which thousands of women lived with across Sheffield.

It wasn't all doom and gloom though. The one thing that struck a chord with me while talking to the women and their families was the way in which they counteracted the harshness life had thrown at them. They created unbreakable bonds with their new female fellow workmates and a camaraderie which even Hitler himself couldn't break. In a determined bid to 'keep up morale' our feisty factory sisters focussed on safeguarding a warm community spirit to keep them all going when times got hard. Friendships were created in the most unlikely of circumstances, often amongst women who would never normally mix; lipsticks were snapped in half and divided between colleagues, and a single wedding dress could be worn a dozen times to ensure a Sheffield bride didn't walk down the aisle without looking her absolute best. It really was the era of sharing what you had with your neighbour and never letting someone in need go without.

Of course, it would be easy to romanticise this period, or hale it as 'the good old days', but the reality is it wasn't that either. It was simply a case of facing head-on the atrocities life was dealing and getting on with it as best you could. Some had it easier than others but no matter what, all these women woke up in September 1939 to a new life and somehow managed to take it in their stride, but they really didn't have much choice. With no savings to fall back on to tide them over, or a welfare state to lighten the load, it was a case of 'cracking on' and doing what was needed.

In 2009, Kathleen Roberts rang the *Sheffield Star* and asked why she and others like her, who had sacrificed so much of their lives had never been thanked, after watching a TV show on the Land Girls. What started as a frustrated phone call, developed into a campaign by the local paper to ensure the women of the city who had worked day and night in the steel works, were finally recognised. Kathleen, alongside Kit Sollitt, Dorothy Slingsby and Ruby Gascoigne, representing this whole generation of women, were whisked down to London to be personally thanked by the then Prime Minister, Gordon Brown. Afterwards a grassroots campaign was launched by the *Sheffield Star* to fundraise for a statue representing the female steelworkers to be commissioned and erected in Barker's Pool, in the city centre, directly outside the dance they would often visit on a Saturday, to escape the drudgery of their lives.

In June 2016, the larger-than-life bronze statue, paid for entirely by donations from the people of Sheffield, was unveiled to the sheer and rapturous delight of the still surviving Women of Steel, their contribution to the war effort now eternally immortalised.

Although the characters in this book are entirely fictional, their experiences a result of my creative imagination having a bit of fun with itself, the truth is every page is based on the interviews I conducted, the factual books I've read from the period and the ongoing research I'm still undertaking. I hope within my books, I can also help keep this generation's memory alive. I interviewed women who flew up crane ladders, others who were scared witless and many who remember only too clearly what it was like to live in absolute poverty, the tallyman a regular visitor to their door. So, despite the poetic creation of Betty, Nancy and Patty, I can envisage their real live counterparts, hear their voices and recall their experiences – the reality of it is, I simply couldn't make the raw bones of some of these stories up. Only after hearing first-hand how terrifying it was to be hauled up to the dizzy heights of the factory heavens in a crane cab or listen to the raw heartbreak of not knowing if your husband was dead or alive in a faraway country, could I put pen to paper and serve our real Women of Steel the justice they rightfully deserve.

I truly hope, as a Sheffielder (well just about – I've been here 26 years) I have served the women of this hard-working industrious city well and you have enjoyed reading this book as much as I have writing it.

Acknowledgements

Firstly, I would like to thank every female steelworker of the First and Second World War and their family members, who over the course of the last four years have so generously given up their time to talk to me, recalled memories and answered my endless questions. Without these women, The Steel Girls series would not be possible. Although the characters are fictional, they are created from the true-life stories, which have been shared with me. I am also very grateful to the women and their relatives for their ongoing and tremendous support, which means so much. At every step of the way, they have been my biggest cheerleaders, and for that I will be forever grateful.

I am indebted to every author, historian, journalist and social commentator who enabled me to look at this period of time in extra detail, allowing me to understand the wider issues and feelings of the women who lived and worked through World War Two, creating a new way of life in the most troubled and hardest of times.

I must say a huge thank you to the fabulous Sylvia Jones, whose own 'little nannan', Ada Clarke, was a Woman of

Steel. Sylvia has become my 'go to' expert on anything Attercliffe based. She never fails to come up with the details when I ask her something specific or something utterly random, at all hours of the day and night, about the area the women of these books worked, and so many lived in. Sylvia took me on a wonderful walking tour of the area, pointing out all the old shops, picture houses and pubs, so I could envisage all these landmarks, which was utterly invaluable. I would also like to say a huge thank you to Ted Evans, whose mum, Doris Evans, was a Woman of Steel also. What he doesn't know about the Sheffield steelworks isn't worth knowing. I'd like to further express my gratitude to Vic Jay, author of *The Mallon Crew*, for helping me so much when I needed to know more about pilot training and Bomber Command. On this point I'd like to add my thanks to the late Dick Starkey, who recorded his wartime RAF memories, in his book, *A Lancaster Pilot's Impression on Germany*, which I have read from cover to cover, after another reader, Sandra Kay, pointed me to it.

I must also say how grateful I am to every book blogger who has been kind enough to support me, in particular Nicola Smith, from Short Book and Scribes, Zoe Morton from Fiction Book Reviews, and Lesley Wilkinson, who have been so kind, continually shouting about the books and offering immense support.

I must also add my appreciation to Ivy & Keith at The Book Vault, in Barnsley, who have offered boundless support since my very first book was published. Local bookshops are so important for authors and often act as our biggest cheerleaders, and for that I am very grateful.

Enormous thanks must be given to my agent, the extremely dedicated Hannah Weatherill, at Northbank Talent Management, who not only believed in me, but offered reassurance, encouragement, and invaluable advice, when I first embarked upon this series. Her dedication is second to none.

I must also offer the greatest of thanks to my incredibly patient and extremely dedicated editor, Katie Seaman at HQ Stories, without whom The Steel Girls series would never have seen the light of day. Not only did Katie believe in me from the very start, when the Steel Girls was just an idea, but as I have said many times has become the wisest and kindest of sounding boards whenever I need a little natter or a brainstorm. Katie's unfaltering and enthusiastic passion for The Steel Girls is infectious. I feel incredibly lucky to be blessed with such a dedicated editor. Our chats around character development and plots (or plot gaps!) never feel arduous or chore like. When I can't see where a storyline is going, Katie is always there to talk it through. It's the epitome of a lovely chat over a cup of Yorkshire tea, while we bash out ideas until they come to life.

Alongside Katie at HQ Stories, I must offer my sincere thanks to my magician like copyeditor Eldes Tran. A huge thank to Stephanie Heathcote for designing the most fitting and beautiful of covers and to the utterly brilliant and all round truly wondrous media extraordinaire Becca Joyce, who has the speediest Twitter typing fingers known to man and is an all-round lovely human being. I'd also like to extend my gratitude to Sian Baldwin for helping create the publicity for The Steel Girls series and to Harriet Williams in sales, for getting this book on actual shelves.

I am so grateful to each and every one of my family members and truly amazing friends, who have offered unfaltering support in writing the book. As always, I can't fail to mention my good friend and long-suffering running mate, Leanne Hawkes, who has very patiently lived every one of my books with me, listening to me three times a week as we pound the hills of Millhouse Green, and kept me sane throughout. I think at least two of my characters are named after members of her family – including Ivy, (Leanne's lovely Mum and now Betty's landlady), which we decided on during one very particular rainy and windy run. I must also thank Ann Cusack for offering relentless support and being the greatest friend anyone could ever wish for.

I would also like to say the biggest thank you to the truly amazing and quite frankly fabulous group of people I work with at The University of Sheffield. Thank you Polly Rippon, Lisa Bradley, Yvonne Illsley, Lindsay Pantry, Lynn Dixon, James Whitworth, and his very lovely wife, Lisa, who arranged for me to have a tour around a Sheffield steel factory.

I cannot end this passage of gratitude without saying thank you to my husband, Iain, who once again, has never once moaned about me turning my laptop on at least four evenings a week to make sure I reach my word count and is there with a ginormous and quite frankly much needed cup of coffee every morning – he knows I'm pretty grumpy without it. As for our two amazing children, Archie and Tilly, they are simply the best, even if my now teenager son rolls his eyes when I mention anything that isn't gaming focused. I sincerely hope I have instilled into them if you work hard enough for something, you can achieve your dreams, no matter how big or insurmountable they might feel.

There is one person, who I constantly think about while writing my books and that is my late mother-in-law, Coleen, a hardy Steel Girl in her own right. I would give anything for her to still be here to see this book. I can imagine her shouting from the rooftops about it, telling all her friends they must read it. Coleen was an avid local history fan and I wished she was still here for so many reasons but would have loved to check the minutiae of this book, the accents, the landmarks, the Yorkshire traditions. I know she would have been there, going through the details with a fine-tooth comb.

But I gain so much happiness and comfort at how proud and excited she would have been to see little old me writing this series, seeped in historical fact about the remarkable women of the city she loved so much. Coleen, like our hard-working and caring Steel Girls, you will never be forgotten.

Make sure you've read all the books in the heartwarming Steel Girls series

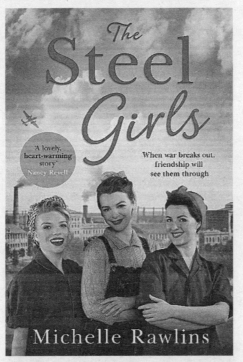

With war declared, these brave women will step up and do their bit for their country . . .

The Steel Girls start off as strangers but quickly forge an unbreakable bond of friendship as these feisty factory sisters vow to keep the foundry fires burning during wartime.

Don't miss this festive tale of courage and friendship on the Home Front

As the Steel Girls face their first Christmas at war, can they come together this winter?

In the harsh winter of 1939, our feisty factory sisters must rally around each other to find hope and comfort this Christmas season.

ONE PLACE. MANY STORIES

Bold, innovative and
empowering publishing.

FOLLOW US ON:

@HQStories